CAST A COLD EYE

BY ROBBIE MORRISON

Edge of the Grave

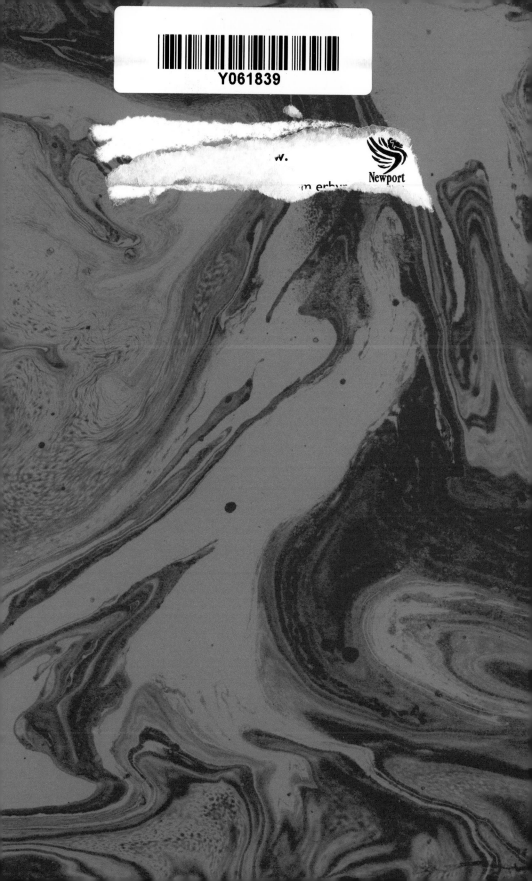

ROBBIE MORRISON

CAST A COLD EYE

MACMILLAN

First published 2023 by Macmillan
an imprint of Pan Macmillan
The Smithson, 6 Briset Street, London EC1M 5NR
EU representative: Macmillan Publishers Ireland Ltd,
1st Floor, The Liffey Trust Centre, 117–126 Sheriff Street Upper,
Dublin 1, D01 YC43
Associated companies throughout the world
www.panmacmillan.com

ISBN 978-1-5290-5406-4

135798642

A CIP catalogue record for this book is available from the British Library.

Map artwork by Hemesh Alles

Typeset in LTC Goudy Oldstyle Pro by Jouve (UK), Milton Keynes
Printed and bound by CPI Group (UK) Ltd, Croydon, CR0 4YY

Visit **www.panmacmillan.com** to read more about all our books
and to buy them. You will also find features, author interviews and
news of any author events, and you can sign up for e-newsletters
so that you're always first to hear about our new releases.

For Deborah, my love,

without whom these books may not exist.

And in memory of her mother Elizabeth/Betty (born 1923),

whom I sadly never met, but whose recollections have helped

to inform the Dreghorn novels.

'Cast a cold eye
On life, on death.
Horseman, pass by!'

– W. B. Yeats, 'Under Ben Bulben'

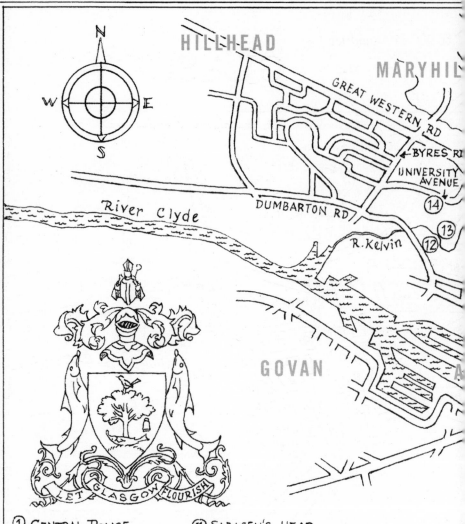

N
W E
S

HILLHEAD

MARYHIL

GREAT WESTERN RD

BYRES R
UNIVERSITY AVENUE
⑭

River Clyde

DUMBARTON RD

R. Kelvin
⑬
⑫

GOVAN

A

LET GLASGOW FLOURISH

① Central Police Headquarters
② Bridgeton Cross
③ Mermaid Bar
④ Glasgow Mortuary
⑤ Court House
⑥ Necropolis
⑦ Central Station
⑧ The Gordon Club
⑨ St Enoch Hotel
⑩ The Barras Market

⑪ Saracen's Head
⑫ Kelvingrove Art Gallery & Museum
⑬ Kelvingrove Park
⑭ Glasgow University
⑮ Hamilton Park Avenue
⑯ Royal Infirmary
⑰ Cathedral
⑱ Duke Street Gaol
⑲ City Chambers
⑳ George Square

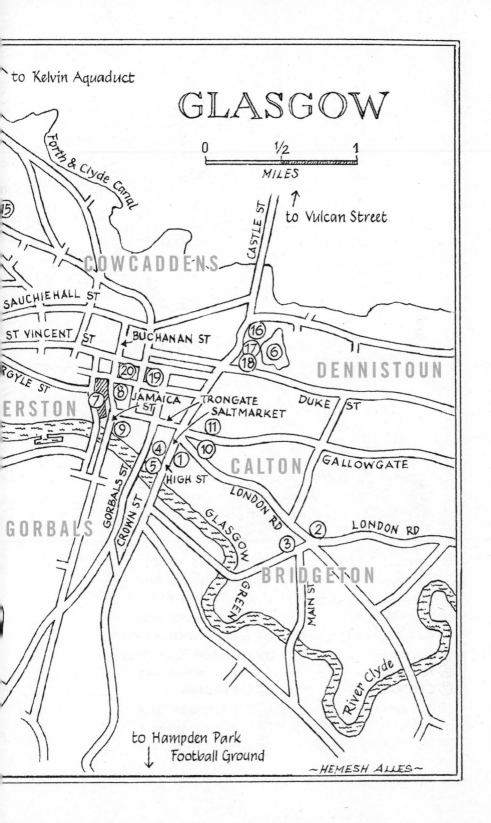

PROLOGUE

At first it's like a prison, an iron fist around my head, but as the horror goes on, it becomes a shield and I raise my hands, pulling it tighter.

There's no escaping the sounds though. The heavier ones buffet me like a storm. The lighter ones scuttle over me, sinking in their claws. They echo inside the metal, writhe within my head.

A rat-tat-tat sharp enough to rend bodies.

A thump-thump-thump, followed by a sickening wet crunch as something gives way that isn't meant to.

There's a fearful whimper, a 'No-no-no!' and then a scream. The whimper is mine. I try not to think of where the scream comes from.

Squelch-squelch-squelch in the mud, coming desperately towards me. A bang, a splash; I jump, startled, as something spatters me, thicker than water.

I hear my name called, cut off by a slap and a curse. Crying, pleading, struggling, a barrage of blows being struck, a guttural mob of encouragement: 'GETINTAETHEM!'

Finally it subsides. Footsteps tramp past. Figures bump me as if I'm not there. Shots ring out occasionally, almost casually. The voices become less monstrous, less bloodthirsty. Just another day's work now.

Liquid sloshes past me in a heavy can.

Frenzied splashes.

Petrol fumes.

A brief, expectant silence.

The flare of a match.

A deafening whoosh. A blast of heat that almost knocks me over. A crackling like a hearth, but fiercer, louder.

Clang-clang! The impact surprises me. I heard no one approach.

'Knock-knock,' says an inhuman voice that I'll never forget. I turn and stumble helplessly, not knowing which way is which. 'Knock-knock,' the voice repeats. 'And you say, Who's there?'

'Who's there?' I stammer.

'That's right. Who's there?' Closer, alcohol on the breath. 'I'm asking you now, who's there?'

'I . . . I don't know . . .'

'Who's there?' Shouted now.

'I don't know!'

'That's right. You don't know. You didn't see anything.'

Hands fall upon my shoulders, turn me away from the voice. A truck engine growls into life.

'You don't know,' the voice says again. 'You didn't see anything.'

The hands free me from my prison, removing my shield.

I see everything.

Every smashed skull, every leaking wound, every twisted body in every muddy, bloody puddle. Every broken man and woman. Every burning house in a street of fire.

I stare into the flames until they dry my tears and burn my eyes.

I scream until my voice cracks and dies within me, 'I see everything!'

CHAPTER I

Glasgow, Wednesday, 29 March 1933

In the countryside, or far out at sea, the water was no doubt clean and fresh, but when it reached the city it was as dark as sin, punctuated occasionally by cheerful rainbow swirls of oil, leaked from the battered boats that plied their trade on the canal.

Inspector Jimmy Dreghorn stopped at the lock gates, glanced one way and then the other. A couple of weans were walking a dog on the opposite side of the canal. One of them threw a stick and the mutt followed fearlessly, launching itself into the water despite the icy temperature, springtime or not.

Dreghorn looked at Police Constable Ellen Duncan, who pointed west, in the direction of the Kelvin Aqueduct, where the canal crossed over the River Kelvin.

'Just along there's where everyone goes winching, sir,' she said authoritatively. 'Or at least, they used to.'

'Notice I don't ask how you know that, constable.'

She gave him a cheeky, knowing look. 'Please, I wasn't always a—'

'Fine upstanding member of society?' Dreghorn interrupted.

'Police constable.' She spoke over him. 'And I do have a life off duty, you know.'

Dreghorn raised his hands. 'Whoa, I'm scandalized enough already.'

The Forth and Clyde Canal cut across the Central Lowlands,

joining the two Scottish coastlines, from the Firth of Forth at Grangemouth in the east to the Clyde at Bowling in the west, both rivers then leading out to open sea. When first opened in 1790, business was booming, with timber, oil and coal transported from one side of the country to the other. Barges and other working craft bobbed happily alongside yachts and pleasure boats, an unlikely camaraderie between the classes as they navigated the locks and sluice gates.

As the influence of the railways grew, transporting greater quantities of freight more swiftly, and the trend in shipbuilding veered towards vessels too large for canals, the Forth and Clyde had fallen into decline, not helped by the Depression, which had engulfed the country four years earlier.

A lumber boat was approaching the lock, heading west towards Bowling, and the lock-keeper emerged reluctantly from his cottage to assist at the gate, breath misting in annoyance as he buttoned up his overcoat. He saw the dog swimming towards the stick, right in front of the boat.

'Get that dug oot my river,' he yelled, 'or I'll chuck you in after it!'

He spotted Dreghorn and Ellen, straightened his cap and asked suspiciously if there was anything he could do for them.

'Aye,' Dreghorn growled, 'don't draw attention to us.'

They walked in the direction Ellen had indicated. Two barges were berthed on the same side of the canal as them, so decrepit they could have been mistaken for derelict, if it hadn't been for the peelie-wallie-looking family glimpsed through the windows of one, and the skipper of the other half-heartedly scrubbing his deck. With a guilty air, he pretended not to notice them as they passed.

As legitimate trade had dwindled, so the smuggling of

black-market goods had flourished along the canal, although that wasn't why Dreghorn and Ellen were there; in piratical terms, it was hardly *Treasure Island*.

They walked a little further, scanning the long grass at the side of the path. The handlebars of a motorcycle came into view, the grass around them swaying and rocking, although there was little breeze. Dreghorn stopped, put his finger to his lips and pointed.

Two pairs of feet, one male, one female, protruded from the grass at the edge of the path; the woman's on the bottom, splayed awkwardly, kicking and struggling, the man's on top, toes down, scuffing the earth to gain purchase. The man rolled away suddenly, revealing the black-and-white sheen of his spats – completely inappropriate for Scottish weather, but easily identifiable as the shoes the suspect they were seeking was described as wearing.

Dixon 'Dixie' White: robbery, assault and battery and, looking increasingly likely, manslaughter, if not murder.

The case had dragged on with painfully slow progress for almost a year. It wasn't an investigation Dreghorn was particularly keen on, but Chief Constable Sillitoe had insisted that he take charge, as it was an important test of the new Fingerprint Department, recently set up to replace the ink-spattered, index-free shambles of the previous regime.

The first robbery had been at the Kingsway Cinema in Cathcart Road, May 1932, with several nights' takings swiftly and efficiently snatched at around 1 a.m., while the watchman enjoyed a supper break that ended up costing him his job. Sergeant Bertie Hammond had succeeded in lifting a full set of fingerprints from the safe, but there was no match with the paltry samples in the files. Hammond, whose eagle eyes Sillitoe had brought with him from Sheffield, dispatched copies of the prints to Scotland Yard in London. Again, no match.

Four more picture houses were robbed over the following months, before the bandit moved further afield with the same modus operandi – to Paisley, Greenock and Troon. At every crime scene, prints were discovered, sometimes fragmentary, but all matching.

The bandit had to be young, fit and something of a daredevil, due to the rooftop acrobatics many of the crimes demanded. He was likely to be a bachelor of no permanent abode, moving freely from district to district and spending time in each as he planned his heists. Beyond that, and the fact that he was a fan of the pictures, they had little to go on.

The case had become more serious on 25 March this year, when the night watchman of the King's Cinema in Sauchiehall Street was found unconscious at the bottom of the stairs that led from the foyer to the auditorium, presumably after encountering the cinema bandit. The man's skull was fractured; doctors feared the worst.

Two days later the manager of the Blythswood Hotel had contacted CID about one of his guests, a young man named White, resident in the hotel for over a week. On check-in, he had asked to be awoken each morning at eight sharp with a cup of tea, a service the hotel charged threepence for. Each day, along with some risqué flirting, White gave the waitress who served him the tea a half-crown tip.

This largesse aroused the suspicions of the spendthrift manager: White didn't appear to work, but wasn't short of money and, in the midst of the Depression, had just bought a new

Matchless Silver Hawk motorcycle, the roar of which disturbed other residents.

Dreghorn's informant Bosseye, a skelly-eyed bookie who boasted that he could see in opposite directions at once, asked around his punters and learned that White was originally from Partick, but had gone off to London in 1927 to make his fortune.

He had recently returned, sporting spats and fancy suits, and was often to be found standing his old pals drinks in the Windsor, the Hayburn Vaults or Tennent's Bar. By all accounts, his newfound gallusness rubbed them up the wrong way, but drinks were hard to come by in the Depression, so if you had to suffer some shite patter to get one, so be it. Patience was wearing thin, though, because of White's habit of tempting the local girls with a flash of his wallet and a ride on his motorcycle.

Dreghorn had recruited WPC Ellen Duncan to question the Blythswood waitresses, figuring they'd be more likely to open up to her than a hardened thirty-five-year-old detective. It hadn't taken her long to establish that White was tipping all the female staff generously and was – unknown to each of the others – 'stepping out' with three of them. Where did they go on these romantic excursions? The pictures.

Hammond had been keen to get a sample of White's prints, but without more substantial evidence, there was no legal means of forcing the suspected burglar to hand them over, although Dreghorn made a couple of illegal suggestions.

Sillitoe snapped testily, 'I know you Scots have a reputation for being tight-fisted, but we can't arrest a man simply because he's a generous tipper.'

'Agreed, sir.' Hammond cocked his head conspiratorially. 'But we can arrest the teacup.'

Ellen had collected the potentially incriminating china from the Blythswood's manager that morning, but by the time identification was confirmed, the dapper White had left the hotel scooting off on his bike.

Dreghorn stationed a pair of uniformed officers at the hotel, in case White returned unexpectedly, then drove to Partick, taking Ellen along, somewhat against regulations, in gratitude for the good work she'd already carried out. They scoured the pubs and cafes White was known to frequent, but animosity towards the police won out over ambivalence to the motorcyclist and they met only a stony-faced silence.

Finally a little fellow slinked out of the Hayburn Vaults after them. Glancing over his shoulder, he whispered, 'If I did know where he was, what's in it for me?'

'A sense of pride at doing your civic duty and helping us apprehend a dangerous criminal?' Ellen suggested.

'Dangerous?' The man thought hard. 'I'm no' a grass, right, but he's up the canal with Wilma Ford.' He thumped his chest, which sounded disconcertingly hollow. 'She was going with me before that prick turned up, swanning about on his fancy bike. She's too good for him.'

'All's fair in love and war.' Dreghorn said.

Dixie should've known he wasn't going to get anywhere the moment she climbed daintily onto the motorcycle behind him and asked, 'But what's to stop me falling off?'

'Hold on to this,' he laughed and clamped her hand between his legs.

Wilma Ford squealed in horror and might well have jumped

off, but he was already roaring up Byres Road, so she had to throw her arms around his waist or she'd have been bouncing along the cobbles in his wake. She was yelling in his ear – telling him how cheeky and wonderful and handsome he was, no doubt – but he couldn't hear properly above the engine and the horns of other vehicles, honking their jealousy and admiration as he weaved in and around their cars, causing them to brake and swerve.

Dixie was lucky with the traffic lights, barely stopping all the way to Maryhill Road. He only slowed slightly as he came onto the canal path, politely allowing an old duffer with a walking stick to stumble out of his way. 'Get yourself one of these, auld yin,' he yelled as he revved past.

After a bit, he turned the Hawk into a small clearing, stopped and threw down the towel he'd sneaked out of the hotel. He lay down, careful not to rumple his suit, and looked expectantly at her.

'Thought we were going to the Blythswood for our dinner?' Wilma asked sourly.

It was a bloody good act, Dixie thought; her face really did look as though it was tripping her, but he knew she was just holding herself back.

'Aye,' he said, 'but I thought we could get some fresh air first, work up an appetite.'

The Blythswood was the last place they'd be going. He'd already taken out three waitresses to cover his reconnaissance of his next cinema target, and there'd be a riot if they spotted him with Wilma. He patted the towel suggestively. 'C'mon, it's a braw day.'

Wilma looked at the grey skies, black smoke pumping from tenement and factory chimneys. She sighed and sat primly beside him, back straight.

I'm in there, he thought, smiling sweetly, giving her his puppy-dog eyes.

'Fanny will be the death of you,' his mates used to say. 'Aye, but what a way to go,' he'd tell them. Better than slogging yourself to death in the shipyards or down the pits – bunch of mugs, wearing away flesh and bone against steel hulls and coalfaces.

In London he'd got in with the Sabini gang, Eyeties with a penchant for protection racketeering rather than fish and chips and ice cream. They'd taken to the cheeky young 'Jock' when they learned he could shinny up a drainpipe faster than Tarzan and was just as deft at safe-cracking. Of course that business with Darby Sabini's eldest niece had obliged him to step lively out of the Big Smoke and keep on the move when he was back in Scotland, in case any of them were sniffing around after him.

Snuggling up to Wilma, he teased her until she relaxed and consented to lie beside him, then he was all over her like a rash, unleashing the full force of his charm: 'You're a wee smasher, Wilma, so you are. You've got all the bits in all the right places.'

He nuzzled her neck, licked her ears, planted slavery kisses on her lips. He tried to slip his hand under her blouse, but she pushed it away. Fair enough, a wee bit more winching first then. He tried to manoeuvre his knee between her legs, angling for a dry hump at least.

She was wriggling a fair bit, thumping his back and bucking her body under his. Trying to shove him away? Surely not. He suddenly remembered struggling with the wee night watchman who had tackled him at the King's, rolling around on the floor. First to his feet, Dixie had clouted the man with his torch, then watched in surprise as he tumbled head over heels down the stairs. At first he'd thought the darkness under the man's head was the pattern on the carpet, until he realized it was spreading, oozing . . .

Dixie jumped to his feet now, gagging, swallowing bile. 'Fuck this for a game of soldiers,' he said. He swung his leg over the Hawk, pointed at Wilma as if it was all her fault. 'You're a dead loss, hen, so you are.' He started the bike, the engine growl matching his mood, and reversed onto the path.

'What, you think you're just going to leave me here?' Wilma followed in outrage, even had the audacity to grab the handlebars.

'You won't want to go where he's going, miss.' Another lassie's voice, firm but with a hint of sarcasm.

Dixie glanced at the newcomer, startled by the sight of her uniform: a polis you wouldn't mind shagging – that was disconcerting. He was less drawn towards the man in the trenchcoat and fedora beside her, short for a polisman maybe, but with a look that didn't invite you to mess with him.

The man flashed his warrant card and said, 'Dixon White, you're under arrest for robbery and assault and battery . . .'

Dixie stopped listening as the detective continued with the legal bumf, and gave Wilma his winning smile again. 'Wilma, sweetheart,' he asked, 'are you a good swimmer?'

'Me? Never learned.'

'Just as well the polis are here to save you then.'

He gave the Hawk a burst of acceleration and nudged Wilma over the side of the canal. He was already turning at speed, spraying the air with gravel and taking off, when he heard the splash as she struck the water, her scream cut off.

CHAPTER 2

Dreghorn instinctively sprinted after White, but the young woman's cries and frantic splashing brought him to a halt. He swore under his breath, turned towards the water and began removing his coat. Something bounced off his chest. He looked down to see Ellen's police hat land on the ground at his feet.

She was already stepping out of her uniform skirt, revealing her slip as it puddled around her feet, and was unbuttoning her heavy jacket. She nodded urgently at White. 'Get after him – you're faster than me.' Dreghorn started to argue, but she cut him off. 'Go! I've got my lifesaving medals.'

Dreghorn had medals too, but they weren't for saving lives. He nodded and started after the cinema bandit again. Glancing back, he saw Ellen launch herself into the water without hesitation.

Dixie laughed like a loon as he sped along the canalside. A daring escape, worthy of Douglas Fairbanks on the silver screen. Granted, filmstar Dougie usually played the goodie, but Dixie didn't view himself as a villain, more a dashing, devil-may-care rebel.

'What're you doing? It's no' your money,' he'd yelled as he fought with the watchman, trying to make the old boy see sense. He'd been sleeping badly ever since, waking well before his early-morning cup of tea, and had avoided the newspapers because he didn't want to know the watchman's name, think of him as a real person or – worse – read that he wasn't ever likely to wake up again.

Dixie figured it was time to get off his mark, wondered if somewhere like France would suit him, the Riviera . . .

He braked as another trenchcoated figure stepped onto the path ahead, this one sporting a more hoity-toity hat, like one of those Churchill wore – a hamburger, or whatever it was called. Everything about the hulking silhouette said polisman. If the first fellow was one of the shortest plainclothes detectives Dixie had encountered, this one was the biggest; he folded his arms and waited, staring straight at Dixie.

Dixie shot a look over his shoulder. The short-arsed polisman was slowing to a halt behind him, about the same distance away as the big yin. The wee detective looked around, then bent down to pick up a discarded two-by-four, weighed it in his hands like some Pictish war club. Dixie looked back at the big man, still as a statue. The engine throbbed impatiently between his legs, 592cc of pure power.

'Fuckin' come ahead then,' Dixie snarled and accelerated. Despite his size, the polisman would soon move, with a Matchless Silver Hawk hurtling at him at full speed. Either that or he'd be flat on his back, with a dirty great tyre mark running from his bawbag to the top of his skull.

The detective calmly took off his coat and placed it carefully on an adjacent bench. He removed his hat, blew a speck of fluff off the brim, perched it on top of a bollard, then ran straight at the motorcycle, cocky bastard.

Dixie wavered for a second, but quickly recovered his grit and went faster, the polisman drawing nearer, getting bigger and bigger, his fists clenched, arms swinging as he ran. Dixie yelled above the roar of the bike, braced himself for the impact.

When it came, it wasn't the one he expected. The detective leapt into the air just before the bike ploughed into him, turning so that his trunk-like body was almost horizontal above the ground. The pattern of the detective's suit, stretched across his shoulder blades, briefly filled Dixie's vision, then everything went black.

Not that he'd openly admit it, but Dreghorn was impressed by Sergeant Archibald McDaid's acrobatics. McDaid had taken bronze in the Heavyweight Freestyle Wrestling at the 1924 Paris Olympics and liked to boast that, at thirty-seven, he was still in championship form, though he'd have difficulty squeezing into his old wrestling trunks these days.

That mental image made Dreghorn wince almost as much as the sight of McDaid landing on top of Dixon White like a felled tree, crushing the robber into the ground. The motorcycle carried on without a rider for a short distance, then veered sideways and rolled into the canal with a drowning splutter. Dreghorn slowed to a saunter, attempting to delay the inevitable McDaid smugness. He had dropped the big man off further along the canal, in an attempt to block White's potential escape routes.

McDaid had stretched out his legs, crossed at the ankles, and had placed his hands under his head when Dreghorn reached them. He smiled and snuggled into Dixie White as if the cinema bandit was the comfiest mattress in Scotland.

'That was how I won the bronze, you know,' he prompted when Dreghorn didn't comment. 'A flying body-slam to you earthbound bums. Speciality of mine – signature move, and that.'

'Bonnie Archie McDaid, the other Flying Scotsman.'

McDaid frowned. He approved of 'Bonnie' when it was applied by ladies who admired the figure he cut while playing the bagpipes in full Highland dress, but was instantly on guard when it was bandied about by sarcastic colleagues. Too many times he'd opened his locker to find a photograph of himself from his uniform days stuck to the inside of the door, but with Jean Harlow or Carole Lombard's face plastered over his own. Or, worse, his own ruddy face – cheeks billowing as he played the pipes with all his puff – fixed to the naked body of a wantonly posed woman, torn from the pages of books they were supposed to arrest people for possessing.

'Is he alive under there?' Dreghorn continued.

'Och, he's fine. Quietly contemplating his guilt, aren't you, Dixie?'

A low, tentative groan emanated from beneath McDaid, as if the slightest reverberation caused untold pain.

McDaid started to sit up. 'Where's the lass that was with him?'

Dreghorn nodded back along the canal. 'He threw her in the water before he took off.'

McDaid tutted and accidentally tramped on White's groin as he got to his feet, prompting an even more despairing wail. 'Beg your pardon, awful sorry,' McDaid cooed politely. 'It's just no' your day, is it?'

'Ellen dived in after her,' Dreghorn said.

'And you let her?' McDaid's sense of chivalry was piqued. 'Gentleman Jimmy Dreghorn strikes again.'

'Ahoy there, inspector!'

Dreghorn almost didn't recognize Ellen without her uniform.

She was saluting him irreverently from the stern of the family barge they had passed earlier, dressed in a borrowed Aran jumper and a pair of man's breeks, the legs rolled up at the bottom. Her hair, usually pinned in a bun under her hat, hung loose and tousled, still damp from her dip, making her seem younger.

Wilma Ford, swathed in an enormous greatcoat, head barely peeking out of the collar, sat beside Ellen, cradling a mug of tea in her hands. Another woman, the lady of the barge, sat with Wilma, though at first Dreghorn thought it was a man from the cropped hair, weathered features and Popeye the Sailor pipe she was puffing on.

'Did you get him?' Ellen asked.

'Aye, Archie's keeping him company – that'll be worse than the prison sentence. Are you both all right?'

Wilma nodded quickly, without meeting his eyes. Ellen gestured gratefully at the other woman, who seemed to be sizing Dreghorn up.

'Mrs Lambie here's been looking after us. Helped us out the water, gave us some of her husband's clothes to dry off and made us tea.' She raised the mug. 'Better than the muck you get at the station.'

Dreghorn frowned. 'You're the one that makes it.'

She lifted an eyebrow conspiratorially. 'Aye, and if I keep doing it badly enough, maybe you lot'll stop asking.'

Dreghorn thanked Mrs Lambie, then addressed Wilma. 'You're better than the likes of him. You know that, don't you?' He paused and she met his eyes sheepishly. 'Don't be fooled by the gift of the gab and a few bob. Sometimes there's not much behind them.' He was pleased with the avuncular authority in his voice, until he saw Ellen's smirk.

'Wise words, sir,' she said. 'Should I get my notebook?'

The three women shared a look at Dreghorn's expense, but at least Wilma seemed less disconsolate.

He raised his hands in submission. 'Aye, aye, you know what I mean. There's a lot of chancers out there. No' everyone's a sweetheart like me.'

He had left McDaid to guard Dixie White, not that the cinema bandit was going anywhere soon. In fact he had howled when McDaid started to haul him up, complaining of chest pains and breathing difficulty. Admittedly he was wheezing, leading Dreghorn to surmise that some of his ribs were cracked or broken. It was a miracle he wasn't as flat as a tattie scone, having had McDaid plough into him.

'The heavy hand of the law,' Dreghorn had said, drawing his eyes off the big man and heading back to their Alvis radio-car to contact Turnbull Street for an ambulance. Specially made for the Glasgow Police by the electronics company EKCO, the car radio could only receive voice messages. Officer responses had to be sent via Morse code or telephoned in from a signal box.

Ellen became serious. 'While you're here, sir, Mrs Lambie has something she wants to tell you.'

The woman had been tamping fresh tobacco into her pipe. She struck a match and stared at him suspiciously through the smoke as she lit it. There was no love lost between most citizens and the Glasgow Police.

'It's about one of the barges,' Ellen prompted.

Mrs Lambie removed the pipe from her mouth, only as much as she needed to in order to speak. There seemed to be little yellow semicircles of nicotine stain on her lips where they clamped around the pipe.

'The *Blue Bonnet*,' she said. 'Moored about half a mile further down the bank. Owner's Rex Smith.'

'What's he done?' Dreghorn asked.

'Nothing – that's the thing.' A short puff. 'Nobody's seen him, and the boat's no' moved for the best part of a week.'

CHAPTER 3

Something about the design of narrowboats – the claustrophobic interiors – made Dreghorn think of coffins, albeit elongated
ones. He hoped it wasn't a premonition. He and McDaid
shared a glance as they approached the *Blue Bonnet*, the rest left
unsaid. The discovery they'd made the last time they boarded
a boat still haunted them.

McDaid said, 'Strictly speaking, we should call in Marine
Division.'

'We're only checking things out.'

'You'll no' be saying that if we find him sitting on the pan
with his troosers at his ankles, deid from a heart attack or
something.'

'Anybody ever tell you you've got the soul of a poet?'

'I'm just saying. On your head be it.'

Ellen had been keen to accompany them, but after the ambulance and escorting officers arrived for White, he told her to
remain with Mrs Lambie. Ellen had fair fizzled with frustration, but while Sillitoe may have been more open-minded about
female officers than other chief constables, he was also a stickler. Regulations stated that WPCs were not allowed to make
arrests or even leave the station, other than on death duty. If
he learned that Ellen had not only taken part in a chase,
but had also been dunked in the Clyde under Dreghorn's

supervision, then the detective would probably be demoted back to uniform alongside her.

The detectives walked the length of the boat – seventy feet from bow to stern, and six feet ten inches wide, just enough that McDaid's feet wouldn't dangle over the side if he lay width-ways. The traditional hull decorations of roses and castles had wilted and crumbled into ruins as the paint peeled and the wood below cracked. If Dreghorn hadn't already been given the name of the vessel, he wouldn't have been able to decipher it from the faded letters.

He noted the flies buzzing in the air and crawling atop the roof as if searching for ingress, but didn't mention them to McDaid, already jittery enough. He knocked politely on a win-dow, shuttered from the inside, as they reached the boatman's cabin.

'Mr Smith, it's the police. Can we have a word?'

Silence. He knocked louder.

'It's all right, you're not in any bother. Some of the other crews have been a bit worried about you.'

Silence.

Dreghorn waved a hand to scatter the flies, looked at McDaid, then stepped onto the small deck, grabbing the tiller for support as he did so. The rounded head of a propeller pro-truded from the water. A missed step or a stumble when the boat was in motion and a steerer could easily lose a leg to the churning propellers. He gave the door a shake. Locked.

McDaid nodded at it. 'If you want me to do the honours, you'll need to step aside. No' enough room to swing a cat in these things.'

Dreghorn reached into his coat, produced a short crowbar with a curved end.

McDaid tutted. 'I forgot; Jimmy's jimmy always does the trick.'

The locks were flimsy; a little pressure and the doors cracked open. Dreghorn recoiled from the smell, steeled himself. He could hear more flies buzzing within. He pushed back the top hatch, not that it improved visibility, and stepped carefully inside.

Wood creaked wearily underfoot as he crossed over the hatch that covered the coal box. He gripped the jimmy, ready to use it as a weapon, reached out his other hand to run along the wall and descended the narrow stairs, the darkness growing thicker. Something soft brushed his face: a Rangers Football Club scarf, suspended from the brass drying rail that ran almost the length of the ceiling. He called Smith's name again, but knew better than to expect an answer.

During the Great War, in the trenches and stalking no-man's-land on night raids, Dreghorn had become attuned to death: the sights, sounds, smells. The stench that slowly enveloped him now, catching at his throat and seeping into his clothes, said that nothing living had been inside the boat for four or five days at least. Apart from flies. He longed for a cigarette, though lighting a whole pack at once wouldn't exorcise the smell.

As his eyes acclimatized to the darkness, his foot nudged something – a bulky shape on the floor ahead of him. His fingers trailed across the window shutter. He dropped the jimmy back into his pocket, fumbled with the bolt and let in a feeble burst of greying light.

It was hard to imagine human habitation smaller than the single tenement rooms that most Glasgow families were crammed into, but the boatman's cabin made them seem spacious. A small range stove with pots and pans suspended from hooks on the ceiling above it, plates racked upright in the alcove around it. A fold-down bench opposite the stove, for seating or sleeping. Another foldaway bed that came down at night to block the door into the cargo-hold. A cupboard door that lowered on hinges to bridge the cabin and form a dining table of sorts.

When the canal first opened, the boats were horse-drawn, and the boatmen and their families lived ashore. Competition from the railways forced them to move on board to save money on rent, where at least the conditions were more hygienic, with plenty of fresh air and a cludgie, admittedly rudimentary, which they didn't have to share with numerous other families in a tenement block.

The shape on the floor materialized into the outline of a body – face-down, with a skin-crawling shimmer of movement upon the head. Dreghorn stepped over the torso as respectfully as he could, crouched down and waved a hand to scatter the flies, the pale light colouring their wings.

The light dimmed and the cabin rocked as McDaid squeezed inside. He waved his arms furiously to try and clear the air.

Dreghorn said, 'Flap any harder and you'll take off.'

'Flying to the moon wouldn't be far enough away from this.' McDaid reached out to open the window that Dreghorn had uncovered. 'Is that our man?'

'Suppose so.' Dreghorn leaned closer to the body. 'I don't envy whoever has to identify him. Gunshot. Back of the head. Revolver probably.'

McDaid pulled a face. Although illegal firearms had flooded the country after the war, brought back as soldiers' souvenirs from battlefields across the globe, actual gun crimes were few.

Ammunition was hard to come by and the penalties were heavy. Why risk it when there were knives, razors, bicycle chains, pick-shafts and good old-fashioned bottles around?

From the way he had fallen, Smith – if it was him – had been on his knees, the killer standing behind him, the revolver at point-blank range. Dreghorn pictured it in his head, a stark newsreel.

There were no signs of a struggle; indeed the rest of the cabin was immaculate, the kitchenware clean and neatly tidied away, the gas mantle and the brass drying rail overhead polished until they gleamed. Dreghorn felt a chill at the preciseness of it, the cold-bloodedness. Most murders and acts of violence in the city were carried out in the heat of the moment, driven by rage. This was an execution. A single shot, well planned, no fuss.

The entry wound was neat, easily visible through Smith's cropped hair. The pulped, gaping maw of the exit wound seemed sunk into the deck, the pool of blood now black and crusted. Dreghorn imagined the sucking noise it would make when the corpse was prised off the deck.

Small, narrow shelves were set into an alcove just before the cross-bed, home to a familiar collection of trinkets and photographs. Familiar because most households held something similar: sweet, innocent mementoes of family life. Smith's were spattered with blood and brains and fragments of bone, clotted and hardened so that the images were impossible to discern.

It seemed like an insult to all families – to the celebration of affection, to normality, to the trappings of so-called civilized society. One photograph seemed to feature men in military uniform, but blotches of gore obscured their faces and any regimental details.

Smith had been kneeling in front of the photographs as if they were a shrine. Was that significant? Had the killer forced him to assume that position for a reason? Or had Smith just wanted to fill his gaze with the comfort of something he loved as he waited for death?

Dreghorn's mother had a similar military photograph on display, of him and his Uncle Joe – young and gallus before they went to war in 1914, safe in the knowledge that they would be back by that Christmas. Dreghorn did not return to Glasgow until 1920: six years of war of one sort or another. His uncle came home earlier, a ravaged man. Dreghorn felt the old rage grind within him, and the helplessness that went with it.

It seemed to take an age to rise to his feet, the walls of the cabin bearing down on him. McDaid was staring at him.

'You and me need to stay off boats, Jimmy,' he said. 'From now on, I'm a confirmed landlubber.'

CHAPTER 4

'I am capable of cooking for myself, you know.'

'Oh, aye,' Mairi McDaid said over her shoulder from the range. 'A regular Mrs Beeton.'

'Well, if you're no' hungry, wee man . . .' Needing no excuse where food was concerned, McDaid reached for Dreghorn's plate, even though he hadn't yet touched his own.

'Get!' Dreghorn raised his fork like a gladiator's trident to defend his mince and tatties. He feinted a couple of times until McDaid retreated, then smiled. 'I can cook for myself, but I'd have to be daft to turn down grub like this.' He reached for a slice of bread, already buttered and on the table in front of them.

Mairi set down her own plate, followed by two bottles of McEwan's Export. She sat beside her husband, opposite Dreghorn, who looked at the pair of them.

'It's just, you don't need to worry about me,' he stated.

'If I worry about anyone, it's myself, having to go around with you.' McDaid shovelled in a huge forkful of food, then gasped in cold air to stop his mouth burning. Mairi absent-mindedly slid a glass of water towards him.

'Archie says you're looking for somewhere else to live,' she said to Dreghorn.

'Does he now?'

McDaid ignored Dreghorn's frown, laughed. 'He's no' got much choice – the Merry Widow's found herself a new man.'

He poured his beer with typical abandon, then lunged forward to sook the overflowing froth from the top of the glass.

'I thought all that was . . .' Mairi left the rest unsaid.

'All that was nothing anyway; your man's imagination gets the better of him sometimes.' Dreghorn lifted his glass, angled it to pour his beer with a perfect head. 'It's true, though, Mrs Pettigrew does seem to have taken a shine to her latest lodger.'

'An educated man: university lecturer, no less,' McDaid stated. 'They go to the theatre together; not the music hall, the posh theatre' – he nodded at his wife – 'the kind you like.'

Mairi ignored him, smiled sympathetically at Dreghorn. 'He's a lodger too? Must be awkward for you and her.'

Dreghorn shrugged nonchalantly, but knew he wasn't fooling her.

McDaid wiped his plate with a chunk of bread. 'Must get the heebie-jeebies whenever they pass in the corridor. And the new man's room's right next to his. Why d'you think he's round here all the time?'

'You're the one that drags me back.' Dreghorn ate a forkful of mince, winked at Mairi. 'He claims all you do is nip his heid if I'm no' here. Bringing me back's the only way he gets any peace. So he says.'

'Peace? He doesn't know the meaning of the word, with those blasted pipes. Woke the whole house up last Sunday morning.'

'Folk pay good money to hear me play, and well you know it,' McDaid straightened like an outraged ramrod. 'You just don't appreciate that I'm an artist.'

Mairi waved a hand, dismissing his pretentions. 'Poor Morag thought Nessie was coming for her.'

New eyewitness accounts and photographs purporting to capture the monstrous underwater denizen of Loch Ness had been published in *The Inverness Courier* a few weeks earlier and were still the talk of the town.

'To be fair,' Dreghorn said, 'there is a resemblance.'

Mairi laughed, reached for her husband's glass as he finished refilling it and took a healthy sip for herself.

McDaid glowered. 'Hen-pecked in the hoose and downtrodden at work.' He thumped his chest. 'Us sporting heroes shouldn't have to put up with this.'

Dreghorn poured himself more beer. 'How's Morag settling in? How're you all settling in?'

In January, McDaid and his family had moved from their cramped tenement house to a semi-detached cottage in Mosspark with a front and back garden. Part of the 'Homes for Heroes' programme – the reality of which fell far short of the political promise – the rent was a stretch financially, but Chief Constable Sillitoe himself had pulled a few strings to accommodate the growing McDaid clan.

Archie and Mairi already had three sons – Wee Archie, Bruce and Kenneth – and had recently adopted Morag Gilmartin from Trinity Village, an orphan community in the Renfrewshire countryside. After months of weekend visits to assess their compatibility, which was never really in doubt, the adoption had been formalized just before the move. The last time Dreghorn had visited the girl had proudly shown him practice attempts at her new signature: Morag McDaid.

'Hard to credit the space we've got,' Mairi replied. 'Almost doesn't seem right, after just a room and kitchen. A bit of decorating to make it more our own' – a barbed look at McDaid – 'but, aye, it feels like home all right.'

'And Morag?'

Mairi had been a teacher before marrying McDaid, her

insight into the children extending beyond the domestic arena. 'She's happy, we think. We told our laddies to watch out for her at school, and she's not been strange with any of us since getting here. Misses some of her pals back at Trinity, but she'll make new ones and we'll make sure she stays in touch as much as we can.' She glanced at McDaid. 'She's stopped wetting the bed . . .'

'Touch wood,' McDaid planted a palm on the table.

'But she still has the bad dreams.'

'No wonder, poor lassie,' said Dreghorn.

The detectives had rescued Morag from a house fire in Trinity Village the year before. Prior to the blaze being set, she had been locked in a wardrobe, cowering in terror as the flames raged closer and the smoke stole her breath.

Didn't seem right to send her back after that, McDaid had said matter-of-factly at the time. He and Mairi now looked at each other with a depth of feeling Dreghorn doubted he'd ever know himself.

Mairi said, 'You can always stay here for a wee bit until you get yourself sorted out.'

Behind her back, McDaid, his eyes on Dreghorn, shook his head so vigorously it was a wonder he didn't get whiplash. He burst into an ingratiating smile as she glanced at him. 'Of course, long as you want,' he said, then paused. 'Or maybe back at the station? The cells are quite comfortable – the prisoners are aye saying so.'

They had remained at the *Blue Bonnet* until the police photographer had finished and the corpse had been transported to the morgue, by which time the light was fading. McDaid had joked that if Ellen was keen, she could get a lift back with the corpse and get dropped off at Turnbull Street on the way. She had elected to return with them in the Alvis. Another ambulance had ferried Dixie White, still moaning and groaning, to the Royal Infirmary.

They dropped Ellen off in Dennistoun and drove off quickly, in case her parents challenged them about the state of damp disarray in which they had delivered her.

Their shift had finished, but they still nipped into the station to file White's arrest. Dreghorn neglected to return the Alvis to the garage and drove McDaid home. The big man – trying to avoid the expense of post-work drinks – suggested that Dreghorn join them for dinner and a wee dram. Dreghorn noted that McDaid had recently adopted the term 'dinner' for an evening meal instead of 'tea'. The children had gone to bed, so they had crept in quietly, and Dreghorn attempted to leave with equal stealth.

Mairi said she'd walk him to the door, but stopped and turned to face him in the corridor.

'How are you, Jimmy?' she asked. 'Really.'

He started the usual answer, but she saw through it, saw the emptiness within him. For a moment her eyes became another's, full of love at first, then fear and hopelessness, and finally a dark nothing.

'I'm fine.' The words caught in his throat.

She nodded as if he wasn't fooling anyone, led him towards one of the bedroom doors and opened it enough for him to peer inside.

In one bed, he could see the form of Wee Archie, asleep, the blankets kicked off. In the other, he could just make out Morag's blonde hair and peaceful features. A soft toy in the shape of a Highland terrier that he'd bought for her rested in the crook of her arm.

Mairi slowly closed the door, keeping her eyes on Dreghorn.

'Whatever else is going on in your life, Jimmy,' she said, 'that wee lassie wouldn't be here if it wasn't for you. Remember that.'

'It was Archie that found her.' He put on his hat and stepped past her towards the front door, saying good night.

'Aye, you too,' she said, a little harshly.

No sooner had she shut the door after him than a gentle knock sounded on the other side. Dreghorn was standing there, having removed his hat. He darted forward with a boxer's speed and kissed her on the cheek.

'Thank you,' he said.

Sometimes it's all just darkness, easy to lose any sense of where you are. What you are, in some cases.

Chimneys, industrial and domestic, heaved black smoke into ebony skies; the air thickened, heavy and oppressive. Shapes gradually formed within the gloom, large swathes of the city's lighting extinguished to save money in the Depression, little thought given to the welfare of those walking the streets.

The hard edges of tenement blocks were etched into the darkness. Scrape the walls with a blade to remove the filth and you'd reveal hues of gold or red sandstone, like some magical artefact on an archaeological dig. More disturbing were the moving shadows, adopting human shape as they came towards you, too late to gauge whether they were harmless in nature and intent or predatory. If it hadn't been for the headlights of the Alvis, illuminating cobbled roads, stray dogs, gang members guarding street corners, it would have been easy to get lost, disorientated.

The steeple of the Caledonia Road United Presbyterian

Church loomed above Dreghorn as he approached the Gorbals and turned onto Crown Street. A house of God; turned black as sin by the world around it. Surely all that darkness couldn't fail to touch people, seep into their souls.

The warmth and reassurance he had gained from the company of the McDaid family was gone, illusory at best, but maybe better than nothing.

As he crossed over Albert Bridge onto the Saltmarket, the darkness lifted, the lights kept burning in the city centre. Dreghorn should have turned right onto Greendyke Street, returned the Alvis to the police garage, but he continued up High Street instead, then turned left at George Street, heading west.

He slowed as he neared Kelvinbridge. Mrs Pettigrew's townhouse was on the right, Hamilton Park Avenue. He accelerated past the turning, hardly even a conscious decision, and carried on until the darkness enveloped him again.

It was clearer now, cleaner, heading out into the East Dunbartonshire countryside, an occasional star glimmering overhead. The headlights flashed over trees and roadside bushes, grass verges, the twin orbs of a fox startled by the light and warning growl of the engine.

He reached Bearsden in less than twenty minutes, fewer tenements now, more spacious cottages and villas, an air of refinement and respectability. That could be illusory too.

Turn right, and Number 14 Boclair Road was a 'posh knocking shop', as McDaid once called it, with customers who arrived in Bentleys, Jaguars and Daimlers, and pretty young lassies who welcomed them with malt whisky or champagne, and flattered with a flair that made their visits seem tinged with genuine affection, not merely some sordid business transaction. The law wouldn't be paying Number 14 a visit any time soon. Many of those who made the laws were frequent visitors.

Dreghorn turned left onto Roman Road, stopped outside Number 36, switched off the engine. A quiet and stillness unlike those of the city. He thought about lighting a cigarette as he looked at the villa, almost obscenely large for a single occupant, especially when entire families were crammed into one or two rooms, ten or more per tenement. Block upon block, the weight of the city slowly crushing them.

Warm light glowed behind the curtains of the reception room on the lower floor. Did one of them twitch slightly? The woman inside also had secrets, a buried past that Dreghorn had uncovered during a murder investigation the previous October, plunging them both into horror and tragedy. He was the only one who knew her truth, and that secret had eventually thrown them together. He shook his head. Not so much togetherness as clinging to the wreckage.

He stared at the road ahead, the emptiness calling again. His hands hadn't left the wheel. He shouldn't be here. Again, it was hardly a conscious decision, more a low gut instinct. For a moment he felt as though he was being watched and looked around warily. Nothing. Just shadows probably, playing with his mind.

He glanced at the house again, then shook his head and sighed with a disconsolate smile. He turned the key in the ignition and started the car.

The front door to the villa opened. A woman stood there, her long hair tinged golden, her nightgown turned translucent by the light behind her. She looked like a bold angel, almost challenging him to cross the threshold.

He turned off the engine.

CHAPTER 5

Thursday, 30 March 1933

Shug Nugent was the fiercest desk sergeant in all of Glasgow. Niceties ricocheted off his implacable features like a pea-shooter fired at HMS *Hood* and were even harder to draw out of him.

'Detectives' meeting in the Lodge,' he said as Dreghorn came through the doors. 'Half an hour. All departments. Chief constable's orders.'

When they had a particularly recalcitrant suspect in for questioning, interrogating officers would sometimes send for Shug, who would simply sit across from the prisoner and stare. And stare. And stare. Bets were laid on how long it would take before the man was a gibbering wreck, ready to confess to any crime on their books.

'Cheers.' Dreghorn stopped at the door to the stairs, craned his neck to try and look over Nugent's counter. 'What are you wearing today?'

The rest of the station so rarely saw Nugent step out from behind his desk that they doubted he bothered to wear the bottom half of his uniform.

'Sequined ballgown,' Shug replied. 'Me and the wife are going dancing later.'

A quick jog up the stairs and Dreghorn opened the door to the Special Crime Squad. He glanced at the tam-o'-shanter pinned to the wood between the two long panes of glass like a Christmas wreath. He considered removing it, as Sillitoe was doing his rounds and wasn't the world's biggest fan of flippancy.

Hell mend you, he thought and left the tartan hat where it was; the chief constable's shameless promotion and mythologizing of his 'elite' team had resulted in various nicknames throughout the city – the printable ones being the Heavies, the Heavy Mob and the Tartan Untouchables, hence the headgear outside their office.

Dreghorn hung up his coat and hat, nodded to Big Fartie and Sammy Stirling, the night-shift detectives that week, who, due to knock off, were guzzling coffee to stay awake for Sillitoe's unscheduled briefing.

'Busy night, lads?' he asked.

A low noise, like a weary trombone note, emerged from Big Fartie as he rocked to one side on his chair. Dreghorn couldn't recall ever having heard Detective Constable Walter Maxwell – Big Fartie – actually speak, but the man's mastery of flatulence rivalled that of Le Pétomane, the tone and volume of his emissions perfectly capturing the mood of any situation.

'So-so,' Detective Sergeant Stirling translated. 'The incident book's on your desk. One thing, Jimmy. We heard a few sleekit whispers that Danny Semple's back in town.'

Daniel Semple, aged twenty-five, a member of the Norman Conquerors street gang, had fled the city the previous month after an assault on a rival gang member that almost left the man for dead. He was rumoured to have headed north, Aberdeen or Inverness, but the local constabularies had found no trace of him.

'Wouldn't be very smart of him,' Dreghorn said, 'but neither's stabbing somebody in broad daylight on the top deck of a busy tram, so par for the course maybe. Cheers, Sammy, I'll follow it up.'

He sat down, flicked through the overnight incident reports for investigations that would be carried through into the day shift. The usual attrition: drunkenness, domestic disturbances, a couple of gang fights brought about by incursions into enemy territory – slights against honour or just for the hell of it.

'No news from Northern on the Garngad gelignite?'

In the early hours of 24 March, 640 sticks of gelignite, 500 detonators and 60 feet of white tape fuse had been stolen from the Garngad Explosives Magazine, distribution centre for collieries across the west of Scotland, and a night watchman clubbed unconscious. Technically it was Northern Division's investigation, but the entire force was on alert because of the potential for casualties. Explosives were a valuable commodity in the underworld, handy for safe-cracking. Or blowing up rivals.

Stirling shook his head. 'Rumour is a couple of Special Branch jobbies are on their way up from down south, in case it's political.'

'Heaven forbid they let us plebs deal with something political.' Dreghorn returned to the book. Another report caught his attention.

'Les Campbell was assaulted?'

Stirling said, 'Aye. Didn't get much out of him, though. Barely conscious for the most part. A right good working over.'

'Where were Bull and the Conks?'

'No sign of them, according to Les's wife.'

'Strange, wouldn't have thought they'd leave Les out on a limb like that. Were they involved in some other stramash last night?'

'We spoke to three constables who were on the beat round about Norman Street and that neck of the woods. Nothing suspicious involving the Conks that they could see or hear.'

'Do you reckon that's genuine or a three-wise-monkeys act?'

'Wouldn't take one of them's word for it, but the other two are straight down the line and don't dish out favours to either side.'

The sectarian battle lines that were drawn between Glasgow's gangs also ran through the police force; natural prejudices or backhanders often resulted in a blind eye being turned. Catholics were a minority in the force, Dreghorn being the only one to reach the lofty heights of inspector, and that was through circumstances beyond the bosses' control. Not that he was first in the queue for Holy Communion. Whatever youthful faith he possessed had been shot to pieces in the Great War. The Great War, the Great Depression. Maybe greatness wasn't the best thing to strive for these days.

He looked up as Ellen Duncan entered the office.

'High and dry again, constable?' he asked.

'Perfectly, sir,' she said, placing a mug of tea in front of him. He eyed it suspiciously, having learned her philosophy towards hot beverages.

She noted his hesitation. 'Only the best for you, sir.'

'That's what Dr Crippen said to his wife.'

The door opened again and McDaid stormed in. Dreghorn marvelled once more at how the big man's shoulders hadn't quite yet worn grooves into the door frame.

'See you,' McDaid pointed at Dreghorn. 'I want a word with you.'

Dreghorn leaned back as if settling in for a cosy story, waved for the big man to continue.

'Morag,' McDaid said. 'Wee, sweet, butter-wouldn't-melt-

in-her-mouth Morag burst our Bruce's nose this morning. I'm
no' saying he wasn't asking for it – he can be a right wee nyaff –
but do you know what she said?' He glanced from Dreghorn to
Ellen and back again. ' "Uncle Jimmy told me to do it." Is that
so, "Uncle Jimmy?" '

Dreghorn shifted awkwardly. 'Aye and no. First time I met
her, at Trinity, there was a big baw-heid of an older boy bully-
ing her. So, I said – only if there was no alternative, like – for
her to . . .' He raised his guard, feigned a punch. 'But I wasn't
talking about your lads.'

McDaid flopped into his chair, grudgingly accepting the reasoning. 'She's got ring potential. Might be better than my own
three, from the shot she dished out.'

Ellen asked, 'What did she hit him with? Was it a. . .' – she
made a chopping motion with the edge of her hand – 'or a . . .'
She drove the heel of her hand straight out, then smiled as
McDaid's jaw dropped. 'Inspector Dreghorn's been instructing
me in self-defence at the police gym.'

McDaid puffed out his chest. 'Well, if you want to learn from
a true master, there's only one man in this station with an
Olympic medal.'

As she walked away, he gave Dreghorn a pious, judgemental
look, his chair transforming into a pulpit. 'Self-defence?'

'It's a tough city to live in all by yourself,' said Dreghorn.

'It's the kind of grappling it might involve that concerns me.'
Only half joking.

Dreghorn gave him a hard stare. 'Nothing like that. And
well you know it.'

'When it comes to houghmagandie, I wouldn't put anything
past you.'

*

'Don't mind me, men,' Chief Constable Percy Joseph Sillitoe said, sticking out like a sore thumb with his ramrod stance, impeccable uniform and English accent. 'DCI Monroe is in charge. I'll have a few words when he's finished.'

Sillitoe removed his hat and stepped to one side, giving Monroe the floor. They were gathered in the Murder Lodge, the name given to the CID offices by the rest of the station. Not so much because plainclothes was regarded as a step up in rank, as because the detectives were all rumoured to be Freemasons and viewed anyone not part of that select club with disdain.

Special Crime was affiliated to CID and the Robbery and Homicide offices, but essentially operated as a separate squad – Sillitoe's personal troubleshooters, with a remit to investigate crime across the city, regardless of divisional borders. The Lodge was crammed with extra bodies, thick with cigarette smoke; some detectives sat behind their desks, others stood with an attitude that in other circumstances would be described as loitering with intent. Dreghorn stood in front of McDaid, who could easily see over his head, and flicked his Ronson Princess, lighting a cigarette of his own, setting off a domino effect of flaring matches and exhaled smoke.

Monroe said, 'For those of you that haven't read your daily reports . . .'

'Or the teuchters that can't read,' piped up DC Brian Harvie with a daring glance at McDaid and Big Fartie, who hailed from Cromarty. The youngest detective in the Lodge, Harvie affected a mouthy gallusness that, if anything, only highlighted his inexperience. Sillitoe silenced him with a hawk-like glare.

'A body was discovered yesterday on a narrowboat on the Forth and Clyde Canal, near Maryhill Locks,' Monroe continued. 'Awaiting official identification, but we're fairly sure that the victim is the skipper of the boat: Reginald Smith, unmarried, no children. The body's been taken to the mortuary; we'll hopefully have initial post-mortem results later today. Smith wasn't found until late in the day, so the light was too poor for a forensics examination. Sergeant Hammond will conduct one today.'

'As long as the Heavy Mob didn't tramp all over the evidence.' Inspector Boyd Strachan's stony face turned towards Dreghorn from where he leaned upon the edge of his desk at the front of the office, as if preparing to usurp the briefing. His crony, Sergeant Orr, grinned in malevolent support. He was a shambling jumble of a man: head too big, arms too long, legs too short, brain too small, as though he'd been sewn together by Salvador Dalí instead of Dr Frankenstein.

'We should get Forensics to comb your 'tache, Boyd,' Dreghorn said. 'Looks like you've got half your breakfast stuck in there.'

Strachan's heavy ginger moustache twitched like a slug sprinkled with salt, the closest thing to a smile he'd ever give Dreghorn. A staunch Orangeman, he was the senior Murder Squad detective, with an admirable conviction record and, it was rumoured, a brutal interrogation technique that was nevertheless considerate enough to leave suspects' writing hands untouched. All the better to sign a forced confession with. He and Dreghorn had clashed dangerously the previous year over Strachan's conduct and subtly licentious harassment of Ellen. Dreghorn had since brokered an uneasy truce. Well, not so much brokered as blackmailed.

Strachan turned back to Monroe, as the chief inspector started again after an impatient pause. Dreghorn noticed him raise a hand to brush his moustache surreptitiously, just in case.

'Smith has no criminal record to speak of, but did appear before a magistrate earlier this year. Nothing major – a dispute over unpaid berthing fees – but terms were arranged and the case was dismissed. We're waiting for full employment records, but he seems to have worked the canals mostly. Assumed ownership of the narrowboat upon his father's death in 1924. An army man before that – served on the Western Front, Royal Highland Fusiliers.' Monroe nodded at Ellen. 'WPC Duncan?'

'I've taken a statement from a Mrs Lambie of the narrow-boat *Rose Red*. She's given me a list of other boats that work the canal and had some acquaintance with the victim, and of men who crewed for Smith, usually on a casual basis.' She waved a handful of papers. 'I've had it typed up.'

'Very diligent, constable,' Strachan complimented, moustache veiling his sincerity.

'Sir,' Ellen responded, coolly concealing her unease at Strachan's attention.

'Thank you, constable,' Monroe continued. 'Obviously the traffic on the canals is transient to a large degree, always on the move, which will make our job harder. Chief Constable Sillitoe has arranged for a Marine Division vessel to be put at our disposal to approach other crews for possible leads and confirm which, if any, need to come in for further questioning.'

'Bear in mind,' Sillitoe stated, 'that some of these vessels may be carrying illegal cargoes and might be reluctant to offer their cooperation. Stress that this is a murder investigation. Any such reluctance will be deeply frowned upon and could result in their cargoes – legal or otherwise – being impounded and their ships grounded. Carry on, chief inspector.'

'We need to find out who Smith's most recent clients were and what cargo he was ferrying, in case that had something to do with his death.'

The bald head and hawk nose of DS Lewis Tolliver rose into view as if his spine was being cranked by an unseen hand. In Dreghorn's head, whatever movement Tolliver made was accompanied by the creaking sound of a coffin lid. A wave of ennui swept through the detectives' ranks; even Sillitoe seemed to deflate somewhat, as Tolliver spoke with the same gravity he employed in his role as a Church of Scotland reader.

'Chief constable, chief inspector, a heinous crime indeed, but why does it require the presence of detectives from other departments?' His eyes rolled towards Dreghorn, as if the other detective was a likely suspect in the killing.

Monroe quickly cut off Tolliver's ministerial monotone. 'Because it's hardly your usual murder. Smith wasn't stabbed in the heat of the moment or bludgeoned to death during a drunken argument. His killing was cold, deliberate and, most likely, premeditated. No signs of forced entry or of a struggle. He was on his knees, with the killer behind him. A single shot to the back of the head. It wasn't some daft wee ned running about, blasting away like a Wild West gunfighter. It was expertly done. An execution.'

Tolliver was about to pass another judgement, but Strachan motioned for him to sit down, saying, 'Save the sermon for later, Tolli.'

'We know that there are guns all over the city, souvenirs from the war – a Mauser lifted from a dead Boche, a Webley pinched from an officer's holster, maybe even the odd Lee

Enfield.' Monroe cast his eyes over the detectives. 'Probably we even have some of them ourselves, those who're old enough. But despite that, firearms offences are rare.'

'Because they know it'd be the long drop for them.' Orr grinned brutishly.

'The Murder Squad will investigate, under Inspector Strachan. The rest of you, continue with your current caseloads, but with an emphasis on possible firearms connections. Anyone you think might know something – informants, suspects in other crimes – come down hard on them. Anyone looking to buy or sell guns or ammunition, bring them in and we'll show them the error of their ways. It's bad enough with chibs and blades, but if the gangs get it into their heads that they need to start pulling guns to maintain their reputation as hard men . . .' He let the observation hang in the air, looked at Sillitoe.

'An expert analysis, chief inspector.' Sillitoe stepped forward, a politely imposing figure, though that balance could easily shift into harsher territory. 'I have little to add beyond this: We're well acquainted with the violence that blights these streets and the terror of the gangs, but this murder crosses a line. I will not have guns in my city.'

Dreghorn could almost see the hair bristling on the necks of some of the detectives and read their thoughts: *His city? Who does he think he is, English bastard?*

Sillitoe gauged their reactions with the briefest of smiles. His voice became keener, like a blade sharpening on a whetstone. 'I may not have been born in Glasgow, but I have come to admire and respect the city. And its people.' A pause, almost daring hecklers to speak. 'I may reside outside its boundaries, but I spend the greatest part of my time here, and my wife and daughter are frequent visitors. I will have the streets safe for them, for your families and for every other law-abiding citizen. I will fight for that, and I will fight for you in the course of your duties. I repeat: I will not have guns in my city. And you will do whatever is necessary to enforce that law. Do you understand?'

'Yes, sir,' the detectives answered in unison, like a smoky, gravelly voiced school assembly.

'Gentlemen, Constable Duncan.' Sillitoe cast his eyes over his officers. 'See it through.'

He turned and talked quietly to Monroe. The detectives got to their feet with a business-like air, discussing the case, dividing tasks between themselves. Ellen moved amongst them, handing out the list of interviewees she had drawn up. McDaid nudged Dreghorn in outrage as she neared Strachan.

Orr snatched the list from her hand with a dismissive 'Aye, cheers, hen.' Strachan accepted the document with an air of quiet ceremony. As Ellen moved away, he placed a hand on her arm to halt her. She did well not to flinch.

'I'd like to review the list with you, Ellen, if you don't mind.' He looked at Dreghorn, gave his moustache a slow, almost sexual stroke with thumb and forefinger.

Dreghorn gritted his teeth and was moving towards them when Sillitoe appeared before him, gesturing at the door. In the corridor outside, Sillitoe nodded to a couple of passing officers, waiting until they were out of earshot.

'This killing, Dreghorn,' he said. 'Do you think it might have a sectarian element?'

'We're in Glasgow, sir. What doesn't?'

CHAPTER 6

Gambling was illegal, but since when did that stop anyone? In the criminal rankings, next to murder, rape, assault and even housebreaking it was viewed as more of a harmless pastime, something to be indulged with a roll of the eyes, an exasperated sigh.

Unless, of course, you were about to get your fingers broken for cheating at cards; or your weans were starving hungry because you'd tossed away the last of the Public Assistance money on a nag so slow it might as well have been hobbled; or your wife was forced out to hoor on the streets to feed the family, shivering and near catching her death because you'd pawned her only coat for a tip that was a sure thing, honest.

Some would say Glasgow was a city of gamblers, whether it was for financial gain – the turn of a card, the pitch of a coin, the first to nose it over the finish line – or more existential: the flash of blades against each other in the moonlight, the swing of a fist, whoever strikes first wins. All fun and games, until somebody loses an eye. Or their homes, their families. Their lives.

But it's worth it for the thrill, the one that reminds you that you're still alive, and for the spark of hope that you can rise out of the Depression, that you might just be the one to beat the odds.

Nobody beats the odds. But once you've started trying, once

that corrosive dice is rolling through your blood, it's too late to stop.

Nobody beats the odds, except of course the person who makes them.

That's what you'd say, Dreghorn reckoned, when you rolled up outside bookmaker Leslie Campbell's Pollokshields villa, with the crunch of Scottish beach pebbles – specially transported from the coast – under your feet as you approached the front door, which chimed like an angel announcing your arrival.

It's what you'd say when the pretty young maid ushered you inside and led you up the deep-pile stair runner to the bedrooms, past paintings of racehorses and bare-knuckle prizefighters in Victorian long-johns. It's what you'd still think as she waved you, surprisingly gravely, into the master bedroom and your eyes scanned the plush decor, slid over the finest of cotton sheets on the grandiose bed.

This conviction might be shaken, however, when you spied the master of the house, propped up stiffly on huge pillows, his head swollen to the size of a beach ball, his skin a patchwork of purple bruising, dotted black with dried blood. One eye was closed over and resembled two bloated leeches, cleaved together to suck from the same wound. The other glared furiously at Dreghorn and McDaid as they entered.

McDaid recoiled, then adopted a Quasimodo hunch. 'The bells, the bells!' he said.

They didn't quite catch Les Campbell's snarled response, although it definitely ended with 'off'.

'We received reports of an assault here last night, Les,' Dreghorn said.

'Somebody made a mistake then, didn't they? It was an accident. I fell.'

'Where from, Ben Nevis?' Dreghorn moved to one side of the bed, McDaid to the other, causing Campbell spasms of pain as he looked from one to the other.

'Outside. Getting out of the car. That bloody gravel's treacherous.'

McDaid leaned over the bed like a visiting surgeon. 'Look, they missed a bit.' He prodded Campbell's temple, causing the bookmaker to yelp. 'Sorry, Les, trick of the light. That's been bashed as well.'

'What do you mean, "they"?'

'Whoever duffed you up,' Dreghorn said. There was no apparent firearms connection to the assault, but the fact that the Norman Conks had left Campbell high and dry was suspicious enough to warrant following up first. Breaking the razor-gangs was the Untouchables' main priority. 'What was it, a robbery? Or is the competition heating up?'

'Nobody touched me. I told you, I fell. Maybe I'd had a few drams.' Campbell fixed Dreghorn with his good eye. 'You two need a warrant to come in here. On your way, or I'll get Garrison on to you.'

Dreghorn and McDaid shared a look. George Garrison was the defence lawyer of choice for those with loose morals, money to burn and delusions that their reputations were worth saving. 'Get me Garrison!' was what they all cried.

Dreghorn put on his most reasonable voice. 'I'm afraid Mr Garrison would have to inform you that we're only doing our job. A crime was reported at these premises and we're duty-bound to investigate.'

'By who?' Campbell demanded.

'Your wife.'

'Aye, well, she made a mistake. Easy done.'

'Seemed pretty sure, from the statement she gave.' McDaid flipped open his notebook, read the notes he'd taken from Sammy Stirling's report, as if giving evidence in court. ' "I was listening to the wireless" – this is your missus talking – "when I heard the Daimler arrive. Must have been half-past ten or so, because Ray Fox and his band had just started playing, live from the Kit-Cat Restaurant. I could tell something was wrong from the speed the car was going. It screeched to a halt, scrunching gravel everywhere. I looked out of the window and saw two men drag Leslie from the back seat and dump him on the ground. He was all limp, just hanging in their arms. I thought he was dead. By the time I got to the door, the car – our car – was racing off again. I called an ambulance, then I called the polis." ' McDaid snapped shut his notebook. 'Sounds like a reliable witness to me.'

'You might not remember,' Dreghorn added, 'but two of our colleagues were here last night. You weren't in a fit state for questioning, though you did refuse to go to hospital. Where is your wife? We'd like to speak to her.'

'Dundee.' It was impossible to read Campbell's pummelled features, but there was triumph in his voice. 'At her sister's for a few days.'

'For her own protection or to stop her talking to us?'

'Family visit. They're very close.'

'Leaving you here in a state like this?' asked McDaid.

Campbell attempted to shrug. 'I'm no' an easy patient, and the wife's no' the most sympathetic of nurses. I'm better off with the maid.'

Dreghorn sat on the bed. McDaid did the same on the

opposite side. Campbell whimpered in pain as the mattress rocked like a storm-tossed lifeboat. Dreghorn offered the bookmaker a cigarette, which he accepted, and lit them both. One puff and Campbell's body was racked with agonizing coughs.

He jammed the cigarette between swollen fingers and wheezed, 'Cheers, just what I needed.'

Dreghorn said, 'Who were the two men, Les?'

'What two men's that?'

'The ones that dumped you off like a sack of tatties last night.'

'Don't know. Couple of good Samaritans, maybe? Is that what the Bible calls them?'

The bed rocked again as McDaid lurched to his feet and looked out of the window. 'Did they take your car as payment for helping out? Don't see it out there.'

'Maybe the wife took it to her sister's.' Campbell managed another draw, didn't cough this time. 'Or maybe it's at the garage. Or parked at the office. I'm no' sure. My memory's playing up. Bang on the heid, y'know?'

The detectives glanced at each other. McDaid leaned on the windowsill and folded his arms.

'Bull Bowman's no' doing a very good job,' Dreghorn said.

'Good job of what?' Too innocent to be true.

'Being your bodyguard.'

'Bull and me are pals from the old days, that's all.' Campbell would've laughed scornfully if it hadn't been too sore. 'I don't need guarding. I'm a shop owner, a grocer – with a wee concession at Ayr racecourse right enough, but that's just a hobby really, a wee bit of fun.'

'You don't look like you're laughing much the day.' Dreghorn stood, picked up his hat. 'So you don't want to press charges for this assault – the one that never happened.'

'Sherlock Holmes has got nothing on you, inspector.'

Dreghorn paused as he and McDaid reached the door. 'We'll put out an alert, see if we can't find your car. Least we can do for a law-abiding citizen with a bad memory.'

'Very kind.' Campbell's reaction could have been a grimace or a smile. 'On your way out, lads, if you see the maid, ask her to come up, eh? My pillows need fluffing.'

They neglected to pass on the request. Walking back to the Alvis, McDaid asked, 'What do you make of all that?'

'I'd say he doesn't fancy the odds of surviving if he tells us anything resembling the truth.'

CHAPTER 7

'You're in with the big boys now, hen.' Detective Sergeant Orr hoicked at the crotch of his trousers as if what they contained was too large and powerful to rest easy. 'Murder, that's where it's at, isn't it, sir?'

'First-division,' said Inspector Strachan. 'A bit of class.'

Ellen could only see Strachan's eyes, reflected in the rear-view mirror as they flicked towards her, but she could imagine the slow, smoothing stroke of his moustache that accompanied the comment. His gaze made her skin crawl under her uniform, but she refused to register any discomfort, gave a professional nod.

'Grateful for the opportunity, sir.'

Orr leaned over, nudged her with his shoulder. Again she refused to react, stared fixedly out of the side window. The towering sign of the Bryant and May matches factory, where the Scottish Bluebell brand was produced, came into view above the rooftops. Like many businesses, it had its own wharf on a corpse-free stretch of the Forth and Clyde Canal.

'She's grateful, sir,' Orr said. 'Are you grateful to Jimmy too? He's aye taking you out and about on wee jaunts away from the station.'

'Even though, strictly speaking, it is against regulations.' In the front passenger seat, DS Tolliver tutted loudly at the thought of flouted regulations. Normally Ellen found his presence as welcome as an open casket in a front room, but now his upright moral piety seemed reassuring.

'So you keep saying, minister.' Orr glared at the back of Tolliver's head, then leered back at Ellen. 'So, how do you show your gratitude, PC Duncan? What do you do for Dreghorn that keeps him panting keen to have you around?'

Ellen said, 'My duty as a police officer.'

'Police wumman.' Orr gave a bark of a laugh. 'Not quite the same thing, making tea and taking notes.'

'Did you enjoy your tea earlier?'

'Eh?'

'The tea you asked for before we left. Did it taste all right?'

'What do you mean?'

'Nothing.' Pause. 'Just, I thought the milk smelled a wee bit funny. I mean, once the bottle's open and sitting there, anybody could do anything to it.'

Orr was silent, his Neanderthal brow deep in a frown.

'But a first-class detective like you would notice if there was anything wrong, wouldn't he?'

'Aye, too true I would.' Orr turned away hastily and looked out of the side window. Ellen could hear his mouth moving like a cow chewing the cud, trying to detect remnants of a suspicious taste.

'Don't worry, Graham,' Strachan said, 'you talk so much pish you wouldn't notice anyway.' His eyes were in the mirror again, an admiring smile in them. Ellen gritted her teeth and turned away. Every time she defended herself or showed some spirit, Strachan seemed more interested, not that he revealed it to anyone else. He was too clever for that. 'Better wash your mouth out anyway, Graham. Be on the safe side.'

They were in a police Alvis, driving up Maryhill Road

towards the Forth and Clyde Canal, where they were to rendezvous with a Marine Division motorboat to stop and question boat-owners travelling along the stretch of the murder scene. She had been thrown when, after the detectives' briefing, Strachan had requested that she accompany them. For the better part of the last six months the inspector had paid her little attention – it was rumoured that he and Inspector Dreghorn had had a confrontation over Strachan's treatment of her – but in the last couple of weeks she had been aware of the odd look, the placing of a supposedly avuncular hand on her arm, shoulder, the small of her back. Her mind hadn't been fully focused on work. The sound of her father's coughing that morning, the gurgling in his lungs and his ashen features as he waved her out of the door in case she was late were all she could think of.

Sandy Duncan had been in the submarines during the war, and whatever had happened to him in the cloying little hellhole of an engine-room at the bottom of the ocean had scarred his insides. When he'd returned home, never speaking of his experiences, all he had wanted was to walk in the fresh air and get to know his daughter again. They'd strolled the parks of Glasgow and hiked the surrounding hills religiously, but even that was growing beyond him now.

Strachan had ordered Ellen to put aside her other duties and join the Murder Squad on their door-to-door – or 'boat-to-boat, in this case'. Any hopes that this might have been some acknowledgement of her abilities was quickly dashed by the banter during the journey. She was little more than a dogsbody when they arrived at the canal, being expected to keep shtum and take notes, saving the other detectives the onerous task of having to actually write in their own notebooks.

Marine Division had stationed their launch in the centre of the riverway to intercept traffic in both directions. They checked the papers and identification of the crew of any approaching ship and instructed them to pull into the canal side for questioning. Any reluctance to comply was quickly dispelled by a threat to check the cargoes they were carrying and the seaworthiness of the vessel. The threat was clear: even if the cargoes were perfectly legal and the boats in tip-top shape, the police would soon discover irregularities and problems, if cooperation wasn't forthcoming.

And so Ellen flipped open her notebook, stifling tuts and shakes of the head as she observed Strachan and Orr's interrogation techniques. Did you know the deceased Reginald Smith? When did you last see him? How often do you travel this way? Have you noticed anything or anyone suspicious on the canal, people or boats that you've never seen before? Has anyone tried to hire you for illegal activities? Did Smith seem scared or worried about anything? What was that? Speak up, you big Jessie. Take your cap off when you're talking to a polisman. If you don't want to answer, we'll fuckin' take you down the station and ask harder – up to you, wee man.

Menace and intimidation, that's all it was. Immerse the suspect – they weren't even suspects, far from it – in a climate of fear and increase the pressure. If they had been hidden away in a police cell, how many of those questioned would have ended up on their knees, gasping for breath after a low punch or a knee to the balls?

It was all wrong, as far as she was concerned, guaranteed to build barriers between the police and the people they were meant to protect. Us and them. And we're the ones with the power. That was Strachan's attitude.

She had sat in on interrogations with Inspector Dreghorn; he was clever, cunning, able to break suspects down psychologically, but there was still an element of confrontation, a battle of wills. Maybe it was simply a male characteristic, a marginally less twisted version of the same drives that saw gangs waging war in the streets, marking their territory with spilled blood. Ultimately those battles were pointless and futile too, a raging at the heartless indifference of the world, but the damage they caused was all too real – physical, psychological, emotional. Generation upon generation of damage.

Ellen imagined that the real way to draw information, confessional or otherwise, from suspects was through empathy: build a relationship, show compassion and understanding. Violence and brutality would only release half-truths and desperate lies, forced confessions. It isn't about us and them, she thought – there's only us.

She wouldn't be getting a chance to test her theories any time soon, though. Strachan and Orr's inquiries shed no further light on the murder of Reginald Smith, each interview ending with Orr glancing disdainfully at her and asking, 'Did you get all that, hen?'

She did, every useless irrelevant detail, all captured in a shorthand that would be impossible for the detectives to decipher without her or one of the station secretaries. Maybe she wasn't that far above games of 'us and them' herself.

Eventually, with Orr's ample stomach grumbling like a bear with a sore head, Strachan gave Ellen a few bob and ordered her to go and find them something to eat – pies, bridies or rolls and sausage, and 'a sweetie for yourself', as if she was a greetin'-faced wean being rewarded for behaving herself.

She left them to clamber clumsily aboard another boat and

walked along the canal bank, stopping for a moment on the aqueduct to admire the view of the River Kelvin as it wound its way through the West End towards the Clyde. There was more police activity further along the waterway: Sergeant Hammond's forensics examination of the *Blue Bonnet*. WPC Jean Malloy emerged from the hatchway, with bagged evidence in her gloved hands. Spotting Ellen, she pulled down the surgical mask that covered her nose and mouth and smiled.

'You drew the short straw the day, hen.'

'I don't know about that,' Ellen said. 'Creeping about a murder scene's no picnic.'

'I'd rather be hobnobbing with a deid body than Strachan and Orr,' Jean stated bluntly. A few years Ellen's senior, and as veteran as a woman on the force could be, she took a materteral interest in her younger colleague. 'Watch yourself. You know where I am if you need me.'

Ellen nodded her appreciation. 'Fancy something to eat?'

'No, you're all right.'

'DI Strachan's paying.'

'Does he know that?' Jean laughed as Ellen shook her head. 'I'll have the works then.'

Ellen carried on towards the lock, but didn't get far before another voice called out.

'Dried off now, have you?'

Ellen stopped, so wrapped up in herself that she hadn't taken notice of the *Rose Red*, still berthed where it had been the day before. Mrs Lambie stood at the tiller, the unlit pipe seemingly a permanent fixture at the side of her mouth.

Ellen smiled and tugged at her lapel. 'Spare uniform. Thanks again.' She looked along the length of the boat. 'Thought you might have moved on by now.'

'No cargo to shunt, nowhere to go. Can't waste what fuel we've got – it's not a pleasure cruise.'

Ellen nodded, unsure what to say. She tried not to look at the woman's ragged clothes and inwardly cursed the Depression. So much unemployment, so many lives hanging by a thread, unravelled by the greed of others.

'Where's the one who was with you yesterday: Dredger or whatever he's called, the no' bad-looking one?'

'Inspector Dreghorn?' Ellen almost laughed at the description. 'On another case.'

Mrs Lambie nodded sourly in the direction of Strachan and Orr, the police launch just visible further along the river. 'Prefer him to this pair.'

'You're not the only one.'

The older woman's pipe jerked up and down, as if she was biting back words.

'Is something wrong, Mrs Lambie?'

'There's somebody who wants to say something.' She jerked her pipe at Strachan and Orr, but kept her eyes on Ellen. Her gaze could have scared off a shark. 'But no' to them. He's a gentle soul, wouldn't hurt a fly. Them? I know their sort. They'd take advantage, twist his words . . .'

Ellen wished she could disagree. 'I could arrange for him to see Inspector Dreghorn at the station. Or –' she glanced around surreptitiously – 'maybe I could speak with him myself?'

CHAPTER 8

For a moment Dreghorn was a wee boy again, transported back to a time of wonder and innocence – before Shanghai, before the war, before the shipyards, even before he had put on the gloves for the first time and danced about a ring, boxing shadows that his imagination turned into Jack Johnson, Bombardier Billy Wells or Tancy Lee.

In those days all it cost to escape the grim, grimy city was the price of a tram ride if his mother was with him, or the shame of being caught trying to dodge the fare if he and his pals were off on an adventure of their own. A tram ride to Kelvingrove Art Gallery and Museum in the West End, an international palace of culture and history on the banks of the River Kelvin, with free entry to fire the imagination and raise the spirits of even the most downtrodden citizens.

Dreghorn smiled at the memory as he gazed up at his favourite childhood exhibit, a magnificent specimen that dwarfed even McDaid: weathered grey skin, legs like tree trunks, yellowing tusks that seemed to curve all the way back to prehistoric times, and dark eyes that seemed soulful, even though he knew they weren't real.

No doubt a taxidermist's nightmare, Sir Roger the Asian Elephant had toured the country with Bostock & Wombwell's Menagerie in the late 1800s, before becoming part of the Scottish Zoo in New City Road.

'You know they had to get a firing squad from Maryhill Barracks to put the big yin there down?'

A wee man in a bunnet had sidled up to Dreghorn, flashing an overly friendly smile. He cocked his head at Sir Roger, one eye on the elephant as if it might suddenly spring to life, the other on the detective. Dreghorn didn't return the smile.

'Aye,' the wee man continued, 'developed some medical condition or something that caused him to go doolally and get all aggressive, start attacking everybody.'

Dreghorn was well aware of this condition. 'It's called living in Glasgow,' he said.

Homburg pushed back on his head, McDaid was seated on a bench, enjoying the sunlight from the arched windows high overhead and scanning the museum crowd – schoolchildren on a trip with their teacher; middle-class mothers pushing prams; older women in pairs, their men lost in the Great War or the Boer War; office staff eating their pieces on a dinner-break; unemployed yard or factory workers looking to fill the long empty hours. No one to raise a detective's suspicions. Until he spotted Dreghorn's companion.

'You're late,' he huffed.

Dreghorn deposited the wee man in the centre of the bench and sat down himself. Squashed between the detectives, the man removed his bunnet, one eye looking straight ahead and the other towards the nearest exit, as if calculating the odds of reaching it before McDaid flattened him.

Calculating the odds was second nature to Hamish 'Bosseye' Balfour, a mathematical skill honed as a child when bullies targeted his lazy eye and he had to gauge whether his sharp patter would deflect them or provoke greater violence, due to the intellectual humiliation. He was another bookmaker, though unlike Leslie Campbell he hadn't ascended to the heights of semi-legality with a government-sanctioned (and taxed) race-track franchise, the only place where gambling in earnest was allowed.

Bosseye was a street bookie, his office an intangible, almost mythical concept, forever changing locations – pub, cafe, back-court, steamie, street corner – to remain one step ahead of the polis. The calm centre of a whirlwind of runners and betting notes, he was the conduit for incriminating gossip and indis-creet asides from across the city, as well as Dreghorn and McDaid's best snitch, albeit a reluctant one.

'This is cosy.' He smiled politely. 'What can I do for you fine fellows today? Always a pleasure.'

'Guns,' said Dreghorn.

'This is about that poor bastard you found on the canal boat?'

The detectives leaned forward to glance at each other. Dreg-horn had bet McDaid that Bosseye would already be aware of the Smith murder, even though details were being withheld. The post-work dram was on the big man tonight.

'You know me.' Bosseye tapped his temple. 'See things that no one else sees; hear things that no one else hears.'

'Aye, well, if you see or hear anything involving firearms, make sure you come straight to us. Anyone looking to buy or sell a heater, or boasting about using one to sort someone out.'

'There's no' a big market for guns round here, inspector, you know that. The sentences for getting caught are too heavy. Most gangs prefer a square go, anyway. Doesn't take a hard man to pull a trigger – any wee ned can do that. And they aren't cheap. There's a Depression on, remember? Why splash good beer-money on a cannon when you can stab someone in the back with a knife from the scullery?'

'What about the victim?'

'Smith? Uh-uh, never heard of him. If he was a gambling man, he wasn't sharp enough to lay bets with an honest bookie like me.'

McDaid harrumphed loudly at the concept of Bosseye's honesty, startling two elderly women as they passed.

Dreghorn said, 'If he worked the canals, he could've been involved in transporting stolen goods or something shady.'

'I daresay I could give you good odds on that.'

'Ask around, see if you can shorten them further.'

'Anything you say, inspector,' Bosseye said, his insouciance level carefully judged.

'Do you have any dealings with Les Campbell?'

'Me? No. Too high up the tree for me. Why?'

'Someone beat him up last night,' McDaid said. 'A right good doing.'

Bosseye seemed genuinely shocked. 'There's a fair few would be happy to see that, but no' many gallus enough to try it. Bull Bowman and the Norman Conks are usually around to watch his back.'

'Not last night they weren't. Heard anything about them having a falling-out?'

Bosseye raised his hands as if at gunpoint. 'I make it a point never to get involved with my competitors. Or someone as heavy-handed as Bull. One time when a horse didn't come in for him, he offered to straighten up my bad eye for me. With a pick-shaft. That's the sort of surgery I can do without.'

'Not everyone appreciates you the way we do,' McDaid pointed out.

'Said the rock to the hard place.' Bosseye rolled his good eye, then had a thought. 'Got your Sweepstake ticket yet? Big jackpot on the horizon. I could maybe, just maybe, get youse a couple. Remember: "If You're Not In, You Can't Win." '

Dreghorn said, 'Nobody should be in over here. Last time I looked, they were illegal.'

'Good cause, though: hospitals in the Free State, sick and needy children.' Bosseye winked cheekily with his bad eye. 'Surely you have to turn a blind eye to that?'

'Maybe. As long as the money's going where it's supposed to.'

The Irish Hospitals' Sweepstake had been set up in 1930 by the Free State government to finance the building of new hospitals, a lottery in which punters hoped and prayed to be matched with the winning horses in major races across Ireland and Britain. Tickets were sold internationally, stretching beyond the Irish diaspora to encompass anyone who liked a bet. The world had gone crazy for the Sweep, human avarice being fuelled by the destitution of the Depression.

There was only one snag. Gambling was illegal in two of the Sweep's biggest markets – the United Kingdom and America – making it a criminal enterprise in those territories. Tickets had to be smuggled in, the gargantuan profits smuggled out, and counterfeiting scams were rife.

Bosseye tutted sadly. 'You have no faith in human nature, inspector.'

'Maybe I've too much faith – in how rotten it is.'

Bosseye looked back and forth at the detectives as if considering doing them a good turn. 'Would you, by any chance, be looking for Danny Semple?'

McDaid said, 'The very man we were going to ask you about. There's a vicious rumour that he's back in town.'

'And you'd appreciate a tip to his whereabouts?'

'Demand it.'

Bosseye flicked through metaphorical betting slips in his head. 'If I was you, I'd park myself – or some lowly plod whose time isn't as valuable – outside the Sarry Heid to see who's nipping in for a dram.'

'It's a fine establishment.' Dreghorn stood up. 'And Sergeant McDaid does owe me a drink.'

McDaid followed, glanced down at Bosseye. 'Watch your back, wee man. Just in case some enterprising outlaw has decided that bookies are an easy target.'

The bookie's eyes sparkled. 'Why, Archie, you do care.'

CHAPTER 9

Callum Baird may have been a gentle soul, but he had a strapping workhorse build that would have made him an asset in any shipyard or dockside on the Clyde, if there had been any work around. Hands like shovels and wide shoulders that would only grow thicker with age and heavy labour, but when he spoke or broke through his crippling shyness to make eye contact, his voice was soft and he seemed younger than his fifteen years.

Ellen asked, 'How did you know Mr Smith?'

'Captain Smith,' Callum corrected her excitedly. 'That's what you call the skipper on a boat. He had a cap and everything.'

'Captain Smith then.' She figured this was more of an affectation on Smith's part than an official title, but played along.

'Known him for donkey's, since I was a wean. I used to come down and watch the boats.'

'Come down from where, Callum?'

'Over there.' He pointed at the dark outline of the tenement blocks on the opposite side of the canal. '1515 Maryhill Road, second floor, third hoose,' he continued as if the address had been drummed into him in case he ever got lost. Ellen understood why Mrs Lambie wanted to shield him from the attentions of Strachan and Orr.

'So, you worked for Captain Smith?'

'Oh, aye!' As if it was his purpose in life. 'Used to carry things on and off the *Bonnet* while Captain Rex had a smoke and supervised. And I'd travel with him when he was picking up cargoes and taking them to other places. He'd let me steer sometimes. And blow the whistle.'

Ellen glanced at Mrs Lambie, who said, 'All casual. And no' exactly paying the going rate, I'd imagine.'

'Callum.' Ellen looked back at the boy, who quickly lowered his eyes. 'You know you're not going to see the captain again, don't you?'

A curtain of despair fell over the boy's features. 'Aye, Mrs Lambie told me. He died.'

'He didn't just die, Callum, someone killed him – do you understand?'

He nodded, lip quivering. She could almost see the lump in his throat.

'Did anyone else work for Captain Smith?'

'Just me. I was his First Mate, that's what he always said.'

'You were obviously good at it. He must have thought highly of you.'

Callum smiled, met her eyes briefly, chuffed at the observation.

'And when did you last see him? Mrs Lambie said it was about a week ago.'

'About that, a wee bit more maybe. I've come down every day since and banged on the hatch, but there was no answer.'

Mrs Lambie said, 'It was Callum who first said to us. He was worried.'

Ellen nodded. 'The people that hired you to transport goods up and down the canal, did you ever meet any of them?'

Callum looked at Mrs Lambie.

'Tell her what you told me, Callum,' the older woman said. 'I know she's a polis, but she's all right. And this is important.'

'Not normally – Captain Rex did all the talking. I just waved when we were picking stuff up or delivering, and there's not been much work lately.'

'For anyone,' Mrs Lambie added bitterly.

'But last week he told me that we had a big job on, but that I wasn't to tell any of the other boats in case they' – a guilty glance at Mrs Lambie – 'tried to steal it from us. He said to come at night too, not early in the morning when we usually started.'

'Do you remember what day it was, Callum?' Ellen asked.

'I'm no' very good with dates and stuff, miss. Last week, maybe Friday?'

Ellen nodded: within twenty-four hours of Smith's time of death, as estimated by the Chief Police Surgeon, Professor Glaister.

'So, I did,' Callum said. 'I came down to the canal that night, could hardly see a thing in the dark, but when I got to the boat, Captain Rex said he didn't need me after all. He said he was sorry and all that, but the people who hired him wanted to crew the boat themselves. That's a wee bit strange, isn't it?'

'Did you see any of them?'

'Oh, aye, they were there – three of them at least, but it was dark, so I couldn't really make them out. I mean, Captain Rex had a lantern, but . . .'

'How did the captain seem – just his usual self or . . .'

Callum hummed and hawed, then said, 'I thought he seemed nervous, talking all quiet and . . . I could smell whisky on his breath. He'd been drinking more and more lately, said he was worried about losing the boat, 'cos there was no work. He must've been getting desperate, to let those men hire him.'

'Why?'

'Well, they were trying to be quiet, but I've got good ears, I could hear them talking. They had' – he leaned closer, conspiratorial – 'Irish accents. Captain Rex didn't like the Irish. He was in the army over there, I think, and was always going on about them. "Dirty fuckin' Irish", that's what he called them.'

'Callum!' Mrs Lambie almost bit the stem of her pipe in two.

'Och, I'm awful sorry, Mrs Lambie.' Callum hung his head, sheepishly raised his eyes to Ellen. 'But that's what he called them.'

CHAPTER 10

'When I was a wean and I heard people mention the Sarry Heid, I thought they meant "Sorry Head" – something to do with a hangover.'

'A born detective, Jimmy, even back then,' McDaid noted. 'You weren't that far off.'

As if on cue, a man with legs bandy enough for a small child to scoot through caromed out of the double-height doors of the Saracen Head pub and stood swaying as if in the midst of a mighty storm and not a surprisingly pleasant spring evening.

Dreghorn said, 'When I learned it was short for the Saracen Head, I had to ask my uncle why it was called that.'

'Because some unlucky ancient Arab warrior got his lands invaded and his head chopped off and served up on a platter to some mad King of England during the Crusades?' McDaid snorted. 'That would've been a cracking holiday abroad, the Crusades. I mean, between that and our war . . .'

'Give me a hangover any day.'

They were in the administrative office of the Barras Market, across the road from the Saracen Head, which was named, rather more mundanely, for the once-adjacent Saracen Lane. It claimed to be the oldest public house in Glasgow, although the original building, demolished in 1904, was actually located on the site next door to where the detectives were currently concealed.

A taxi pulled up outside it. Three men got out, all well dressed, two in fedoras, one in a wide-brimmed bunnet.

'Is that Bull Bowman?' Dreghorn leaned closer to the window, raising a pair of dainty opera glasses to his eyes.

'Top-quality surveillance equipment, by the way,' McDaid complimented sarcastically.

'Mrs Pettigrew's. She'd be pleased to know they've been drafted in to help the forces of law and order in their war against crime.'

'You nicked them then.'

'Borrowed.'

The slab-like figure of Bull Bowman sharpened into focus through the lenses, as he opened the Saracen's door and gestured affably for his companions to enter. Dreghorn couldn't identify the other men, who had their backs to him.

'Give us a shot.'

Dreghorn carefully handed over the glasses, which looked dangerously delicate in McDaid's hand. 'Watch you don't break them.'

The big man scoffed and placed the glasses, pinched between thumb and forefinger, precariously on the bridge of his nose. He leaned so far forward that his forehead almost touched the window.

'What's going on, d'you think?' he asked. 'Annual General Meeting of the gangs?'

They'd arrived shortly before the Sarry Heid had opened for the evening and had observed the comings and goings for nearly two hours. They hadn't spotted their target, Danny Semple, but had noted the arrival of several high-ranking members of the city's Catholic gangs. Bull Bowman, leader of the Norman Conks – self-styled conquerors of Norman

Street – was the most powerful of these figures, so it was fair to assume that the others were waiting for him.

'Whoa!' McDaid shot bolt upright as if someone had stuck a gun in his back. He turned and cried, 'Will you please stop that,' with a prim-and-properness unlikely for Glasgow's biggest polisman.

Maggie McIver laughed, one hand extended as if still grasping an invisible portion of the big man's right buttock in a pincer-like grip.

'You're a fine big mountain of a man, Archie McDaid,' she said.

'A fine big married mountain,' McDaid stressed.

'Don't you come all coy with me.' She flashed Dreghorn a conspiratorial wink. 'Bent over like that, you knew fine well what you were doing . . .'

She moved to the window, McDaid backing away, spluttering in his defence. She gazed out at the Sarry Heid, asked, 'Find what you were looking for?'

'Police business,' McDaid stated, on safer ground now.

'My office. My word is law in here.' She glanced at Dreghorn as he fished a pack of Capstans out of his pocket. 'A lot of faces being shown today.'

Dreghorn nodded, exhaling smoke. 'Do they cosy up together often?'

'Not outside of match day.'

The Sarry Heid was a well-known Celtic pub, supporters of the football club gathering there from across the city for a pre-match bevvy before heading further into the East End to Parkhead.

'Any idea what's going on?'

'None whatsoever. They don't bother me, and I don't bother them.'

Maggie McIver, possibly the sharpest business brain in Glasgow, was the owner of the Barras Market, which operated every Saturday and whose profitability and popularity seemed to increase on a weekly basis, despite the Depression. It was named after the barrows from which hawkers sold their wares. Maggie had a roof constructed over the market in 1926, concerned about the toll the brutal Scottish weather was taking on her clients. Her approach was compassionate more than cutthroat and she was always quick to smile, but her eyes, like those of her policeman father, missed nothing.

'We agreed an hour, but you've been here nearly two.' She folded her arms. 'I believe a small renegotiation may be in order.'

McDaid drew himself to his full height. 'You've already got me for half my usual rate, and no' even offered so much as a cup of tea.'

Maggie's daughter or niece – Dreghorn had ignored the negotiations – was getting married in a couple of months and McDaid had agreed a cut-price piping fee, in return for her allowing them to use the office to spy on the Sarry Heid.

'This is for something else, a bigger do.'

'Bigger than your daughter's wedding?'

'Oh, aye, it'll be the talk of the town.' She examined the detectives, weighing up their trustworthiness. 'You know how the Corporation wouldn't let me hire the Merchants House for the market's Christmas party last year? Double-booked, so they claimed, but I didn't come up the Clyde in a banana boat; they were just looking down on us – not hoity-toity enough. Well, I'll build my own hall. That'll show them.'

'Whereabouts?' Dreghorn asked.

'Here.' Maggie stabbed a finger skywards. 'Right on top of the market, on great big muckle stilts. A "Palais de Danse" to beat them all.'

'A dance hall,' Dreghorn said to McDaid.

'I know what it is,' the big man hissed out of the side of his mouth, before smiling sweetly at Maggie. 'And you want me to play for the punters, like a residency or something?'

'No chance,' Maggie said, affronted. 'I want to get the young yins in – jazz, jive, swing, all that big-band stuff, that's where the money is.' She gestured dismissively at McDaid. 'But I'd want you for the opening, a bit of pomp and ceremony. The Lord Provost and all the old farts from the Corporation love that sort of thing.'

McDaid struck a diva-like pose. 'I hope you're not including me in your definition of old farts?'

'It is what your playing sounds like,' Dreghorn said, heading for the door. He tipped his hat to them with exaggerated politeness. 'I'm off. Listening to youse two's enough to drive a man to drink.'

CHAPTER 11

The teeth were drawn back, either screaming or laughing; it was hard to know which was more disturbing. The darkness within the eye sockets was deep and enveloping and spoke of ancient evils, of curses and cruelty and torture. The surrounding surface had been corrupted, discoloured, an ivory hue darkened to the colour of dried blood.

The owner of the skull, one Maggie Wall, had died – if the completely unbiased legends were to be believed – screaming curses at her tormentors atop a funeral pyre; the last witch to be burned at the stake in Scotland in 1657.

Just the sort of thing you wanted to look at when you stepped into the pub for a quiet drink, Dreghorn thought. Although, judging by the popularity of the Sarry Heid, a lot of punters preferred facing Maggie than going home to their wives.

The Sarry Heid wasn't shy about playing on its history. After their famous voyage of discovery around Scotland, James Boswell and Dr Samuel Johnson – notoriously fonder of the road out of Scotland than the one into it – had stayed overnight. And got blootered. National poet Rabbie Burns had been another guest, writing the pub its own personal poem. After he'd got blootered.

The ode in question, scrawled on notepaper, was kept on display in a glass case, although Dreghorn doubted the authenticity of the spidery handwriting, suspecting it was the work of an opportunistic bartender of old. He veered more towards the pragmatic than the poetic, so was unable to judge whether or not the words reached the giddy literary heights of the bard's, but never let the truth get in the way of a good story. That could have been the motto of the city.

Leaving Maggie McIver and McDaid, Dreghorn had crossed the road like a man on a mission and entered the Sarry Heid. He didn't scan the faces of the clientele as he shouldered his way to the bar. At least he didn't make it obvious.

'Hauf and a hauf,' he said. 'Please.'

The two barmen glanced at each other to register their disdain for the detective, then one moved lazily to fetch his drinks. Dreghorn remembered one of his mother's favourite sayings from childhood – 'You've got two speeds, James Dreghorn, dead slow and stop' – usually directed at him as he reluctantly carried out household chores like emptying the chanty or transferring ash from the range to the midden in the back court.

The barman placed a half-measure of whisky and a half-pint of beer on the bar. Dreghorn knocked back the whisky in a oner, reached into his pocket as he drained half the beer, handed over the money as he set the glass down and said, 'Same again.' He pushed his hat back into a rakish angle and undid his top button, making it look like he was just popping in for a much-needed drink after a tough day at work.

He faced the bar, not making eye contact, and waited for fresh drinks to arrive. Maggie Wall's skull continued to stare at him, but in the mirrored surface behind her he could spy out suspicious activity amongst the other drinkers. Many seemed to take no notice of him, even though he, McDaid and the rest of the Untouchables had something of a name about town. A decent number, however, were doing their best to keep their heads down, bunnets shadowing their faces.

In a booth to his left he could sense Bull Bowman watching him, shifting in his chair as if he had ants in his pants. Dreghorn finished his first beer, picked up the second whisky and turned from the bar, resting an elbow on the counter, a heel on the foot-rail.

Bowman was up like a shot, unable to hold himself back any longer. He powered bullishly – nicknames in Norman Street weren't subtle – across the spit-and-sawdust floor, other customers stepping aside, making sure they didn't accidentally bump him or give him an excuse. He stopped in front of Dreghorn, rolled his neck to loosen the tension.

'Off duty, inspector?'

'Still deciding.' Dreghorn sipped his whisky.

'Don't often see you in here.'

'I'm no' a stranger.' Dreghorn looked around for the first time, taking everything in; certain faces hurriedly looked away, exchanged shifty glances with one another. 'You can't beat the atmosphere – pulls you back every time, like a magnet. Have you seen Danny Semple? I hear he's another one who just can't stay away.'

'Danny? No, not since before he did a runner from your lot. You'd know if I had, inspector. As a law-abiding man, I'd be obliged to get in touch after what he did. Must've been aff his heid.'

'Not acting on your orders?'

'Me?' Bowman feigned a shiver. 'When it comes to violence, I'm a shrinking violet.'

'Speaking of violence,' Dreghorn said, 'someone battered Les Campbell last night.'

'I heard – shocking, isn't it? There's an awfy amount of crime around these days. You'd think the polis would do something.'

'I thought he put his faith in you to protect him. And his takings.'

'Me?' Bowman shook his head. 'Les is an old pal and, aye, I've helped him out in the past, but, y'know, people change. Don't see each other much now.' He looked around. 'The big man no' with you the day?'

Dreghorn seemed surprised to note McDaid's absence. 'Must've misplaced him.' He cast his eyes over Bowman's clothes. 'You're looking very swish, Bull. Just come from Connell's Tailors?'

Bowman didn't have the build for an elegant suit, his slab-like body solid and angular, like a shithouse in tweed.

'Cheers,' he said, opening his jacket to display the waistcoat, a watch-chain hanging artfully from one pocket. 'You've got to keep up appearances, even when the world's going to hell in a hand-cart around you.'

'Not cheap, though, a new suit.'

'Been saving my pennies.'

'Aye, but where've you been getting them from in the first place?'

'And here's me thinking this was just a friendly conversation, not an interrogation.' Bowman extended his wrists, fists clenched, the knuckles gnarled and scarred, inviting the handcuffs. 'If you want to take me down the station, on you go, but you're the one who'll end up with a riddy – I'm as clean as a whistle.'

'I could find something,' Dreghorn said. 'No bother.'

'Aye, I bet you could.' Bowman's face flushed with sudden anger. Perhaps it was too many years of shovelling coal into a foundry furnace, but his skin seemed almost lobster-red, burning from some inner fire always on the verge of erupting. His wide, craggy features were almost flat, sculpted with all the finesse of a riveting hammer.

'Nice try, though.' Dreghorn raised his whisky in a toast.

'Eh?'

'Popping over for a chat to try and divert my attention from the folks you're in with.'

Taking his drinks, Dreghorn stepped around Bowman and walked towards the table he had come from. The two men who had entered the Saracen with the gang leader displayed little more than mild curiosity at Dreghorn's approach. The others reacted with wariness, hostility and exasperation, a couple swearing under their breath. Vinny Wylie, leader of the Cheeky Forty, Bert Rowan of the Calton Entry, Paul 'Dagger' Kane, main man of the San Toy: loitering with intent, drunkenness, assault and battery, disturbing the peace, destruction of property, housebreaking – their criminal records were virtually interchangeable.

There was another couple in their company, seated intimately close to each other: a woman with quick, pale-blue eyes and a thick-necked fellow who hunkered over the table as if he favoured arm-wrestling to conversation. Or strangling.

'Mind if I join youse, lads? Miss?' Dreghorn sat in the chair that Bowman had vacated without waiting for an answer, placed his drinks on the table.

One of the unknown men smiled and waved a hand. 'The more, the merrier.' An Irish accent – Dublin, maybe further south, if Dreghorn had his bearings.

Bowman nodded for a punter at an adjacent table to move, picked up the man's stool and set it down opposite Dreghorn.

The detective reached for his cigarettes. 'So, what's this, your AGM – Annual Gang Meeting?' he asked, shamelessly stealing and embellishing McDaid's joke.

'No gangs here, inspector,' Bowman answered, tongue-in-cheek, the others nodding agreement. 'Just a few old mates enjoying a wee drink.'

'New suits, drinks with the lads? No' many can afford that sort of thing these days.' Dreghorn lit a Capstan, stared through the smoke at the smiling Irishman. 'I keep hearing there's a lot of money going around your crowd the now. Have to wonder where's it's coming from.'

'Prudence and clean living.' Bowman grinned as he lifted his pint, took a deep gulp.

'What business is it of yours, sir?' The Irishman wasn't smiling now.

'Oh, he's aye got our best interests at heart, our moral welfare.' Bowman slammed down his empty glass, a hint to whoever's round was next. 'Inspector Jimmy Dreghorn, one of Sillitoe's Heavy Mob, the Tartan Untouchables.' A flash of malice. 'How is the chief cuntstable, anyway? Settling in nicely?'

'A lot of neds locked up in Duke Street Gaol and the Bar-L – been there yourself, recently, Bull – so I'd take that as an aye,' said Dreghorn. 'And you are?'

'Tracy, Conall Tracy.' The Irishman nodded respectfully. 'A pleasure.'

Tracy's companion looked like someone had taken sandpaper to his skin, then forgotten to blow the dust away. He was glaring at Dreghorn, but when he blinked, only one eyelid moved, the other frozen by faint scarring, the glass eye within unseeing.

'And this is Mr Dempsey,' Tracy continued. 'He's a little

shyer than me, especially around – no offence – the peelers. Where we come from, if you're of, shall we say, a different persuasion to them, it can be a little hairy sometimes. Pays not to say much of anything, in case it gets taken the wrong way.'

Bowman nudged Tracy. 'Jimmy here's different; he's an endangered species. One of us in amongst all of them. A lone Tim. Proddies to the left of him, Proddies to the right.'

'And a big posh English bastard sitting on top.' Dagger Kane slurred, alcohol talking.

Tracy smiled. 'Isn't that always the way of it.' A cynical, bittersweet statement, not a question.

Dreghorn changed tack, glanced at the woman.

'Are you all right, miss?'

She gave him a caustic look, as if his attempt at gallantry was naive at best.

'How do you mean?' Irish as well, Belfast most likely.

'Sitting amongst a bunch of hairy-arsed Scotsman, all talking shite.'

'I might like it.'

'Hairy arses or talking shite?'

The man beside her flinched. 'You've no call to speak to her like that.' Belfast again, harsh and bitter.

Dreghorn's needling had finally worked. He marked the man down as jealous and short-tempered, the easiest to goad into slipping up, if necessary.

The woman laid a hand on the man's arm, calming him, though Dreghorn reckoned she was also quite capable of doing the opposite.

'It's fine, Pat, look at him, he's just full of devilment. Nothing wrong with that now and again.' She smiled at Dreghorn, cocked her head at the pub. 'It's a man's world, but sometimes

I like to show my face to remind you all that's just what we let
you think.'

'And if anyone can do that,' said Tracy pleasantly, 'it's Nora.'

She raised her glass to him with a smile.

Dreghorn reached for his drink. 'Fair enough, as long as
you're happy. I was just concerned for your reputation amongst
this lot.'

'How kind,' Nora said. 'And what about your reputation?'

'Shot to pieces long ago.' Without a pause, Dreghorn shifted
his attention, added an edge to his voice. 'Where're you from,
Mr Tracy?'

'Kerry man, originally, County Kerry, but now I'm in Dublin's fair city, the Irish Free State. It suits my temperament, so it
does, freedom.'

'How's it going? That's what, over ten years now?'

'Well, we could argue the nature of freedom till the cows
come home, but I'm on holiday and amongst friends, so I'll
be magnanimous and say' – he smiled cheerfully – 'grand.
Like walking on air.' The smile faded quickly. 'Rather be there
than the north, where they've still got the lead boots of the
Brits weighing them down.' Tracy's dark eyes narrowed. 'Can't
be easy being the lone Tim in an army of Prods. Why would a
man want to do that? He'd be hated by his own side because
they'd think he was betraying them, and he'd be hated by the
other side, well, for the pure and simple love of hating something different.'

Dreghorn liked eyes, liked to examine them during
interrogations – the windows to the soul, if you wanted to get
all fancy and philosophical about it. Bull Bowman's eyes were
easily read; if he was about to charge or rip your lungs out,
you'd know it. Tracy was different. Whatever emotions lay

within him didn't reach his eyes. They stayed blank, the true depths unrevealed.

'Suits my temperament,' Dreghorn said. 'What're you doing in Glasgow?'

'Just visiting.' Bowman was a little too eager, Dreghorn thought. 'He's my cousin.'

'Mother or father's side?'

Bowman looked nonplussed, but Tracy didn't miss a beat. 'Not blood as such,' he said. 'Our da's and uncles were friends in the old days, before Bull's folk came over here. You know what it's like when you're a nipper in a tight-knit community – just about everyone's your auntie or uncle.'

'Where are you staying?'

Dempsey shifted angrily in his seat, but Tracy radiated a calm so serene you couldn't help but notice the sarcasm in it.

'We've not long arrived, wanted to catch up with some old friends before anything else. Guess we hoped some of these fine fellows might put us up for a night' – cue a chorus of welcoming offers from the gang leaders – 'after that, a hotel or a boarding house.'

'Sleeping on a tenement floor dressed like that?'

'Oh, Mr Dempsey and me are used to roughing it.' Said almost as if Tracy was making a promise.

Dreghorn took a final draw of his cigarette, crushed it underfoot. 'Well, when you find somewhere, drop into Turnbull Street police station – Bull knows the way – and let us know the address. For your own safety. We like to take care of our visitors.'

'Anything to oblige, inspector.'

Dreghorn resisted another cigarette. Another whisky would've gone down well too. He asked, 'What do you do, back in the Free State?'

Tracy rolled his eyes as if the workings of the world were beyond him. 'I'm a sort of businessman, a sort of politician, but not elected, not now anyway.' He smiled and shrugged. 'All boring and legitimate, inspector.'

'Things never stay boring for long around here.' Dreghorn cocked his head to one side, but kept his eyes on Tracy. 'Danny Semple,' he said over his shoulder, 'I wouldn't use that door if I was you.'

One of the drinkers who'd been avoiding eye contact with Dreghorn when he was at the bar had been creeping towards the Saracen's exit. He froze and whispered, 'Fuck!' as Dreghorn turned to face him. He threw a quick glare at the detective, bolted through the doors like a racehorse off the starter's line . . . and then ricocheted back through them like a human cannonball. He landed on his arse, sliding through sawdust, spittle and cigarette douts, almost tripping a couple of other drinkers.

Dreghorn, on his feet now, said, 'That was an official warning, by the way.'

The pub doors opened and McDaid's bulk filled the doorway. He paused for a moment, stepped inside as Danny Semple scrambled to his feet.

'Daniel Semple,' he said, 'you are under arrest for assault with a deadly weapon and attempted murder. You are not obliged to say anything, but anything you say may be used in evidence.'

Semple looked from Dreghorn to McDaid, then darted to the side, as if attempting to go round the big man.

McDaid skipped nimbly to block his way. 'Are you dancing?' he asked, the favoured chat-up line from Palais de Danse across the city.

'Are you asking?' Semple answered, one hand reaching into a pocket, closing round something.

The pub crowd was enjoying the unscheduled entertainment, offering sarcastic encouragement: 'Ya beauty – better than the pictures.'

'Gaun' yourself, Danny.'

'Aye, attempted murder's pish – go for the big yin.'

Semple drew out his hand, tore away a makeshift cardboard sheath to reveal a small paring knife: dangerous and easily concealed, but hardly a machete.

'Is that it, wee man?' McDaid almost laughed. He raised a hand, dangled his pinkie like a worm wriggling on a hook, the inference clear.

The detectives made sure they stayed on either side of Semple. He waved the blade menacingly between them.

'Wondering who to go for first?' Dreghorn asked. 'I'd say Archie; he's the biggest. The bigger they are, and all that . . .'

'True,' McDaid agreed. 'But if you get me, then Jimmy'll get you. I'm a gentle giant; he's a vicious wee swine. You might no' make it to court.'

'Just have to take the both of youse then, won't I?' Semple said, the tremor in his voice overcoming the bluster.

He lunged for McDaid, thrusting the blade at the big man's belly, but Dreghorn had read the intent in his eyes and was also moving. He grabbed Semple's wrist with his right hand, slipped his other arm around the elbow joint and snapped the limb straight, applying an armlock.

Semple's gasp of pain was cut off and his struggles ceased, the knife dropping from his trapped hand. Dreghorn turned to see panicked eyes popping out of a rapidly purpling face. McDaid, one arm wrapped around Semple's neck in a chokehold, was swaying from side to side to music that only he could hear. Semple, lifted almost off his feet, balanced desperately on his tiptoes.

'He did fancy a dance,' said McDaid.

He let out a whoop and started dancing around the bar as if he was at a ceilidh back on Skye, his reluctant partner tiptoeing frantically to follow him. He sang as he danced, Semple accompanying with strangled gasps:

> '*Oh, you beautiful doll,*
> *You great, big beautiful doll!*
> *If you ever leave me how my heart would ache—*'

'He's going blue,' Dreghorn warned as McDaid waltzed past.

> '*I want to hold you,*
> *But I fear you'd break.*
> *Oh, oh, oh, oh,*
> *Oh, you beautiful doll!*'

McDaid executed a final pirouette and deposited the unconscious Semple in a chair. There was a hush in the pub as he then retrieved Semple's bunnet from the floor and placed it back on its owner's head, low over the eyes, as if he was just having a nap.

The hostile silence was broken by a burst of laughter. Bowman and Tracy were on their feet, not quite applauding.

'I do love Glasgow,' Conall Tracy said. 'It's like Belfast's more dangerous big brother.' He tipped his hat to the detectives. 'Rambunctious, that's the word.'

CHAPTER 12

Friday, 31 March 1933

The last place Jimmy Dreghorn expected to fall in love was at a hanging.

Fortunately, the object of his affection wasn't the person around whose neck the executioner had just tightened the noose. In the long run, it might have been simpler if it had been.

The hanging bell had already sounded, alerting the rest of the prison to the imminent execution, yet Thomas Pierrepoint's movements were unhurried, dignified, even compassionate. There were few words, communication being exchanged between the executioner and his nephew and assistant, Albert, through almost reverential nods and glances.

At the last moment the condemned man, Thomas Bryce, had refused any religious succour, although the minister had opted, somewhat ghoulishly, Dreghorn thought, to remain in the viewing gallery, as if keeping score between heaven and hell.

The route to the execution block was screened off, so that prisoners were unable to observe as the Death Watch Officer led their fellow inmate to the gallows. The hanging bell was rung fifteen minutes before the event and fifteen minutes afterwards to mark its successful completion. Was it kinder or crueller to leave things to the imagination during that half-hour of deathly silence?

Duke Street Prison was located at the top of High Street, with the Gothic spire of Glasgow Cathedral and the adjacent mausoleums of the Necropolis visible from some cells, to add cheer to a sentence. Listen closely and the hanging bell could be heard across the city centre, the toll muscling aside the sounds of trams, cars and horses' hooves to give warning to citizens of dubious morality.

Surprisingly, if you read the lurid criminal tales that scorched newspaper pages, Glasgow didn't carry out enough executions to justify a permanent hanging shed, the most recent being two murderers in 1928. When necessary, a gallows was erected in one of the prison workshops. The only clue to this grim extra-curricular activity was the curious outline of a trapdoor in the centre of the floor, nimbly avoided by superstitious prisoners.

Thomas Pierrepoint had quietly and expertly positioned Bryce upon that hatch. As his assistant stepped back, Pierrepoint placed a hand on Bryce's shoulder and said something that no one else could overhear. Bryce blinked and nodded gratefully, the only emotion yet to touch his pale features.

When asked what he said to his charges in those final moments, Pierrepoint would respond only that they were 'private words' between executioner, prisoner and their maker.

Without ceremony, Pierrepoint produced a white hood. As it slid over his head, Bryce's eyes met Dreghorn's, but were unreadable. The detective had been present at only one other execution, a firing squad during the war. Many years later the victim had been proved innocent of the crime, and that thought still haunted Dreghorn. Thomas Bryce's death wouldn't trouble him, though the memory of his young victim still did.

A glass screen had been erected between the gallows and the

observers, as if to offer some measure of protection. Dreghorn would have preferred a steel hull from Pagan's or Fairfield's shipyards, but had felt unable to refuse the unofficial request to attend.

The tension in the gallery – the moral unease about bearing witness to a legally sanctioned killing – was heightened to surreal levels by the fact that someone appeared to have brought along their mammy.

The woman was perhaps fifty, well dressed in a tweed jacket and skirt and slouch hat, which, unlike the men, she hadn't removed. She wasn't tall and was maybe beginning to grow a wee bit 'broad across the beam', as Dreghorn's mother might have said, but in a way that somehow seemed to promise strength of character as well as a formidable physical presence.

Dreghorn had arrived late, the final chimes of the hanging bell echoing as he entered the execution block, so he hadn't been introduced to everyone. He felt he knew the woman, maybe from the old days, before the years he'd spent in Shanghai, but the name and face refused to click. She had given him a cursory glance as he slipped in, and an exasperated raise of the eyebrow at his reaction to her gender.

'Martha Hepburn,' said the man beside Dreghorn, a reporter he vaguely recognized from court appearances. 'Magistrate. No need for her to be here. Just sticking her oar in. Bloody women! I've got one sitting across from me in the newsroom. Not a typist. A real, live reporter. Supposedly.'

Martha Hepburn stood in the front row of the gallery, with the prison governor on one side of her and Chief Constable Sillitoe on the other, head and shoulders above most of the other observers.

The governor looked agitated, half turned towards her, hands cupped like a goalkeeper's as if to catch her when she fainted. Sillitoe was a calm, attentive pillar of support, upright as a police truncheon. He cocked his head occasionally, speaking with quiet authority, explaining the procedure to her.

A stillness descended as Pierrepoint fitted the noose around his victim's neck, a tremor going through the body, and checked the knot. A formality. The mechanism had already been tested several times with a sand-filled mannequin of equal weight to Bryce. Done correctly, execution was an exact science: the neck snapped instantly. Done incorrectly, it was a comedy of terrors.

Pierrepoint stepped away from Bryce, took his place beside the lever that operated the gallows and gave the viewing gallery a grave nod.

Dreghorn fancied that he heard the crack of Bryce's neck breaking, but it was probably the sound of the trapdoor release. A blur of movement and Bryce was gone, the gallows rope whipped taut. To be fair to Martha Hepburn, she didn't jump any more than Dreghorn did.

No one moved, no one spoke, watching as Pierrepoint stepped over to the hatch and peered into the unused cell below, where a physician waited to confirm the condemned prisoner's demise. Pierrepoint acknowledged the communication from below with another grave nod.

The hesitancy to speak first, a contemplation of fragile mortality, was broken by the journalist, who flipped his notebook shut and clamped his hat on his head. 'Hold the front page,' he said to Dreghorn, 'I can make the evening edition.'

The gentlemen of the press. Dreghorn resisted the urge to follow and trip him up at the top of the stairs.

Sillitoe had glanced around for him, so he moved towards the chief constable, nodding to a couple of ashen-faced observers on the way. The governor was addressing Martha Hepburn with ingratiating concern, asking how she was.

'Shaken to the core,' she replied. 'I'd be appalled at myself if I was anything less.'

'It went well, if you'll pardon the expression.' The governor cocked his head in admiration. 'The Pierrepoints are true professionals.'

'Dreghorn,' Sillitoe said pointedly, 'I saved a space for you beside me.'

'Thank you, sir. Very considerate, but I'm more at home in the cheap seats.'

Sillitoe drew his eyes off Dreghorn's sarcasm. 'Mrs Hepburn, this is Detective Inspector Dreghorn, the arresting officer in the Bryce case.'

She turned to him with interest. Looking past the sombreness of her attire, she was perhaps a few years younger than Dreghorn had first thought, attractive in a daunting fashion that wouldn't suffer fools gladly. 'A tragic, terrible business, but you brought him to justice at least,' she said.

Dreghorn glanced at the gallows rope, taut with Bryce's dead weight. Sometimes justice left a bad taste in the mouth.

She kept her eyes on him. 'Is it normal practice for the arresting officer to attend the execution?'

Sillitoe answered with a hint of reproach. 'Like you, Mrs Hepburn – and also against my advice – Dreghorn is here voluntarily.'

'Normally wild horses couldn't drag me to a party like

this . . .' Dreghorn shrugged as if he'd had no choice. 'A favour to the condemned man's wife.'

Dreghorn hadn't seen Peggy Bryce since the previous October, when her husband had been convicted of murdering their young son Tommy. The execution had originally been scheduled for November, but was delayed after Bryce had fallen ill with pulmonary tuberculosis and the authorities reckoned it would reflect badly upon them if they had to stretcher him to the gallows, delirious and coughing up blood before the noose even touched his neck. Two days ago Dreghorn had returned to Central Police Headquarters in Turnbull Street to find Peggy Bryce waiting. She asked him bluntly to attend the execution for her, to make sure 'the bastard stretches the full length of the long drop'.

Martha Hepburn searched his eyes. 'What will you tell her?'

'What she thinks she wants to hear.'

'Do you think your account will give her some sort of solace?'

Dreghorn paused. 'Why are you here, ma'am?'

'I've been appointed magistrate. If I'm to be involved in legal decisions that could lead to capital punishment, I think I should fully understand and experience the consequences, at least once. I hoped a crime as heinous as Bryce's would make it rest easier with me.'

'And did it?'

'No.' A darkness in her eyes. 'As I'm sure you're already aware, inspector.'

'It won't make things any better for Peggy Bryce, either, but at least she'll know he's dead and buried.'

The hanging bell sounded again, the signal that the execution had been carried out successfully. As was tradition, Bryce's corpse would be taken down from the gallows and buried in an unmarked grave in the prison grounds; no one to mourn him, no headstone to visit. Not that they would have been queuing.

Sillitoe spoke with what Dreghorn thought was an air of amateur-dramatic theatricality, though it might have been just his English accent. 'Send not to know for whom the bell tolls . . .'

There was an understandable awkwardness to the post-execution small talk, like a funeral wake where no one had liked the deceased but didn't want to let rip with their true feelings. Sillitoe and Martha Hepburn wished to express their respect to Thomas Pierrepoint for the dignity with which he'd carried out his grim task, and Dreghorn found himself beside the younger Pierrepoint, Albert.

'Bad enough having to tell folk you're a policeman sometimes,' he said, 'but "executioner's assistant" must make it tough to get a lumber at the end of the dancing.'

'A lumber, sir?' The Yorkshire accent always sounded friendly to Dreghorn's ear.

'A lassie on your arm at the end of the night.'

Albert smiled with surprising cheer. 'Oh no, I tell people I'm a delivery manager at Pennington's grocer's – which I am.' He nodded at the gallows. 'We're paid by commission; not enough condemned souls to make it a full-time occupation.'

'There's a pub called The Hangman's Rest, Wilson Street, not far from here, if you and your uncle need a drink afterwards.'

'No, no, straight back home to Yorkshire for us. Hanging needs a steady man with good hands. If you can't do it without whisky, don't do it at all, Uncle Tom says.'

Albert's father, Henry, had been removed from the list of

executioners in 1910 for arriving drunk at Chelmsford Prison the day before an execution and starting a brawl with his own assistant. A strange profession for a family to follow in, although it was rumoured that as a child in school, Albert had written of his wish to become an executioner like his father and uncle.

'Good advice for most things,' Dreghorn said, not intending ever to follow it himself.

Sillitoe announced that he had some business with the governor and suggested, with an uncharacteristic flash of humour, that Mrs Hepburn escort Dreghorn to freedom, as if there was a good chance that the prison officers would lead him straight into a cell.

The prisoners' morning exercise had been delayed because of the execution, so an officer led them through the yards for the most part, rather than the forbidding corridors of the gaol. There were furtive movements behind the barred windows that loomed over them, the high walls blackened as if the badness was leaking out from within. Following the construction of Barlinnie Gaol in 1882, Duke Street functioned primarily as a women's prison, and only a few higher-category male inmates – murderers, terrorists – were held within its walls. Nevertheless, a handful of male voices yelled insults at Dreghorn, and lewd comments at Mrs Hepburn.

She laughed them off. 'At my age, when they ask' – her accent grew broader – ' "Are ye awright, hen?", it's usually genuine concern about my health, not anything licentious.' Her expression grew serious. 'You and your flying squad had a busy first year, inspector.'

'Just a bit. Hopefully this year'll be quieter.'

'You're in the wrong city for that. And the wrong profession.'

She gave him a disarming smile. 'What do you think of Chief Constable Sillitoe?'

'A prince among men, ma'am. Best man for the job.'

'And you wouldn't say otherwise, even if you didn't believe it.'

'Honour amongst thieves, ma'am,' Dreghorn said. 'Works both ways.' He nodded thanks as the prison officer unlocked a heavy door for them. The smell of the prison – a damp, oppressive Victorian mustiness tinged with cold sweat, rolling tobacco, stale cooking, the acrid whiff of latrines – and the hopeless gloom silenced them as they stepped inside.

CHAPTER 13

Bonnie Archie McDaid was the biggest man on the Glasgow Police Force, and they hadn't yet built a car that could comfortably contain him. Frankly, a Vickers-Armstrong tank would have been a tight fit.

As Dreghorn escorted Martha Hepburn through the prison gates, he could see the big man waiting with surprising patience. Their Alvis police radio-car was parked on the opposite side of Duke Street, outside Alexander's Public School for Boys, Girls and Infants.

'What eejit would build a school across the road from a prison?' McDaid had asked earlier.

'Good for discipline,' Dreghorn had told him, then adopted a schoolmarmish voice. 'Behave yourselves, boys and girls, or—' He had choked off, jerked his head to the side as if his neck was suddenly stretched by an invisible rope. Gallows humour that seemed a wee bit too close to the bone now.

Drawing closer, Dreghorn realized that McDaid wasn't so much waiting patiently as lost in his own world, his features contorting through a series of eye-rolling, cheek-billowing, lip-pursing facial gymnastics. Exercises for his other great passion besides policing – the bagpipes.

'Do you believe in the chief constable's reforms?' Martha Hepburn resumed the conversation. 'You're in the front line, so to speak, so you see how effective they are. Do you think they'll be successful in the long run?'

'If he gets the right support from the high heid-yins.' Dreghorn manoeuvred himself into her line of vision, hoping she wouldn't notice his great galumph of a partner's gurning mug.

'Why, inspector, are you implying that having an Englishman in charge of a Scottish institution might be ruffling the feathers of our fair-minded city?'

After considerable success at breaking up criminal gangs in Sheffield, Sillitoe had been appointed chief constable, primarily to mete out similar punishment to Glasgow's even more infamous razor-gangs, who had turned large sections of the city into war zones, battle lines drawn along sectarian grounds – Protestant and Catholic. Other religions were brushed aside with an air of incredulity: 'Aye, aye, aye, but are you a Catholic Jew or a Proddie Jew?'

The first of Sillitoe's many reforms had been the formation of the Special Crime Squad. Plainclothes detectives attached to the Robbery and Homicide Division, they were the biggest (apart from Dreghorn) and toughest (he didn't do too badly in that respect) police officers that Scotland had to offer. Working in pairs, they patrolled the city in high-speed radio-cars that cut regular response times massively, although the breathtaking expense of acquiring the vehicles during the Depression had Corporation penny-pinchers scrabbling for the Vicks VapoRub.

With his gentlemanly bearing, Sillitoe had arrived in Glasgow like a polite earthquake, firmly shaking your hand and holding you steady as the ground threatened to tear itself apart under your feet. If necessary, his officers were to meet violence with greater violence. As far as Sillitoe was concerned, the biggest gang in the city was the Glasgow Police Force, no matter what they had to do to prove it.

'Don't worry, I'm one of his champions.' Martha Hepburn glanced along the road and waved to a motorcar parked on the same side of the road as the prison. 'I was on the Police Commission that appointed him. I had the casting vote.'

Dreghorn said, 'Oh, they must have loved that.'

After decades of protest by the Suffrage Movement, the government had reluctantly passed the Equal Franchise Act in 1928, finally granting women the same voting rights as men. Actively welcoming women into the corridors of power, however, was still a step too far for most politicians, harrumphing in outrage in a gentlemen's-club miasma of cigar smoke, brandy and gout. Martha Hepburn was one of the few women to hold authority in the Corporation of Glasgow. Male officials were wary of her, but she enjoyed huge popularity amongst the female population, thanks to her prominence in the Rent Strikes, the Suffrage Movement, the Women's Peace Crusade and other idealistic campaigns.

She laughed with delight. 'They were livid. I rather enjoyed it, actually. Perhaps I'm going power-mad.'

'I thought that was a job requirement in politics.'

'Spoken with just the right amount of disrespect, inspector.'

A car door slammed. Dreghorn looked round to see a woman coming towards them from the vehicle the magistrate had waved at.

'Uh-oh, more disrespect. Here comes my assistant to keep me in line,' Martha announced. 'She claims I could talk for Scotland, says I should aim for Westminster next, put the wind up Maxton and Shinwell's kilts. And MacDonald's – if anyone needs geeing up, it's Gentleman Mac.'

'Jimmy? Jimmy Dreghorn?'

Dreghorn had only glanced at the woman at first. Now, as she came closer, he looked beyond her elegant and expensive attire and the years fell away, until he was twelve years old again, standing shame-faced in wet trousers without a drop of rain in sight.

'Rachel?' Even his voice suddenly sounded younger, as if coming from that innocent time before the war when everything seemed possible, no matter how much the world tried to convince you it wasn't.

She smiled, and he realized he was too, without sarcasm or cynicism, holding nothing back. The prettiness of her youth had matured into a beauty that could have been daunting, if not for the warmth of her eyes and the dimple in one cheek, her dark hair bobbed and styled in a Marcel wave.

'You know each other?' Martha Hepburn looked back and forth between them with suspicion.

Rachel McAdam said, 'We went to school together.'

'About a hundred years ago,' said Dreghorn, 'though you're wearing a wee bit better than me.' Was it his imagination or did her eyebrows shrug slightly to say she disagreed?

'I heard you were back in Glasgow. I mean, I read about what happened last year in the papers. You're all right now?'

'I'm fine.' Dreghorn removed his fedora, his tone warm, but indicating that he'd rather not talk about those events – Kelpie House, the Lockhart family, the deaths he'd failed to prevent. Rachel understood, a flash of empathy in her eyes, but Dreghorn's expression continued to darken.

'I'm sorry, Mrs Hepburn,' he said, 'but if this woman is in your employ, then it's my duty as a Glasgow police officer to inform you of her heinous criminal record.'

'Criminal record?' Martha Hepburn frowned.

'Aye. St Brendan's Primary School, 1908. Playing "Kiss, Cuddle or Torture".' He nodded accusingly at Rachel. 'The cruellest torturer going. Torquemada had nothing on her.'

Rachel laughed. 'Is that why you kept getting yourself caught?' She glanced at Mrs Hepburn. 'Do you remember Jimmy's mother, Betty Dreghorn? You served together in Mary Barbour's Army.'

In 1916, with the men of many families away at war, ruthless landlords had tried to exploit their tenants by imposing swingeing rent increases on the poor helpless women who remained. The poor helpless women had proven themselves anything but, organizing a campaign of mass resistance, which saw collection agents humiliated, pelted with fish-scraps, flour and the contents of chamberpots or stripped of their clothing and sent fleeing, bare buff, through the streets. Such was the outrage that the government stepped in, forcing landlords to maintain post-war rent levels. Mary Barbour, a founder of the Govan Women's Housing Association, had become the figurehead of the movement and had gone on to serve as a Labour councillor, magistrate and Justice of the Peace, before retiring in 1931.

Martha Hepburn's face lit up. 'I thought I recognized the name. A fine woman. Witty, articulate and not afraid of a good argument, if I remember correctly. Is she well?'

'Aye, still likes a good blether.' Dreghorn rolled his eyes in mock exasperation. 'And a good argument. She'll be pleased to hear I met you.'

'Please, give her my regards and tell her not to be a stranger if she's ever passing the City Chambers.' She glanced at her watch. 'What time is this talk at: midday? We'd better show our faces or it'll be the strap.' She gestured at the entrance to

Alexander's Public School. 'A good friend teaches at the school. I made the mistake of telling her I'd be in the vicinity and she tricked me into giving a talk to some of her pupils.'

'You're an inspiration, Mrs Hepburn,' Rachel teased, then added sincerely, 'You come from the same tenement closes as most of these weans, and look at you now.'

'Oh, aye, fresh from a hanging – there's something to aspire to.'

Dreghorn warned Mrs Hepburn that she might regret her invitation to his mother, then looked at Rachel.

'How about you?' he asked. 'What have you been doing?'

Are you married? was the real question in his mind. Despite legislation against such prejudice, most employers had yet to embrace the concept of equal opportunities, and women still had to resign from their jobs upon marriage, although Dreghorn reckoned Martha Hepburn would take satisfaction in bucking that tradition.

Rachel gave a self-deprecating smile, started to answer, but was interrupted by Martha peering curiously around her and asking, 'What is that man up to . . . ?'

She strode off without waiting for an answer, crossing the road towards the Alvis, with the gurning McDaid oblivious inside. She knocked sharply on the driver's window, causing him to jump. She leaned closer as he lowered the window, then spoke with magisterial authority.

'Are you all right, sir? Do we need to call a doctor?' A barbed pause. 'Or the police.'

'I *am* the police.' McDaid was opening the door, stepping out as Dreghorn and Rachel approached. 'Is there some sort of problem, ma'am?'

'Well, it's just that from the faces you were making, it looked like you were suffering some sort of fit or seizure.' She raised an eyebrow sternly at him. 'Or something more sinister, parked outside a school, the car shuddering suspiciously.'

'What? You think I was—' McDaid bit down on the next words, flabbergasted.

Dreghorn tried to keep a straight face. 'I think there's been some sort of misunderstanding. Sergeant McDaid here is one of the finest officers on the force, a man of outstanding character, happily married with three – no four – children.'

There was a flash of humour in Martha's eyes as she glanced at Dreghorn, then turned back to McDaid. 'So, what exactly were you doing, sergeant? I could hear all sorts of strange noises.'

'Breathing exercises,' McDaid stated, as if it was perfectly normal.

Dreghorn attempted to explain. 'Archie plays the bagpipes; you need to keep your lips and lungs limber, don't you?'

McDaid nodded vigorously at Martha and Rachel. Like Dreghorn, they were trying hard to conceal their amusement.

'I have a friend who's a music teacher,' Martha said with a slow smile, 'and I don't hear him huffing and puffing like a constipated elephant.'

McDaid bristled at the comparison, then said proudly, 'I devised them myself.'

'And I'm sure the rest of the world will catch up eventually, but until then perhaps you should consider practising in private, to save yourself further embarrassing misunderstandings.' She switched the smile to Dreghorn. 'Rachel, we'd better be getting along to our talk. It was good to meet you, inspector. May we speak again on another occasion? I found your view from the streets very enlightening.' She nodded politely at McDaid and walked off, Rachel hanging back slightly.

McDaid let out an exasperated sigh, then nodded at the prison. 'If Pierrepoint ever hangs up his cloak, she'd be a shoo-in for public executioner.'

For a moment, Rachel McAdam looked as though she was going to mount a spirited defence of her boss, but the car radio crackled into life before she could speak. McDaid straightened as if on parade and said pompously, 'Duty calls.'

As he squeezed himself back into the car, Rachel looked at Mrs Hepburn, now mounting the entrance steps to the school. 'I'd better catch up,' she said to Dreghorn. 'It's good to see you, Jimmy.'

Dreghorn willed himself to say something witty and interesting that would make her stay longer, but all he came up with was, 'You too.'

Rachel smiled and said she'd telephone to arrange an appointment with Mrs Hepburn. She took a few steps, then stopped and looked back. Did she realize, Dreghorn wondered, that he hadn't moved and had just been watching her?

'Should've chosen "Kiss", Jimmy,' she said.

'Aye. Story of my life.'

She turned away with a fleeting smile, leaving him wondering where the years had gone and how he could possibly feel young and old at the same time.

'Who was that you were talking too, then?' McDaid asked innocently as Dreghorn got into the car.

'Martha Hepburn, magistrate of our fair city.'

'No' her – the young one. The one you fancy.'

'I don't recall making any statement to that effect, Sergeant McDaid.'

'Away, man, it was written all over your face. Your eyes lit up like Piccadilly Circus.'

'We went to school together.' Matter-of-fact.

McDaid laughed. 'Another one that got away then.' His face darkened as he realized what he'd said. 'Sorry, I didn't . . .'

Dreghorn had been involved with a woman the previous year, against McDaid's advice. It hadn't ended well, whatever tenuous future they might have had together cruelly destroyed.

'Don't worry,' he said, 'I live for your blunders and *faux pas.*' He let the big man stew for a bit, then nodded at the radio. 'Was it my imagination or did we not just receive an urgent call?'

'Aye!' McDaid brightened with relief. 'A sighting of Les Campbell's car on Buchanan Street, heading towards Argyll Street. A PC just called it in. Might be worth a daunner down there, see if we can spot it?'

Dreghorn gestured at the road ahead. 'Lead on, McDaid.'

CHAPTER 14

'Get me Garrison!'

He snarled the word as if it was more of a threat than an order, rolling the rr's into a predatory growl. He wasn't usually present when the phrase was uttered, but he liked to imagine the fear and intimidation it instilled in the listener.

'Get me Garrison.'

He tried the phrase again, softening his tone into a contented purr, raising an eyebrow suggestively. His reflection in the rear-view mirror reciprocated. He liked the sound of that too, especially when delivered in the honeyed tones of several women that he knew. None of them his wife. They were on speaking terms again, but not sleeping-together terms. He wasn't exactly bereft on that front, but there was a contract of sorts between them, and he liked to follow the letter of the law where it applied to him. Elsewhere, it was open season.

'Get me Garrison!'

The battle cry of the Glasgow guilty, from knife-wielding neds to politicians or Corporation bigwigs on the graft. George Garrison was the *prremierre* – another roll of those rr's, please – defence lawyer in the city, nay, in the West of Scotland, if not the entire country.

Hated by the polis, feared by the procurator fiscals, grudgingly admired by judges, whose ranks he might deign to join one day, and loved by his clients – until he cleaned them out of every penny they had. Garrison's brand of justice didn't come cheap. Amongst the Glasgow Police there was one cast-iron method of knowing when a suspect was guilty: if he yelled, 'Get me Garrison!' Proving it, of course, was another thing entirely.

'Get me Garrison!' George Garrison said again, now adopting the bombastic tone of a newsreel or trailer for the latest Hollywood epic. 'The truth, the whole truth and nothing but the truth.' He liked that too, mainly because it would cause a right hullabaloo amongst his detractors.

He turned his Bentley 4½ Litre coupé off London Road onto James Morrison Street, aware of heads turning admiringly to follow his progress. Since January he had been contributing a weekly column to *The Glasgow Herald*, lifting the lid on the shenanigans of the Scottish legal system. It had proven popular, as much, Garrison felt, because of his own charismatic personality as the scandalous nature of the cases he presented, with names altered to preserve the modesty of those originally involved – and spare him the poetic justice of a legal challenge.

With the contract up for renewal, the column was gaining interest elsewhere. Rival publishing houses Collins and Macmillan were sounding him about a book deal and, more interestingly for someone who prized his oratory skills so highly, the British Broadcasting Corporation had expressed interest in the possibility of a weekly radio show that would expand on the column. He was lunching with producers that afternoon to discuss options, hence his attempts at different linguistic approaches. No actor would voice George Garrison, not when the genuine article was available.

He took a left at St Andrew's Square and parked at the rear of the church. Garrison's car was distinctive, as it should be, and leaving it directly outside a police station was courting trouble. On too many occasions the crimson paintwork had been badly scratched; the scarring, he suspected, would match the grooves of handcuff or police-box keys, wielded by some jealous or disgruntled officer. A hazard of the job, but perhaps deserving of admonishment in his next column.

He crossed Turnbull Street towards Central Police Head-quarters, glancing first through the archway into the motor yard, where a couple of Thorneycroft police vans were parked, then up at the statues of Law and Justice on either side of the building's central gable. Law was bearded and a bit too Presby-terian and bloody-minded-looking for Garrison's liking, while Justice reclined coolly with her scales in one hand and her sword-hilt clasped to her breast. He flashed her a cheeky wee wink. Always best to keep in with the ladies.

Inside, he and Shug Nugent played their usual game: Garrison gave the details of the prisoner he was there to see and requested a private interview room, as was the suspect's legal right, and Nugent, with excruciating politeness, took as long as humanly possible to arrange it.

'When are you due for retirement, sergeant?'

'Oh, you've a few years left in which to savour my company, sir.' Nugent smiled with the implacability of an immovable object.

'Just wondering,' Garrison mused. 'I might be in the market for a private inquiry agent to help with the investigative side of my caseload. That friendly manner of yours would be perfect for encouraging people to open up.'

Nugent raised an eyebrow. 'Would you be suggesting I stop working on the side of the angels?'

A stocky WPC came through the doors that led to the

interview rooms, which weren't much more ostentatious than the cells, and called out Garrison's name.

The lawyer tipped his hat to her as he answered, 'There's not many angels in this town, sergeant.'

'No,' Nugent said, not quite under his breath, 'that's why you do so well.'

Garrison followed the WPC through the doors.

'This way,' she said.

'I'm in your hands, constable.' He checked his watch, determined not to be late for the BBC meeting.

Doors at the other end of the corridor opened. He heard a familiar voice greet the WPC and felt a looming presence.

'Sergeant McDaid,' he beamed, 'I'm here for a meeting with one of your recent arrests, to determine whether or not I represent him.'

'And who would that be?'

'Semple – Daniel Semple. Attempted murder, I believe.'

'More than one count,' McDaid said. 'He also tried to stick a knife in my belly.'

'And missed?' Garrison laughed as if they were the best of friends. 'I'll see you in court.'

'Hold my hat while I jump for joy.'

Dreghorn sighed as he climbed the stairs, suddenly weary. You'd think a day that started with a hanging could only get brighter, but events continued to play out unsatisfactorily.

He and McDaid had patrolled the streets in question and those surrounding it, but there was no sign of Les Campbell's errant vehicle. Giving up the search, they had returned to Turnbull Street, where Dreghorn told McDaid to check with Shug Nugent whether the constable who had reported the sighting could give them a description of the driver. He then headed for the Murder Lodge to find out what progress, if any, had been made on the Smith murder.

He was hoping to find Ellen there, but she was 'Helping Inspector Strachan with his inquiries,' DC Brian Harvie said, voice dripping with innuendo.

Dreghorn concealed the slow burn of anger that rose in him; he and Strachan had had words about the inspector's interest in Ellen. Maybe it was time for a gentle reminder of that conversation. Or a not-so-gentle one.

Despite the rivalry between the Tartan Untouchables and the rest of CID, Harvie liked the sound of his own voice more. He explained that he was going through the interview statements gathered the previous day, but had so far found nothing of significance. A bullet had been retrieved from the deck of the *Blue Bonnet*, but the ballistics report was outstanding. He had been told to expect post-mortem results shortly, as Professor Glaister was currently at work on the corpse in the mortuary. Bertie Hammond had conducted a forensic examination of the crime scene and taken various samples for testing. Another report due soon.

'I'll tell WPC Duncan you popped in to see her,' Harvie finished, aiming to get a rise out of Dreghorn. 'If she plays her cards right, she could be Inspector Strachan's protégée.'

Dreghorn said, ' "Protégée" implies that you have someone's best interests at heart – Strachan hasn't got one.' He nodded at the messy sprawl of documents on Harvie's desk. 'If you don't play your cards right, you might get the heave-ho in her place.'

Dreghorn wandered back to the squad room, loosening his tie, the walls closing in. He would rather have been on the move, noising up gangsters and informants, but was due in court early afternoon to give evidence for the prosecution in an assault case at the High Court. He was flicking through his notebook to reacquaint himself with the details when McDaid appeared in the doorway, jerked a thumb over his shoulder.

'I bumped into George Garrison downstairs, gallus bastard. Looks like he's defending Danny Semple, said he'd see us in court.'

'Hold my hat while I jump for joy.'

McDaid shook his head exasperatedly. 'You and me spend too much time thegither.'

They questioned Danny Semple for the better part of an hour, but failed to elicit a confession, the suspect being buoyed by the presence of George Garrison in his corner. Even when the evidence against them was damning, criminals had faith that Garrison was capable of working miracles, and the lawyer did little to dissuade them of the notion.

Semple would go before a judge on Monday, when a trial date would be set. Until then he would find himself kicking his heels – or having them kicked out from under him – in Duke Street Gaol or the Bar-L.

'He's guilty, why drag it out?' Dreghorn said to Garrison when Semple was carted back to the cells. He knew full well that Garrison charged by the hour, though the lawyer had been checking his watch during the interview. 'There are eyewitnesses who won't be intimidated. And the fact that Danny pulled a blade on me and Archie won't endear him to the court, either.'

'You may think that, inspector, but hope springs eternal, and every accused man is legally obliged a defence.' Garrison

smiled and tried to step past, but Dreghorn shifted to block his
way.

'Very noble of you,' he said, 'but where does a wee ned like
Danny Semple get the money to pay for you?'

'I'm afraid those details stray into the realm of client confidentiality.' The lawyer glanced at his watch again.

'In a rush, Mr Garrison?'

'Actually, yes. A prior appointment. The world is calling,
and far be it from me to disappoint.'

The court case was adjourned until the following week. Cru-
cial witnesses failed to turn up to testify – the usual story.
Witness intimidation was a huge problem in a city as congested
as Glasgow, especially when the gangs were involved, with witnesses, victims and perpetrators living cheek-by-jowl in the
same streets, same tenements.

Dreghorn emerged from the shade and shelter of the grand
Doric portico that fronted the court house into a light drizzle
and crossed the road onto Glasgow Green, taking the scenic
route back to Turnbull Street. He cupped his hand against the
rain, lit a Capstan and smoked and walked until his frustration became sanguine, which usually didn't happen without an
accompanying dram or two.

At the station he finished the arrest report for Danny
Semple and was considering the best way to make inquiries
about Conall Tracy when the telephone rang. Magistrate
Hepburn was on the line, the telephonist informed him. He
leaned back in his chair, intrigued, and said to put the call
through.

'Jimmy?' He recognized Rachel McAdam's voice immediately.

'Magistrate Hepburn's office?' He played dumb. 'You're not taking me to court, are you?'

'Guilty conscience, inspector?' Laughter in her voice. 'It's Rachel, Jimmy, following up on your blether with Mrs Hepburn. She would like to invite you to lunch, pick your brains a little more about procedure, your feelings towards the system, where it works, where it doesn't.'

'The view from the trenches?'

'Something like that.'

'Will you be there?'

'I don't know, Martha hasn't said. I'm not sure I'd be needed.'

'Tell her I'll only say yes if you come along too. I'll be showering her with so many nuggets of information that she'll need a secretary to take them all down.'

'A secretary? Is that what you think I am?' Playful.

'That's what I figured, I suppose.'

'I'm her personal assistant, legal clerk and inquiry agent – a Girl Friday, they'd call me in the talkies.'

'I've got one of those,' Dreghorn said as McDaid entered the squad room after nipping out for a pee. 'Well, more of a Man Friday, always breaking things, putting his foot in it and embarrassing me.'

McDaid frowned: *who's that?* Dreghorn cocked his head sharply: *mind your own business.* The phone on McDaid's desk rang. He reached for it the way a farmer grabs a chicken whose neck he's about to wring.

'I'll pass on your suggestion and see what she says.' Rachel paused. 'You do realize you've just asked me to luncheon when someone else is paying.'

'You can take the boy out of the Gorbals . . .'

Another laugh, warm and infectious, as she said goodbye, the years falling away again.

Dreghorn hung up at the same time as McDaid.

'Sillitoe wants to see us,' the big man said. 'Pronto. Sounded serious.'

CHAPTER 15

The chief constable's office was in the turreted gable end on the top floor, with a double aspect that allowed Sillitoe to gaze out at both St Andrew's Parish Church and, across the rooftops, at the High Court opposite Glasgow Green, giving him a view of the entire moral gamut. Dreghorn suspected that this was why Sillitoe chose to base himself at Central, despite his duties taking him all over the city and, more often than not, into the political arena of the City Chambers.

Walking through the moral gamut was a tightrope, though, and as he and McDaid entered Sillitoe's office, Dreghorn felt it looming as ominously as the long drop had for Thomas Bryce. It stemmed partly from Sillitoe's expression, which looked as though he was wrestling with some inner demon, his true feelings barely suppressed by his authority.

Deputy Chief Constable Sydney McVicar stood just behind the seated Sillitoe, with that brand of loyalty that was devotional until the moment your superior officer fucked up and the opportunity to step into his shoes arose. His upper lip twitched into an involuntary sneer, as if the detectives had trailed an unpleasant aroma in with them.

Another two men, dressed in almost identical black suits, were seated opposite Sillitoe's desk. They turned in unison to look at Dreghorn and McDaid. Both had death in their eyes. Not a bloodlust, but the casually pragmatic understanding that comes from having seen and breathed and delivered it in all its forms. A sense of mortality and the fragility of life, especially someone else's, when it was in your hands. Dreghorn recognized the look. He'd seen the same in his own eyes, hoped it didn't walk with him still.

Sillitoe stood up. 'Inspector Dreghorn, Sergeant McDaid, these gentlemen would like a word.'

The dark-suited men rose to their feet at Sillitoe's introduction, the taller of them with a military formality and barely any other acknowledgement of the detectives' presence.

'Superintendent Haldane, Special Branch, and—'

'Quinlisk – Eugene Quinlisk,' the smaller man interjected slyly, as if expecting Sillitoe to forget his name. He followed with a short, courteous bow, the sincerity of which was open to question.

'No rank, Mr Quinlisk?' Dreghorn asked.

'Not here, inspector,' Quinlisk said almost wistfully. 'Not today.' He was about Dreghorn's height, with an air of sated corpulence, strangely disconcerting because he wasn't particularly overweight.

Sillitoe continued, 'It involves the arrest you made last night.'

'Danny Semple?' McDaid said, flabbergasted. 'Wouldn't have thought he'd be of much interest to Special Branch.'

Special Branch was the arm of the police charged to combat terrorism, subversion and threats to national security. While the police were supposedly independent and apolitical, Special Branch by its nature was enmeshed in politics and skulduggery, a blunt instrument of His Majesty's Government.

'Not Semple.' In contrast to Quinlisk's warm southern Irish tones, the Scottishness in Haldane's accent had all but been ironed out by a ruthless mix of public schooling and officer training, the cold detachment of which was written all over him. 'The other man you had dealings with in the Saracen Head – Conall Tracy. And his accomplice, Gabriel Dempsey.'

Dreghorn glanced at Sillitoe before answering. 'I wouldn't say "dealings with", sir – a conversation. A short one.' The chief constable's expression was unreadable. 'You said, "accomplice" – are they wanted for some crime?'

'Persons of interest, Dreghorn,' Haldane snapped, not out of malice, simply his manner. 'Persons of interest.'

'To us,' Quinlisk pointed out, almost apologetic. 'Not to you.'

Sillitoe sat down again, Haldane and Quinlisk following his lead. Dreghorn and McDaid stood to attention, more because their hackles had been raised than out of deference. McVicar folded his arms like a eunuch at an orgy, surplus to requirements but determined not to show it.

'There were others too,' said Dreghorn. 'A man and a woman. Looked like they were together.'

Haldane and Quinlisk shared a calculating look.

'Pat and Nora Egan, Belfast's Bonnie and Clyde.' Quinlisk smiled at his own wit. 'Though it's Nora who wears the trousers.'

'What did you converse with Tracy about?' Haldane asked.

'The usual,' said Dreghorn. 'Who he was, what he was doing there.'

'Why the sudden interest? You were on the hunt for another suspect, no?'

'Aye, but Tracy was in the company of persons of interest to us.'

'Whom exactly?'

Dreghorn glanced at Sillitoe, who nodded cautious assent. 'Prominent members of some of the criminal gangs in the city.'

'We can supply names and addresses,' McVicar volunteered a little too eagerly.

'All in due course, Sydney.' Sillitoe drew his deputy a cold glance. 'If required.'

Haldane ignored the exchange, kept his attention on Dreghorn. 'From my understanding, Glasgow gangs are organized along sectarian lines,' he said. 'Which side do the ones that Tracy was consorting with favour?'

'Catholic, sir.'

'No surprise. What did he say when you questioned him?'

'To be honest, he was evasive. Claimed he was visiting cousins, but not blood relations; it was just a turn of phrase.'

There was an amused twinkle in Quinlisk's eyes. 'It doesn't sound as though you found his answers very satisfactory, inspector.'

'Tell the truth, I didn't.' Dreghorn reckoned the Special Branch men knew fine well what had happened in the Sarry Heid, but were testing him. 'But I had no real grounds for further suspicion, and the original matter that brought us there came to a head.'

'Dreghorn and McDaid apprehended a knife-wielding felon,' Sillitoe elaborated. 'A dangerous man, currently residing in the cells downstairs on a charge of attempted murder.'

Haldane responded with a sour twitch of a smile. 'Oh, for the days of knives, eh, Quinlisk?'

'Simpler times, sir.' Quinlisk's eyes, on Dreghorn, hinted that he was merely humouring his superior.

Haldane reached for his hat, which lay on Sillitoe's desk. 'That appears to tally with what our sources reported. Thank you for your time, gentlemen.'

Dreghorn said, 'I don't recall seeing either of you in the Saracen Head, sir.'

'You wouldn't, Dreghorn, we've been doing this for a long time.' Haldane brushed a speck of dust from the brim of his hat, as if the comment warranted little further attention. 'Quinlisk here has men who could blend into a sultan's harem, who could lift the wallet from your pocket without you noticing.'

McDaid cocked his head insouciantly at Dreghorn. 'Not Jimmy, sir – that mousetrap he keeps in there would take their fingers clean off.'

'Not the time or place for joshing around, McDaid,' McVicar stated, though Dreghorn detected a glimmer of amusement in Sillitoe's expression.

'Why are you keeping Tracy under surveillance?' he asked.

'Defence of the realm, inspector,' Haldane said. 'That's all you need to know. Stay away from Conall Tracy. We can't risk you jeopardizing our operation.'

'If he's a threat to the public, that's something we should be aware of. Our streets, our people.'

Haldane's silence warned that Dreghorn was overstepping the mark.

Sillitoe let the statement stand for a moment, then said, 'With respect, my officers are nothing if not dedicated, as I'm sure your own men are. The protection of the city of Glasgow and its citizens is their prime directive and they'll move hell and high water to do their duty. We all know there have to be boundaries, lines of demarcation between departments and investigations, but there also has to be cooperation and a sharing of information, to understand exactly why those boundaries should not be crossed.'

Haldane nodded reluctantly, turned to Dreghorn and McDaid. 'No further than this room,' he warned, then glanced at Quinlisk.

'He's a card, is Conall Tracy,' Quinlisk said with an admiring smile, like a big-game hunter about to pull the trigger on a beast he'd stalked for a long time. 'A fierce Republican in his time. Still is, though nowadays we suspect he might not be above feathering his own nest too.'

'I thought it was all Happy Families after the Partition,' said Dreghorn.

'I'll assume that's sarcasm and not ignorance, detective,' Haldane remarked impatiently. 'Not everyone supported the Partition. There's plenty that didn't give up the gun and the bomb, and have been trying to tear it apart ever since.'

Under the terms of the 1921 Anglo-Irish Treaty, the twenty-six-county Irish Free State remained part of the British Empire, but was self-governing, with its own army and control over taxation and foreign affairs. The other six counties were still under British rule – the Unionist-dominated state of Northern Ireland.

Quinlisk's smirk didn't fade. 'Tracy was involved in the Easter Rising in 1916, but didn't start making a name for himself until later, during the Anglo-Irish War. Him and his sister Bernadette were in the Post Office siege with Pearse and Connolly. You'll have heard of them?'

Patrick Pearse and James Connolly were two of the leading figures in the Easter Rising, an armed rebellion to overthrow British rule in Ireland and declare an Irish republic. They seized control of the General Post Office building in Dublin, beginning a week-long conflict that saw much of the city centre destroyed by British artillery fire. On 29 April 1916 the rebels were forced to surrender.

Mired in the bloody slaughter of the Great War and concerned that their handling of the 'Irish Question' – that 'old family quarrel', as Lloyd George called it – could set a precedent for calls for Home Rule and self-determination in other areas of the Empire, the British government acted with characteristic ruthlessness.

Over a two-week period after their surrender, Pearse, Connolly and thirteen other leaders of the Rising were executed by firing squad in the grounds of Dublin Castle, the shots echoing ominously over the city. The executions were a serious miscalculation on the part of the British government. Disgust and outrage at the killings increased support for Republicanism, shattering any previous ambivalence to the cause. Soon afterwards, Sinn Fein were elected with a massive majority in the Catholic south. To the north, with the exception of Donegal, in the mainly Protestant six counties of Ulster, the Unionists remained the biggest party by far.

With these divisions firmly entrenched, Ireland was plunged into a maelstrom of political turmoil and brinkmanship, subterfuge and sabotage, atrocity and assassination, guerrilla warfare and internecine conflict. First in the Anglo-Irish War – rebellion or War of Independence, depending on your point of view – and then in the bitter, bloody civil war that followed, between those who supported the Treaty, however reluctantly, and those who viewed it as compromise at best, betrayal at worst.

'Tracy was imprisoned with Michael Collins in Frongoch internment camp in north Wales,' Quinlisk continued, 'fomenting unrest together in fine style, no doubt. Firm friends, thick as thieves. When Collins was made IRA intelligence chief a few years later, Tracy was right beside him, and helped spring Éamon de Valera from Lincoln Jail. He served in the assassination squad Collins formed, targeting loyal servants of the Crown, and took part in Bloody Sunday. Thirteen British agents shot dead – some in their beds, some in front of their wives and children. They called themselves the Twelve Apostles, though there were a good deal more than twelve of them, which shows . . . what: delusions of grandeur?'

Quinlisk neglected to mention that in retaliation for the Bloody Sunday killings on the morning of 21 November 1920, members of the Auxiliary Division of the Royal Irish Constabulary, recruited from the ranks of former military officers who had served in the Great War, had, that same afternoon, attacked Croke Park Gaelic-football stadium during a Dublin–Tipperary match. Acting on the unproven assumption that some of the assassins were at the game, and claiming that they were shot at first, the Auxies opened fire on the 40,000-strong crowd. Twelve people died, another eleven were seriously injured, shot or crushed in the panic of the stampeding crowd.

Always the same, thought Dreghorn. However noble or ignoble the cause, violence breeds violence, smothering the original cause until only the violence remains. Right or wrong, innocent or guilty, once the blood starts flowing, it's hard to tell whose it is.

'Tracy's something you don't get very often,' said Quinlisk sarcastically, 'a hero to all men. After the formation of the Free State, he got himself elected for Sinn Fein and was even Minister of Agriculture for a while. But Conall's not really the sort for rules or bureaucracy; he's the kind who likes to shoot at you from rooftops or plant bombs under cars. He quit the Cabinet and resigned his seat after a year and a half, though he still maintains connections. He supported the Treaty on the surface, but we always suspected that he hadn't given up the fight and was working both sides during the civil war – and afterwards, all the way up to the here and now. Not so much a double agent, as a triple one – with the third party being himself, if you know what I mean?'

Haldane grunted disdainfully, eyeing Dreghorn and McDaid. 'You've heard of the Irish Hospitals' Sweepstake?'

'Hard not to, sir,' McDaid answered, admirably straightfaced. 'It's all the rage.'

'A raging scandal. Criminally condoned by the Free State government. Tracy is one of the main organizers.'

'Some say it was his idea to sell tickets outside the Free State,' Quinlisk elaborated. 'There is a touch of twisted genius to it, playing on all those romantic feelings people have about the "old country", making them nostalgic about a place they've probably never been to, and which their ancestors couldn't get away from quickly enough.'

Dreghorn said, 'Most of them didn't have much choice in the matter. It was either that or die. And they were travelling on what ended up being called "coffin ships", no' the *Mauretania.*'

Quinlisk's eyes flashed at this telling glimpse of Dreghorn's sympathies. 'Certainly no picnic for them.' A crass remark, considering that the majority of those he was referring to were fleeing famine or being forcibly repatriated, their homes burned to the ground in the dead of winter on the orders of ruthless landlords.

'Conall Tracy,' Haldane took over impatiently, 'is in charge of smuggling the Sweepstake tickets into other countries, and the profits – substantial – back out, employing a network of distributors and agents on the ground.'

'A bit out of Special Branch's territory, surely?' Dreghorn said.

'It's the money that concerns us. The profits are supposed to help the cash-starved Free State pay for hospitals and medical care. Some of it does, but nowhere near the sums the scheme is generating, by our estimation. We suspect Tracy is siphoning off money to finance the procurement of arms for a planned campaign of terror, either in Northern Ireland or here on the mainland. No shortage of sympathizers or Sinn Feiners amongst the Irish slums in Glasgow, elsewhere as well. Tracy's travelled here a great deal recently, we think to set up secret hiding places for weapons, safe houses for agents.'

Haldane stood up, set his hat on his head, the meeting over as far as he was concerned. 'I reiterate: stay away from him. These are issues of national security. If you do encounter him again in the course of your duties, come straight to us.' He extended a hand to Sillitoe. 'Thank you for your time, chief constable. I have it on good authority that Westminster is impressed with the job you're doing up here.'

Sillitoe shook Haldane's hand, said nothing more than 'Superintendent'.

Quinlisk opened the door for Haldane, gave a short bow to the room.

'What about the other one?' Dreghorn said. 'Dempsey.'

Quinlisk smiled. 'Likes to blow things up.'

Dreghorn glanced up at McDaid as the door closed. 'Something tells me that wasn't quite the truth, the whole truth and nothing but the truth.'

'Technically, inspector, they are your colleagues,' said McVicar, a stickler for bureaucratic detail. 'Are you accusing them of deliberately trying to mislead us?'

'Wouldn't be the first time.'

Sillitoe tapped a fingernail three times on his desk, slow and steady, to silence them.

Dreghorn sighed. 'See it through, sir?'

Sillitoe ignored the detective's insouciance. 'In my experience, Special Branch often acts as if they're above the law, not upholding it. Use your own discretion in regard to this fellow Tracy. We are the City of Glasgow police. If they step out of line, we will show them the error of their ways.' He raised an eyebrow at Dreghorn. 'See that through, inspector.'

CHAPTER 16

Leaving Sillitoe's office, Dreghorn headed for the Lodge again to press for an update on the Smith case.

He froze as he reached the door, spotting Haldane and Quinlisk inside. Haldane and Strachan were shaking hands like old comrades, the Special Branch man's attitude considerably warmer now. Orr was beside Strachan, smiling and nodding obsequiously, with Ellen standing nearby, no one taking any notice of her as introductions were made.

Dreghorn stepped back, trying to discern what connection there could be between Strachan and Haldane. Had they worked together on an earlier case or was it something deeper? He hoped no one had seen him, but suspected that Quinlisk's amused glance had clocked him as he retreated.

Even though they hadn't discussed it, the habit becoming ingrained, they walked to the Old Empire Bar after work. Entering the lounge, McDaid ordered them each a hauf and a hauf and they took a seat in the corner. Normally they stood at the bar, but a day of relative inactivity had tired them out more than knocking neds' heads together and chucking them into the back of a Black Maria.

No sooner had they sat down than the door opened and Ellen peered in gingerly. She spotted them, rolled her eyes a little – that may have been Dreghorn's imagination – and stepped inside. She was still in uniform, the sight of which inspired the other patrons to hunch over and avoid eye contact, disappearing into the depths of their drinks.

'Brian Harvie said you were asking for me, sir.'

Dreghorn gestured at her uniform with his whisky. 'Is it no' knocking-off time, constable?'

'Thought it'd be best, considering the venue, sir.'

'Respectable young ladies do not socialize with heathens like us,' McDaid trilled in a disquietingly convincing schoolmarm voice.

Dreghorn asked, 'How did Strachan get on, up at the canal?'

Ellen sat on the stool opposite. 'Him and Sergeant Orr ask a lot of questions in a manner that's guaranteed to make people clam up, so nothing much to report.' She thought for a moment. 'I did talk to one lad who used to crew for Smith.' She told them about Callum Baird and the men who had seemingly hired Smith on the night of his death.

'Irish eyes are smiling at us from every direction,' McDaid said. He downed half his beer, set the glass down loudly.

Ellen frowned, and Dreghorn related the details of their encounter with Conall Tracy, his glass-eyed compatriot Dempsey and 'Belfast's Bonnie and Clyde'. He then told her about Haldane and Quinlisk, but asked her to keep shtum about it around Strachan.

'Do you think there's a connection between all that and Smith's murder?' Ellen asked.

'There's no shortage of Irish accents in Glasgow, so . . .' Dreghorn shrugged, then nodded at her. 'Good work, though. Why don't you go and change and join us for a drink?'

Ellen looked around. The pub was stark and cold and unwelcoming. The few drinkers who were there remained silent; no laughter, no tall stories, the apathy of the Depression settled like a shroud.

'Thanks, sir, but I'm off to the pictures tonight.'

McDaid's gossip-antennae twitched. 'Are you winching, hen?' He started patting his pockets for one of the shamelessly patriotic business cards – enough to out-tartan Harry Lauder – that advertised his services as a piper. 'Because, you know, if romance and potential matrimonials are in the air . . .'

Ellen was already standing up, getting off her mark. 'With a friend, Archie,' she said. 'A lassie. And I've already got one of your cards. So have all my pals. And my ma and my aunties, and they're already married.'

'Cheeky wee besom, that yin,' the big man said as she left, unable to keep the smile off his face. It faded as he looked at Dreghorn. 'So what do you make of all that Special Branch shite then?'

Dreghorn shrugged again. 'Seemed to be going out of their way to draw our attention to something they didn't want us to have anything to do with.'

'Didn't take to the wee man, Quinlisk. Sleekit, eyes everywhere. Didn't take to the other one, either, but he's just your typical pole-up-his-arse officer. Seen enough of them to know not to trust them.' The big man took a modest sip of whisky; usually it was down in a oner. 'There was some stuff here a few years ago, back when you were still hobnobbing around the Whore of the Orient – cases of rifles being smuggled over to the IRA, a load of explosives nicked from a colliery in Stirlingshire. Big search; I was part of it when I was still in uniform. Some eejit took them down to London to do a Guy Fawkes and nearly blew himself up because they'd nicked instantaneous fuses instead of slower-burning ones.'

'You want another?' Dreghorn nodded at McDaid's glasses. Neither of them had finished their drinks, but it was something to say.

'No, I fancy getting home – a night in. Come back for your tea, if you want?'

'You're all right, thanks.'

'How's the house-hunting going?'

'Nowhere at the moment. Scared I'll take Mairi up on her offer?'

'Nae fears.' McDaid drained his glasses in rapid succession. 'You'd run a mile first.' He went to the bar, replenished Dreghorn's drinks without asking, set his homburg on his head and said, 'A night in might no' do you any harm, either.'

'I'll take it into consideration.' Dreghorn toasted the big man as he left, but put down the whisky without drinking.

If he did leave now, he could make it back to Mrs Pettigrew's for the evening meal that was included in his rent, but he didn't feel like polite company. He could, of course, grab a fish supper from the Coronation chippie round the corner on the Gallowgate, or head to the Savoy cafe in Cowcaddens. It was more a haunt of officers from Northern Division, but the food was good and he was on friendly terms with the owner, Joe, and his family, keen boxing fans who originally hailed from Palermo, Italy.

After that, he could go back to Hamilton Park Avenue and head straight to his room, put on the wireless or gramophone and not listen, pick up a book and not read, the words and sounds washing over him, blocked by the residual barrier of the day, the job, his dark thoughts.

From John Smith & Son's on St Vincent Street he had recently added Ernest Hemingway's *Fiesta* and Lewis Grassic

Gibbon's *Sunset Song* to the pile of half-read books that failed to offer an escape from the real world. An ex-soldier with a war wound that stopped him shagging all the chic Parisian women who kept throwing themselves at him. A young woman's miserable existence in rural Kincardineshire under the unsavoury attention of a succession of men, from her father to her husband. Disillusionment, disconnection, dourness and misogynistic misery. He should have bought a copy of *Amazing Detective Stories* instead; that might have given him a laugh at least.

He could return to Turnbull Street, sign out a car and make his way to Bearsden, sit outside that same villa, reproaching himself until the door opened, and then pretend that it was all normal, that the world wasn't the way it was. Or he could simply drive the streets, soak up the city, the good and the bad, until one or the other won him over.

One of the day's few bright spots returned to him now: the laughter in Rachel McAdam's voice when they spoke on the telephone. What was she doing this evening? Her laughter became another woman's laughter, a smile that he didn't want to be reminded of, a smile that twisted into a memory of terror. Longing and loneliness hollowed him out as surely as a razor.

'A half and a half – that is the drink of choice in these parts, isn't it?'

Eugene Quinlisk stood over him, two half-pints of beer and two half-measures of whisky cupped in his meaty hands. He had made no sound as he approached – or was Dreghorn just too lost within himself? As Quinlisk sat down, Dreghorn noticed that the drinks McDaid had bought him were almost gone, although he had no memory of touching them.

Quinlisk slid two glasses towards Dreghorn. 'A whisky and a beer,' he said. 'I like it. One burns, the other cools. Soft and hard. Like two sides of the same coin. I haven't been in town long – does that say something about the Scottish character?'

'Maybe it just means we like a dram. Why have one drink when you can have two?' Dreghorn found himself brightening, more comfortable with the prospect of conflict than the ennui that had been closing in. 'Were you following me and the big man?'

'Not at all, inspector. I asked around some of your fellow officers to find out where a man might enjoy a little libation if he so wished.' Quinlisk glanced around the pub; the levity had not risen. 'We may differ on our ideas of what constitutes a night's entertainment.'

Dreghorn raised his glass to Quinlisk. 'So, we've had the official warning. This is the unofficial one?'

'More of an apology, if anything. Superintendent Haldane's a dedicated officer, but very much King and Country, very black-and-white. He doesn't really see the grey in between, the no-man's-land. He doesn't really understand . . . well, men like us.'

'Like us?'

'Men who see' – Quinlisk picked up his drinks as if weighing them – 'both sides.' He chose whisky, sipped and savoured it. 'After the war you were freezing your arse off in Russia, Murmansk, part of allied forces helping the White Army against the Bolsheviks during the Civil War. You were seconded to Military Intelligence.'

Dreghorn said nothing, knocked back his whisky.

'Your commanding officer said you were an effective interrogator. Insightful. Good at breaking people.'

'There's an epitaph for the gravestone.'

Quinlisk gave the comment a bigger smile than it deserved. 'Did you think about sides then?'

'The army doesn't pay you to think.'

'No, but the revolutionaries, the people you were fighting against, were socialists, communists, peasants. Stick them in a tenement and surely they're no different from the vast majority of Glaswegians.'

'There's a few of them ended up here.'

'So I hear – quite the melting pot. Wonder if they think it's an improvement.'

Dreghorn downed half his beer like a man leaving once it was finished.

'Those you were protecting – the Whites – were more supporters of the old Tsarist order,' Quinlisk continued. 'Corrupt and over-privileged aristocrats, pissing and preying on everyone below them like it was their God-given right. You weren't ever tempted to give the other side a helping hand, strike a blow for the common man?'

Dreghorn didn't answer.

Quinlisk tried another tack. 'Did you enjoy it, feel proud about doing your duty?'

'Not particularly. Wondered what the fuck we were doing there, to be honest. Protecting what we thought was our own interests probably, not theirs. Whatever it was, it didn't do much good. Just ended up with both sides hating us. Didn't take long for you to gather all this information. Military records?'

'Special Branch. The "Special" part helps to grease the wheels nicely.'

'How long have you been with them?'

Quinlisk smiled. 'I don't recall anyone saying I was. I've known the superintendent for a long time. He brings me in every now and again when he needs someone to navigate the grey areas, so to speak.'

'Where's the grey area here?'

'Well, I'm hoping to reassure him that it's not you.'

'Me?'

'That you haven't changed your position on taking sides, since Murmansk.'

Dreghorn cocked his head, awaiting further explanation. 'I think all this cloak-and-dagger shite's going to your head.'

'The colonel imagines a man of your persuasion might sympathize with men of a similar outlook. You're a Roman Catholic officer in a largely Protestant force and, just over the water, those two sides have been at each other's throats for as long as anyone cares to remember.'

'They're no' exactly snuggling up for a bit of houghmagandie over here.' Dreghorn laughed. 'Your boss doesn't trust me because I'm a Tim? My membership of that club is well and truly lapsed.'

'To be fair, he's paid to have a suspicious mind, and there were plenty of infiltrators and informers in the Royal Irish Constabulary when he was over there helping to keep the peace. The danger is, if you're not careful, you start to see enemies everywhere. Personally I think it's wise not to trust anyone but yourself. And some people can't even do that. Some people just don't know which way they're going to turn.'

Dreghorn said, 'Tell your boss he can trust me to do what's right.'

Quinlisk watched coldly as the detective stood up. 'And whose definition of what's right would we be talking about?'

Dreghorn tipped his hat to Quinlisk and headed for the door.

'That might be one of those grey areas you seem so fond of.'

CHAPTER 17

Saturday, 1 April 1933

The Hampden Roar surged through him, the exhilaration threatening to lift him off his feet.

On the pitch below, Jimmy McGrory, clad in the navy blue of Scotland rather than the green-and-white hoops of his regular club Celtic, turned away from the goal and spread his arms as if to embrace the crowd. Four minutes into the match he'd intercepted a low cross and booted the ball into the back of the net, outfoxing Henry Hibbs, the England goalkeeper.

The goal sent memories of a legendary earlier encounter crackling through the vast crowd crammed into Hampden Park – a new world-record attendance, the tannoy had announced pre-match. Five years ago Scotland had hammered England 5–1 at Wembley. The sense of jubilation and solidarity that the 'Wembley Wizards' had inspired couldn't have been greater than if William Wallace had risen from the dead and sewn himself back together to score the winning goal.

Dreghorn glanced at his Uncle Joe, the joy in the older man's eyes, the porcelain solidity of his jaw, and felt a rush of affection for him, for the city, for the beautiful game and the way it could bring them all together.

Well, for ninety minutes, at least. Normally the sectarian divisions that ran through every stratum of the city, from the Corporation and industry to law enforcement and the underworld – deciding which job you could do, which yard or factory you could work in, which street you lived in and which pub you drank in – also dictated which football team you supported. Rangers or Celtic. Protestant or Catholic.

Despite often being at the very heart of the conflict, football – like Dreghorn's own passion, boxing – could occasionally transcend it, albeit in favour of a convenient villain everyone loved to hate: England.

Beyond following the fortunes of the national team, Dreghorn wasn't as fitba'-crazy as the vast majority of his fellow countrymen or even, indeed, his family – diehard Celts on his father's side, rampant 'Gers on his mother's. More divisions: a fiery mixed marriage, the volatility ending only when his father died. Or jumped ship in Australia for another woman, depending on whom you believed.

At school Dreghorn had been a half-decent footballer; not the best, but never last to be picked for playground teams or stuck ignominiously in goal. He enjoyed the game, which was just as well, as it was ubiquitous. Everyone played, especially as weans – end of story. When he discovered boxing and his own natural fluidity of force and thought and movement in that noble art, football assumed less significance in his life. He still followed the ups and downs of the League, especially Old Firm games, and enjoyed the banter that went along with it, even if he did sometimes play devil's advocate.

Joe Dreghorn loved it, though, and Jimmy loved his uncle, so he tried to accompany him as often as he could. The tickets to today's match were his treat. Joe thumped his back and leaned close, nodding at the players celebrating on the park. 'Ya dancer!' he cried, although only Dreghorn could understand the muffled, garbled words.

Before the war Joe Dreghorn had been one of the most

renowned jokers and patter merchants in Lockhart's Shipyard, able to talk the hind legs off a donkey and have his fellow workers in stitches for so long they begged him to shut up. That mischief, that quick wit was still there, but the words were trapped, cut off by the Boche sniper's bullet that had shattered his jaw. The doctors of the Masks for Facial Disfigurement Department – the Tin Noses Shop, the soldiers called it – in the Third London General Hospital had built him a new jaw made of sculpted clay and copper, painted to match his skin, and held in place like a ventriloquist's dummy's that had jammed shut by wires around the ears.

Amongst the supporters, any initial askance looks at his uncle's disfigurement were quickly absorbed by camaraderie and the excitement of the match. Glasgow was a city of scars – missing limbs and digits, flesh knitted back together in signature white welts that never faded. Not just from the war. The industrial landscape could be as brutal as any battlefield. Dreghorn had plenty of his own.

Joe had retreated from the world after the war, self-conscious of his physical appearance and lacerated speech, fearing folk would recoil from the monster he'd become or, worse, pity him as a victim. Football, supporting his beloved team, was one of the few things that could make him re-engage with society. Most Saturdays during the season he plugged himself back into the human race, laughed and cried and cheered with the best of them.

On these days he followed a routine that was established from when he was first able to pass for drinking age: meet the lads – all, frankly, far too long in the tooth to meet that description – for a few bevvies in the Sarry Heid and then stride to Parkhead, if Celtic were at home.

Even though today's destination was Hampden Park in Mount Florida, home of the national team, Dreghorn didn't have the heart to ask if they could buck tradition and sample the wares of some other establishment, and so he had found himself slinking through the familiar double-height doors behind Joe, hoping no one would spot him. He had opted for a bunnet instead of his usual fedora in the hope that it would help disguise him.

An elbow nudged him halfway to the bar.

'Just can't stay away, can you, Jimmy?' Bull Bowman said.

Dreghorn didn't stop, but glanced over his shoulder. 'Missed your filmstar looks, Frankenstein.'

He smiled as Bowman thrust two fingers up at him and joined Joe and his cronies at the bar, most of whom he knew from his own apprentice days in the yard.

Despite one war, extended by a jaunt to the frozen wastes of Murmansk, seven or eight years on the crime-ridden streets of Shanghai and his well-publicized investigations as a Tartan Untouchable, it was as if Dreghorn was back to being a fourteen-year-old virgin on his first day in the Black Squad again. He called them a bunch of fannies and made sure he got in the first round.

He soon relaxed, as much because of the company as the alcohol. It had been a while since he'd socialized with anyone other than police officers. Maybe Joe wasn't the only one plugging back into the human race. He enjoyed the chat and the banter. Where better to set the world to rights than in a good pub? They battered through some pressing issues of the day:

'That wee shite Hitler,' sworn in as Chancellor of Germany in January and promising to rearm the country and make it an imperial power once again. A rumour that Glasgow University had offered Albert Einstein a position, following the physicist's relinquishment of his German citizenship due to the rise of Hitlerism. The imminent collapse of the once-mighty Palmers' shipbuilders on the River Tyne, and the repercussions it might have for Clydeside yards. Another rumour – that the National Party of Scotland and the Scottish Party were considering joining forces to continue their campaigns for independence. And most important, the finalists in the *Daily Record*'s search to find Scotland's Prettiest Girl – Dreghorn's personal preference was for Miss C Burns, first in the Factory Girl Section.

He also liked the way the old shipyard squad, what was left of them, surreptitiously closed around his uncle whenever Joe reached for his glass, sparing him the shock or horrified expressions of other customers when he shifted aside the copper jaw to take a drink.

At one point his uncle, eyes smiling, put an arm around Dreghorn's shoulders. 'You look like you're enjoying yourself,' Joe said, the words half-formed, rolling grunts, though Dreghorn was attuned.

'I am.' It was the truth. For the first time in months, pain and grief and rage didn't writhe in his guts.

'You should get out more often.' A chorus of approval and clinked glasses from Joe's cronies.

'So should you,' Dreghorn told his uncle.

Come on, look at me, Joe's eyes said sadly.

Dreghorn widened his eyes in exasperation, gestured at the faces around him. 'Away, man. You'd have to lose your whole head to look worse than this lot.'

He left them laughing and went to the gents, popped a Capstan in his mouth on the way back and reached for his lighter. A match flared in his face, deftly struck by a thumbnail.

Dreghorn stared at Conall Tracy as he puffed on his cigarette to light it.

'Looks like we're both incognito, going back to our roots.' Tracy raised his eyebrows towards his headgear. Like Dreghorn, he was wearing a bunnet, blending in with the crowd. Bull Bowman, Nora and Patrick Egan and a couple of Norman Conks were seated behind him.

'You're going to the match?' Dreghorn asked.

'When in Rome, though I'd rather it was the Celts. That's your duty as a good Catholic.'

'I'm no' in the running for that award.'

'Or a bad one.'

Nora Egan blew Dreghorn a kiss as she approached, offering to give Tracy a hand with the drinks.

Tracy nodded towards Joe. 'The old boy – family of yours? There's a resemblance.'

Dreghorn said nothing, but it didn't deter Tracy, who tapped his own jaw. 'War wound? Hell of a thing to happen.'

'Good-looking fellow too,' Nora said sadly. 'Kind eyes.' She smiled at Dreghorn as she started back towards her seat. 'Not like yours.'

'You were over there as well?' Tracy continued.

'Start to finish.'

Tracy nodded as if that said something in itself. 'Dodged that bullet myself, though we had other wars to fight.' He looked at Joe with what seemed like genuine sympathy. 'That's what happens when you serve in the British Army. Come back a cripple, but still expected to rise to your feet for His Majesty when they play the national anthem, dirge that it is.'

'If you've got a leg left to stand on.'

Tracy smiled. 'Careful, inspector, that's almost rebel talk.'

Tottenham Hotspur's George Hunt had equalized for England at the half-hour mark, and play continued at a frantic pace. The players returned to the pitch after half-time and the game was in full swing again when Dreghorn spied Willie Kivlichan at the end of the row, gesturing urgently. He told his Uncle Joe that he'd be back soon and, muttering apologies, made his way across the crowded stand to where Kivlichan waited in the aisle, his face like grim death. As well as being team doctor for both Celtic FC and the national team, Kivlichan acted as a police surgeon under Professor Glaister, so he was an expert in grimness and death.

'Enjoying the game?' It was Kivlichan who had given the tickets to Dreghorn.

'I was, until I clocked your cheery mug. What's up, Willie?'

The doctor leaned closer to avoid any curious fans. 'We've found a body.'

'No' surprised. That last goal probably caused a fair few heart attacks.'

'Nothing as natural as that.' Kivlichan nodded for Dreghorn to follow him.

They walked up the steps, heading for the nearest exit, Dreghorn glancing at the sea of bunnets, tam-o'-shanters and bated-breath expressions, marvelling at the scale and the passion. Every now and then supporters would recognize Kivlichan and nod or reach out to shake his hand: 'Are you all right, doc?' 'Some game, eh?' 'Wish you were playing, doc.'

Dr William Kivlichan was something of a legend, having played for both Rangers and Celtic in his day, something of an own goal, considering Rangers' denied and derided unofficial policy of not signing Catholics. In the spirit of face-saving sporting detente, Rangers had eventually exchanged Kivlichan for Alex Bennett, a Protestant who had been playing right-wing for Celtic. Kivlichan had studied medicine at Glasgow University while still with Celtic and, despite being Dreghorn's elder by a decade, remained handsome and athletic. A medical officer in the King's African Rifles during the war, he sported a shock of white hair above one temple, from a German bullet that had creased his skull.

They walked along the corridor under the stands, the drumbeat of stamping feet and the cheers and songs of the crowd overhead. Dreghorn asked where the body was discovered.

'The outhouse,' Kivlichan stated flatly.

'Charming. You don't get that in your Agatha Christies.'

'Have you been drinking?'

Dreghorn shot the doctor a look that mixed incredulity and sarcasm into a potent cocktail. 'Feel free to wait for Lord Peter Wimsey or someone more salubrious to come along,' he added. 'Or somebody who's actually on duty.'

'You're all right, this'll soon sober you up.'

The lavatories were a brick-built bunker at ground level. A young police constable blocked the entrance, arms folded. A shaken man in his forties leaned against the wall opposite, his face pale and covered by a sheen of cold sweat, a spattering of vomit on the ground near his feet. Two other men, match stewards, hovered around uncertainly.

'The lavvies are out of order, that's all you say,' Dreghorn instructed them. 'Nobody uses them, doesn't matter how desperate they are.'

He introduced himself to the polisman and flashed his warrant card. He was still carrying it, even though he was off duty – what would Dr Freud and the new science of psychotherapy say about that?

The officer gestured at the man opposite. 'Mr Thompson over there discovered the body, sir.'

Dreghorn nodded sympathetically at Thompson and said, 'Sorry, you'll have to stay here and make a statement. The constable will take your details for now.'

He looked at Kivlichan, who gestured politely. 'After you.'

CHAPTER 18

The smell of communal urine hit him first. Nothing unusual there, but above that he detected the coppery whiff of fresh blood.

Sure enough, the trough flowed red, not the usual shades of yellow, spiralling down the drain. The body was sprawled at a slant, legs on the ground, torso on the low platform that you stood on to pee, and head turned to the side, resting in the trough. The man's hands were still at his groin, shrivelled penis now shrunken out of his grip. The face was destroyed, wet and pulped, startlingly red against the white of the tiles. Dreghorn crouched, examined the neat entry wound on the back of the skull.

'Gunshot,' he said.

Kivlichan nodded. 'Pistol or revolver. Point-blank range.'

Dreghorn sighed, positioned himself at the corpse's feet and extended his arm, thumb and forefingers cocked like a revolver.

'The killer came in while the victim was peeing – he probably didn't hear him over the sound of the match.' He discharged his imaginary weapon. 'A gunshot would have echoed in here, though. Surely someone would have heard it?'

The Hampden Roar filled the air suddenly, almost deafening.

'Not over that, Jimmy,' Kivlichan said. 'Reckon we just equalized.'

'And us down here. Typical.'

He stared at the raggedly circular spread of blood and tissue where the victim's head had been driven into the tiles by the impact of the shot. He briefly imagined he could detect the victim's features within it, like the Shroud of Turin.

The smear arced downwards, following the victim as he had slid lifelessly down the tiles, then rolled half onto his back. Not as precise as a mathematical graph, but a record nevertheless of the man's expiration. Dreghorn jumped at a sudden shrill sound: the final whistle, ending the game. Almost immediately the crowd would be heading for the exits. It would be impossible to hold them within the ground, impossible to question and search more than 134,000 people. Not that the murderer was likely to have gone back to watch the rest of the match after pulling the trigger.

He hunkered down beside the man, started to pat his pockets, searching for some form of identification.

'How long do you reckon?'

Kivlichan glanced at his watch. 'Within the last half, maybe less. The body's still warm, the blood hasn't started to coagulate. Fifteen minutes tops since the stewards fetched me. I conducted a quick examination, then came straight to you.'

Dreghorn lifted the lapel of the man's jacket, fished out a wallet and flipped it open: a ticket for the match; a welder's union card in the name of Harold Beattie plus a handful of coins; a Bureau of Unemployment card in the same name; side-by-side portraits of a plain-faced woman and a heavily moustached man; and another photograph of the same couple dressed in their Sunday best and proudly posed with three children. He got to his feet, slipped the wallet into his pocket and asked Kivlichan, 'Is there somewhere you can call this in for me? I'll question our witness.'

When they left the toilets, the young constable was facing off against a group of fans eager to use the facilities.

'Out of order,' he repeated, slapping his truncheon into one palm for emphasis.

'C'mon, big man, I'm bursting,' one of them protested.

Another shifted his hips uncomfortably. 'Have a heart. I've got a turtle's head peeking out here.'

'Aye?' The officer gestured with his truncheon. 'Well, I can knock it back in with this, or you can use the other loos. Up to you.'

The first man tutted and headed for the exit; the second man waddled off like a penguin, buttocks clenched.

Dreghorn nodded to the constable, then offered the shaken Thompson a cigarette. 'Not exactly what you want to see when you're bursting for a pee.'

Thompson exhaled smoke as if trying to exorcise the memory, shook his head.

'You don't know a Harold Beattie, do you?'

'No.' Thompson looked at Dreghorn with wide eyes. 'Is that the poor fellow in . . .'

Dreghorn changed the subject. 'Did you see anyone else when you came down, on the stairs or before you went into the toilets?'

'Aye. Somebody was coming out as I was going in. "Good game, eh?" I said, but he never answered, just barged straight past me, head down. I pegged him for a Sassenach who'd lost his way and ended up in the wrong end and was getting off his marks quick.'

'Would you recognize him again? Can you describe him?'

Thompson thought hard, his excitement fading. 'Well, maybe no'. I mean, he was just like everybody else here, y'know. Bunnet, taller than me. Didn't really see his face. About your age, maybe a bit older, but hard to say . . .' His eyes locked on Dreghorn's as he took a last draw of the fag. 'It must've been him, though, eh? The killer. Why else wouldn't he have said anything? He could've done me in too . . .'

Dreghorn offered Thompson another Capstan to calm his nerves. 'I think he knew exactly who he was after.'

He stepped away from Thompson as Willie Kivlichan returned; more officers and an ambulance were on the way.

'I read Glaister's report on the body from the canal,' Kivlichan said. 'Same modus operandi, by the looks of it. You and Archie found that one too?'

'Aye.' The doctor had been right; Dreghorn was well and truly sober now. 'A magnet for murder, that's me.'

CHAPTER 19

Sunday, 2 April 1933

Without thinking, he kissed the crescent-shaped scar on her upper arm. As his lips touched the puckered white skin, he could almost feel the memories it released in her. She flinched, but recovered well as he drew back, ignoring his apologetic look and pushing the covers down to his hips.

She poked a finger into the circle of scar tissue on his side. A kiss from a madman's bullet.

'You win,' she said with a bittersweet smile.

'Aye, but I'm thick-skinned,' Dreghorn said.

As she stepped out of bed and slipped into a silk robe, she gave him a look that said she could write a book on that particular subject.

'You'll be going soon, I trust?'

'Prior engagement.' He watched her cross the room. 'With another woman.'

'Scandalous. And I thought you were a gentleman.'

Dreghorn flopped back down onto the pillow as she left, stared at the ceiling rose overhead. The pretence was wearing thin; it always did in the cold light of day. Easier to maintain at night, in the shadows and the gaslight, when they were both happy to be someone else.

'Sarah, Sarah, Sarah,' he said to no one.

Not that Sarah was her real name. Or at least not what the world knew her as these days. Now she was Catherine

Fraser – Kitty to her friends – almost an honest woman, if you discounted the brothel on Boclair Road that she'd inherited from her late husband, and her semi-legitimate partnership with Teddy Levin, one of the city's most powerful gangsters. Number 36 Roman Road was a recent purchase, so business was obviously booming.

Before that, though, in another life, she had been Sarah Catherine Hunter. Six months previously Dreghorn had put her estranged brother Billy in prison, but they didn't talk about that. They didn't talk about the horrors and tragedies that had pushed her and Billy closer together than they should ever have been and then torn them apart. They didn't talk about Isla Lockhart or Molly Raeburn, or all the other ghosts that hovered around them, the pain and grief and guilt that they tried to numb with their secret liaison.

In their private little world of broken hearts and what-might-have-been, of sex that almost overwhelmed the memories, she was simply Sarah and he was . . .

Dreghorn wasn't quite sure what. A means to an end. An escape from reality. Someone who knew all her secrets but didn't judge, who almost matched her damage and sadness with his own.

It was madness, and all for 'a wee bit of houghmagandie', he heard the big man say in his head. If discovered, it could destroy his career and it wouldn't do Kitty – Sarah, whoever – any favours with her own underworld connections. Sillitoe would view his judgement as flawed and his integrity as a detective irrevocably compromised, open to manipulation and blackmail by the very criminals the Untouchables were formed to destroy. Dreghorn would be drummed out of the force in disgrace. At best. And without the force, what did he have?

Occasionally when he arrived at her villa, late at night in a squad car or, like yesterday, having taken a train and walked from the station, he felt as though he was being watched. His own conscience, probably.

The safest thing, the healthiest thing for both of them, would be to end it. He doubted he was what she wanted him to be, and she couldn't be what he wanted, because that woman was dead and would never have been his anyway, not when barriers of class and race and religion rebuilt themselves faster than you could tear them down.

She was standing over him again. As he pushed himself onto one elbow, determined to tell her, she let the robe slip free. His eyes travelled up, over the dark hair at the top of her inner thighs, her slightly rounded belly and breasts to her face, her eyes and sly smile telling him that she had felt every inch of his gaze.

He glimpsed the white scar again as she slipped back under the covers and rolled towards him, but he wasn't thinking with his head now, and his high morals had gone out the window.

Dreghorn was indeed meeting another woman that sunny Sunday morning, just not an *other* woman.

Betty Dreghorn skipped off the tram like a woman fifteen years younger, following what looked like a suspiciously flirty exchange with the tram driver. She scowled in surprise on seeing Dreghorn already waiting on the entrance steps of the Kelvin Hall, hands in his pockets and grinning gormlessly at her.

'Early for once,' she said, turning her cheek for his kiss, then darting forward to examine his chin. He was washed and clean-shaven and had nipped back to Mrs Pettigrew's to change his shirt and swap his bunnet for his fedora – nothing to suggest he had spent the night anywhere other than at his lodgings.

He could have sworn that his mother was almost disappointed to see him looking so respectable, robbed of the chance to point out new shoots of grey in his stubble, or to lick a finger and wipe at some stain, real or imagined, on his clothing.

'When henpecking's made a crime,' he'd tell her, 'don't think I won't be the first to slap the handcuffs on you.'

She slipped her arm through his and led him towards Kelvingrove Park for their regular constitutional, and towards Frederick Risi's cart for ice cream or hot chestnuts, depending on the season.

Crossing Argyle Street, they strolled past the Art Galleries and turned left onto Kelvin Way. As they entered the park, Betty delved into her handbag and produced a piece of paper with a flourish.

'A Sweepstake ticket for you,' she announced proudly. 'They're like gold dust, you know.'

Dreghorn examined it closely: Irish Free State Hospitals' Sweepstake Ticket, number 26358, bearing an official watermark and valid for the Epsom Derby of 31 May. It was authentic all right.

His mother misread his expression. 'I've already given your brother and sister theirs. There's no favourites in this family, Jimmy, you all get the same.'

'It's no' that, Ma,' He waved the ticket sternly in her face. 'These are illegal.'

'Och, away with you. It's no worse than a raffle ticket. For helping out sick children and hospitals? We could do with one over here.'

'Aye, no, but . . . strictly speaking, it's gambling. Which you don't approve of, by the way.'

Betty was having none of it. 'Well, if that's what the law says, then the law's an arse.'

'Mother, it's Sunday!' Dreghorn said in his best priest-voice, then 'And it's an ass.'

'Eh?'

'An ass. The correct saying is: "The law is an ass".'

She hmphed loudly. 'Well, I said arse and I meant arse. Say what you mean, and mean what you say.'

'All right, all right.' He made a show of reluctantly slipping the ticket into his inside pocket.

'You'll no' be greetin' about it if your number comes up.'

'A pokey hat or a wafer?' They had reached Frederick Risi's horse-drawn ice-cream cart and the queue wasn't too bad. Dreghorn sometimes wondered if the hokey pokey man, with his cheery cries of 'Ice-A-Cream-A!', had a Corporation licence to sell his goods in the park, as he seemed to set up shop wherever took his fancy, rather than in the same spot each week. Mind you, there would be an uproar if the Corporation ever dared deprive the public of ice cream; the Scottish sweet tooth was so prevalent that the ice-cream maker could probably have got away with murder.

'Your Uncle Joe enjoyed the day out with you yesterday,' she said. 'Called in to see me after the game.'

'Did he now? What time was that?'

'The back of seven. He'd had a wee dram on the way back – you leading him astray, no doubt.'

'Not guilty, Your Honour, he must have done that all on his lonesome. I left the accused at about five.'

'Why?'

'Police business. A bit of trouble at the game.'

Dreghorn had returned to the stands as the stadium emptied, where his Uncle Joe was waiting, flabbergasted that his nephew had missed Jimmy McGrory's winning goal in the final minutes of the match. Dreghorn had apologized, said he couldn't join Joe and the lads for a post-match drink and dissection of the game, explaining that a body had been found. He revealed nothing about the cause of death, but the story would get out quickly enough. Gossip would have been spreading amongst the match stewards even before he and Willie Kivlichan were alerted. By the time the crowd had dispersed, it would be all through the city, embellished and exaggerated to God-knows-what degree.

Chain-smoking cigarettes to the end of the pack, he had remained at Hampden to supervise the crime scene. The police photographer arrived first, then Bertie Hammond, who didn't hold out much hope for forensics evidence. Whether chosen deliberately or through good fortune, a public lavatory made a perfect execution spot, with chemicals, flowing water, gallons of pish and the trampling feet of thousands of desperate football fans effectively destroying any potential clues.

An ambulance removed the body for transport to the morgue just after 7 p.m. Kivlichan said his goodbyes and Dreghorn travelled back to Turnbull Street in a Black Maria with the uniformed officers who'd been on match duty and would now be clamouring for overtime because of the murder.

'Don't you ever leave here?' he said to Shug Nugent as he passed the reception.

'I was just about to ask you the same question,' the desk sergeant replied.

Dreghorn quickly wrote up a report on Harold Beattie's

murder and left it for whoever was on duty the next day, with instructions that a copy be sent to the Murder Lodge. Two corpses with their brains blown out was too much of a coincidence. Possible connections between the victims would have to be explored. But not tonight, he said to himself. It was 9 p.m. No sign now even of Shug Nugent.

He should have gone back to Mrs Pettigrew's, sat in his room with the wireless playing and a few nips of whisky, though the bottle was getting dangerously low. Or to one of the bars frequented by police officers or some of the few friends he had outside the force, but he was weary of banter and bravado. After the sad indignity of Harold Beattie's corpse and the chill wind that had whistled through the empty football ground, cutting to the bone, he needed something more.

He had left the stadium and headed straight for Sarah Hunter. That too was illusory, but there were worse lies to tell yourself.

He thought back on all this, not noticing that the queue for ice cream had dwindled before him, until Risi asked what he wanted, his original southern Italian accent now tinged with Scots. As Dreghorn ordered – two large cones with raspberry – he realized that things had come full circle.

A few weeks earlier he had turned from Risi to see Kitty Fraser strolling towards him and his mother. He hadn't seen her since the previous November, her hand then bandaged from an injury that had quite possibly saved his life. She had been blunted by pain and grief, but seemed to have recovered and was drawing admiring glances from both men and women.

She greeted him as if they were old friends and explained that she'd been for a walk with her sister and niece. Betty

Dreghorn was intrigued and raised an expectant eyebrow at her son. Reluctantly Dreghorn started to make introductions, gesturing towards Kitty. 'And this is—'

'Sarah,' Kitty had said before he could finish, extending her hand with a dazzling smile. 'Sarah Hunter.'

'You better lick that quick or it'll dreepy all down you.' Betty Dreghorn's warning brought him out of his reverie, and he quickly lifted the melting ice cream to his mouth. 'You're away with the fairies today,' she continued, rescuing her own cone before it too started dripping.

They walked, tracking the course of the River Kelvin through the park. Follow it far enough and it would almost take them to where Reginald Smith's body was discovered, but Dreghorn neglected to mention that to his mother.

'Guess who I met the other day,' he said.

'Some reprobate or other.' Betty Dreghorn had little faith in the power of police work to raise her son's social standing.

'Old friend of yours, Martha Hepburn.'

Betty took a bite out of her cone before answering. He didn't see quite the level of affection that he expected in her expression.

'Watch you don't get on the wrong side of her, Jimmy. She's fond of a good argument.'

'Funny, that's more or less what she said about you.'

CHAPTER 20

Monday, 3 April 1933

The reprisals, the newspapers reported, began almost immediately after the discovery of Harold Beattie's body, violence bubbling over in pubs and streets throughout the city.

If pressed, the journalists who used the word would probably admit that 'reprisals' was intellectualizing the situation too much, hinting at some genuine justification for the beatings and stabbings and slashings. 'Any old excuse' would have been a more accurate summation of the motivation behind the attacks. And it would take a skilled mathematician to differentiate between that and the regular Saturday-night rammies.

Glasgow lived and breathed news, served by four daily newspapers – *The Glasgow Herald*, the *Daily Record*, *The Bulletin* and the *Scottish Daily Express* – and three evening ones – the *Evening News*, the *Evening Times* and the *Evening Citizen*. With that sort of competition, headlines had to be eye-catching: *GLASGOW GUNMAN STRIKES AGAIN*; *SUDDEN DEATH AT HAMPDEN PARK*; *SECTARIAN EXECUTIONER STALKS CITY STREETS?*

The headlines were inflammatory in a town that was a tinder box at the best of times. Even if the facts were essentially correct, the words were malleable according to religious bias and took on a fierce life of their own when they rose from the newsprint and sprang out of people's mouths, propelled by cheap whisky and warm beer to become outright lies. Two plus two equals five in alcoholic arithmetic. Proddie victims equals Catholic killer. Only one thing for it, lads, go out there and get them before they get us.

Two members of the Cheeky Forty, Catholic, were set upon by a marauding squad from the Protestant Baltic Fleet, beaten black and blue, stripped naked and dumped in the waters of the Doulton Fountain on Glasgow Green. Lucky for them it wasn't the dead of winter.

In retaliation, the Forty rampaged through Bridgeton Cross, heartland of the Billy Boys, the city's most powerful Protestant gang. Taking advantage of the leadership void caused by Billy Hunter's incarceration, they smashed the windows of the Mermaid Bar, cracked three skulls with a variety of chibs, and left countless slash-wounds in their wake. To be fair, they suffered an equal number of casualties themselves, leading both gangs to claim victory, instead of reflecting on the ultimate pointlessness of the endeavour.

After that, it all escalated: same old story. Catholic, Protestant. Proddie, Tim. Punch, kick. Stab, slash. 'Mon then, yah orange bastard!', 'Come ahead, yah Fenian cunt!'

No matter what God they supposedly worshipped – technically the same one, but don't go there, that's a whole other can of worms – what team they supported, what colours they wore, they all bled red.

DCI Monroe read out the list of weekend affrays that could theoretically have been instigated by the two shootings, to stress the urgency and importance of solving the crimes. 'If we don't make progress, and quickly,' he said, 'there's a good chance we'll be conducting our investigation in the middle of a full-scale gang war, with all the fun and games that brings.'

'The Wouldnae-Touch-Them-With-Bargepoles can deal with

CAST A COLD EYE   153

that,' Graham Orr said with a sleekit glance at Dreghorn. 'Leave the real work to us.'

The initial forensics results and ballistics report on Smith had come in: a .45-calibre round, fired from a handgun, the bullet prised from the deck of the narrowboat after passing through the victim's skull. Any fingerprints found in the cabin either belonged to Smith himself or didn't match those of any known criminals held on file. With such a precisely planned, cold-blooded murder, it was likely that the assassin would have worn gloves anyway.

Despite Calum Baird's witness statement, the Captain's Log of the *Blue Bonnet* – if Smith's scrappy notebook could be called that – held no details of journeys or cargoes in the days leading up to his murder.

Dreghorn asked if the examination of the hold had uncovered anything.

'It was empty,' stated Strachan bluntly.

'If there were traces or fragments of what it had been carrying, that might give us some inkling of who he'd been having dealings with,' Dreghorn said.

Strachan consulted the report. 'Only pieces of sacking. Ellen, chase up Sergeant Hammond to see if it's been analysed.' He raised his eyebrows at Dreghorn: *satisfied?*

Post-mortem and ballistics reports on the second murder were imminent, though not expected to yield any new information. The nature of the killing pointed to the same murder weapon and the same finger on the trigger, but, as Dreghorn had already surmised, the location made the collection of forensic evidence almost impossible.

Official identification of the second victim had been confirmed. A follow-up interview with the deceased's widow was required, as she had been too distraught to answer questions. Dreghorn volunteered to conduct the interview, asked Ellen to accompany him. She glanced at Strachan, who was staring impassively at Dreghorn, giving nothing away.

'Is that wise, sir?' Orr asked Strachan. 'If someone's going around shooting Proddies in the head, maybe having a Tim muddy the waters isn't wise. Might make people resentful, make them clam up.'

Dreghorn said, 'I'm a detective first and foremost. You remember what that is, don't you?' He looked at Strachan. 'I found the body. It should be me.'

Strachan stroked his moustache, nodded assent. Dreghorn leaned close to Orr as he left.

'Don't worry, Graham,' he said, 'you're not in any danger. There's not a marksman alive good enough to hit your brain.'

Excused from the briefing by other duties, Archie McDaid was enjoying a late breakfast of square sausage, bacon, tattie scone, fried eggs, baked beans and a clootie dumpling in the Rialto Cafe.

Or would have been if his dining companion hadn't been attempting to turn his plate into a Surrealist masterpiece, with a hunk of fried bread as the brush and egg yolk, brown sauce and swirling grease as his paints.

'Don't stand on ceremony, Denny,' McDaid suggested, 'just pick it up and lick it clean.'

Denny Knox laughed as he chomped, his glasses steaming up from the effort. He freed his mouth enough to say, 'Sorry, big man, no dinner last night. Could eat a scabby dug.'

By no dinner, Knox obviously meant nothing solid. An evening's drinking in the Press Bar, swapping stories and information or trying to send rival reporters shooting off in pursuit of false leads. With a touch of shame, McDaid realized that despite having known the man for many a year, he couldn't recall Knox's domestic circumstances. McDaid was sure he had been married at one point, but whether there were children, he had no idea.

It was hard to imagine any self-respecting woman allowing Knox to leave the house in his current state – crumpled shirt, tie askew, a day's growth of beard. A scabby dog wasn't a bad description of his appearance. He had a nervous, whippet-like energy, his eyes forever searching for giveaways and signs of someone being less than truthful with him. That unrelenting doggedness would be hard to live with.

Knox wiped his mouth with a napkin, already scrawled upon with notes and pithy phrases that had come to him over break-fast. 'So, is this a social call or are the Glasgow Police buying me brekkie, because if they are, I'm having a jam doughnut as well.'

'Can't it be both?'

Knox removed his specs, started cleaning the lenses with his tie, which had fallen into his plate more than once. McDaid waved to the waitress and ordered a jam doughnut. He sat up straighter, breathed in to create a slimmer silhouette. 'Make it two, please,' he said.

'Fighting weight's gone by the wayside then?' Knox popped his glasses back on and was startled to find them more smeared than they had been before cleaning.

'I can still hold my own, don't you worry.'

'Aye, against a doughnut.'

McDaid finished his tea. 'Jimmy and me encountered a

couple of fellows that we thought you might be able to give us some extra information on – you being a top reporter and all that.'

'Who?' Acting casual.

'A fellow named Haldane – don't know his first name – and a disagreeable wee shite called Eugene Quinlisk.'

'Irish?'

'Quinlisk, aye. Haldane's Scots, but so posh that he almost sounds English. Superintendent in Special Branch, but we reckon maybe Military Intelligence in the past. No' too sure about Quinlisk.'

'Special Branch?' He was focused now. His days as a war correspondent, sifting through casualty reports, briefings and military jargon that reduced men's lives and deaths to dry, emotionless statistics, had left Denny Knox with a healthy disrespect for authority and an unhealthy dependency on alcohol. A post-war stint as a sports journalist, during which he first met McDaid, covering the big man's medal-winning exploits in the 1924 Paris Olympics, hadn't provided him with the necessary adrenaline boost, so he had switched to the crime beat. All forms of power were to be regarded with suspicion and held to account, even his long-suffering bosses at the *Scottish Daily Express*. Knox believed a good reporter should be an irritant to those in power, though arguably he carried that attitude a little too far into other areas of his life.

'Isn't that simply another department of the fine institution you serve?' he asked. 'Sounds like you're being a wee bit sleekit. Why not just ask officially?'

'Might set alarm bells ringing, and me and Jimmy want to play nice. For now.'

'Has it got anything to do with the shootings?'

'Don't think so, but . . .' McDaid liked to be enigmatic with Knox, letting the reporter's nose for a story lead him on.

'How close are you to catching the killer?'

'We're following strong potential leads. Can't say anything more than has already been released, at this stage of the investigation.'

Knox removed his glasses, breathed on the lenses and started wiping them again. 'What do I get out of it, sergeant? Your last exclusive wasn't very exclusive.'

McDaid looked hurt. 'I was on death's doorstep, injured in the line of duty. Otherwise I'd've been singing like a canary.'

Knox remained silent.

'There's probably nothing in it – the usual red tape and rigmarole – but if there is anything newsworthy, we'll make sure you hear about it first.' He paused for Knox to nod agreement. 'What do you know about Ireland?'

'Partial to the odd half of Guinness, why?'

'There's a man named Conall Tracy in town. Bigwig in the Free State and the Sweep, by all accounts. It'd be nice to know if there are any other hobbies he's fond of.'

'One man's terrorist is another man's freedom fighter. Is that what we're talking about here?' Consciously or not, Knox had lowered his voice.

'See me?' McDaid pointed at his own face. 'Inscrutable.' He saw the waitress approaching and leaned forward before she reached them. 'We're talking about nipping things in the bud so that nobody gets terrorized or terrified.'

'Two jam doughnuts.'

The big man leaned back to smile his thanks at the girl as she placed the plates on the table.

'Do you want forks?' She nodded at the hulking, sugar-encrusted dollops of deep-fried dough.

'You're all right, hen, we'll live dangerously,' McDaid said, taking a reckless bite, then lurching forward desperately as a globule of jam burst out the other side, failing to catch it before it plopped stickily onto his crotch.

'*Mhac na galla!*'

CHAPTER 21

With a small nod to Ellen, Dreghorn removed his hat, chapped the door and waited for Diana Beattie to answer. Diana Beattie, thirty-seven years old, whose husband had waved cheerio two days previously to attend a football match and never returned.

Dreghorn hated death-calls, especially of unnatural causes. You never knew how the bereaved would react: shock, hysterics, numbness, tears, denial, silence, rage, withdrawal. The shades of grief that coloured those broad strokes were infinitesimal. Everyone was different, yet everyone was the same. Loss was life; life was loss.

Diana Beattie's eyes washed over them emptily. There was a smear of black lead-polish on one cheek, a similar handprint on her pinny, and strands of hair hung loose over her face, slipped free of the severe bun she'd pulled it into. She turned away before either of them could speak and drifted dazedly back into the house, leaving the door open.

Dreghorn let Ellen go first – avoidance, not gentlemanly manners – and followed, closing the door quietly.

Some tenement families were fortunate enough to have two rooms. The Beatties weren't one of them. The front door opened straight into their sole living space. The range, for cooking and heating, was on one wall, polished to an ebony sheen, embers burning in the hearth, a kettle on the ring above.

A gleaming sink and shining swan-necked water-pipe and tap, the limescale scoured off, sat to the left of the range, beneath the only window. The alcove bed opposite the range was neatly made, the wheelie bed below, which the children slept upon, equally tidy. Every inch of the linoleum-covered floor had been swept vigorously, and a dustpan and brush set beside the door.

Diana Beattie had been cleaning – religiously was the word that came to Dreghorn's mind – preparing for one thing: the return of her husband's body. All the chairs were pushed against the walls and the table was placed at the centre of the room, awaiting the coffin. She stared at the table as if his presence was already there.

Ellen spoke with warmth and sympathy. 'Mrs Beattie – Diana? I'm Police Constable Duncan. This is Inspector Dreghorn.'

'I don't know what else I can tell you.' Her voice sounded querulous, lost. 'I've already spoken to you . . . yesterday . . . Saturday . . . I don't know . . .'

'I know, Mrs Beattie, but we have to ask.' Dreghorn stepped to the opposite side of the table. 'Sometimes folk remember things afterwards, details that could be important.' She gave no sign of having heard him, so he said reluctantly, 'I was there, Mrs Beattie, when they found your husband.'

She blinked, focusing on him for the first time. 'They said he wouldn't have suffered.'

'That's right, ma'am. He wouldn't have known what was happening, wouldn't have felt a thing.' Dreghorn couldn't know that for sure, couldn't know if the killer had alerted Beattie to the fact that his life was about to end, but there were good lies and bad lies. 'Scotland had scored not long before, so he'd have been pretty chuffed at the time.'

She gave Dreghorn a weak smile. 'He loved the football. And the Rangers. More than us, I thought, sometimes.'

Ellen said, 'I'm sure that's not true, Mrs Beattie.'

'A different kind of love,' Dreghorn offered, immediately wincing at the triteness.

Diana Beattie looked him straight in the eye. 'When will I get him back? Everything's ready.'

Death didn't haunt the tenements so much as exist there like an unwelcome guest that folk ignored until they no longer had a choice. It was such a part of life – babies lost at birth; children dead of disease and malnutrition; mothers from sheer exhaustion; fathers and sons in industrial accidents; grandparents, aged and worn down beyond their years – that people became inured to its frequency.

Practically, few in the tenements could afford to store bodies at the undertaker's until the day of the funeral. The dearly departed lay in the house they'd previously lived and breathed in, their families eating and sleeping around the coffin, the surrealism of the situation soon becoming almost normal.

Dreghorn recalled the first corpse he'd seen in this fashion, the grandmother of a childhood friend who lived in the same close. He'd followed his mother into the single end, the coffin laid out on the table, the sides too high for him to see anything. As his mother spoke hushed condolences to the bereaved, his childish curiosity had got the better of him.

He started jumping up and down to gain fleeting glimpses over the edge of the coffin, the silver hair and pale frozen features stirring a strange fascination. A skelp around the ear halted his bouncing and he was ushered out in shame: 'Away and let her rest in peace, yah cheeky wee besom!'

Meeting Diana Beattie's gaze, he said, 'I'm sorry, ma'am, we can't say for sure when the body will be released. It's a murder. There are procedures to be followed, a post-mortem to be carried out.'

The comment seemed to drain her. She swayed unsteadily and Ellen took her arm, offering gentle support, suggesting they sat down.

'Are you on your own?' Ellen asked as Dreghorn brought over chairs.

'No,' Diana said, 'my sister's staying, but she's gone for some messages.' She looked around. 'Took the weans with her, gie them some fresh air instead of . . .' She looked around the room, suddenly lost.

'That'll be good for them, but you've got to take care of yourself too, aye? For the weans, if nothing else.'

Not for the first time, Dreghorn was impressed by the easy rapport Ellen had with members of the public, most of whom viewed the polis as little more than blunt instruments of the state, there to keep them in their place. He sat down opposite the two women, asked, 'Mrs Beattie, are you aware of anyone who might have wanted to hurt your husband?'

Diana took a breath. 'No, everybody liked Harold. He didn't bother anyone, and nobody bothered him.'

'No gang affiliations?'

She gave him a look: *daft question.* 'He was a bit old for that, do you no' think?'

'Maybe, but what about in the past? Some folk in this town have long memories.'

'He was never into that malarkey. The army, that was his gang. Loved it, joined up as soon as he was old enough, before the war, like.'

She nodded at a chest of drawers in one corner of the room,

framed photographs resting on the surface. Dreghorn couldn't make them out in detail, but one of them appeared to be an image of men in uniform, posing with their rifles like conquering heroes of the empire.

'What regiment was he in?' Dreghorn knew that Diana and her brother-in-law had already formally identified Beattie's corpse. Fortunately she hadn't had to look at her husband's destroyed features, identification being made from a small birthmark above his left nipple and what the autopsy report described as an 'army tattoo of indeterminate origin on right bicep', the ink faded so as to be largely indecipherable.

'The Royal Highland Fusiliers. The weans and me just laughed and yawned and took the mickey whenever he started going on about the war – "When I was in the army . . ."' She'd doubtless have given anything to be bored by those stories now.

Dreghorn gestured at the photograph. 'May I?'

He crossed the room, picked up the picture, felt his stomach tighten as he examined the men, their uniforms and weaponry. Ellen smiled at Diana in the silence.

'Did your husband know Reginald Smith?' he asked.

'Is that the man who got shot up at the canal?' She thought hard, shook her head. 'Not that I know of, but he had a few pals that he used to meet once a week at the King's Arms. The lads, he called them. Lads, at his age!' Her voice cracked, something that had been a source of disdain and exasperation now unbearably poignant.

Dreghorn returned to the seat, the photograph still in his hand. 'What about work? Did he talk much about that, have problems with anyone there?'

'He'd only been there since Christmas, a stock-man for

Petershill Brewery.' She nodded at the picture. 'Ronnie Anderson – the one on the left – got him the job, or put in a good word anyway. Ronnie's the manager of the King's Arms.'

'On Bath Street?'

'Aye. Before that, Harold'd been on the buroo for nearly two years. He was a welder at Springburn Locomotions, but nobody's building anything now. I know he thought making deliveries was below him, but he'd rather that than be on the buroo. Never been out of work in his life before. Always made sure he supported us. Didn't smoke, didn't drink much.' Tears came to her eyes. 'Who could do something like that? Who could just walk up to somebody and . . .'

Dreghorn said, 'We don't know, Mrs Beattie, that's why we have to ask questions, dredge things up. He might just have been in the wrong place at the wrong time.'

Diana leaned forward suddenly, eyes red with tears, burning with rage. 'When you find whoever did this, hang them high – hang them fucking high!'

'Ma?' A fragile wee voice.

Dreghorn pulled back, glanced over his shoulder. A girl of about twelve stood in the doorway beside a woman a couple of years older than Diana. Wipe away the stresses of life and age, and the girl was almost the double of her mother. Two younger boys huddled close to their sister, all staring at Dreghorn with fear and uncertainty, their world unravelled.

Diana's anger changed to shame at the capacity for hatred that her children had seen within her. She opened her arms and they rushed to her. Dreghorn quickly stepped back, feeling like a ghoul. He nodded to Ellen, who leaned close to Diana and said they were leaving, thanking her for her time and apologizing for intruding.

'Can we take this?' Dreghorn raised the photograph. 'It might prove useful. We'll make sure it's returned safely.'

Diana nodded, huddled amongst her weans, not even looking at him. Dreghorn slipped the photograph free and placed the frame back on the chest of drawers, its grey emptiness matching that of the room.

Dreghorn examined the photo as they descended the stairs. 'If we needed a connection between Smith and Beattie beyond the bullets in their heads, we've got it now.' He handed the image to Ellen. 'They served together.'

'During the war, you mean, in the Fusiliers?' She looked at the photo; the faces of both Smith and Beattie stared out at her with a gallus arrogance that she found inherently menacing. Men with guns, fired up by the power and swaggering confidence.

'That an' all. But see those hats – the tam-o'-shanters – that's not the uniform of the Fusiliers.' He gave her a distasteful look. 'That's from a different war – if you can call it that. They were in the Black and Tans.'

Ellen's expression was blank, too young to have much awareness of events across the water more than a decade earlier. Dreghorn himself had been in Shanghai at the time.

He explained: 'The Tans were a paramilitary force recruited by the British government as reinforcements for the Royal Irish Constabulary during the Anglo-Irish War – before the Treaty and the Partition of Ireland. Sent there to keep the peace, supposedly, except they weren't very peaceable, by all accounts.' An understatement: the Tans acted with a brutality that made a mockery of the term, pouring fuel onto the flames of conflict.

'A lot of them were ex-soldiers, demobbed after the war, with it all still in them. Quite a few Scots amongst them.'

'Including Smith and Beattie?'

'Looks that way. When we get back to the station, contact the Ministry of Defence to request their military records and those of any other Glaswegians they might have served with. Knowing our luck, the killer might have his eye on more that just these two.'

CHAPTER 22

'Well, this is a nice change from the police canteen,' Dreghorn said. 'A better class of companion and considerably easier on the eye.'

He should have left it at the first comment, but sometimes insouciance was irresistible. Rachel McAdam and Martha Hepburn met it with a roll of the eyes and a shake of the head that acknowledged the cheeky glint in his eyes. The lunch appointment had slipped his mind until he arrived back at Turnbull Street after interviewing Diana Beattie, and he'd set off immediately, leaving a scrawled note for McDaid.

There was another place set at the table, deliberately, it seemed. Dreghorn nodded at the empty seat. 'I should have brought DS McDaid with me, Mrs Hepburn. You could have continued your musical debate.'

'I am expecting another guest,' Martha said, 'but I'm sure you'll enjoy his company. He's keen to meet you and pick your brains. As am I.'

'You may be disappointed, ma'am. I'm not sure there's all that much there to pick.'

Rachel McAdam hadn't touched the notepad and pen she'd brought to take shorthand notes. She was smiling at Dreghorn as she said, 'And here I thought you were the brains and thon big bonnie fellow was the brawn.' She turned to Martha. 'Jimmy was one of the patter merchants at school, always ready

with a smart-aleck comment. Not picking on anyone or anything like that – the opposite, if anything. Just gallus, full of fun.'

'Fun,' Dreghorn said wistfully, 'I remember fun.'

'I think we can all be guilty of being too serious these days,'
Martha Hepburn mused.

'It's been a hard few years,' Rachel agreed. 'Difficult sometimes to see how things can get better.'

Dreghorn sensed the comment was personal to her, looking
deeper within, rather than an observation on the world.

'Did we order an extra helping of despair with our afternoon
tea or do they throw it in for free?' he asked.

Martha whooped with laughter. 'The inspector's right. We
sit and debate and wring our consciences from positions of
relative privilege, compared to most. He's the one who lives
and breathes it on the streets, but still maintains a sense of
humour.'

'All you've got, sometimes, ma'am.'

She picked one of the remaining cakes from the stand and
placed it on his plate with a smile. 'A Victoria sponge to show
our appreciation.'

It wasn't to Dreghorn's taste, but he decided it would be
impolite to refuse; one of the waitresses could secretly scoff it
when they cleared away the china. The luncheon appointment
had been rescheduled slightly later and became afternoon tea
at the Rhul Tea Room in Sauchiehall Street instead.

'We were talking about Chief Constable Sillitoe's reforms
when we met at Duke Street, inspector,' said Martha.

'You were, ma'am.'

'Please, call me Martha.'

Dreghorn nodded, didn't comment.

'Do you feel his approach is reaping benefits?'

'Things don't happen overnight, ma'am. It's an ongoing battle.'

'A battle. Interesting choice of words.'

Dreghorn glanced at Rachel, her expression diplomatically impartial.

'Would you say there's been a decrease in violence between the gangs, thanks to the chief constable's tactics and your own actions in the Special Crime Squad?' Mrs Hepburn continued.

'I don't spend my evenings totting up the arrest sheets, ma'am. They certainly know they can't run riot the way they used to, not without the Heavy Mob coming down on them.'

'That sense of us against them, the mystique of your "Tartan Untouchables" . . . isn't there a danger that will only increase the allure of the gangs?'

'There's nothing alluring about them, ma'am. It's not Hollywood out there, it's seedy and brutal and violent and cowardly. We can do our best and arrest them, but does that deter impressionable weans on the street from wanting to take their place?' Dreghorn shrugged. 'And it's up to the courts to convict them. We can offer protection and try to stop witness intimidation, but it's hard when the whole city lives on top of itself. And there's nothing we can do about bastards like George Garrison getting them off, pardon my language.'

Martha shared a telling glance with Rachel. 'Mr Garrison has an unenviable reputation in certain quarters of the court system.'

Dreghorn said, 'You wouldn't envy him some of the things he's called back at the station, either.'

'It's all still violence, though, isn't it?' Martha's voice hardened, becoming magisterial. 'You're fighting fire with fire, not water. Feeding it, making it worse.'

'Some people, that's all they understand.'

'Now, now, inspector, you can't palm us off with that. I don't think you believe it anyway. We're all familiar with the effects of violence.' She gestured at herself and Rachel. 'We've seen men – brothers, fathers, husbands – go to war and not return. Or come back changed, broken, inside and out. Women have to live with the consequences of your violence as much as you do; more in some ways, because we often become the victims of it.'

'Sorry, ma'am, it wasn't my intention to be flippant or dismissive, but—'

'I've seen bombs and bullets at first hand, inspector, just like you. I know what they can do to bodies, and to hearts and minds also.'

Dreghorn suddenly saw a look in Martha Hepburn that veterans of the Great War shared – a cold eye cast over life and death, an understanding of the fragility of humanity.

'You were in the war, ma'am? A nurse?'

'Another war.' Her eyes softened, saddened.

'Mrs Hepburn was in Dublin in 1916 during the Easter Rising.'

Martha Hepburn gave her assistant an annoyed glance. 'It was after the Rent Strikes. I was visiting my aunt, who was unwell. Her son, my cousin, just a daft boy, was marching with the rebels. On the day of the Rising I went down to the Post Office to try and spirit him away and I got caught up in the siege.'

Dreghorn said respectfully, 'I was at the Front at the time. News seeped through, of course, and there were Irish lads over there who were rattled by the fact that there they were fighting in France and Belgium for the British Army, while back

home the British Army was firing on their countrymen...'
He shrugged, a touch sheepishly. 'Can't say I took too much
notice beyond that at the time.'

Rachel came to his defence. 'To be fair, you did have the
German Army trying to kill you.'

'Not a bad excuse,' he said.

'While I was there I met Pearse and Connolly, and Countess
Markievicz,' Martha continued. 'All dead now. History is
always written by the victors, and the right people don't always
win. I ended up helping with the wounded, not that we had
much in the way of medical supplies. A lot of them were just
boys, probably a lot like you in the war, inspector, scared half
to death, but trying not to show it. Fear isn't manly, is it?'

Dreghorn said, 'I don't do much to hide it these days.'

'I was wounded myself – thankfully taken care of by real
nurses in St Vincent's Hospital. I lay there listening to news of
the so-called trials of the leaders of the Rising. And then the
executions. Connolly had been badly wounded, but they carried him out into the yard tied to a chair and shot him anyway.'
She was silent for a moment. 'The executions sickened and
horrified the population. Instead of crushing the rebellion,
they only increased support for it.

'So the killing went on, both sides. And then there's compromise and negotiation and you start fighting amongst
yourselves, friends and families against each other. And you
end up with a divided country instead of a free one. No one
really wins, but each side claims they did ...' Her voice tailed
off, lost.

'Violence breeds violence, Jimmy,' said Rachel. 'Chief Constable Sillitoe sends you out against the gangs. A gangster pulls
a knife on you and you knock him down with your truncheon.

His friends see that and want revenge. And so it goes on: a vicious circle, a vicious cycle.'

Martha brightened unexpectedly, waving to someone across the tea room. 'Blessed are the peacemakers – that's what we need here.'

Dreghorn turned to witness the least priest-like priest he had ever seen approaching the table. If you'd replaced his clerical collar with a bow-tie, he'd have looked as though he was about to sweep some Hollywood starlet off her feet and onto the Copacabana dance floor.

About Dreghorn's height, handsome, slim and elegant in his dark suit, his hair swept back but for a stubborn kiss-curl that kept falling over his left eye, he was turning heads, from the youngest waitress to the most matronly customer.

He stopped at the empty chair, nodded cheerful greetings to the women and extended his hand to Dreghorn.

'Father Owen Gerrity, inspector,' he said. 'Pleased to meet you.' He had a vivid, infectious smile; the clergymen of Dreghorn's youth possessed all the warmth of tombstones.

Martha Hepburn said, 'Father Gerrity is in charge at the Church of the Immaculate Conception in Maryhill. I asked him to join us.'

Dreghorn rose to his feet, shaking the priest's hand. 'Are you not a wee bit young to have your own church?'

'That's just Aunt Martha being kind. I'm not long ordained, it's true, but the parish priest's been taken ill, so I'm holding the fort. Fortunately the congregation haven't run me out of town – yet.'

A waitress came over to take Gerrity's order: walnut cake and a pot of tea. Dreghorn took the opportunity to frown at Rachel, hoping for some clue as to what was going on. She smiled inscrutably and, he figured, rather mischievously back at him.

There was a short silence. Realization dawned in Gerrity.

'They haven't told you why I'm here, have they?' He nudged Martha affectionately. 'Aunt Martha likes to be enigmatic sometimes, loves a good mystery. Her shelves are all Agatha Christie and Dorothy L. Sayers – *Murder at the Vicarage, Murder at the Races, Murder Here There and Everywhere*.' The priest's dazzling smile was almost beatific.

'Father Gerrity's been doing sterling work in his church,' Martha said, 'but he has interesting ideas that go beyond parish boundaries.'

Gerrity nodded his thanks, addressed Dreghorn earnestly. 'You're part of the squad responsible for dealing with gang violence. A lot of those problems derive from sectarianism. I often see them attending Mass, with their bruised knuckles, slashed faces. It's hard not to notice when they're standing in front of you with their tongues out, waiting for communion.' He sighed. 'They're there, but they're not really there, if you know what I mean, just giving their faith lip service, repeating prayers parrot-fashion. The Catholic Church isn't reaching them any more, inspector.'

'I suppose slashing, stabbing and thieving isn't exactly following the spirit of the Ten Commandments.'

'They need to believe in something again.'

Dreghorn said, 'Say their prayers at night instead of going on the randan?' and felt Martha Hepburn's glare, Rachel's flash of disappointment.

Gerrity took no offence. 'The bishop might give me a clip around the ear for blasphemy, but I don't necessarily mean God. They have to believe in themselves, what's inside them, not' – he gestured towards the heavens – 'what's out there. Otherwise nothing will change.' He noted Dreghorn's interest, pressed on. 'No jobs, no money, no way of providing for your family, empty day after empty day. Is it any wonder they turn to the gangs? We need to make them feel that they can rely on themselves, stand alone, not be swept along by gang mentality. Individually they wouldn't dream of doing half the things they do as part of a gang.'

'In my experience, folk have to want to change, you can't force them.'

'No, they have to believe change is possible – change for the better – otherwise what's the point?'

He paused to let his words sink in, with Martha observing him proudly, then carried on. He explained that he had spoken to the archbishop, and the diocese had agreed to release funds for him to start up an athletics club to try and draw young men away from the lure and temptation of the gangs, through activities such as football, boxing, running.

'Creating a similar camaraderie to the gangs, but healthier in mind and body and without the propensity for violence and bigotry,' Gerrity said. 'What do you say, inspector?'

'It's been tried before.' The young priest's ambition and sincerity were admirable, but hadn't quite cracked Dreghorn's shell. 'It's still being tried.'

'I know. Reverend Warnes of St Frances-in-the-East and Reverend Peddie of Hutchesontown Church in the Gorbals are doing sterling work in reforming the gangs in their areas. And so is the police court missionary Robert Black, with this Govan Pals organization.'

'Aye, they're doing well all right – good men.' Dreghorn played devil's advocate. 'But there's others that have tried turning gangs into social clubs and ended up battered senseless and robbed blind.'

'I'm under no illusion that it'll be easy, inspector, and I've spoken with those who have started similar initiatives. They all agree that these schemes should be non-denominational, open to Catholics, Protestants, Jews, any religion. It's the only way to succeed. In fact I'd propose that instead of individual clubs in separate districts, we should form some sort of cooperative, working together for the same ideals.'

'It sounds like a grand plan,' Dreghorn said diplomatically, his suspicions growing.

'I knew you'd think that, inspector,' Martha Hepburn piped up. 'That's why I asked you here. We're hoping you'll agree to help us.'

Dreghorn glanced at Rachel before answering, 'I don't see what use I could be. They're more likely to view me as the enemy.'

'Exactly,' Gerrity agreed. 'But what better way to break down barriers and foster understanding.'

Martha said, 'I raised the issue of your involvement with Chief Constable Sillitoe. He offered his wholehearted support, but said that as it would be outside police duties, it would have to be your own decision.'

Dreghorn shook his head. 'I'm not really a man for making speeches.'

'We were thinking of something more practical – a boxing coach, maybe.' Gerrity said. 'You used to fight professionally, didn't you? Quite the reputation too, I hear.'

'A long time ago.'

' "Gentleman" Jimmy Dreghorn.' Rachel smiled.

Dreghorn felt cornered, ambushed by good intentions,

though he was pleased by Rachel's unexpected admission that she had followed what passed for his boxing career, way back when.

' "Gentleman"?' Martha scoffed.

'You don't think I'm the epitome of good breeding, ma'am? The name wasn't my idea, but it stuck at the time.' Dreghorn looked at Gerrity. 'Are you sure this isn't just a clever recruitment drive for your club? Roll up, roll up: take a legitimate swing at your friendly neighbourhood polisman!'

Gerrity said with a smile, 'We just think you're the right man for the job.'

A chorus of approval around the table, an expectant hush descending afterwards. Dreghorn eventually raised his hands in semi-submission.

'I'll think about it – no promises.'

'Thank you, inspector.' Gerrity placed his palms together, eyes twinkling with a humour that would have his female congregation fluttering their eyelids and feeling faint. 'I'll pray for the Almighty to nudge you towards the right decision.'

'In my experience, his – or her – nudges are usually from the frying pan into the fire.'

Gerrity laughed, and the conversation drifted into small talk amongst the priest and his 'Aunt' Martha. Dreghorn turned to Rachel, who gave a small, apologetic shrug.

'So,' he said, 'you enjoyed my patter at school? I didn't think you noticed.'

'Didn't want to encourage you too much. Nobody likes a show-off.'

Before he could respond, Martha gripped his arm melodramatically and nodded towards the entrance doors.

'Inspector, there's a strange man lurking over there . . .'

Dreghorn looked. McDaid stood outside, a hulking shape on the other side of the window, making faces at Dreghorn to try and catch his attention.

He rose to his feet, motioning for the waitress to fetch his hat and coat. 'Duty calls, I'm afraid,' he said.

Father Gerrity stood up as well, reaching for an inside pocket. 'Thank you, inspector. I'll give you a card so that we can discuss things further.'

Dreghorn lifted a hand, nodded at Rachel.

'It's probably best if we go through Miss McAdam,' he said. 'That way, everyone will know what's happening.' He hoped this ploy to remain in contact with Rachel didn't appear too contrived, but did note Martha Hepburn's raised eyebrow. 'If we go ahead,' he said to Gerrity, 'I'll make sure I wear my St Jude's medal.'

The priest frowned, still smiling.

'Desperate cases and lost causes,' Dreghorn said.

CHAPTER 23

'Police work's so hard when you're a detective inspector, isn't it?' McDaid observed as they crossed George Square, passing between statues that celebrated Scotland's heritage.

On their left, Walter Scott towered imperiously on his column in the centre of the square; on their right, Robert Burns was relegated to a considerably lower plinth, possibly due to the earthier nature of his work.

'Hobnobbing with magistrates and priests like some bastion of morality,' he continued. 'Well seeing they don't know what you're really like.'

'They were a wee bit sneaky themselves,' Dreghorn said. 'If they'd told me what they really wanted to talk about, I'd have given it a swerve, and I think they knew it.'

'That'll be your new fancy woman – what's her name, Rachel? – giving them inside information.'

'She's not . . .' Dreghorn started to say, then gave up, knowing it would only encourage the big man. 'They're trying to rope me into a scheme to reform young gang members and show them the error of their ways.'

'Is that no' what we already do?'

'Aye, but this time by peaceful means, not punching them in the mouth and hurling them in gaol.'

'How then?'

'By starting boys' clubs, encouraging them to develop hobbies. Supposedly I'd be an ideal boxing coach.'

'They must never have seen you fight then.' McDaid laughed. 'So, the neds can have a free go at punching you in the mouth?'

'That's what I thought – I recommended you instead, said you were the very man for the job. Mrs Hepburn will be in touch. Quite taken with you, so she is.'

'Away!' McDaid jerked a thumb over one shoulder. 'They'll no' see me for dust.'

They waited for a tram to pass along St Vincent Place, then crossed onto Cochrane Street.

'Just as well some of us have been engaged in vital detective work.'

'Who?' Dreghorn asked.

'Well, Bertie Hammond,' admitted McDaid. 'But, y'know, I listened intently.' He became serious. 'The results came back from the examination of the sacking fragments found in the *Blue Bonnet*'s cargo hold. Some innocent stuff, but also traces of guncotton, nitroglycerine, wood pulp and saltpetre.'

'Gelignite,' Dreghorn said.

McDaid nodded gravely. 'Made me think about the Garngad heist, so I telephoned Northern Division CID, spoke to a DS Travers – know him?'

Dreghorn shook his head. Explosives were a valuable commodity in the underworld, mainly used for safe-cracking or the occasional bombing of a rival gangster's car or pub, and coal fields and quarries carried a ready supply. Security was tight at industrial armouries, but bribery and violence still led to frequent thefts, and the sheer number of workers who had access to explosives made it difficult to keep accurate tabs on the quantities that were being used in the underground darkness.

Dreghorn thought about Superintendent Haldane and Eugene Quinlisk; one of the British government's greatest fears was of those explosives falling into the hands of organizations such as the IRA.

McDaid said, 'The robbery was on 24 March, which roughly corresponds to the date of Smith's murder.'

'So the gelignite could have been transported by Smith in his boat and the thieves murdered him afterwards to make sure there were no witnesses.' Dreghorn sighed. 'Have Northern got anything else?'

McDaid shook his head. 'They figure it was more than likely an inside job. No signs of forced entry on the gates or perimeter fences, and the night watchman was jumped on his rounds, which leads them to think the thieves knew his schedule. Minimum of violence. Whacked him on the noggin and tied him up out of sight. Four or five of them, he reckoned.'

'Which ties in with what the Baird lad told Ellen. Did the watchman mention anything about hearing accents of any sort?'

'Claims they never made a sound. Said he got the impression that it wasn't the first time they'd done it. Professionals. Cut through the chain on the explosives store with bolt cutters. Northern reckoned they moved the gelignite by truck, but when I mentioned Smith's narrowboat, Travers's ears pricked up. Explosives tend to be transported by road or rail these days, but back in the day it was done by barge, and he reckons there's still ready access to the Monklands Canal, from an old wharf or the St Rollux Basin.'

'And Monklands joins up with the Forth and Clyde . . .'

McDaid nodded. 'Travers is taking a team there tomorrow. They'll let us know if they find anything.'

'The watchman,' Dreghorn said, 'did they check if he's clean?'

'Seems to be. And they did almost crack his skull open.'

'And they've interviewed the workers – any ex-employees who might be disgruntled enough to break in?'

'Plenty of them around in the Depression, but aye. I was going to ask for a copy of the transcripts and a list of names in case any of them rang a bell, but Travers jumped in first. Wondered if we could help track down a fellow who was given his jotters last year and has gang connections and a criminal record – Paul Kane.'

'Dagger Kane?'

'The very jobby. Travers reckons he's lying low, trying to avoid them, though that might be down to Dagger's other nocturnal activities . . .'

Dreghorn pictured Kane in the Sarry Heid, sitting with Bull Bowman and Conall Tracy. 'How much gelignite was stolen again?'

'Six hundred-odd sticks, give or take,' said McDaid. 'Plus detonators and fuse tape.'

Dreghorn came to a halt at the corner of Virginia Street and Argyle Street, fished out his cigarettes and lit one. He breathed out smoke in a long sigh, glanced along the Trongate to the Steeple, then in the other direction towards the Hielanman's Umbrella at Central Station.

The pavements were busy with people: shoppers, schoolchildren enjoying hijinks at home-time, workers finishing for the day or starting a late shift; the roads were filled with trams, trucks, cars, horses and carts, bicycles; and, above the rooftops, the towering cranes of the shipyards on the River Clyde loomed just a few streets away. For the first time in his life, the mighty city that he loved and hated in equal parts suddenly seemed innocent and vulnerable.

He pushed his hat back, looked at McDaid.

The big man said, 'They might've transported the boxes to the open sea, had another ship waiting to pick them up.' He didn't sound hopeful.

'Aye, or they might be hidden in the city, waiting for some bampot to light the fuse. And we're no' short of them.'

CHAPTER 24

Life was cheap on the margins, the edges.

Down by the docks and wharves that neighboured the shipyards – the sprawling Queen's and Prince's Docks, the Broomielaw, Anderston, Lancefield and Finnieston Quays – Dreghorn always felt a heightened tension, a keener sense of danger. It was as if the closer they got to the Clyde, that roiling age-old elemental power, the more primal and lawless things became, especially at night.

Perhaps it was the nature of the work: a runaway barrel from an unloading ship could shatter a spine; a snapped rope and a crate plunging from a crane onto the docks would crush a man instantly; a red-hot rivet missed by a clumsy catcher could penetrate a skull like a bullet and burn through the brain. Wouldn't everyday risks like that make it seem as though you had nothing to lose? Work hard, play hard. Live hard, die hard.

The same abandon was seen in the sailors arriving in port after months at sea, with a thirst for vice and little fear of being caught if they crossed the line, because they'd be sailing off into the horizon again in a matter of days, broken bones and broken hearts in their wake.

Adding to the heady brew of sectarianism that already divided the yards, a cacophony of accents and languages filled the air like birdsong, rising from ships that docked from all across the world. Lascars, as well as Black and Chinese seamen, were a regular sight in the ports looking for work and dossing in riverside flophouses, from which emanated exotic cooking smells that would have seared the limited Glaswegian palate. Racial tensions bubbled alongside sectarian ones in the competition for employment, the battle for survival.

Aye, life was cheap along the Broomielaw. Especially the parts that should have been the most precious.

The girl had caught his eye a couple of times, but he hoped he'd looked away quickly enough to indicate that he wasn't in the market for her attempt at an alluring smile. His heart fell as she finally started across the bar towards him, looking younger with every step, her seductive sashay marking her naivety. The other women in the place had abandoned that malarkey long ago, becoming pragmatic and business-like, or numbing themselves with drugs and alcohol until simply walking straight was an achievement.

She sat on the stool across from him, shifting it out from behind the table to give him a clearer view. She crossed her legs with the same smile, twirled her ankle playfully.

'Looking for business, mister?'

Dreghorn glanced at the figure chalked on the sole of her shoe, gave her a gentle smile.

'You're all right, hen. Too dear.'

Betty's Bar on Lancefield Quay made the Sarry Heid look like the Savoy, apart from the fact that there were more women in it. It wasn't going to win any egalitarian awards, however, because they weren't customers, although they were on the hunt for them, and what they were selling was themselves.

There was a subtle system of communication at work. Eyes would meet, glimmers of interest noted, then the prostitutes would cross their legs to reveal the prices chalked on the soles of their shoes. No words need be exchanged; handy when a large chunk of your customers comprised foreign seamen with a precarious grasp of English, let alone Scots. Dreghorn suspected the prices lowered over the course of the evening, as drunkenness and desperation set in.

'I might be able to knock it down a wee bit,' the girl flirted. 'Good-looking lad like you's a cut above the usual in here.'

Lad. He was a decade older than her if a day, probably a good bit more.

'Nice of you to say so,' Dreghorn told her. 'But I meant too dear for you, hen, in all sorts of ways.'

She raised an eyebrow, confident in her ability to change his mind. In another world, another life, she'd have been modelling Paris fashions, taking screen tests.

'I'm the polis,' he continued.

She uncrossed her legs hastily, scuffed her sole against the floor to scrape away the chalk mark. Dreghorn nodded at some of the other whores, watching with amusement from a table across the way.

'None of the others told you? They know my face.'

She flashed them a dirty look. 'Flint-faced cows,' she snapped. 'Jealous 'cos I'm getting more attention than them.'

'That's no' really something to aim for.' He knocked back the whisky he'd been nursing; it didn't burn enough. 'You'll only end up like them. Sooner than you think. Find something else to do – anything.'

Her eyes told him what he could do with his advice and noble platitudes.

'Fuckin' easy for you to say, officer. You think I told my mammy this is what I wanted to do when I grew up?'

She stood up, knocking the stool over, and walked away, her

back straight with pride. That would go too. The old anger flared within him as he set the stool upright, the rage that had writhed all through the war and Shanghai, and now, at the way the world worked, no matter what you did.

The anger was still in his eyes when they met Dagger Kane's. The gangster had just entered the pub and was approaching the bar with two other men that Dreghorn didn't recognize. His gallus gait grew wary as he clocked the detective.

Kane was a hoormaister, not that you'd know it to listen to him. He made it sound like a gentlemanly pursuit – altruistic even – just protecting a few lassies o' the night as they plied their trade. Except that he was the one they needed protecting from, if business wasn't brisk enough to fill his pockets more than theirs.

He whispered something to his companions and started backing towards the door as Dreghorn got to his feet. The other two moved to block the detective's way, but he flashed his warrant card and shouldered through them without breaking stride, noting their faces as he passed.

He stepped out on the quay, looked around. No sign of Kane. The industrial murk that clouded the city was thicker by the Clyde, mixed with the fog that rolled in off the river.

A splash from across the road, by the edge of the water. Footsteps on the damp, dank cobbles. A figure slinking through the shadows between the quays where, as a wee boy, Dreghorn caught steamers 'doon the watter' to Largs, Dunoon or Rothesay, on the rare occasions when his mother could afford a day out. A surreptitious glance around and the figure stepped quickly into the centre of the road, striding determinedly in the opposite direction to Dreghorn. The detective recognized

Kane's streetwise strut, matched the pace, making sure his own footsteps could be heard, loud and clear in pursuit.

Almost running now, Kane mounted the pavement, but before he turned the corner onto Elliot Street, a hulking shadow seemed to detach itself from a doorway to block his way.

Kane collided with the shadow at full pelt, staggered back, rocked by the impact, Dreghorn extending a hand to steady him. McDaid stepped into the light.

'Did you see that, inspector?' he asked, appalled.

'Aye, assaulting a police officer. Serious offence.'

'What're you on about? I just bumped into him.' Kane shook his head at McDaid. 'You jumped out in front of me.'

Dreghorn shoved Kane face-first against the tenement wall. 'Looked like assault to me. Poor Archie's terrified.'

'Shaking in my shoes,' McDaid agreed.

Dreghorn carried out a brisk but thorough weapons search, patting pockets, torso, sleeves, trouser-legs, socks. Despite his nickname, Kane wasn't known as a knifeman, although he usually carried a weapon of some description. 'Dagger' came from the fact that he was sharp-witted, a snappy dresser, though most people who listened to his patter, which was mediocre at best, reckoned he had coined the name himself.

'Nothing,' Dreghorn announced.

'There's a first – must've turned over a new leaf,' McDaid said. 'I mean, there's no way that splash we heard could've been him tossing a chib into the Clyde.'

'Or even a pistol.'

'Pistol? What're you on about?'

'There's a gunman loose in the city, Dagger: two men shot dead.'

'You're no' pinning that on me, no way.' Kane started to turn around, but Dreghorn pushed him back against the wall.

'No? The big man fancies you for it, and he's got a nose for these things. What do you know about the victims – Reginald Smith, Harold Beattie?'

'Never heard of them. Proddies, weren't they? We don't exactly mix.'

'Except when you're trying to kill each other,' McDaid pointed out.

Dreghorn said, 'There were traces of gelignite found on Smith's boat, stolen from the Garngad Explosives Magazine.'

'Where you used to work.'

'Aye, *used to*.' Kane craned his head to look over his shoulder. 'Laid me off, didn't they? 'Cos of the Depression, they said. No' been near the place for donkey's.'

'Then why have you been giving the Maitland Street polis the slip. It's their investigation and they wanted to ask you a few questions – eliminate you from inquiries, if you're lucky. They've sent officers round to your hoose, left word with your wife.'

Kane snorted disdainfully. 'She must've forgot to pass the message on.' He mimicked slugging from a bottle. 'The gin, y'know?'

'Drive her to drink, do you? Anyway, they asked me and Jimmy to track you down, seeing as we're old pals, let you know they wanted a word.'

'Cheers for letting me know, big man. I'll pop in and see them tomorrow—' Kane finished with a curse as cold metal encircled his wrists.

Dreghorn clicked the handcuffs shut. 'We'll drop you off tonight, no bother.'

CHAPTER 25

Tuesday, 4 April 1933

McDaid always liked to knock politely at first, not batter in with the heavy hand of the law immediately. 'Gives everyone a chance to behave with a little decorum,' he liked to reason.

He stepped back after a gentle rap on the door of the King's Arms, smiled with what Dreghorn recognized as a misplaced faith in human nature. Across the road, at the King's Theatre, Matheson Lang's run in *Wellington* was winding down to make way for Noël Coward's *Words and Music*.

'Fuck off, yah alkie bastards!' a voice cried from inside. 'We're closed!'

McDaid's smile didn't falter, but he battered his fist against the door in response. Dreghorn could have sworn the windows all along the pub front rattled dangerously.

The voice inside cursed again, this time more of a low growl. There was a clatter, a tinkling of glasses, heavy footsteps. The door was flung open and a man glared out at them, a pick-shaft gripped in his hands. Presumably not the sort of welcome that greeted sophisticated theatre-lovers popping in for a pre-show drink, or Reginald Smith and Harold Beattie on the regular visits that Diana Beattie had informed Dreghorn of the previous day.

'Are you deaf or daft? We're closed. C-L-O—'

He was a big man, broad with it, but his anger and confidence took a knock when he saw McDaid. The bigger man held out his warrant card, so close that the other man nearly went skelly trying to read it.

'Polis,' McDaid announced. 'We're not here for the bevvy or the theatrics.'

'Ronald Anderson?' Dreghorn asked.

'Aye.' Anderson lowered the pick-shaft, stepped back from the doorway. 'Sorry, there's aye some chancer pestering me for an early dram or a late-night lock-in, but there's none of that shite on my premises. Those hours are sacred, far as I'm concerned.' He pointed at the opening-hours sign on the pub door: 11 a.m.–3 p.m., 5.30–10.30 p.m.

'You've been fined twice for after-hours drinking,' Dreghorn reminded him. 'One more and we'll have your licence.' He had checked Anderson's record before leaving the station.

'Dishonest and untrustworthy staff,' Anderson said. 'And they were out on their arse as soon as I found out about it. That should be taken into consideration, you know, my decisive action to follow the letter of the law.'

'Decisive action?' McDaid glanced at Anderson's pick-shaft as he entered the pub. 'Hope you weren't thinking of being decisive with that? We might have been the Sally Army, out collecting for widows and orphans.'

'Ignore me,' he said, 'I'm all talk.' He raised the pick-shaft as he stepped back behind the bar. 'This is just for show, keeps the punters in their place. Don't want them getting too rowdy when they're on the razzle.'

'That's what we're for,' said McDaid.

'Fine job you do, too.'

Dreghorn said, 'Do you know a Reginald Smith and a Harold Beattie?'

Anderson made a show of racking his brains. 'No, sorry,

inspector, doesn't ring any bells.' He set a couple of tumblers on the bar. 'Wee dram, gents? On the house.'

'Out of hours, sir,' McDaid pointed out. 'And we're on duty.'

'Aye, but this is a private chat, and you two make the laws, so . . .'

'No, we make sure nobody breaks them.'

Dreghorn laid his hat on the bar. 'So you don't know either of them?'

'Did somebody say I did? I mean, maybe they drink in here. I don't know everybody.'

'Busy place you run then?'

'No' bad, busy before and after a show, but theatre-goers are not always the biggest drinkers, and the Depression, y'know? Shite for business all round.'

Dreghorn drew the photo he'd taken from Diana Beattie from his inside pocket and placed it on the bar, facing Anderson. 'That is Reginald Smith. That is Harold Beattie. And bang in the middle of them' – he tapped the figure sandwiched between the men he'd just named – 'is you, Mr Anderson. Or Private Anderson, as you were back then.' Dreghorn looked at Anderson, whose mouth hung open, waiting for words to form. 'Or maybe my eyes are playing tricks on me. What do you think, Archie?'

'Spitting image, if you ask me.' McDaid leaned against the bar.

Sunshine weeped through the grimy windows, giving the sparse pub interior a jaundiced feel, motes of dust glistening within the light like fool's gold. It smelled of stale tobacco smoke and male sweat, a ghostly aroma of earlier customers.

The landlord glanced from Dreghorn to McDaid, made a show of studying the photo, then burst into a smile.

'Oh, you mean Rex and Harry. Aye, I know them all right. Course I do. We go way back. You threw me, though, using their full names like that. Fuckin' tragedy what happened to them. I hope you're after the bastards that did it.'

'Black and Tans.' McDaid gestured at the image. 'That's the uniform, isn't it?'

'If you can call it that. You could've got better from Paddy's Market. When we got over there at first, they never had enough supplies for us – uniforms, rifles, anything. Shambles. That's why we ended running about like Harry Lauder with those on our heids. Steel helmets was what we needed. Under fire all the time: bricks, bullets, bombs.'

'So you served in Ireland with them?' said Dreghorn.

'And in the war before that, when we were young and daft. You two must've did your bit an' all.'

'From start to finish. For our sins.'

A moment of quiet solidarity, grim understanding.

'Aye, well, last thing I wanted to do when I got back was sign up for another war, but there was fuck-all work – a bit like now– and they were offering £3 10 shillings a week the Tans, plus allowances. I had a wife and weans.' Anderson shrugged as if he had no choice.

Dreghorn lifted the photo. 'You all joined up again at the same time?'

'We'd kept in touch back in Civvie Street. All pals together, y'know.'

'Such good pals that you didn't even recognize their names,' McDaid scoffed.

'I told you, that's no' what I knew them as.'

'Diana Beattie said you had regular piss-ups together, thick as thieves.'

'Oh aye, I got them in here much as I could – it was my beer they were buying. But I was usually behind the bar, y'know? A few niceties, a wee bit of a laugh for old times' sake, but it was just work really.'

'Touching. They should get you to do the readings at the funeral.'

'I'm just telling you the truth. People change, y'know? The past's the past. Some folk cling to it, but no' me. Onwards and upwards.'

Dreghorn fished for his cigarettes, offered Anderson one. He held out his lighter, asked, 'So when did you last see them?'

'Last week.' Anderson shook his head, exhaled smoke. 'No, tell a lie, the week before.'

'Did either of them seem worried or behave unusually?'

'How do you mean?' Too innocent.

'Like they were scared they might get shot in the heid sometime soon,' McDaid said sharply.

'I think I might remember that topic of conversation.' Anderson rolled back the sarcasm in response to the big man's glare. 'No, same as they always were, poor bastards. Nobody's exactly jumping for joy, these days. Harry'd been out of work for donkeys, 'til I helped him out, and nobody was hiring Rex and his boat. "Half the time I just float about like a jobbie that won't flush," he said. He was even up in court no' long ago for failing to pay his berthing fees, but had a sympathetic magistrate, so I think they worked something out.'

'What about the other men in the photo?'

Anderson pointed out his old comrades in turn. 'Wullie Cameron's deid – cancer of the something-or-other, three years ago maybe – and Tam Stark moved up north to Aberdeen about the same time, which is just as bad, if you ask me.'

Dreghorn asked, 'Where were you on the night of 24 March?'

Anderson rolled his eyes in disbelief. 'Aw, come off it, you're kidding me on?'

Dreghorn smoked and waited, raised an eyebrow.

'Here, more than likely,' Anderson continued. 'I'd need to check the roster.'

'On you go,' said McDaid.

Anderson shook his head, reached into a shelf under the bar and came up with a big hardback diary. He flicked back through the pages.

'What about Saturday afternoon, around two o'clock?'

'I can tell you where I'd like to have been – watching us hump the Sassenachs. But no, I was right here, pulling pints.'

'And you can corroborate that?'

'If corroborate means what I think it does, aye. So can the missus, my barmen and all the punters I was serving.' Anderson turned the roster-book around to face the detectives – pointed at the entry for 24 March to show his name listed alongside three others. 'See?' A note of triumph. 'You can't just pin it on me.'

Dreghorn tutted in mock disappointment. 'Shame, I fancied you for it.'

'Me, too,' agreed McDaid. 'It would've been a doddle.'

Anderson smiled humourlessly. 'Cunny funts, aren't you? Comedians or detectives, I don't know what's worse.'

'You have to admit,' Dreghorn said, 'it's a wee bit suspicious that the only connection between the dead men – apart from the bullets in their heads – is that they served with you in the war and the Tans. Also makes me think that you and this fellow in Aberdeen should maybe watch your backs.'

Anderson paled; it was a thought that hadn't occurred to

him until now. He sucked so hard on his Capstan that it burned his fingers. He dropped the dout behind the bar, stamped on it.

'Better safe than sorry,' McDaid advised. 'I'd keep our number handy, if I was you.'

Dreghorn said, 'Did anything happen over there – Ireland? Something that might cause someone to hold a grudge after all these years, come after you?'

Anderson looked away for a moment, grinding his teeth. 'Plenty, I'm sure, but...' He shrugged. 'Can you remember every shot you fired in the war, every order you followed, every dead body?'

'The ones I was close enough to see,' Dreghorn said quietly. He felt McDaid give him an uneasy glance.

'Well, bully for you, inspector. Some of us don't want to remember.' Anderson deftly poured a whisky, downed it in one and grimaced. 'Drunk half the time we were over there, anyways. It wasn't like regular soldiering. Least, then, you knew where the enemy was, even if you couldn't always see them.

'Over there, they were all in civvies, the way we're dressed now. There were no battlefields; they were shooting at you from bushes and rooftops and alleyways. Guerrilla warfare. You never knew where you were. Scared to nod at a lassie and say hello in case she stabbed you in the back, or to look in some wean's pram in case it was full of fuckin' dynamite and ready to go off in your face.

'At least in Ulster you had the Unionists on your side, all for King and Country, but in County Kerry, where we were stationed?' He shook his head. 'Never knew where you were, so you started seeing every Mick and Paddy as the enemy. And treating them like it.'

He fell silent, poured another whisky. 'So, aye, I put the boot in more than I should've, shot at people before they shot at me, burned down hooses.' He swilled the liquid in the glass, contemplating it. 'I was a cunt all right, roaring drunk most the time, like I said, but that was the only way to get through it. Hate every one of them.'

He stared at Dreghorn, daring the detective to challenge him, judge him.

Dreghorn said, 'Was there anyone else from Glasgow with you, other than the ones in the photo?'

Anderson knocked back his whisky to hide his hesitation, but Dreghorn caught the wary, near-fearful glimmer in his eye. Anderson set the glass down with a sigh. The sort of thirst that requires whisky tends to be deep in the soul, festering away, not so easily quenched.

'Sure there was, but nobody I knew – not in my company.' He said no more.

Dreghorn nodded, lifted his fedora from the bar. 'That'll do for now, Mr Anderson. Thanks for your help.'

Anderson emerged from behind the bar, following the detectives as they headed for the door. 'Oh aye, no bother. Pop in any time, brighten up my day.'

The pub door crashed shut as Dreghorn and McDaid stepped into the street. Bolts thudded into place with the force of rivet hammers, as if Anderson was preparing for a siege.

CHAPTER 26

'That was about as close to a bum's rush as he could get away with,' McDaid observed.

Dreghorn grunted agreement as he stepped off the pavement, crossing to the Alvis, parked on the other side of Elmbank Street. 'And he went out of his way to make us think he hadn't heard a dickie bird about two murders that the whole city's talking about – his own mates at that.'

McDaid thrust his hands into his pockets. 'Did you notice him trying to sling us a deafie when you asked if there was anyone else around from his Tan days?'

'Aye, not exactly up there with Ronald Colman in the acting stakes, was he? Either way, we'll find out when the military records Ellen's requested turn up.'

A message came through the radio as Dreghorn started the engine, asking if they were receiving. McDaid tapped back in the affirmative. The dispatcher came back on, informing them that a vehicle with number plates matching those of Les Campbell's missing Daimler had been spotted entering the car park of the St Enoch Hotel by a PC. The detectives looked at each other.

'Is Big Tam Guthrie still at the St Enoch?' Dreghorn asked.

'Big to you, wee to me,' McDaid said, 'but, aye, far as I know.'

Dreghorn shifted into gear and drove off, saying, 'Get back

to Central. Tell them to call Tam and have him meet me at the back of the hotel.'

McDaid tutted at the Morse-code transmitter in his hand. To him, a message of that length was like writing a novel. 'Bloody hell,' he said. 'We'll be there by the time I've finished.'

'Tradesmen's entrance, Jimmy? And here I thought you were going up in the world.'

'Low profile, Tam,' Dreghorn said, extending his hand.

'Never my style.' Tam Guthrie was – no matter what McDaid claimed from his loftier heights – a big, bloody-minded ex-polisman who'd never risen beyond constable rank, largely because of that bloody-mindedness. An incident of 'insubordination' towards a superior officer had seen him forced into early retirement six months before he would have been eligible for his full pension. He still had plenty of friends in the force, though, who were black-affronted at the treatment he had received.

'Is that why you're the bouncer here?'

'Hotel detective,' Guthrie corrected Dreghorn, stepping back to let the policeman admire the cut of his suit. 'Better tips than walking the beat. What can I do for you?'

'There's a vehicle in your car park that's of interest to us.' Dreghorn gave Guthrie a number plate. 'Can you check if the driver's a guest?'

'No bother.'

Guthrie nodded for Dreghorn to follow and started up the stairs towards the hotel reception desk. When Sillitoe had arrived in Glasgow to take charge as chief constable, McDaid had tried to convince Guthrie to re-join the force, saying he would grow soft in his current job. 'Maybe it's about time,' Guthrie had responded.

When they reached the foyer, exiting from a discreet door that only staff used, Guthrie told Dreghorn to wait while he checked with the reception desk.

Dreghorn scanned the foyer. Quiet, apart from a well-to-do couple haughtily directing a porter on how best to transport their excess of luggage, and another man and woman seated separately, the man with a glass of whisky on the low table before him, the woman pouring a refill from a pot of tea. The newspapers on their laps might as well have been upside down for all the attention they were paying them, eyes focused on the entrance, alert to any sudden movements.

Dreghorn stepped behind a marble column as the woman glanced in his direction. He recognized them immediately: Nora and Patrick Egan, Conall Tracy's companions from the Sarry Heid. 'Belfast's Bonnie and Clyde,' according to Eugene Quinlisk. He glanced around cautiously, but saw no sign of Tracy or the one-eyed Gabriel Dempsey.

'Been there an hour or so, haven't moved, apart from the odd polite nod to coming-or-going guests.' Dreghorn hadn't heard Guthrie approach. 'I've been keeping an eye on them. Doing a good job of pretending they don't know each other. Figured they might be checking out potential robbery victims. I mean, they're well dressed, but that could be part of the act.'

'I reckon they're on guard duty,' Dreghorn said, then nodded at reception. 'Any joy?'

'Aye, the car's registered to one of our guests. A Mr Tracy – Conall Tracy. Irishman. Checked in on the 22nd.'

'That'd be about right. And using his real name, so he at least wants to appear legitimate.' Although Tracy had lied in the Sarry Heid, trying to make Dreghorn think he'd only just arrived in town.

'Mr Tracy's currently dining in the restaurant. Want to play "I Spy"?'

Guthrie led Dreghorn to another staff door on the opposite side of the reception desk. They went down the corridor a short way, then turned into the hotel kitchen; a hive of activity, with harried cooks and waiters somehow managing not to collide with each other or with towers of dirty dishes, the air cloying, filled with bubbling and sizzling.

They moved through the melee until they had some standing space, and Guthrie cracked open the swing doors into the restaurant a fraction. 'Over there.'

The detective craned his neck and peered into another world, one that on first impression appeared untouched by the Depression. The St Enoch was the first building in Glasgow to have electric lighting fitted, and those same lights seemed to illuminate the restaurant in almost too great detail. The thickness of the make-up on the women's faces, the forced jollity of the men's expressions, cracks along the facade of wealth and prosperity.

For some reason he had an image of a baw-jawed Roman emperor caterwauling a fiddle as his city burned to the ground around him. Inexplicably, that shifted into a mental picture of McDaid playing the bagpipes while dressed in a toga. He forced himself to focus.

The only people who didn't seem defined by artificiality were seated at the table Guthrie had motioned to.

Conall Tracy was talking with an easy charm, as at home here as he was in the Saracen Head. Across the table from him was the woman with whom, a few days earlier, Dreghorn had watched a man being executed: magistrate Martha Hepburn. Her expression now was only slightly less solemn than on that occasion.

'Gallus sort, by the looks of him, and the woman seems familiar,' said Guthrie indicating the diners. 'Do you know her?'

'No,' Dreghorn lied.

Dreghorn didn't mention Martha Hepburn's presence to McDaid when he returned to the Alvis. The big man was keen on chivalry, so he could use that as an excuse, if it ever came to it. Dreghorn had observed Conall Tracy and Martha Hepburn as they finished their meeting. They shook hands and Mrs Hepburn departed via the main entrance. Tracy nodded at Nora Egan and walked off, heading – Guthrie reckoned – for the car park.

Dreghorn thanked the hotel detective and exited again via the rear of the hotel, where it adjoined the railway station, the glazed train sheds running the length of North Carriage Drive on one side, Howard Street on the other. Guards' whistles shrilly pierced the air; he felt the judder of trains underfoot, setting off for Dumfries, Stranraer and St Pancras station in London, upon which the St Enoch had originally been modelled. He avoided the wide-open ramped thoroughfare that led to the hotel entrance, kept to the shadows of the arches below, with Burgoyne & Co. Wine Merchants and the double frontage of Ivie Hair & Co. blurring as he hurried past.

He ran across the square, weaving through punters entering the subway station, which looked to him more like a grand townhouse or hunting lodge than the gateway to Glasgow's circulatory underground railway. A large expanse of emptiness since the demolition of St Enoch's Church in 1928, the square had become a chaotic and unofficial taxi rank, car park, dropping-off point for the station and layby for delivery drivers to stop for a fly-break.

McDaid was parked next to the streamlined shape of a Castlebank Laundry van, the curving hood above the windscreen emblazoned with the legend 'Here comes the Castlebank Man.' A clever move on the big man's part, if deliberate, for the eye-catching Deco design was bound to draw attention away from a policeman on surveillance.

From where he sat, McDaid had a clear line of vision to both the hotel entrance and North Carriage Drive. As Dreghorn related what he had learned, Les Campbell's Daimler emerged from the car park, coming towards them. Dreghorn tapped the dashboard, said, 'Step on it.'

The Daimler paused for a break in traffic to turn onto Argyle Street. McDaid started the engine and moved off, slowly and surreptitiously to begin with, accelerating as the Daimler began moving again.

There was a screech of tyres as another car – a big, heavy Wolseley – pulled in front of them and jerked to a violent, deliberate halt. McDaid swore in Gaelic, slammed on the brakes and thumped the horn, three explosive blasts. Light reflected obliquely off the windows of the offending vehicle, obscuring their view of the occupants.

McDaid swore again, threw open his door. 'I'm no' having this.'

Dreghorn followed, ignoring the horns of the cars trapped behind them. The rear doors of the Wolseley opened and two big men in dark suits and hats stepped out with confident and practised menace. Dreghorn slipped a hand inside his coat for his detective baton. McDaid shook his head in exasperation.

'If I was you, I'd get right back in there and lock the doors,' he said and hauled open the front passenger door.

Eugene Quinlisk sat inside, calmly tamping fresh tobacco into his pipe. He glanced at the stalled Alvis, then looked up at the big man with a whimsical smile.

'If you remember our meeting with the chief constable, I think you'll find we have right of way.'

CHAPTER 27

McDaid was still bealing when they got back to the station. He almost ripped the door off its hinges as he entered, a passing WPC skipping back in alarm to avoid being bludgeoned by it. He kicked the nearest thing that wouldn't collapse under the impact: Shug Nugent's reception desk.

Nugent burst out from the back office, yelling, 'Whoa! Do you want a hammer?' He looked surprised to see Dreghorn and McDaid and not some outraged crime victim. 'There is a bell, you know.' He gestured at the paraphernalia on the counter.

'Away and bile your heid, Shug,' McDaid snapped, then looked around in disgust. 'You're lucky I don't kick the whole place down about your ears, for all the good it does the world.'

As desk sergeant, Shug Nugent was nothing if not proprietorial about Central Police Headquarters, as if the reputation of the station was synonymous with his own personal honour.

'Do you want me to step out from behind this desk, Archie?'

'Heaven forbid! And do some actual police work?'

Nugent's leonine features grew fiercer. Dreghorn was just as angry, but it was part of an old rage that never quite went away and would burn far longer than the big man's. He threw a short, sharp jab into McDaid's arm.

'Get a grip,' he ordered.

McDaid flinched and glared at him, then sighed slowly. He raised his hands in apology to Nugent, not quite trusting words just yet. Nugent glanced at Dreghorn and asked, 'Who rattled his cage?'

Dreghorn shook his head as he removed his hat. He had stepped between McDaid and the Wolseley before the big man had hauled Quinlisk out by the throat. From the way the other Special Branch men held their hands close to the pockets, he figured they were armed with something stronger than detective batons, not that that would have discouraged McDaid.

'Right of way?' Dreghorn had said. 'Shouldn't we be going the same way?'

Quinlisk had shrugged with his eyebrows. 'If only the world was that simple. You mean well, inspector, your heart's in the right place, I understand that. Admire it. But sometimes you have to leave things to the experts.'

'It's an offence to obstruct a police officer in the course of his duties. I could arrest you.'

'I could do the same to you. And then we'd be all locked up together like a bunch of clowns, while the real miscreants run amok outside. You've had your orders, boys. Best you follow them.'

Car horns sounded behind Dreghorn, joined by shouting and swearing.

Quinlisk cocked his head at the open door. 'Do you mind,' he said, 'you're letting in a draught.'

Dreghorn had stepped back. McDaid still had one hand on the car door. He slammed it shut as if trying to overturn the vehicle. They had watched in frustration as the Wolseley drove off, then reluctantly returned to the Alvis.

'Those Special Branch jobbies.' Nugent nodded in

understanding as Dreghorn finished explaining. 'They've commandeered an office on the second floor. Put a few noses out of joint already, swanning about as if they own the place. A couple of other big fellows came up from London on the sleeper to join them yesterday. I had to send a car to Central Station to pick them up.'

McDaid growled, 'I'm thinking of sending them back.'

'They're keeping themselves to themselves,' Nugent continued. 'Doors either locked or always someone on guard.' He reached under the counter. 'You're the ones that brought in Danny Semple, aren't you?'

Dreghorn nodded. McDaid slumped listlessly against the desk, hands in pockets.

Nugent flipped through his report book. 'Something for you, maybe. A complaint from one of Semple's neighbours about excessive noise in his house: a wireless blaring, people clumping about at all hours, individuals she doesn't recognize, coming and going.'

McDaid said, 'Semple's wife is meant to have taken off for Ireland with the weans – to escape the shame of his criminal exploits or with a new man, depending on who you talk to. That's why our Danny came back, he claims, to try and stop her.'

'So the house should be empty,' Dreghorn added.

'That's what I figured,' Nugent said. 'I checked with the Housing to see if they'd given it to another tenant. Uh-uh. Still listed under Daniel Semple and family.' A pointed look at McDaid. 'Police work. Normally I'd send round a uniform to make inquiries, but seeing as he's up for attempted murder and is being defended by gorgeous George Garrison.'

*

Sometimes you got a fleeting glimpse of how it was all meant to work – a society in harmony, a people alive to joy and beauty in whatever elusive form it took, a city that was civilized and hopeful, not crumbling into entropy.

The sun was shining when the detectives arrived in Vulcan Street, parking outside MacMillan's Bar, a short distance from Danny Semple's tenement. It was half-past four, the schools not long released. Children, mainly still in uniform, filled the road: boys playing football with a tennis ball; girls skipping or dancing along a hopscotch grid; a mixed group playing Kick the Can, hiding behind the few parked cars and in shadowy doorways. A few women were seated on hard chairs outside their tenements enjoying the sun, a brief interlude between housework and making the tea for the family.

As Dreghorn and McDaid stepped out of the Alvis, shouts and laughter swirled in the air. Even the usual looks of suspicion and resentment were absent, the carefreeness of the moment taking over.

This was what the politicians and social commentators didn't see or understand, drinking in only the deprivation and not the simple joys of being together, tightly knit. The triumph of putting a ball between a set of goals chalked on a wall, or leaping from your hiding place and booting that empty can to kingdom come, freeing your captured pals. The almost ecstatic release gained from the parties and sing-songs that unfolded throughout the tenements during the weekend, after the pubs had shut, sometimes before.

Dreghorn was startled by a sudden shimmering memory of coorieing half-asleep into his mother during just such a party, late at night or early into the morning, while his father sang Robert Burns's 'Wantonness' – a clue if ever there was one to the man's nature. Or would that have been someone else? His Uncle Joe, perhaps, who would never sing again. Dreghorn couldn't know for sure, his long-missing father now little more than a shadow cast across dreams and remembrances. A lump rose to his throat. He forced it back down, deep within himself.

He intercepted the boys' ball as it bounced across the cobbles, dribbled around one lad, shouted, 'For the wing!' to McDaid and passed it to the big man. McDaid trapped the ball under his foot, clamped a hand on another boy's head to hold him at bay and returned the pass. Quick as a flash, a nimble wee lad swept the ball away from Dreghorn, making him look like a big, lumbering tumshie.

McDaid laughed as Dreghorn re-joined him, said, 'Stick to the boxing – you might actually have a chance against a bunch of wee squirts like this.'

Dreghorn grinned back, removing his hat to better feel the sun on his face. He gestured at Danny Semple's house as they approached the tenement.

'Here we go,' he said. 'First floor.'

And the building opened up to welcome them, splitting apart with a battlefield roar and a surging blast of disintegrating sandstone, shattering glass and hailing debris that scoured their eyeballs, deafened their ears, tore them from their feet and smothered their world in darkness.

CHAPTER 28

Something brushes his lips. A kiss, he thinks, but there's no warmth in it, no love. The movement continues. Urgent. Insistent.

He is lying face-down, his arms spreadeagled, something cold and wet and cloying all around him. He tries to breathe, inhales the scent of freshly turned earth, tainted with another smell, one he recognizes but doesn't want to acknowledge. Maybe it would be best to lie still, to surrender to the darkness, the silent escape it seems to offer.

He pushes himself up with difficulty, blinks as his vision begins to return. A face materializes in the soil under him, like a mirror image. At first he thinks he's leaving his body, looking down upon his own dead self. But then he realizes that the lips are moving and that the face is that of an enemy who became a friend, but should now be nothing, a rotting skeleton in a far-off land.

'Fuckin' hell, Jimmy,' Rab Hunter whispers. 'Fuckin' hell. Fuckin' hell . . .'

He sobs, scoops soil frantically with his hands and pushes it over Rab's face, burying him, silencing the litany. Rolling off the body, he scrabbles to get away. His back comes up against something unyielding, a wall of soil. A grave? A trench? Both?

He looks up, the dark walls too high to scale, the debris of warfare partially unearthed within them – abandoned helmets, discarded rifles and bayonets, soil-darkened bones. Overhead, where there should be sky, a thick, jaundiced fog churns.

He staggers to his feet, the soil sucking under them. He is still in his suit, but the colour has changed to the khaki of his old soldier's uniform, the cloth itching like a hair shirt.

In one direction, the trench seems endless, fog creeping into it. In the other, he sees what he thinks is a turning, the trench snaking in another direction. He stumbles along uncertainly, but when he reaches the corner, it is gone, sealed into a dead end.

He claws at the soil, raging like an actor in a silent film, no sound coming from him. The wall of earth crumbles easily, slowly revealing a slim form, buried upright.

He sees Titian-red hair, elegant, beautiful features, and her eyes, which blink lovingly. Or is it with pity? He sees the long, deep cut across her neck and his heart tears apart again. She tries to speak, but her mouth is filled with earth, a trapped centipede writhing within it.

He kisses her anyway, cupping her face in his hands, his tongue searching for hers. Her eyes remain open but are cold now, the life gone from them.

The trench shudders and heaves, the walls collapsing without a sound. He feels the earth rising around his body, cold and heavy and oppressive.

His mouth fills with soil – choking, gagging – but he keeps his lips on hers, desperate not to lose her again . . .

Dreghorn choked and gagged; the back of his head cracked against the cobbles. He rolled onto his side, coughing, the inside of his mouth crawling with a film of dust and grit. He leaned on his elbows, waited until the coughing subsided, his throat sandpapered raw by the feel of it. He needed a cigarette.

Memories flooded back: a roar and a blast, the likes of which he hadn't experienced since the war; blinding, smothering smoke and dust and flying rubble; a shockwave that battered the air from the lungs and burst eardrums; a sudden sickening image of how busy the street had been beforehand, full of fragile, innocent bodies.

He raised his head, looked around. Rab Hunter was Kitty Fraser's brother, the resemblance haunting. He'd died before Dreghorn's eyes in the war, scared and confused, stomach torn open. The woman with the red hair was dead as well, haunting Dreghorn's dreams as if neither of them could let go, her name too painful for him to speak. Dreghorn had seen that too, seen too many deaths.

'Archie?' he said.

The big man lay on his back a few feet away, his clothes and hair red with sandstone dust. Dreghorn crawled towards McDaid, shook the sergeant's arm. No reaction. He shook again, more violently.

'Archie!'

The big man suddenly woke with a roar, leaping to his feet with the speed and power of a felled tree in reverse. He raised his fists towards imagined enemies, looked around dazedly. The shock of what had happened hit him and he staggered.

'Jimmy?'

'Here.' Dreghorn was clambering to his feet. He put a hand on the big man's arm to steady himself. Neither of them spoke, just watched in horror as the dust swirled like a crimson mist, slowly settling to reveal the carnage.

The walking wounded were first to emerge, dusted pink by sandstone dust that turned a deeper, dirtier red where blood seeped through. The boys who had been playing football, the skipping girls, now drifted like lost ghosts. Next to materialize were the forms on the ground, little bodies lying twisted on the cobblestones, some writhing helplessly, others deathly still, jagged chunks of masonry scattered around them. And on them, limbs crushed beneath.

Individual horrors punctuated the tableau: a girl seated on the barely visible hopscotch grid, staring at her torn and bloody legs; another girl, older, unmoving, entwined in a skipping rope; the boy in goal still standing there, frozen in shock, hands raised, now caught in a deadlier game; the dog that had been chasing the ball now prone on its side, head pulped under rubble; the ball rolling as if still in play.

At first there was only silence, as if the explosion had stolen all the sound in the street, expelled it in that great monstrous roar. But then someone screamed, yelled their child's name, and everything was released in a cacophony – hacking coughs, weeping, shouts, whimpers, howls of pain, cries to God and Jesus.

Dreghorn pointed at the Alvis, far enough away to remain undamaged. 'Get onto Headquarters, get them to send ambulances,' he rasped. 'Then start moving the casualties, the ones that can be moved.'

'Where are you going?'

Dreghorn nodded at the tenement. 'There could be people trapped.'

McDaid shook his head. 'Watch yourself. The gas mains could be ruptured.'

They split up, McDaid heading for the car, Dreghorn for the

tenement. The damage was extensive. All the windows in the building were shattered and the entire first-floor wall had been blown away, leaving a giant jagged oval, like the maw of some dark monolithic deity. The homes within were torn to shreds, no movements to disturb the ruined shells. He hoped the occupants had been out, safe in the streets or at work, and reckoned Danny Semple's house was the epicentre of the blast. Streams of rubble cascaded from the crumbling edges of the blast-hole.

Dust was still thick in the air. As he walked, Dreghorn realized he was unsteady on his feet, disoriented. His eyes teared up as he moved, placing his hands on the frail shoulders of shell-shocked children as he passed, directing them towards McDaid. Neighbours were flooding out of the other tenements now, pushing through their shock and horror to help.

He wondered if he was concussed. Sights came to him in jagged splinters, triggering other thoughts and images, dredged up from within. He stepped over the dead dog, saw again the corpse of a war horse that had decomposed over weeks in no-man's-land, trapped upright in barbed wire. The weeping and wailing echoed in his mind, became the sounds of a field hospital he'd once lain wounded in, operations and amputations all around, anaesthetic a long-gone luxury. Occupants from the tenement staggered out as he tried to enter, and their faces were those of soldiers he'd served with, soldiers he'd killed, their voices the desperate babble of fearful refugees, fleeing in terror from the very forces he was marching towards.

He gritted his teeth, drawing blood from the inside of one cheek, swore and told himself to get a grip, focus on the here and now.

The voices became Scottish, though the alarm in them remained the same. He found his own voice again as he went up the stairs, barked instructions amidst the coughs. He stopped outside Danny Semple's house, the door still partially intact, checked the injuries of those coming down, whether they could walk unattended or needed aid. From what he could make out, the injuries weren't too severe. The blast seemed to have been contained mainly on the first floor, barring the fact that the exterior wall had been blown out.

'Is that everyone from upstairs?' he asked a shaken young man who had been supervising the evacuation from the upper floors.

'I think so. What happened? What caused it?'

'Don't know yet.' Dreghorn patted the man on the shoulder. 'Go on downstairs, get clear. You did well.'

He checked the door once the man was out of sight. Locked, but with the damage from the explosion, it wouldn't take much. He put his shoulder to it, the force taking him over the threshold as the door sprang open.

A sickening, sulphurous odour clawed at his throat, caused his eyes to tear up again. Gas. McDaid was right: the gas mains had been ruptured, but surely that meant the tenement should be ablaze, unless leaking gas wasn't the cause of the initial explosion, but the mains had been damaged by it.

He searched his pockets for a handkerchief, covered his nose and mouth and scanned the room. The slightest spark could turn the building into an inferno, so best stifle the urge to light a cigarette.

The room was devastated, torn apart, daylight streaming in from the collapsed walls. Debris littered the floor, twisted and shredded together. The sink had been ripped free by the blast, a trickle of water gurgling from the broken pipe. The range had been blown backwards, half embedded in the wall, the gas mantles ripped from their fittings, probably the source of the escaping gas.

He took a couple of steps further, but the floor creaked and swayed, near to giving way. He could hear thumps and crashes, rubble falling unseen elsewhere in the building.

In the centre of the room, half buried, was what initially looked like a hunk of freshly butchered beef, bloody and dusty, shards of wood embedded in it. Dreghorn's stomach lurched as he realized it was a human torso, clothes and skin shredded, the limbs blown off, no doubt scattered somewhere around him. Again his body cried out for a cigarette to excoriate the tastes and smells seeping into him.

Danny Semple had a wife and child. Was there just one body or more than one? The thought made him ill and he staggered, the floor scrunching underfoot like rotting twigs. Something solid pressed into the sole of his shoe – small and round and hard. He brushed away debris with his toe. A flash of white. A child's marble, by the looks of it.

Something drove him to reach down and pick it up, glassy and strangely sticky to the touch. He rolled the object in his palm and examined it.

It stared back at him.

CHAPTER 29

Ellen Duncan's reward for having gleaned information from Callum Baird was to be demoted once again to charwoman by the detectives of the Lodge. She'd just returned from the cafeteria, placing a mug of tea in front of Orr with a butter-wouldn't-melt smile, when news of the Vulcan Street explosion reached Turnbull Street.

Strachan took the call, raising a hand for silence and repeating the details out loud for his team. His moustache twitched distastefully at the concern on Ellen's face as he said that Dreghorn and McDaid had been caught in the blast.

'Minor injuries only,' he said after a malicious pause.

'Nae luck there then, eh?' said Orr, eying his tea suspiciously.

Danny Semple's house was, it seemed, the source of the explosion. There were five confirmed fatalities so far: whoever was in Semple's house – thought to be Gabriel Dempsey – a man and woman in the street, and two children, one boy, one girl, all yet to be officially identified. The death toll was expected to rise. There were dozens of casualties, many weans having not long returned from school, their injuries ranging from minor cuts and bruises to critical and life-threatening, with a fleet of ambulances ferrying them to hospitals across the city.

Uniformed officers, including Jean Malloy and other WPCs, were dispatched to help evacuate the street in case of further explosions, cordon off the site and take witness statements. Ellen was readying herself to accompany them when Strachan said, 'No, you're needed here' and told her to assemble for a detectives' briefing in the Lodge.

Dreghorn and McDaid arrived not long afterwards, refusing medical treatment until they recounted their story. There was none of the usual sarcasm or barbed comments, just a terse silence as they talked.

Ellen was surprised when Chief Inspector Monroe didn't take charge, although his expression said that he wasn't happy with the fact. Instead two of the Special Branch officers who had commandeered offices on the second floor stepped up: Superintendent Haldane and Quinlisk, the smug Irishman who'd raised his hat to her a couple of times in the corridor.

They explained brusquely that they had been carrying out surveillance on suspected members of the Irish Republican Army and their sympathizers amongst Glasgow's Roman Catholic street gangs. They believed this squad was responsible for the recent theft of explosives from the Garngad Explosives Magazine and that these explosives, whether deliberately or accidentally, were the cause of the carnage in Vulcan Street.

One of the suspects, Gabriel Dempsey, was an explosives expert, having been a miner in his youth and served with the Royal Irish Fusiliers in the Great War. He had been arrested for dynamiting roads and bridges during the Anglo-Irish War. Official identification was pending, but courtesy of the glass eye that Dreghorn had discovered, it seemed likely that Dempsey was the corpse ravaged by the blast at Danny Semple's house.

Conall Tracy, the leader of the squad, had a long history of insurgence, but was now masquerading as a legitimate businessman. He had taken a suite at the St Enoch Hotel, which hardly seemed like subterfuge to Ellen – more like hiding in plain sight.

Quinlisk handed out photographs of Tracy and the other suspects: Nora and Patrick Egan, a husband and wife from Belfast; and Frank Cleary and Gerard Byrne, long-term associates of Tracy's. All were thought to be embedded to some degree within the gangs, specifically the Norman Conks. Ellen noticed Dreghorn shake his head almost imperceptibly as he examined the last two mugshots. Tracy, the main target of the operation, was currently 'in the wind', having eluded his shadows.

'Aye, and whose fault was that?' McDaid piped up.

Haldane ignored him, but Ellen noted the look of enmity that passed between Quinlisk and McDaid.

'Tracy's an old hand at this game. We can't discount the possibility that he may already have identified me and my officers' – Haldane nodded at Quinlisk and a couple of Special Branch men – 'so we're entrusting his arrest to Inspector Strachan and his team. We're presuming he'll return to the hotel before he leaves. We believe he'd already have made good his escape if the detonation of the explosives was deliberate, so that may give us the element of surprise.' He looked at Dreghorn. 'Inspector, you recently apprehended the man whose house was the centre of the explosion. Are you up to interrogating him again? We need to establish a connection, gather as much evidence as possible.'

Dreghorn, smoking a Capstan, nodded and muttered hoarsely, 'Aye.'

'Gentlemen,' Haldane snapped, dismissing the meeting. Quinlisk smiled, gave the room a short bow and added, rather too earnestly, 'A pleasure to be working with you.'

Ellen tried to catch Dreghorn or McDaid's eye as they left, to ask if they were all right, but they were off their mark too quickly, focused on other matters.

She turned back to find Strachan alarmingly close. 'Dennistoun, aren't you, constable?' he said. 'We'll take a detour past your house, so you can get done up to the nines – you and me are going out on the razzle.'

CHAPTER 30

'Fuckin' hell, you two look rough. Been down the pits or something?'

Danny Semple seemed to have been brushing up his gallus-ness since his arrest. Either that or, having been in and out of approved schools, borstals and prisons all his life, he was genu-inely more at home behind bars. If he was in any way curious about why he'd suddenly been removed from his cell and brought to an interview room, he didn't show it. Gallus or simply contented, it wasn't going to last.

Neither Dreghorn nor McDaid answered as they entered, the big man nodding to the prison officer to leave them alone. They had cleaned up to an extent after the explosion, but were still wearing the same clothes and looked as though they had been to hell and back.

Semple was seated at a table, two empty chairs opposite. Grim-faced, Dreghorn set a half bottle of Bell's and a tin cup before the prisoner. He cracked the seal as they sat down, poured a generous measure and slid the cup over to Semple.

'Take a drink, Danny. You're going to need it.'

'The service in this hotel's looking up.' Semple drank it in one, coughed as the whisky caught his throat and slammed the cup down again.

Without a word, Dreghorn refilled it, then glanced at McDaid. The big man seemed reluctant to speak.

'C'mon then, spit it out,' said Semple, reaching for the cup.

McDaid said, 'The night we arrested you, Danny, did you speak to anyone else in the Sarry Heid?'

'Shooting the breeze with a few of the lads. That's what you do in pubs, isn't it?'

'Who?'

'Nobody in particular, just the usual faces at the bar, all talking shite like they do, putting the world to rights.'

Dreghorn said, 'You might not find that easy any more.'

'Eh?'

'Putting the world to rights. Your world at least.'

'So, you didn't chat to Bull Bowman then?' McDaid continued.

'No. I mean, I saw him and nodded hullorerr, but we didn't speak.' Semple kept his eyes on Dreghorn, growing uneasy. 'He was sitting with a bunch of other folk, looked like a private party.'

'Vinny Wylie, Bert Rowan and Dagger Kane.'

'Aye, might have been.'

'Anyone else?'

'A couple of fellows that I didn't know, maybe.'

Dreghorn nodded for Semple to have another drink as McDaid asked, 'But you didn't speak to any of them?'

Semple shook his head as he lifted the cup. He sipped warily this time. 'What's this all about?'

The detectives glanced at each other. A difficult subject.

Dreghorn said, 'Did you hear any alarm bells earlier?'

'Aye, a right curfuffle. What was it – polis, fire?'

'Both,' said Dreghorn. 'And ambulances. From all over the city.'

'Why, what happened?'

'There was an explosion, bad one. Surprised you didn't hear it.'

'Don't hear much in a cell, inspector,' Semple said. 'Gas?'

'That's what we hoped at first.'

'Hoped?' Semple, appalled, laid down the cup.

Dreghorn topped it up, leaned back, stared at Semple.

'It was at Vulcan Street, number fourteen, second floor,' he said.

The colour drained from Semple's face.

'Your hoose, Danny.'

'No, but . . .' Semple shook his head. 'It can't be, there's no one there – Audrey's in . . .' He tailed off, doubts festering.

'The blast knocked the whole front wall out. The schools were no' long out, kids playing in the street. Came down right on top of them.'

Semple drank more whisky, gagged, coughing and spluttering liquid down his front. McDaid glanced at Dreghorn, shifted uncomfortably in his seat.

Dreghorn continued, 'They weren't all killed, but we're still counting. Poor wee souls. All for a game of football.' A pause. 'The Fire Brigade went in first, to make sure everything was safe. We all thought it must have been a gas main, but they said no, did all the checks. There were two bodies in there.'

Semple was shaking his head again, pushing his chair back from the table.

'I saw them,' Dreghorn said. 'A woman and a boy of about seven. Not that you could tell, after the blast. It was the doctors that confirmed it. It was them, Danny. Audrey and Michael. Your wife and son.'

Semple howled, sweeping the cup off the table, Dreghorn snatching the whisky before it went as well. The prisoner staggered back, overturning the chair. He cried out, picked up the chair and hurled it against a wall. McDaid slowly rose to his feet, raised his hands, a mix of reassurance and warning, not that Semple noticed. He was pacing from one wall to the other, trapped, arms flailing, sobbing and talking to himself.

'They weren't meant to be there, they . . . They weren't meant to be there . . .' He slammed his palms onto the table, glared, eyes red with tears. 'They went to Dublin, to Audrey's granny's.' He sounded like he was trying to convince himself.

'They came back when they heard you'd been caught.'

'No . . .'

'We had Dublin send a polis round to her grandma's to check, and your neighbours confirmed it.' Dreghorn shrugged. 'Perhaps she wanted to get back together with you. Or maybe she figured it was safe to come back, seeing as you were being put away.'

'Fuck up, Dreghorn!' Semple turned away, found himself facing the blankness of the wall, the plaster stained and cracked.

'What did you do, Danny?' Dreghorn asked. 'We did tests – there were explosives in your house. How did they get there?'

'Bastards! They said it was nothing, they just needed it for a few days.' Semple stayed staring at the wall.

'Who said that?'

Semple turned, tried to speak, but couldn't. He paced the room again, roughly pushing away tears with one palm.

'Who was it, Danny? Bull Bowman? The men with him, the Irishmen?'

Semple's shoulders slumped, the energy draining from him. McDaid retrieved the chair, set it by the table again and gently guided Semple to it.

'They said they'd help me get out of the country safely, get to Ireland, to Audrey and the wee yin.' Semple's voice cracked, but he carried on. 'Give me some money as well. They just wanted to use the hoose for a few days.'

'What for?'

'They never said. To lie low, I thought. Nothing like this.'

'Who was this: Bull?'

'He made the introductions, but no, he wasn't doing the talking.'

'So it was the Irishmen, Conall Tracy and Gabriel Dempsey, the one with the glass eye?'

Semple nodded. 'I never asked their names. When you two picked me up, I never thought any more about it. The game's a bogey, you know. Then Garrison turned up. He said he'd been hired to defend me, on condition that I agreed to abide to the prior arrangements I'd made with his client. Those were his words. He never mentioned any names or talked about what the arrangement was; said he didn't know and didn't want to know.'

McDaid said, 'You can always rely on George to cover his own arse first.'

'And you agreed,' Dreghorn said to Semple.

' "Get me Garrison?" Of course I did. If anybody could get me off, he's your man. I jumped at it. My ma's got spare keys to the house. I wrote him a note to give to her, saying to hand them over. My ma . . . Oh, Jesus, when she finds out . . .' He hunched over, in pain, head in his hands. 'I got them killed, I fuckin' got them killed! I'm sorry, I'm sorry.'

McDaid stepped towards Semple, but Dreghorn warned him back with a sharp look, then leaned forward, spoke quietly.

'Danny, the men you made this arrangement with – they're

the ones who killed them, not you.' He reached into his inside pocket and laid two photographs on the table: old prison mug-shots of Conall Tracy and Gabriel Dempsey.

Semple raised his head with a sigh, stared long and hard at the faces. 'Aye, that's them.'

Dreghorn nodded his thanks, slipped the photographs away and stood up.

Semple buried his face in his hands. Sobs racked his body, a barrage of invisible blows.

The detectives shared a glance. McDaid shook his head, placed a hand on Semple's shoulder. The prisoner looked up the second time McDaid spoke his name.

'Danny, the explosion,' the big man said. 'There was only one body – a man's. Your wife and weans are still in Dublin. We checked to make sure.'

Semple blinked disbelievingly, shrugged off McDaid's hand and stared at Dreghorn.

'You bastard!'

'It's no' me,' Dreghorn said. 'It's the city.'

McDaid said nothing as they left the interview room, nothing as they were escorted through the prison corridors, nothing until they stood outside in the drizzle, the skies grey overhead and his voice bitter with accusation.

'That was cruel, Jimmy.'

'No' as cruel as blowing up a street full of weans,' Dreghorn said. He only wished it made him feel better.

CHAPTER 31

'One lump or two, Miss Duncan?'

'Just milk, thank you, insp— Mr Strachan.'

Ellen smiled politely, but really wanted to shake her head in exasperation at the surreal situation. All hell was breaking loose in Glasgow and here she was 'enjoying' high tea in the St Enoch Hotel with Boyd Strachan, who appeared to think they were engaged in some elaborate courtship ritual.

He had ordered a pricy glass of claret – 'Expenses' – but she had opted for a pot of Earl Grey. A delicious meal was growing cold in front of her, her normally hearty appetite having dwindled drastically. Her stomach lurched further as Strachan's hand fell on hers. She tried to pull away, but his grip tightened.

'For appearances' sake, Ellen. We're undercover, remember.'

'I don't think people expect fathers and daughters to be sitting holding hands and staring into each other's eyes. Sir.' She whispered the last word.

Strachan's moustache twitched, which she took for a smile. 'That wasn't the film I was seeing in my head.'

She freed her hand with a little jerk. 'Aye, well, one glance at the age of us and I think everyone else'll be buying the same ticket as me.'

'What age do you think I am?'

'Old enough to know better. Sir.'

'You'd rather be here with Dreghorn, I suppose.'

'At least he behaves professionally.'

'Jimmy seems quite proprietorial towards you.'

'Hopefully he just thinks I'm good at my job.'

'So do I, Ellen, so do I. But you have to take things slowly. The likes of Jimmy have a tendency to burn out quickly. They rub people up the wrong way, don't know how to play the game.'

'I don't view police work as a game.'

'Figure of speech. You need to understand how things work. Pin your colours to his mast and you might go down with the ship.'

She raised an eyebrow. 'You think I'd be better off pinning my colours to yours?'

Strachan stroked his moustache, the unintended innuendo hanging in the air. He glanced away, suddenly business-like, at a movement in the hotel lobby, their table being positioned to view the comings and goings. He examined the man who'd just approached the reception desk.

'Not our suspect,' he said. 'Are you winching, constable?'

'I don't think that's an appropriate question, sir.' Ellen wondered if the sudden changes of topic were designed to fluster her.

'Cheeky choice of words, perhaps, but relevant if I'm evaluating your future.'

She frowned.

'Whether you're serious about being a police officer – meet some young blade, fall in love, get married and you'll have to give up your job. Then all that training's for nothing.' Strachan raised his hands innocently. 'I'm just raising the issue. It's partly why duties for your lot are restricted. Must be a dilemma for you.'

'There's no one at the moment.' Not that she'd tell him, of all people, if there was.

'On the other hand' – moustache-stroke – 'it'd be a crime if you ended up like some of those old trouts haunting the corridors.'

'I'll pass your compliments on to the other WPCs, sir.'

Strachan laughed. 'Aye, but they know their place.' His eyes washed over her appreciatively. 'You're different.'

Ellen tried not to squirm. Or jab her fork into his eye.

'What about you, sir?' she asked instead. 'The job must have an impact on male officers' family lives as well, especially a murder detective's.'

'I don't talk about it with them.'

'Never?'

'They don't need that sort of thing in their lives. I could tell them stories that would turn their stomachs, terrify them, make them never want to leave the house, but I don't – I keep it in here.' He tapped a fist to his chest. 'Where it belongs.'

She nodded sympathetically. 'You've got two daughters, haven't you? About my age?'

'A good few years younger – fourteen and eleven.'

'What would you advise them to do if they encounter men whose intentions aren't honourable? Have you told them how things work?'

'There's time enough yet.' He seemed uncomfortable. 'Their mother can do all that.'

'How is Mrs Strachan?' Ellen had eavesdropped on Orr and a couple of the other detectives discussing Strachan's domestic life once. She knew his wife suffered from some sort of illness – seizures, perhaps – that occasionally required Strachan to take time off work, but no more beyond that.

'Fine and dandy.' The harshness in his voice was like a portcullis coming down. He nodded almost imperceptibly towards the lobby. 'He's here.'

Ellen smiled and rolled her eyes as if he'd said something amusing, glancing surreptitiously at their target: Conall Tracy, easily identifiable from the photographs supplied by Eugene Quinlisk.

In the flesh, Tracy was handsome, his suit tailored to his athletic frame, and looked far more reputable than the detectives sent to apprehend him. If he was agitated in any way, he hid it well, politely waving an elderly couple to go ahead of him in the queue for the reception desk.

The lobby was busy now, which was what they had most wanted to avoid. There was a strong possibility Tracy would be armed; he was known as a crack shot, and they didn't want to risk civilian casualties – especially not ones who could afford to be guests at the St Enoch. Ellen noted that, while he smiled and nodded politely to staff and fellow guests, Tracy kept his right hand in the pocket of his coat. His stance was casual, relaxed, but that could change with the draw of a gun, the pull of a trigger.

She leaned closer to Strachan, feigning an intimacy that made her skin crawl. 'He doesn't look bothered, but he hasn't taken his hand out of his pocket.'

'I can see that for myself, thanks.' Strachan's condescension was back. He had made it explicit that no one was to approach Tracy except on his orders. Graham Orr was seated on a stool in the hotel bar, hopefully not getting pie-eyed; Lewis Tolliver was doing an alarmingly accurate impersonation of a visiting

Church of Scotland minister, seated with a Bible on a lobby armchair; and Brian Harvie stood at the entrance, having borrowed the ill-fitting uniform of a doorman for the operation. Harvie was the weak link as far as Ellen was concerned, though the other detectives thought the disguise was a brilliant ploy.

'If Tracy gets into the lift or makes it to his room, it'll be harder to get him, sir.'

'Aye. And if he starts shooting or takes a hostage, we could have a bloodbath on our hands.' Strachan kept his eyes on Tracy, then muttered under his breath, 'C'mon, take your hand out your fuckin' pocket.'

Ellen glanced at Tracy, now almost at the reception desk. 'At the briefing, they said Tracy fancied himself as a ladies' man, didn't they?'

'Aye,' Strachan shot her an angry glance. 'But what's that got to do with—'

Ellen stood up, knocking over her chair, and threw the contents of the wine glass into Strachan's face. He rocked backwards, spluttering.

'Dirty besom!' she cried, then stormed into the lobby.

Strachan got to his feet, speechless with fury, with all eyes in the restaurant and lobby turned towards him, including Conall Tracy's, though they moved to Ellen as she drew closer.

'Are you all right, miss?' Tracy asked, amusement tinged with polite concern.

'I'll be fine once I get my coat and leave.' She gave Tracy an appreciative nod. 'I didn't find my dinner companion's suggestion for pudding very appetizing, whether he has a suite here or not.'

Strachan was still on his feet, looking around with what

everyone would think was embarrassment, though Ellen knew his gaping was directed at his detectives, unsure what to do.

Tracy stepped forward protectively. 'Don't worry,' he said, 'I'll make sure he doesn't bother you any more.'

'Thank you, sir. It's good to know there are still some gentlemen in the world.'

He had his back to her now, his hand still in his pocket. Ellen remembered her ju-jitsu training with Dreghorn in the gym: arm-locks, leg-sweeps, the technique of using an opponent's strength and weight against him.

She grabbed Tracy's elbow and wrist, jerked his hand out of his pocket and twisted his arm up his back. Something fell from his grasp with a flash of red, landed by her feet, but she couldn't see what. She pushed Tracy forward, bending him over the reception desk, his face slamming into the guest book. She felt the power in him as he struggled, wondered how long she could hold him.

Orr and Harvie were suddenly beside her, Orr driving a short punch into Tracy's left kidney. They took the suspect's arms, kept him pinioned against the desk.

Ellen bent down to retrieve the object Tracy had dropped: a Ward, Lock & Co. *Illustrated Guidebook to Glasgow and the Clyde*, the city's coat-of-arms stamped on the vivid red cover. She smiled; after all that!

Strachan was standing over her as she rose, his eyes hard, moustache still dripping. 'We'll have words back at the station, constable,' he promised. He produced a set of handcuffs, locked them tightly around Tracy's wrists, saying, 'Leaving us so soon, Conall? We'll need to see if we can't better our hospitality.'

Orr and Harvie straightened Tracy up, turning him away

from the desk as Strachan continued, 'Conall Tracy, you are under arrest on suspicion of . . .'

Tracy didn't listen as Strachan listed the charges, but simply shook his head and smiled in admiration at Ellen.

'You're a police officer, miss? Now there's a thing. Isn't progress grand?'

CHAPTER 32

Arriving back at Turnbull Street after interrogating Danny Semple, Dreghorn and McDaid had witnessed a handcuffed Conall Tracy being escorted out of a Black Maria by the Special Branch officers who had been in the Wolseley with Eugene Quinlisk. Tracy caught Dreghorn's eye, nodding with a casual 'Evening, inspector' as he was led past.

Another two cars were pulling into the vehicle courtyard, with Haldane, Quinlisk and another two Special Branchers emerging from one, and Strachan, Orr, Tolliver and Ellen Duncan, looking as though she'd just been attending a film premiere, from the other.

Realizing that they were being sidelined, Dreghorn demanded to be involved in Tracy's interrogation. Without stopping, Haldane said, 'Eugene, please inform Inspector Dreghorn that Mr Tracy is our prisoner and is being held under the Defence of the Realm Act, which means restricted access for anyone other than Special Branch.'

'I'm afraid you'll have to get in line, lads.' Quinlisk shrugged helplessly. 'Good work, though. You should be proud.'

The procession continued, Strachan looking them up and down as he passed, stroking his moustache.

'Big arrest, boys, better get yourselves spruced up,' he said. 'McVicar and Sillitoe'll be along to share the glory, and the Vicar'll have you on a charge if he sees you looking like something the cat dragged in. I'll give you the name of my tailor, if you're stuck.'

'Better get him to bring you a clean shirt and all, Boyd,' McDaid said. 'Looks like you've been bilin' your heid in Vimto.'

Strachan ignored the comment; Orr gave the big man the two fingers as they mounted the entrance steps.

Ellen stopped to explain what had happened, getting as far as hurling a glass of wine in Strachan's face – all in the line of duty – before the man himself called out impatiently, 'Save the gossip for later, constable, we've got reports to file.'

The detectives stared at each other.

Dreghorn said, 'Ever feel like you're not being invited to a party you wouldn't want to be seen dead at anyway?'

To add further insult, as Shug Nugent was booking Tracy in and filing away his personal effects, the Irishman said, 'On the question of legal representation, I was advised, if any misunderstandings arose, to ask for a Mr Garrison. Would one of you gentlemen be kind enough to contact him for me?'

Catching sight of them trudging wearily up the stairs, Chief Inspector Monroe ordered them to go home. 'You're no use to man or beast, dead on your feet like that.'

McDaid asked Dreghorn back to Mosspark. Initially tempted, he declined to spare Mairi McDaid. Having your husband turn up looking like he'd been rummaging through a midden for clues was bad enough, without him inviting another tramp along for tea.

With all the fuss, Dreghorn didn't take a car for the night and walked down to St Enoch again to catch the subway to Kelvinbridge. He briefly thought about a train to Bearsden and Kitty Fraser, but the sight of him would be a distinct passion-killer.

He encountered Mrs Pettigrew as he entered his lodgings, gave her a weak smile and a shrug. After a pause in which he thought she was going to give him his marching orders, she said that she'd heard about the explosion and would run him a bath and bring him something to eat afterwards.

He soaked in the bath, staring at the ceiling, washing away the dust and grime, but not the memories, old and new. He thought of Martha Hepburn lunching with Conall Tracy, tried to gauge if the meeting looked strictly business-like or a friendlier affair. The suspicion made him feel grubbier, but he determined to raise it with Tracy, if Special Branch let him near the Irishman.

A tray of sandwiches was waiting in his room when he returned. He knew he should eat something, but only had an appetite for whisky. Fortunately the bottle was at as low an ebb as he was. One glass finished him off, and he slept for ten hours straight and ate the sandwiches for breakfast when he woke.

CHAPTER 33

Wednesday, 5 April 1933

Catching a tram into the city centre seemed a more attractive prospect than the underground, the top deck offering fresh air and a view of the city streets. A view Dreghorn didn't then take advantage of, examining first the mugshots of Frank Cleary and Gerry Byrne that Quinlisk had handed out, and then the photograph of Harold Beattie and his fellow Black and Tans, which he had removed from the inside pocket of his ruined suit. He had shaken his head angrily during yesterday's briefing, recognizing Cleary and Byrne as the men in Betty's Bar with Dagger Kane.

He studied the faces and uniforms in the Beattie image, remembered the blood-spattered photo in Smith's narrowboat. Similar certainly, but the same image? Hard to say for sure. He made a mental note to check, Smith's photo having been collected as evidence and held either in the Lodge or in Hammond's forensics lab.

Dreghorn ran events through his mind like a newsreel, searching for connections, things they might have missed, the excised scenes on the cutting-room floor that no one wanted him to see.

For once McDaid had made it into Turnbull Street before Dreghorn. He expected the big man to make a crack about it, but McDaid just glanced up from the incident book, frowning.

'Busy night?' Dreghorn asked.

'Just the opposite.'

'Surprising, considering what happened.'

'Suspicious. Tensions should be running high, not low. A wee word might be in order.' McDaid tapped the message pad by the side of the telephone. 'And Denny Knox called. Wants to see us.' He frowned. 'Speaking of seeing things, we haven't heard hide nor hair of Bosseye.'

'That's no' like the wee man.'

'No,' McDaid agreed, 'he puts on an act, but he loves a good gossip with us. Track him down?'

'Later,' said Dreghorn. 'What about Les Campbell's car? Have they brought it in yet or is it still at the St Enoch?'

'Parked downstairs, waiting for Bertie to examine it.'

'Only polite to let Leslie know, seeing as he was having trouble remembering where he'd left it.'

'Sir?' Ellen Duncan was peeking gingerly around the door.

'Aye,' Dreghorn and McDaid answered, then looked at each other.

'I'm the "sir", here,' Dreghorn pointed out.

'Aye, but I'm a sergeant and she's a constable, so I'm a "sir" as well to her.'

' "Sir" implies respect, big man.' Dreghorn winked at Ellen. 'Who were you talking to, Constable Duncan?'

She smiled. 'Both of you?'

'Well played,' said Dreghorn. 'And for yesterday. The hero of the day, single-handedly apprehending a dangerous criminal, a suspected bomber and terrorist no less.'

'Suspected,' Ellen stressed. 'Special Branch have been at him all night, but haven't made much progress. And Deputy Chief Constable McVicar didn't offer much in the way of congratulations; said I was lucky he didn't suspend me for breaking regulations and taking an active part in an investigation.'

'The Vicar's a stickler all right,' McDaid said.

Ellen looked at both of them. 'I just wanted to say sorry I couldn't talk last night. Everything was moving so fast.'

Dreghorn waved a hand dismissively. 'Away – you did a good job, that's what counts. Never mind what the Vicar says.' He thought for a moment. 'Any sign of the military records we requested – Smith and Beattie, the soldiers they served with?'

'Nothing so far, I don't think, but I'll check the post.' She hesitated, looking troubled.

McDaid asked, 'Are you all right, hen?'

'Inspector Strachan and the Murder Squad . . . It's like they're getting a bit blasé about the investigation. Tracy's been arrested, he's a suspected IRA commander, and Smith and Beattie served in Ireland, so Tracy's obviously the killer. I mean, he might be, but . . . Do you not think they're jumping the gun?'

'Probably,' Dreghorn said.

'Aye, but don't worry, hen – we won't,' McDaid said with a determined nod that encompassed all three of them.

'They're already organizing a drink-up tonight, even invited me.'

'How're you getting on with Strachan these days?'

Ellen shrugged. 'I'm not sure if he's getting better or if I'm just getting more used to his shite. Pardon me.'

'No bother, I usually come up with stronger than that when I think of him.' McDaid gestured at himself and Dreghorn. 'Just remember, you know where we are if you need us.'

*

If he wasn't still stechie from his injuries, Les Campbell would have bolted from his house like Brown Jack or Phar Lap or some other speedy thoroughbred that he would have given his punters atrocious odds on. Instead he scrunched across the gravel drive towards the taxi at snail speed, the weight of his cases almost pulling his arms from the sockets.

'Hey,' he yelled at the driver, 'no tip if you don't gie us a hand with these.'

There'd be no tip anyway, but as a bookie, Campbell was a past master at preying on people's hopes. He dropped the cases for the driver to pick up, then climbed gingerly into the back seat.

'Central Station,' he snapped when the luggage was loaded, and began flicking through *Sporting Life* as the car rolled off. He was flung forward, almost off the seat, as the taxi braked suddenly.

'Whoa,' he grunted, 'who taught you to drive – the Dunfee Brothers? And I mean the one who crashed.'

'It wisnae me, pal.'

The driver gestured at the windscreen. A black Alvis blocked the driveway, with Dreghorn and McDaid stepping out of it, the teuchter waving cheerily. Campbell reluctantly rolled down the window.

'New motor, Les?' McDaid asked, impressed.

'It's a taxi.' Campbell tried to keep the irritation out of his voice. 'A taxi.'

'Oh, aye, where you off to?' Dreghorn now.

'Station.'

'Going on your holidays?'

'Going to join the wife.'

'Where is she again, Timbuctoo?'

'Dundee.'

'Well, she'll have to do without the pleasure of your company for another few days.'

'Or maybe a few years,' McDaid stated ominously.

'Because, as of now, you're helping us with our inquiries.' Dreghorn jerked his head towards the house. 'Back inside. Quick smart.'

Les Campbell seemed to deflate as he lowered himself onto the sofa. Dreghorn sat across from him, while McDaid paced the lounge, hands behind his back like a receiver assessing a rapidly collapsing business.

Dreghorn lit a Capstan, then leaned back and crossed his legs. 'Remember your car, Les?' he said. 'You couldn't recall where you'd parked it or whether your wife had taken it, or what?'

Campbell wavered, trying not to commit to an answer either way.

'We found it. Parked in the garage of the St Enoch Hotel,' Dreghorn continued. 'Though we've taken it down to the station now.'

'For safekeeping,' said McDaid, 'so it doesn't get misplaced again.'

'Cheers,' Campbell chanced a bit of sarcasm.

'So, is that where you left it then?' Dreghorn said.

'Well, things are still a wee bit foggy.' Campbell tapped one temple apologetically. 'You know what it's like with a bang on the head. Guess it must be.'

'Strange, because it was registered in the hotel to one of their residents – Conall Tracy, over from Dublin on business. Do you know him?'

Campbell answered with a curious snaking movement that was both nodding and shaking his head. 'Conall Tracy, aye,' he said, then elaborated, 'I know him from the racing – the Irish love the gee-gees.'

'So, he stole your car?' McDaid's tour of the room had taken him behind Campbell, forcing the bookmaker to twist painfully to answer.

'What?'

'He beat you up, stole your car and dumped you outside for your wife to find.'

'No, no, nothing like that.'

Dreghorn said, 'What then, Les?'

Campbell rubbed his brow, then looked up as if having a revelation. 'He borrowed it. I mean, I gave him a loan of it. Aye, it's all coming back now. I lent it to him.'

'You must be thick as thieves to let him drive off with a luxury motor vehicle like that.'

'Aye, no – well, I was just doing him a favour. A visitor to our fair city, and all that. And he's placed some big bets with me. All legitimate, of course.' Campbell was growing in confidence, the patter coming back.

'So you gave your consent for him to take the car.'

'Aye, happy as Larry, so I am.'

'I think we've got everything then.' Dreghorn looked at McDaid, satisfied. 'Archie, do the honours.'

McDaid collared Campbell and hauled him to his feet. 'Leslie Campbell, you are under arrest on suspicion of terrorism, destruction of property, grievous bodily harm and five counts of murder, though the death toll might be rising.'

'Eh?' Campbell struggled like a headless chicken in the big man's grasp.

'You are not obliged to say anything, but anything you do say may be used in evidence.'

'What do you mean? What're you talking about?'

Dreghorn stubbed out his cigarette in an ashtray that looked as though it had never been used. 'Conall Tracy's in the cells at Central. We believe he's responsible for the explosion in Vulcan Street – five people killed, all those weans in hospital.' Dreghorn let the rage reach his eyes. 'You being good enough to let him scoot about the city in your car makes you an accomplice, especially if the scientists at the lab find traces of gelignite in it, which may be quite possible.'

'No, no, no, I don't know anything about that.' Campbell looked back and forth at the detectives, eyes popping with alarm.

'Don't worry, Les,' McDaid reassured him, 'Jimmy only said an accomplice. You'll no' get the death penalty, just life in prison.'

Dreghorn said, 'Should've stuck to bookmaking, not bomb-making.'

'Hold on, you can't believe I've got anything to do with that.'

'We just follow the evidence, Les.'

Campbell sighed and raised his hands, promised he'd tell them the truth. Dreghorn considered the offer, cocked his head at McDaid. The big man plonked the bookie back onto his bahookie.

'I don't know anything about bombs or gelignite, all right?' Campbell said. 'Politics isn't my thing – all I read is the sports pages.' He sighed. 'I mean, I'm no' daft. I know Tracy has connections, or used to, but I'm no' involved in any of that, none of it.'

'What are you involved with then?' McDaid loomed over Campbell, his arms folded.

'The Sweep, that's all, the Irish Hospitals' Sweepstake – and no' even that any more. I've known Tracy for a few years. Like I said, I met him at the racing. He visits regularly, got a niece or a nephew living over here or something. He aye goes to the races when he visits and we got friendly. He likes a flutter, and I like a punter who likes a flutter.

'Couple of years ago he had a wee proposition, told me all about the Sweep, how he was setting it up, with the backing of the Free State government. But he didn't just want to sell tickets on their home turf, he wanted to punt them all over the world. Here, America, Canada, everywhere the Irish went. The Paddys and Micks are as bad as us – they all love the old country.'

'Aye.' Dreghorn reached for his cigarettes again. 'Even though the old country was full of famines and clearances and oppression that drove them and their ancestors away in the first place, if they even had a choice in the matter.'

'A lot of romantic old shite it might be, but romance sells. I think they were shocked by how many tickets they sold, how much money they were raking in, especially here and in the States. Tickets are like gold dust, but because of our outdated and frankly uncivilized gambling laws . . .'

'You're not legally allowed to sell them, so it all goes under the table. Tickets smuggled in; profits smuggled out. Which means you need some sort of black-market network to sell them through, like a bookmaker's operation, with runners and punters already raring to go.' Dreghorn smiled cynically. 'You're the Sweepstake agent in Glasgow.'

'West of Scotland. Well, I was.' Campbell winced, either from memories of lost earnings or from residual pain. 'We came to a mutual agreement that my services were no longer required.'

McDaid said, 'Aye, right, you gave up one of the most profit-able rackets in town?'

'Money isn't everything,' Campbell argued, humble as a church mouse.

'Get the handcuffs on him, Archie,' Dreghorn ordered.

The big man reached for Campbell; the bookie scurried out of reach, raising his hands.

'Awright, awright! They accused me of skimming off the profits.'

'And were you?'

'No' as much as they said,' Campbell said, his honour impugned. 'Perfectly reasonable unforeseen expenses.'

'So, Tracy took your car as payment of the debt and had his boys work you over into the bargain.'

'I never said that. We might have parted ways, but I let him borrow the car as a gesture of good faith.'

'And then fell down on the gravel outside.'

'Think so, but you know – the bang on the head, it's all still a bit foggy.'

Dreghorn stood up. 'A night in the cells will soon bring it all flooding back.'

Campbell squirmed in McDaid's grip as the big man hauled him to his feet.

'Hold on a wee minute, I'm cooperating here.'

'Debatable.'

They had Les Campbell charged with illegal bookmaking at Maitland Street Police Station, avoiding Turnbull Street in case the paths of the bookmaker and Conall Tracy somehow crossed. The arrest was mainly a ploy to stop Campbell high-tailing it the moment they left his villa and to buy them time to gather further evidence against Tracy. They didn't really expect the charges to stick. As he was led away, the detectives heard Campbell demanding, 'Get me Garrison.'

'What do you reckon?' McDaid asked as he started the Alvis. 'Is he telling the truth?'

'Half-truths at best,' said Dreghorn. 'Lies are always more convincing when there's an element of truth in them. He's got nothing to do with the bombing, I'm sure of that, but the Sweepstake stuff I believe. And that Les would be creaming off the top. The car and the beating were punishment for that – probably got off lightly. I reckon he's trying to get himself off the hook by incriminating Tracy a wee bit, but not enough to convict him.'

'If Les has been given the heave-ho, who's taken over?'

'Well, considering Bull and the Conks are supposed to act as Les's bodyguards, they've been noticeable by their absence.'

'The Conks, the Forty, the San Toy, the Calton Entry, they were all cosying up together in the Sarry Heid the night after Les got his doing.'

'Armies of neds in pubs and on street corners might be a useful alternative to bookie's runners for selling tickets. Maybe we should raise that very question with some of them?'

'Lead on, McDaid.'

They patrolled the usual streets and haunts of various gangs, Protestant and Catholic, but saw little activity, few recognizable faces. It was quiet; too quiet, as some Hollywood cavalry officer might observe, just before ten thousand Apaches on the war path suddenly appeared over a nearby hill.

Any gang members that they did spot skittered away like cockroaches caught in a spotlight, doing their best to look innocent and nonchalant. No defiance, no cheek, no acting-the-big-man, no giving them the Vicky. Now that, the detectives agreed, was suspicious.

'Let's be sleekit about it,' Dreghorn suggested.

Driving past at a discreet distance, they spotted some of the Cheeky Forty gathered as if in vital conference on the Garngad Road. McDaid dropped Dreghorn out of sight just behind the adjacent block, then circled around the next two blocks and drew to a halt, engine running, at the opposite side of the street from his partner.

Dreghorn strolled nonchalantly along the pavement, hands in pockets, hat pushed back rakishly, trying to look as little like a polis as possible. He got close enough to identify some of their number before they recognized him and scattered, whistling innocently and looking like butter wouldn't melt.

Dreghorn chose the likeliest target and yelled, 'Midge McConnell, where's the fire?', which turned a harried stride into a full-blown sprint.

Michael 'Midge' McConnell, named for his irritating nature as much as for his short stature, was a veteran of the Cheeky Forty, more because of a dogged propensity to hang around like a bad smell than a reputation for violence. He glanced back furtively as he ran. The fact that Dreghorn was still engaged in a casual stroll should have made him suspicious, but by the time that thought occurred, McDaid was pulling up to the kerb in the Alvis. The big man threw open the door, the upper edge striking McConnell in the face and the lower corner catching him hard enough in the groin to make Dreghorn wince.

McDaid was out of the car in a shot, rushing to help, voice soothing.

'Sorry, Midge! Jimmy's aye saying I need to look where

I'm going – I'm like a bull in a china shop. Here, you rest up against the side of the car. Nothing worse than a bash in the baws, takes the wind out your sails every time. There, deep breaths, that's it.'

Dreghorn joined them. 'Looks like your pockets are full to bursting, Midge,' he said. 'Let's clear them out. Don't want to risk anything else banging against your knackers, do we? Sensitive state they're in now.'

Dreghorn rifled expertly through McConnell's pockets. He fished out a pack of Capstan Full Strength – pocketed, as he was running low – a lighter, a few shillings, a suspiciously stained handkerchief, house keys, a cut-throat razor, a set of knuckledusters and a wad of Sweep tickets, which he passed to McDaid.

The big man flicked through the book of tickets curiously. 'Wait a wee minute, what have we got here: Irish Hospitals' Sweepstake tickets? Tut-tut-tut, is that what you were dishing out to the lads? Aren't these illegal, Jimmy?'

'Gambling, Archie, that's what they are,' Dreghorn said. 'And all gambling is illegal outside of a licensed bookmaker's at an official racecourse.'

McDaid nodded over McConnell's shoulder into the road. 'There's a big dod of shite on the cobbles over there that some old cart-horse must've dumped on the way past, but I don't think that qualifies round here as a racecourse.'

'I don't know how they got there,' McConnell wheezed. 'Never seen them before – you must've planted them on me!'

'Expensive way to incriminate a weasel like you, Midge. If the winning ticket's in here, you'd be onto a fortune. We're far too cheap for that sort of palaver.'

Dreghorn flicked open the razor in front of McConnell's

face, the gangster going cross-eyed as he stared at the blade's edge.

'What are you carrying this for?'

'In case I needed a shave.'

'You're bum fluff at best, all you need is a strong wind.' Dreghorn clicked the razor shut, reached out over the edge of the pavement and dropped it down the drain. There was a rattle as it slid through the stank, a splash as it struck water below.

He moved to do the same with the knuckleduster, changed his mind and slipped it into his pocket.

McDaid waved the tickets as a reminder. 'Where'd you get these from, Midge? Who's taken over the Sweep from Les Campbell? Come on, we saw you selling them.'

McConnell shifted his hands from his groin, clasped them sincerely to his chest. 'Don't know what you're talking about, cross my heart. I bought them off some fellow in the pub.'

'Who?'

'Never caught his name. He was just passing through, stopped off for a quick swally.'

The detectives shared a weary look.

Dreghorn sighed. 'The standard of lies just isn't what it used to be.'

McDaid slapped a hand onto the back of McConnell's neck, bent him double, slipped an arm around his waist and lifted him off the ground so that he dangled upside down, the blood rushing to his head.

'Whoa! Whoa!' McConnell yelled like a cowboy on a runaway horse, struggling as wildly as he could. 'What're you going to do?'

McDaid stepped into the road, strode across the cobbles, carrying his prisoner as easily as a child. He stopped at the pile of horse manure that he'd pointed out earlier. McConnell coughed and spluttered, his hair almost brushing the muck.

'You've been talking so much shite, Midge, that I thought you might need to replenish your supply.'

'Who's taken over the Sweep?' Dreghorn repeated. 'Who're you selling them for?'

'I told you – I don't know anything!'

McDaid shrugged to lift McConnell higher, then dunked him into the still-warm pile. His gagging, choking, horrified cries carried all along the street, bringing curious faces to the windows. McDaid eventually brought him up for air.

'Bosseye, it's Bosseye!' McConnell gasped, almost tripping over his words. 'He's running it along with Bull and the Conks! Les was ripping everybody off and lying to Bull about how much money he was making.'

The detectives stared at each other over the worn soles of McConnell's shoes.

'Hears things that nobody else hears, sees things that nobody else sees,' McDaid muttered.

'He certainly saw us coming,' Dreghorn said.

McDaid plonked McConnell down on the road, nudged him with a toe. 'Beat it,' he said. 'Count yourself lucky we're feeling charitable.'

'Charitable!' McConnell clambered to his feet – hard done by, in his own eyes at least. Backing away, he nodded at McDaid. 'What if you've got the winning ticket in there?'

McDaid smiled and patted his pocket. 'We'll send you a postcard from Monte Carlo.'

CHAPTER 34

Denny Knox leaned forward like a predator scenting prey. In his case, a good story. Either that or it was the beer McDaid was bringing back from the bar that had his nose twitching. He nodded thanks as the big man laid the drinks on the table, but didn't reach for his glass, just stared inscrutably.

'Must be important,' he said, 'for the organ grinder to turn up as well as the gorilla.'

'I resent that,' McDaid said as he sat beside Dreghorn. 'We're partners.'

'Exactly, we complement each other.' Dreghorn pointed at himself, then McDaid. 'Brains and brawn.' He became serious before the big man could take umbrage. 'Haldane and Quinlisk, what've you got for us?'

Knox picked up his notebook, which he'd been scrawling in when the detectives had arrived, his handwriting so bad that rivals would never be able to decipher it. They were in the Press Bar, next door to the *Scottish Daily Express* building, where Knox worked the crime beat. Dreghorn couldn't decide whether having a pub devoted to reporters next door to a newspaper office was a help or a hindrance – alcohol fuelling frantic writing as deadlines loomed.

Knox said, 'I'm still suspicious about why you want to avoid the official channels.'

'We're a couple of rebels,' said McDaid.

'Provocative term when bandied about this pair of honeys.' Knox tapped his notebook against the edge of the table, then started reading from it. 'Superintendent Alexander Haldane, born Edinburgh 1890, grandson of Menzies Haldane, who built the family fortune as the owner of Caledonia Distilleries – you've probably tried the whisky.'

'Aye,' McDaid grunted in exasperation, 'and it'll be going down the sink when I get home.'

'Educated at Eton, where he was disciplined and nearly expelled in his senior year for breaking the arm of a younger pupil, probably his fag. He entered the Grenadier Guards in 1909, later transferring to the Life Guards, and seems to have taken to soldiering like a duck to water.

'He was wounded on the Western Front in 1915 and transferred to Military Intelligence, having impressed Generals French and Tudor. Something of a tactical genius, supposedly, though his critics said he was a wee bit laissez-faire with his men's lives when it came to achieving military objectives. At the end of the war he was dispatched to Ireland to set up a secret-service organization to destabilize the IRA. Counter-intelligence, bribery, torture – all the gentlemanly pursuits.

'He endeared himself to the Republican movement fairly quickly and was one of Michael Collins's main targets. Survived a couple of assassination attempts, one a car bomb, the other from a pair of gunmen. Haldane shot and killed one of the assassins himself. The bomb detonated prematurely; just as well because someone had got their information wrong, and it was Haldane's wife and daughter who were due to use the car that day. The driver was killed in the blast, but they were close enough to be injured and needed treatment for burns and shrapnel wounds. The daughter seemingly still bears the scars, and his wife – a society beauty in her day – has to walk with a cane.'

Knox paused to let that sink in, watched the detectives glance at each other, silently acknowledging the tapestry of violence that was weaving its way around them.

'It's here that Haldane meets your other man: Eugene Quinlisk, a Head Constable of the Royal Irish Constabulary in County Mayo, who was drafted in to organize an effective on-the-ground resistance to Collins's network of agents in Dublin. They operated out of the intelligence room at Dublin Castle – "the knocking shop" they used to call it, because of the number of prisoners who got their teeth knocked out during interrogations.' The reporter in Knox couldn't resist adding the odd dramatic detail to hold his audience's attention. 'This is all through 1920. The Black and Tans and the Auxiliaries are already deployed, but their actions are raising eyebrows back in Parliament, especially the burnings of Cork and Tralee.

'It's guerrilla warfare on the part of the IRA. As well as ambushing British soldiers on patrol and attacking barracks, they formed squads of gunmen whose job it was to assassinate British agents, informers or traitors. The Dublin squad, who called themselves the Twelve Apostles, even though there was more than twelve of them, were commanded by Michael Collins, then the IRA's chief of intelligence.

'Quinlisk's mission mirrored that of Collins's hit squads – identify and capture, or kill, IRA operatives. He and his men were in plainclothes, undercover. Effectively you had opposing teams of assassins hunting each other through the city.'

'The government ordered this?' Dreghorn didn't sound surprised.

Knox sipped his beer, untouched so far, amazingly. 'All

records are covered by the Official Secrets Act, some of them not allowed to be opened until well into the twenty-first century. In Quinlisk's case – possibly to avoid the controversy of admitting the British government was officially sanctioning murder in the streets – quite a few of the men they arrested were subsequently "shot while trying to escape".'

'Handy for him,' said McDaid.

'Afterwards the Whitehall Tribunal, which decided compensation levels for agents like Quinlisk, praised his "loyalty and devotion to duty in the face of quite exceptional danger" and granted him a pension of fifteen hundred pounds a year.'

'What!' McDaid exclaimed. 'Geezo, we're in the wrong business, Jimmy.'

'We all are,' Denny Knox agreed. 'As Quinlisk would probably be unable to reside in Ireland for fear of reprisal, a condition of the settlement was that he should be able to draw this pension anywhere in the world, no questions asked. The story is that he still works as an undercover agent for Britain's interests, when required. Very courteous, though, that's what everybody says about him.'

'A smiling assassin,' said Dreghorn. 'What about Haldane? Special Branch seems like a bit of a demotion for someone of his background.'

'He's a man on a mission. Stamp out Irish terrorism. He didn't agree with the partition of the country. As far as he's concerned, the government should never have given in and allowed the formation of the Irish Free State. Said it was a war that wouldn't stop for some – including himself. Too much bad blood around. He transferred to Special Branch in 1923 and has obviously kept up his association with Quinlisk.'

Knox drained his beer in a thirsty gulp, set the glass down with an interrogatory gleam in his eye.

'So,' he said, 'the fellow you've got in Central, it's Conall Tracy, isn't it?'

The identity of the suspect arrested for the Vulcan Street explosion had been withheld from the press, but it was only a matter of time before someone at the hotel blabbed. Dreghorn was surprised the secrecy had lasted this long.

'No comment.'

'Archie's already asked about him, so you might as well come clean.'

'No comment. For the now.'

'He's got family in Glasgow, a nephew studying for the priesthood, his sister's son, so he visits here regularly.' Knox carried on, hoping to draw more information from them. 'On the surface, Tracy seems to have moved on – member of parliament, briefly, successful businessman and one of the main organizers of the Sweep. But I imagine Haldane would say a lot of that bad blood he was referring to is flowing through Conall Tracy's veins. Rumour is that even though Tracy sided with Michael Collins in accepting Partition, he still maintained strong ties with those Republicans that didn't, and that his allegiances have shifted further in that direction of late. There's evidence that the IRA are stockpiling weapons and explosives for a new campaign of sabotage and unrest. Tracy was one of Collins's Apostles, so he, Quinlisk and Haldane know each other.'

Knox checked his watch and stood up, surprising McDaid with his punctuality. 'Time, gentlemen. Stories to write, scandals to uncover.' He put his hat on. 'A couple of things you detectives should be aware of, if you're not already. Conall Tracy's sister was badly injured during the siege of Tralee in

November 1920 by the Black and Tans. Died not long afterwards. And the car bomb that almost killed Haldane's wife and wean was ordered by Conall Tracy.' He let that sink in. 'They're not men possessed of an overwhelming fondness for each other.'

Dreghorn thanked Knox, then glanced at McDaid. 'Just what we need – another grudge in Glasgow.'

CHAPTER 35

Jab. Jab. Cross. Slow at first, not making much of an impact.

Jab. Jab. Cross. Picking up the pace.

Jab. Jab. Cross. Jab. Jab. Cross. Faster now, hardly any time elapsing between the punches, the impact loud and heavy, rocking the bag, a small grunt of effort from the other side of it.

'Are you all right there, Father?' Dreghorn asked with a quick wink at the boys who were watching, their initial suspicion shifting into admiration as they watched him practise combinations on the heavy bag suspended from a ceiling chain in the Immaculate Conception church hall.

The hall was a newer structure built to the rear of the main church, normally used for charitable and community events, but now playing host to a bunch of gallus street lads, who were acting up for the news photographer who was recording Dreghorn's assault on the bag. Across the hall, reporters were interviewing Martha Hepburn about her and Father Gerrity's new initiative. A couple of them had tried to question Dreghorn about the Smith and Beattie murders and the Vulcan Street explosion. He'd said he was off duty, but would happily grant an exclusive to whoever could last a couple of rounds of sparring with him. Their curiosity quickly cooled.

'I said are you all right there, Father?' Dreghorn repeated.

Father Gerrity peeked out from behind the bag, cheeks

flushed, strands of his slicked-back hair knocked loose by the impacts. He kept his hands on the bag, trying to hold it steady.

'Fine, thanks,' he said unconvincingly, then grunted again as Dreghorn drove a mischievous right-cross into the bag before he had braced himself.

'Remember,' Dreghorn addressed the boys, 'the jab's your best friend. Everybody steams in swinging madly first time around, looking for that knockout punch, but it's wild and knackering and leaves you open for the counter-punch.'

He started moving again, dancing lightly on the balls of his feet, throwing jabs and then skipping back out of range of an invisible opponent.

'Better to use the jab,' he said, 'especially if you've got a longer reach than your opponent.'

He was weaving around the bag now, firing jabs into the leather, increasing the speed and force.

'It wears them down, irritates them, and that means they make mistakes. Hit and run. Then, when you spy your chance – go for it!'

Dreghorn launched a frenzy of blows upon the bag, hooks and uppercuts to the body, finishing with a powerful right-hook to the jaw.

'That was a hook,' he told the audience. 'A good powerful punch if you're inside someone's guard or up close. And if you mistime it' – he missed deliberately with another right hook, shifted his weight to compensate and drove his elbow into the bag with a sharp crack – 'you can always follow through and smack them with your elbow instead.'

Dreghorn straightened up and wagged a disapproving finger as he saw Rachel McAdam approach behind the boys.

'But that's a dirty trick, so I don't want to see any of you using it.' He nodded with integrity at Rachel; she raised an eyebrow back, seeing straight through him.

One of the boys swung his elbow into his own palm as if striking a mortal enemy. 'Fuck you!' he cried.

Dreghorn clipped him around the ear. 'Watch the language,' he warned. 'There's ladies present.'

Father Gerrity pointed at the lad. 'Ten "Hail Marys", Gerry Keenan.'

'Thought it was meant to be non-denominational in this club, Father? No Proddies, no Tims, no nothings – just one, big, happy family.'

'He meant to say ten press-ups, didn't you, Father?' Dreghorn said.

'I meant to say twenty!'

'You heard the man, Keenan. Hit the deck. Twenty press-ups.'

'Aye, that'll be right!' Keenan could feel the tide turning against him.

Dreghorn said, 'Of course if you're too weedy for that, you could always join Miss Toner's dance school down the road.'

Keenan, eager to show them up, dropped to the floor, did two press-ups rapid-fire, but struggled with the third as Dreghorn placed his foot on the boy's back for added resistance. His cries of 'That's no' fair!' were drowned out by his comrades' laughter.

Rachel nudged Dreghorn as if to say: have a heart.

He removed his foot. 'Gaun yourself, Keenan. Lucky for you Miss McAdam is here.'

Keenan continued his punishment unencumbered, counting out the repetitions loudly. Gerrity tapped the heavy bag with his fist as he stepped towards Dreghorn and Rachel.

'You're a natural, inspector,' he said.

'A natural what, Father?'

'With the boys. Strict but fair. A mentor.'

Rachel nodded at Dreghorn. 'They're just scared he'll arrest them.'

'They're not the only ones I might arrest,' Dreghorn retorted. 'And I think you can call me Jimmy, Father. We're both out of uniform.'

They had removed their jackets and rolled up their shirt sleeves. Dreghorn had taken off his tie, loosened his top buttons, and Gerrity his clerical collar. The priest smiled; its removal seemed to add a playfulness to his eyes.

'I suggested to our housekeeper and some of the congregation that they call me Father Owen, instead of Gerrity. They looked at me as if I was the devil in disguise.'

'A scandalous suggestion, Father,' Rachel said. 'You can't possibly be on first-name terms with God's earthly representatives.'

Keenan finished his count and leapt cockily to his feet, trying to disguise his peching and panting. 'Nae bother at all,' he claimed.

'Well done.' Dreghorn clapped the boy on the back, then indicated the still-swaying heavy bag. 'All right, lads. Thirty-second bursts each on the bag. One holds, another hits. Remember what I showed you earlier: keep your guard up and maintain your stance. Well, what're you waiting for? Get stuck in!'

He raised his gloves to untie the laces with his teeth. Almost absent-mindedly, Rachel reached out to help with a quiet 'Here, let me.'

They watched as the boys gathered around the bag, Keenan shoving his way to the front. Dreghorn had run through the basic punches, taught them the correct stance, how to breathe and pivot and distribute their weight. All of which would no doubt go out the window as soon as their blood was up.

He remembered his own tentative first steps into the ring when taken to Dougie McGinn's Boxing Gym, upstairs from Morris Greene's Dance Hall, by his Uncle Joe, after being humiliated by a razor-wielding Rab Hunter. Rachel had also been there that day and had defended him better than he had himself.

She caught him smiling at her. 'What?'

'Nothing,' he said. 'Daydreaming.'

As if reading something in the air between them, Gerrity astutely excused himself, saying that he had to make sure that he had all the attendees' names and addresses.

'A nice man,' Rachel said as he left. 'Do you think being closer in age might give him more of a connection to some of these boys?'

'More than some fire-and-brimstone Bible-basher like Father Nolan?' asked Dreghorn, referring to their old parish priest, a lanky scalpel of a man with a sniper's accuracy for pinpointing impure thoughts and delinquent devotion. 'As long as they don't take a loan of him – I don't know how streetwise priest-school makes you.'

'You don't sound very hopeful about this venture then.'

'Hard to solve the problems of the world by putting on the gloves. I know.'

She looked him in the eye. 'Then why are you here?'

'Because you asked me.'

Her hands rested on the unlaced glove. Dreghorn became

aware of how close she was. So did she. She pulled the glove off his hand and turned away with a look of admonishment.

'That was Mrs Hepburn. I just pass on the messages.'

By the time Dreghorn had knotted his tie and put his jacket back on, the gaggle of reporters had dispersed throughout the hall, a couple talking to Father Gerrity as Rachel listened, the rest doing their best to corral the excited boys, who were still attempting to outdo each other in the gallus league table.

Smiling, Martha Hepburn complimented him on his pugilistic skills, nodding at the heavy bag. 'Impressive. I don't know much about the noble art, but you certainly looked the part.'

'Product of a misspent youth,' Dreghorn said, rolling down his cuffs. 'Comes in handy occasionally, though.'

'You understand these lads then – what they're going through, how to talk to them.'

'A couple of years older than them, I was in the trenches. War makes you grow up fast. I'd rather keep them here, where they belong.'

'That is the talk, though, isn't it? War.'

'Let's hope it is just talk.'

The solemnity between them remained.

Dreghorn commented, 'I didn't say anything.'

'Say anything about what, inspector?' Martha Hepburn frowned.

'Conall Tracy, ma'am.' He kept his voice low to avoid being overheard. 'The man you luncheoned with in the St Enoch Hotel yesterday.'

'What about him?'

'Why were you in his company?'

'You're talking to me as if I was a suspect, inspector.' Her expression was implacable, but he could sense the outrage. 'Am I under arrest?'

'Just a few friendly questions, ma'am.'

Martha Hepburn snorted. 'With friends like that . . .'

They stood silently for a moment, then each broke away from the other's gaze. Dreghorn saw Rachel look over and frown. He gave her a reassuring smile that curdled in his stomach.

'Mrs Hepburn . . .' he began.

She looked back at him, defiant. 'To my knowledge, Mr Tracy is a respected businessman and former politician in the Free State government. The Westminster government has imposed trade restrictions on the Free State, which harm businesses there – and over here. We're both Celtic nations in the grip of a Depression. We should be working to help each other recover, not clashing heads and wallowing in political tit-for-tat. I have friends in the Corporation and in government who would like to see us engage in a more, if not amicable, then pragmatic business relationship. Mr Tracy has the same, over the water. We were asked to meet to investigate whether it would be possible to establish common ground for more substantial negotiations. Discreetly. Of course I wasn't aware I was under surveillance by the Glasgow Police.'

'You're not,' said Dreghorn. 'He was. Conall Tracy's currently under arrest on suspicion of being involved in the Vulcan Street explosion. We're not quite calling it a bombing yet, but this lot' – he cocked his head at the reporters – 'will, given half a chance. And if a pillar of Glasgow society like yourself is involved? Well, there's nothing they like better than pulling down our idols, so it'd be a good idea if you told me exactly what you were doing with him.'

She regarded him coldly. If he'd been the accused in the dock, he'd have been for the rope. 'Aren't you compromising yourself by withholding the fact that you saw me with Mr Tracy?'

Dreghorn didn't answer.

'Why go out of your way to protect me?'

He shrugged with his eyebrows. 'My mammy likes you.'

She laughed, but it was cynical and untrusting. 'Inspector Dreghorn, my meeting with Conall Tracy was perfectly innocent. There was nothing criminal or corrupt about it. You have my word on that. If that's not enough, then please proceed with whatever action you deem necessary.'

'If someone up before you used that as a defence, would you accept it?'

'You may have had a misspent youth, inspector, but there's no excuse for trying to carry it into adulthood.' She drew her eyes off him. 'Good evening.'

Dreghorn shrugged into his coat and removed his fedora from the hat stand as he watched Mrs Hepburn walk away. A couple of the cheekier lads quickstepped warily out of her path, on seeing her expression. She said a curt good night to Father Gerrity and continued towards the door. Rachel McAdam grabbed her coat and rushed after her boss, casting a confused look at Dreghorn.

'Is Aunt Martha all right?' Gerrity asked. 'She seemed in a rush to leave.'

Dreghorn fixed his hat at a rakish angle. 'I sometimes have that effect on people, Father.'

CHAPTER 36

'So you're off hobnobbing while I stay here and do the donkey work?' McDaid had said as Dreghorn prepared to leave for the Church of the Immaculate Conception.

'The detective work, Archibald,' Dreghorn had corrected him, straightening his tie, running his hands through his hair. 'Vital tasks. Don't put yourself down, big man.'

'I suppose that secretary of Mrs Hepburn's will be there?'

'What makes you say that?'

'Your blatant attempts to spruce yourself up – no' that it's making much difference.'

McDaid had walked Dreghorn down to the reception desk as he left, then carried on to Bertie Hammond's forensics laboratory.

'Ey up, Bertie 'Ammond,' he announced in the world's worst Yorkshire accent.

'Hoots, mon, och aye the noo, Bonnie Archie McDaid, whit can Ah dae fur ye?' Hammond responded in far superior Scottish tones, albeit exaggerated.

'Go back to Sheffield with an accent like that,' McDaid said, miffed that the Yorkshireman's impersonation was more accomplished than his own.

'I'm like a native now, Archie, soaking up your culture.' Hammond gestured at the filing cabinets that held his fingerprints and evidence files. 'Stabbings, shootings, break-ins, you'll be in the *Guinness Book of Records* soon.'

McDaid mimicked drinking from a pint glass. 'Guinness might be behind a few of them.'

'Or other beverages – you Scots aren't a fussy lot.'

Uninvited, McDaid bent over the microscope Hammond had been tinkering with and examined the fingerprint that the lens was focused on. His eye followed the swirly lines, none the wiser.

'Jimmy asked me to check something – there was a photograph in Reginald Smith's boat, looked like it might be of him and some others in military uniform, but was spattered with you-know-what. Was it taken as evidence for examination?'

Hammond said yes, opened a file marked with a case number on his desk, lifted the picture with a pair of print tongs and displayed the image to McDaid.

'It's still minging,' the big man said.

'Being in the vicinity of a gunshot wound tends to make things a little messy.'

'Aye, but I need to look at what's under all the blood and gore.'

'Give it here, you big girl's blouse.' Hammond reached for the photograph. 'It's been dusted for prints, and blood and tissue samples have been taken and sent to Professor Glaister for analysis. I'll have it cleaned and sent up.'

When McDaid returned to the squad room, Ellen Duncan was standing hesitantly by Dreghorn's desk with a large brown envelope in her hand. She waved it at the big man.

'The military records Inspector Dreghorn requested have arrived from the Ministry of Defence,' she said.

'He's out reforming the wayward youth of our city,' McDaid told her. 'I'll have a look. Something wrong, hen?'

She was still hesitant. 'The Murder Squad have invited me to join them for a drink at the Steps Bar.'

'Aye, to celebrate solving a case that isn't actually solved yet.' McDaid stepped behind Dreghorn's desk, flopped into the chair. 'Are you going?'

'Perhaps for a wee bit. Feel I should, but . . .' She made a face.

'If you need a chaperone to gatecrash the party with you . . .'

'Thanks, Archie. I should be safe enough in a pub full of polis.' She smiled, didn't sound convinced.

McDaid gave her what he hoped was a reassuring nod, but the thought of Strachan and Orr made him uneasy. 'Keep your guard up and you'll be fine. Or stick close to Tolli; he's a pillar of sobriety, though he might then bore you to death.'

He watched with avuncular affection as Ellen left, admired her determination to prove herself, and thought of Mairi and her former career as a primary-school teacher, which she'd had to give up when they married. What would the world be like if the gender roles were reversed or allowed to exist in equal measure?

The country hadn't fallen apart when war was raging, the men fighting on battlefields across the world, the women manning the home front. They'd held it all together so that there was something more to return to than the government's empty promises. And he couldn't imagine warfare erupting quite so readily if the likes of his Mairi had a say in it.

Opening the envelope, he laid the typewritten documents on the desk. A list of Glaswegian ex-soldiers who had volunteered for the Black and Tans or the Auxiliaries during the Anglo-Irish War, and their accompanying military records. Back from one war and straight into another one. In neither case, McDaid suspected, did they fully understand what they were getting themselves into. One driven by manipulated patriotic ideals that were quickly shattered, and the other by poverty and desperation, quickly descending into bitterness and brutality – beatings, burnings and shootings.

McDaid sighed, read through the list: ordinary, mundane names in alphabetical order. The home addresses given for the men would be out of date in many cases, but it was a good starting point. He crossed off those that were listed as 'killed in action', more than he expected, and put a mark beside the murder victims as he reached them – *Smith, Reginald* and *Beattie, Harold* – as well as their crony *Anderson, Ronald.*

Halfway down the third page, one name jumped out at him. He rocked back in his chair, stung by the implications, blinked, read the list again to make sure, then leapt to his feet as if the chair had caught fire under his bahookie.

He loosened his tie, looked around for some form of reassurance, wondered if he should seek out Sillitoe, in Dreghorn's absence. Everything suddenly seemed askew, shadows formed in the dim light where usually there was clarity. He didn't so much pace the room as stomp.

'Archie?' WPC Jean Malloy stood in the doorway, holding a brown envelope. 'Sergeant Hammond sent up a photograph from the lab.'

'Sergeant McDaid,' the big man snapped. 'Why's he "Sergeant Hammond", but I'm always "Archie" or "big man" to everybody?'

'Sorry.' Jean bristled. 'Sergeant.'

McDaid wilted guiltily, lifted his hands.

'No, I'm the one who's sorry, hen. I'm just a wee bit

scunnered – something I read. Call me Archie, call me what-ever you want. Call me a big bawheid, because that's what I am.' He took the envelope from her. 'What am I?'

She hesitated. He raised his eyebrow.

'A big bawheid.' Mischief in her eyes.

'Exactly.' He dismissed her with a smile and sat behind Dreg-horn's desk again, waiting until she was gone before opening the envelope and examining the newly cleaned photograph. The chair burst into flames again.

'*Mhac na galla!*'

CHAPTER 37

'A small port, imbibed with one's colleagues to celebrate the successful conclusion of an investigation or taken at Hogmanay to ring in the New Year, is all the alcohol a man requires.' DS Tolliver treated himself to an imperceptible sip of his drink. 'Don't you agree, Miss Duncan?'

Ellen wavered her head from side to side, not expressing an opinion either way. The question was pointedly rhetorical; she was already on her third port, which no doubt plunged her into scarlet-woman territory in Tolliver's eyes.

She had followed McDaid's advice for the Murder Squad's excursion to the Steps Bar and stayed close to Tolliver, but the sergeant's overwhelmingly humourless piety was enough to make anyone become a justified sinner. She wondered if he realized how much of a figure of fun he was to the other detectives, frowning at their sarcasm, increasingly colourful language and lewd comments about the busty barmaid who was serving them backchat along with their drinks.

Tolliver apologized again for their behaviour. 'Men together are boys,' he said, as if it was a law of the universe.

Graham Orr lurched over, though it was hard to tell if his gait was natural or down to the bevvy. He thrust two more glasses of port at Ellen and Tolliver.

'It must be my round,' she said.

'No, no, no,' Orr slurred. 'Keep your hand out your purse, you're our guest the night, you hear me.'

Tolliver held up a hand as if directing traffic. 'Thank you, Graham, but I'm fine. As fine as I was on the previous two occasions.'

Orr looked momentarily bemused, then did exactly what he'd done on those previous occasions and knocked back Tolliver's port in a oner.

'Bleurrgh!' he exclaimed. 'Get yourself a real drink instead of this muck and you might fancy more than one.' He focused on Ellen as she removed the other glass from his hand and placed it on the bar.

'Sergeant Tolliver reckons we're celebrating the solving of a case,' she said before Orr could drum up some other inane comment. 'Has there been any news on Tracy? A confession, or admission of complicity even?'

'No' that I've heard, hen, but Special Branch keep their cards close to their chests.' In his head, this seemed to constitute a good reason to glance at Ellen's breasts. 'Stands to reason, though, doesn't it? An infamous Fenian like Tracy, a couple of our boys who were keeping the peace over there murdered, a fuckin' bombing in the town? It's got to be down to him, nae fears.'

'But the explosion was in a Catholic area. He's hardly going to bomb his own people, is he?'

'Gelignite's dangerous stuff, hen. Light a match at the wrong moment and pouf!' He mimicked the burst of an explosion with his hands. 'Serves the bastards right, if you ask me. Anyway, it's Special Branch's case now. They'll get him blabbing all right. They don't mess around. National security and all that.'

'But the evidence linking Tracy to it is mainly circumstantial so far.'

'"Circumstantial!"' Orr guffawed. 'Spoken like a real polis, eh, Tolli?'

Tolliver nodded gravely, the equilibrium of the world threatened.

'You did well yesterday, though, hen,' Orr continued. 'Quick thinking. Ignore what the Vicar said – it's what we think that counts.' He nodded over her shoulder. 'Stick with Boyd, he'll soon get you out your uniform.' He leered. 'Into plainclothes, I mean.'

Ellen didn't bother looking over to where Strachan stood with the other officers, holding court in the adjacent snug, but she could feel his eyes on her. She had done for the entire evening. She hoped it was anger from having thrown a drink over him, but deep down she knew it wasn't. The bar was clad in dark mahogany, intended to evoke the plush interior of a luxury liner, but all it made Ellen think of was a coffin.

Earlier in the evening she'd heard one of the other detectives talking to Brian Harvie about her: 'I'd fire in there if I was you, wee man.'

Harvie, closest to Ellen's age in the Murder Squad, had said, 'Wouldn't mind, she's a wee stoatir, but I think the boss has got the barbed wire out around her.'

And not to protect me, Ellen had thought, remembering once again Strachan's eyes on her in the rear-view mirror of the car as they drove to the canal.

She finished the port in her hand, set down her glass, left the one Orr had given her untouched. She thanked Tolliver for his company and said she was going to slip out quietly. He complimented her wisdom and admitted he would shortly do the same, adding, 'Discretion is the better part of valour, especially where alcohol is concerned.'

Discretion is easier said than done, though, when you're the only woman in the pub who's not behind the bar. She nodded in solidarity to the barmaid as she made her way through the throng to the coat-stand, careful not to bump anyone or catch a wandering eye. She retrieved her coat and slipped out, putting it on as she walked away.

It was cold, the air damp, the smell of smoke heavy in the air. Visibility was beginning to fade, although the view along Glassford Street was still relatively clear. Ellen picked up her pace, but not even Willie McFarlane of Glasgow winning the Powderhall Sprint would have been enough to outrun the telltale creak of the door behind her.

She didn't look round, but envisaged Strachan smoothing his moustache as he said, 'Hold your horses, Miss Duncan. Can't have a young lady walking home unescorted. Not when it's my job to keep the streets safe.'

CHAPTER 38

'So, what did you say to Mrs Hepburn?'

'Me?' Dreghorn recoiled, too innocent to be true. 'Nothing.'

'She stormed out with her battleaxe face on, I've seen it enough times to know,' Rachel McAdam said.

'That usually happens when I chat to women.' He checked his watch. 'Surprised you're still here.'

'Not for long, if you don't answer my question truthfully.' She raised an eyebrow, sipped her sherry, letting time stretch.

Uncomfortable now, Dreghorn broke away from her gaze, glanced out the windows at George Square, framed by the mist-shrouded outlines of the City Chambers on the east and the General Post Office to the south. A man and woman were crossing the square, arm-in-arm, another couple huddled together on a bench under the statuesque eye of Queen Victoria, on her high horse. He could almost feel them shivering. Romance in a cold climate and an overcrowded city. Mind you, when he was young he'd have braved an Arctic blizzard for a quick winch. Probably still would, he realized, catching Rachel's reflection in the glass.

They were in the North British Station Hotel, one of the city's finest, opened only a few years earlier and favoured by visiting dignitaries and Corporation bigwigs. It was Dreghorn's first time inside, though of course he acted as if he spent all his spare time in such splendour.

Rachel had re-entered the church hall minutes after following Martha Hepburn out, announcing that the magistrate desired some fresh air and was making her own way home. She had then asked if Dreghorn was driving back to Turnbull Street. He told her no, he'd be walking the beat tonight. She offered to drive him, suggested that they stop for a drink on the way. Dreghorn briefly considered McDaid, unfairly toiling away back at the station. And accepted without hesitation.

He looked back at Rachel now, smiled reassuringly. 'Really, it was nothing. A minor connection to another case. Can't discuss the details, but, aye, sometimes I should be more tactful. A polisman's lot, I suppose. You get so used to dealing with the bad yins that you expect the worst of everybody.'

'Mrs Hepburn's usually the one who does the cross-examining.' She tailed off, then said, 'Has someone made a complaint? Or threatened her?'

'No, nothing like that. She's not in any bother or danger.' He put on his policeman's voice. 'It'd probably be better if you asked her.'

'I did. She said, "Your friend was doing what he thinks is his job."'

'Friend? That's a bit presumptuous.'

'It wasn't me that said it – you're on rocky ground just now.' A pause as she became serious. 'I've known Martha since I was a bairn, all through the Rent Strikes and up to now. It's not been easy for her. She's had to fight every step of the way. She's the most upstanding person I know, Jimmy. If she's in some sort of trouble . . .'

'I like her too, Rachel. And if she is ever in trouble, you'll be the first person I come too, but she's not. All right?' He glanced towards the bar, started to rise. 'I'll get us another drink, shall I?'

She wasn't letting him off that easily. 'They come to the table, Jimmy,' she said, gesturing for a waiter.

With tips in mind, the man was over like a shot to take their order: a large Talisker for Dreghorn, another sherry for Rachel, the second for each of them. A stubborn silence descended as he went away.

Dreghorn broke first. 'What are Mrs Hepburn's circumstances outside of work? The job must bring a lot of responsibility. Is she married?'

Rachel slammed her hands on the table, leaned forward mischievously. 'So that's it, you've got your eye on her. Did you ask her to step out with you? Is that why she stormed off?'

'Away, she's old enough to be, well, not my mother maybe, but an auntie or something.'

'Nobody would bat an eye, the other way round. You might be one of those – what do they call them? – gigolos, lurking around wealthy widows. Being a polis would be good cover for that sort of malarkey.'

'Oh, aye. Detective by day, dance-hall devil by night. Lock up your daughters. Or your grannies, judging by your opinion of me.'

Rachel laughed. 'Martha's husband was killed in the war. They had a son, but the Spanish flu got him, just a bairn. She has had' – she seemed to consider the wording – 'relationships since, but nothing at the moment that I know of. Really, she's devoted to the job. I like to think we're friends, but we don't talk too much about that sort of thing. It's a good few years off, but she's not looking forward to having to retire. I'm not looking forward to her going, myself. There's not many would've given me the chances she has.'

'You could take over from her. I'll put in a good word.'

'I doubt it's as simple as that, Jimmy, but cheers anyway.' Rachel raised her glass to his offer.

'I'll arrest them if they don't.'

'On what charge?'

'Lack of common sense. Though we'd probably need to lock up the whole Corporation then.'

'It's a deal, inspector.' She reached forward and they clinked glasses.

Dreghorn leaned back in his chair, sipping his whisky, feeling content for the first time in . . . he couldn't remember how long. He looked away because he didn't want to stare too long. The couple on the bench outside were wrapped in each other's arms now, winching, in their own world.

'You know,' Rachel said, 'at school I always thought you were going to ask me to the pictures, or to Risi's Ices for a pokey hat. And during the Rent Strikes your ma said she'd get you to call on me when you came home from the Front. But you never did.'

Dreghorn shrugged forlornly. 'I figured you were too classy to fall for, "Get your coat, hen, you've pulled."'

She raised the back of her hand to her forehead as if swooning at his romanticism, then smiled enigmatically. 'You'll never know now.'

Emboldened by the whisky, he was about to ask if she was sure about that, but the waiter was suddenly back at the table, delivering fresh drinks, though they'd hardly touched the last ones. He nodded across the bar before Dreghorn could speak.

'Compliments of the gentleman, sir. Said you were old friends.'

Dreghorn looked over his shoulder to see Kitty Fraser, elegantly dressed and seated at another table with a lithe, dapper man. She nodded in sombre acknowledgement; the man smiled like the cat that got the canary and lifted his glass in a toast.

Dreghorn glanced at Rachel, returned the toast almost theatrically with the drink the man had sent over, then poured it into the nearest plant pot. The fern it held seemed to shudder, unacclimatized to straight whisky.

Rachel was smiling curiously when he turned back. 'Someone else being presumptuous with the word "friend"?'

'Teddy Levin,' Dreghorn said, as if it explained everything.

'The businessman?'

'He'd be delighted to hear you say that, though business – legitimate business – is just the tip of the iceberg. You know how what we usually call gangsters here are often just wee neds running about the streets with chibs and knives, while in America they race about in cars firing tommy guns? Well, Teddy would fit in nicely with Capone and his cronies.'

'You know him, then?'

'We've stepped on each other's toes.'

On the legal side of the street, Teddy Levin owned the Gordon Club – favoured by high heid yins throughout the city – and numerous other businesses, including menodge societies, pubs and cafes. Skip over to the shady side, though, and his acumen extended to blackmail, bookmaking, bribery, money-lending, prostitution and drugs.

The previous year, Levin had been the main suspect in a brutal murder. He was cleared, though not before he sent four bruisers round to tap dance on Dreghorn's head for the inconvenience of the accusation. Not that the detective held a grudge. Vendetta would be more accurate.

'Maybe I should throw it in his face.' She nodded at the drink Levin had bought her. 'Who's the woman he's with – his wife?'

'Never seen her before, I don't think.' Dreghorn reached for his glass, changed the subject. 'So how did you end up fighting in Mrs Hepburn's Army?'

'I helped her organize the resistance during the Rent Strikes, along with your mother.' She smiled at the memories. 'I worked in the Royal during the war, driving an ambulance, but after that I managed to get a scholarship to study law at Glasgow University from the Lady Jane Lockhart Educational Trust – you must have heard of it?'

The contentment curdled within him. He nodded, not trusting himself to speak without his voice cracking.

'My da' had lost money when his shop went out of business. Watching it all collapse, he figured that the only people who profit from just about everything are lawyers. Of course getting a degree and getting to practise law are two different things when you're a woman. I worked as a legal secretary, but not as an actual lawyer, though I like to think I'd have made a good one. Then I got married and had to give that up too. As you do.' A bitter pause, understandably. 'About five years ago Martha looked me up out of the blue and asked me to come and work for her.' Rachel spread her arms as if to say: and here we are.

'And your man was fine with that?' Dreghorn had slipped on his interrogator's face since she mentioned marriage, not wishing to give anything away.

'It wasn't his decision.'

'Do you have children?'

Rachel's face brightened. 'A girl and a boy. In fact' – she glanced at the large clock over the bar – 'I'll have to be getting back to them after this. We have a nanny; well, my auntie; we pay her to look after them during the day.'

Dreghorn was quick to ask more about her husband, but she was quicker, saying, 'You've never married, Jimmy, a good-looking man like you?'

He pretended to choke on his drink. 'Good-looking? Can I quote you on that?' He looked in the direction of the nearest newspaper offices: *The Glasgow Herald* on Mitchell Street. 'Hold the front page!'

She waited for his answer.

'A couple of close calls in the past.'

'Interesting that you make it sound like a life-or-death situation.'

'With one of them, it probably would have been. The other . . .' Wistfulness softened his voice. 'I'd like to think we could've been happy.'

'What happened to her?'

'I don't know. It was in Shanghai.' Again, as if that was answer enough.

He said no more, and she didn't press him, looked towards the bar. Turning back, there was a smile on her face. 'Are you sure you're not married?'

'I think I'd remember.'

'Not even an . . . I don't know, an unorthodox union?' She glanced over his shoulder. 'It's just that every time I see you, that big fellow turns up. He can't stay away from you.'

Dreghorn turned to see McDaid glaring at Teddy Levin as he padded his way through the bar, like a semi-trained lion who'd just eaten his tamer and was considering whether or not to embark on a full-scale rampage. He stopped at their table, ignoring Dreghorn's fierce look, and removed an envelope from his inside coat pocket.

'Apologies for interrupting, miss, but it's important.'

'How did you know where we were?' Dreghorn asked, accepting the envelope.

'Went to Immaculate Conception and spoke to Father What's-his-name. He said he thought he heard you mention coming here.'

Dreghorn shook the contents of the envelope onto the table: a photograph, a typewritten list of names and addresses, and other documents that he recognized as the military records he'd had Ellen request from the Ministry of Defence.

McDaid said, 'No particular details, but Smith, Beattie and Anderson were all dishonourably discharged in December 1920 after taking part in an operation in Tralee.'

Dreghorn frowned. 'Where Conall Tracy's sister was injured?'

'It gets better.' The big man nodded at the photograph.

It took Dreghorn a moment to realize that it wasn't the image Diana Beattie had given him, but the one from Reginald Smith's narrowboat, cleaned of gore from its murdered owner. Obviously photographed around the same time, Smith and Beattie, in their Black and Tan uniforms, rifles at the ready, were in the same position. Ronald Anderson was gone, though, replaced by another soldier, who sneered more than smiled at the camera. He was burlier than the other two and almost seemed to stand apart, despite having an arm around Beattie's shoulders; young, but with an impressively thick moustache hedging his upper lip.

'His name's on the list as well,' McDaid pointed out.

Dreghorn shook his head. The likeness was unmistakeable,

the same quiet arrogance, the same bristling moustache: Boyd Strachan.

'Fuckin' hell!'

'More or less what I said.' McDaid glanced at Rachel. 'Begging your pardon, ma'am.'

CHAPTER 39

'You can take my arm, I don't mind.'

'I mind, inspector,' Ellen said. 'People might get the wrong impression.'

'What people?' Strachan asked, making her acutely aware that they were alone in the street. 'And if you don't mind me saying, Ellen, you're looking at things the wrong way. You shouldn't care what people think. You're a police officer. People have to care about what *you* think. You've got the law on your side. They don't.'

'Isn't the law for everyone, sir?'

'Of course it is. But it's for some people a wee bit more than others. Don't be shy of that. Embrace it.'

He started walking again, and Ellen cursed herself for allowing him to set the pace of their progress instead of taking charge herself. As ambiguous and oblique as Strachan's games sometimes seemed, the implication was always that he was the one in charge, the one with the power, and there was nothing you could do about it.

He stopped to cross the road, waved ahead. 'You're this way, aren't you? Roebank Street.' Which meant that he had checked up on where she lived. Thrown, she nodded and stepped off the pavement, not looking.

She jumped as a bell dinged, was momentarily dazzled by a bicycle lamp, the rider a hazy silhouette coming towards her in the mist. Strachan grabbed her arm to pull her back, left his hand there too long. Always too long.

She thanked him sharply, pulled away as the cyclist passed, bunnet tugged low, collar up. Minding his own business.

'Now,' said Strachan, keeping a little more distance as they crossed the road, 'I could arrest him if you wanted, give him a night in the cells to teach him some respect – dangerous driving, drunk in charge of a moving vehicle, whatever we wanted.'

'It was my fault. I stepped out in front of him.'

Strachan shrugged, tapped his thumb to his chest. 'We're the law. And you've got to follow the law.'

He sidled closer now that they were on the opposite pavement. The lights of an approaching tram seemed ghostly in the distance, gliding through the mist. She knew fine well that Strachan's 'we' wasn't as inclusive as he tried to make it sound.

'So you've taken a shine to Jimmy?'

'Who, sir?' Too innocent to be true.

'Dreghorn.' Strachan bit down on the name.

'Oh, Inspector Dreghorn,' she said. 'He strikes me as a good detective.' In a way that you don't.

'In his own way, I suppose. He tries.' He adopted a conciliatory tone. 'But he'll no' last the pace. He'll burn out. His kind always do. He's too much his own man. Or likes to think he is. See, he doesn't know how to play the game. It's a police force. We're a team, no' a one-man band.'

'He and Sergeant McDaid seem to work quite well together.'

Strachan waved a hand dismissively. 'Archie's just a big teuchter. Point him in the right direction and tell him to start punching and you'll be fine. Left to his own devices, he's just another numpty promoted out of uniform beyond his gumption.'

Ellen said nothing, letting him talk, wondering how much he'd had to drink.

'You won't believe me, but I've got nothing against Jimmy. No' really. I just think he's dangerous to be around. Big Percy keeps him on a long leash, but that's because he's from over the border and doesn't know the score up here, though the chief'll watch his own back in the long run. Sooner or later, if he doesn't get it in the street, Jimmy's bound to get some Corporation bigwig's knickers in a twist and then he'll be out on his arse.' Strachan cocked his head as if offering avuncular advice. 'And so will anyone too closely associated with him.'

Ellen shrugged her eyebrows. 'Won't make much difference, for all the respect and responsibilities WPCs get.'

'Aye, but the world's changing, Ellen.' Magnanimous now. 'With the right support behind you, who knows? Sky's the limit.'

The tram was drawing nearer, the electric thrum of the lines suddenly more apparent. It was half full and brightly lit, the passengers seen in dazzling clarity, some reading, a couple chatting animatedly, others gazing disinterestedly into the hazy gloom around her and Strachan.

'Talking of what people think,' Strachan mused, 'anybody on there'll think we're a courting couple.'

Another cyclist was following in the wake of the tram, lamp lit, buttoned up against the elements, bunnet on his head: the uniform of the city.

'Only if they've forgotten their specs,' Ellen said.

Strachan laughed, loud and unnervingly genuine. It occurred to Ellen that her attempts to deflect his advances might be making her more attractive to him. A challenge. A battle to be won. She stifled a shiver that crept up her back like a spider testing its web and wished she was home already, fielding questions about her day from her parents.

He seemed to read her mind as they started along Duke Street. 'You still live with your folks, don't you?' She didn't answer, but he carried on anyway. 'Must be at an age when you fancy a wee bit more freedom – not being stuck in listening to the wireless with you ma and da' every night. I've got a wee house in the southside that I sometimes rent out, no tenants the now. Perfect for a young lassie about town.'

A flash of anger made her stop, turn to face him. 'And how exactly would I be paying you to stay there, sir? That is what you're suggesting, isn't it?'

Strachan smoothed his moustache with a thumb and forefinger, then reached out and stroked the back of the same hand slowly down her cheek. Gently, but the knuckles were big and gnarled, easily turned to a heavier touch.

'Well, we maybe wouldn't call it paying, so much as playing.'

His hand carried on from her cheek onto her coat lapel, brushing her right breast. Ellen flinched and stepped away. Her back came up against the window of Coia's Cafe, a family favourite for fish suppers and ice-cream wafers since it opened five years earlier. It was closed now, no lights, no customers. No witnesses.

'What about your wife?' She hoped her voice didn't tremble. 'Sir.'

'It's a loveless marriage, Ellen.' As if that was excuse enough. 'It's the way they all go – sorry to dispel any romantic notions.'

'Is that how your daughters see it?'

'That's different.' A raw nerve touched again.

'I should be going. My folks will be getting worried. They're still fond of each other.' She started to step around him, but he blocked her way, keeping her hemmed in against the cafe window.

'Well, aren't they the lucky ones? Gives the rest of us hope,' he said, then sighed. 'Don't be like that, Ellen. A young lassie on her own, a mother and a sick father depending on her. Don't spite yourself. Don't spite them.'

'How do you know my da's not well?'

Strachan smiled, his moustache expanding like a bloated leech. 'Just taking an interest. I can help you out, Ellen. We can help each other out.'

'I'll get by on my own. Goodnight, inspector.'

He gripped her arm, fingers digging in, holding her where she was. The smile was still there, but there was no humour in it, only threat.

'What're you saving yourself for, Ellen? Gentleman Jimmy Dreghorn? You wouldn't be, if you knew where he's been spending his nights.'

She could smell the alcohol on Strachan's breath, felt nauseous.

'With Kitty Fraser,' Strachan continued. 'They used to call her man Johnny the "Who's Who of Hoors" when he was alive, and she's no' much of a step up. The polisman and the Queen of Hoors, now there's the romance of the century. Never mind Romeo and Juliet. Sillitoe wouldn't have much time for antics like that. Compromised, that's what he'd say. All it would take is a few wee words and Jimmy's done for. And then he wouldn't have the law behind him. There'd be a lot more razors and chibs with his name on them, if that was the case.' He relaxed his grip on her arm, moved slowly closer. 'If you won't help yourself, maybe you'll help him?'

He tried to kiss her. Ellen twisted her head away. He leaned forward with his weight, pressing her against the window. She struggled, tried to keep her head, keep her voice reasonable and authoritative, told him to stop it, to leave her alone.

On the opposite side of the road yet another cyclist rode past quietly, this time with no lamp on. How could he just pass by, minding his own business? Couldn't he see she was in trouble?

She tried to call out, but Strachan's mouth was on hers, the moustache scratching her skin. She gagged, but forced it down, held the panic in, tried to think of the training she'd done with Dreghorn in the police gym.

Strachan was too close for her to knee him effectively in the groin, with one of his legs forced between her thighs. She remembered another technique. She lifted her leg and stamped down with all her strength. The outside of her foot scraped down his inner shin, buckling his leg and forcing him to go over on his ankle, her foot thumping onto his instep. He grunted and lurched to the side, not quite releasing her. She tried to push Strachan away, but he resisted, swearing through the pain.

A movement caught Ellen's eye: the cyclist turning in the road and coming towards them now. In her head she said she was sorry for what she had thought earlier. The cyclist came to a halt, leaping off his bike without braking and reaching into his jacket as the momentum carried him towards them. He drew something from his inside pocket, extended his hand. Ellen's stomach lurched, the world thrown off-course again.

She yelled – a scream more like – and threw her full weight into Strachan. The gunshot and his shocked cry sounded at the same time. He crashed into her, slamming her against the glass, and then fell, body spasming, a dead weight.

The gunman was still coming forward, swinging his gun to

follow Strachan. Ellen had observed firearms practice on the police shooting range, but only at a distance, female officers being barred from that as well. The firearm was like the ones you saw in newsreel footage of the Great War, the handguns carried by officers as they led men over the top in a doomed charge against enemy cannons. She thought it would flare or spit fire with each shot, but there was only a blunt bang and a burst of smoke that dissipated into the mist.

She sensed, rather than saw, Strachan shudder as the gunman fired again, because she was already moving, moving without thinking, lunging for the cyclist.

She grabbed his wrist with both hands, forced his aim awry as the pistol fired again. How many bullets did it hold? Five, six? There was a shriek of shattering glass, cracks shooting across the cafe window, splintering the owner's name emblazoned upon it. Ellen wrenched the gunman's arm, tried to swing him further away from Strachan. He wasn't as strong as the inspector, with less heft behind him. She tried to shake the gun free, but he swung punches over her shoulder from behind, pummelling her cheek, her temple.

In the gym Dreghorn had told her that she was small – he was no heavyweight himself – so she had to be clever in a fight, strike at the sensitive points, the testicles, the eyes, the nose, the throat, or turn an opponent's height and weight against them.

Breathing hard now, adrenaline rushing, she shifted her weight, getting her shoulder under the gunman's arm, then stuck out her hip and flung him over her shoulder. The pistol fired again, and she saw the explosion of debris as the bullet ricocheted off the slab between her feet.

She had mastered judo throws fairly quickly in training, but now lost her footing and went down too, the gunman half on top of her, knocking the breath from her lungs. She gasped like she was drowning, but somehow kept a grip of the man's wrist. Something heavy slammed into the back of her head, jarring her neck like whiplash.

The gunman tore his hand free. Vision blurring, Ellen flailed to try and catch it again. The gun swung high out of reach, then sliced back down again. She gasped, the pain searing across her cheek, the opposite side of her face suddenly hard and cold against the pavement. The gun came down again. Once, twice. On her temple, the back of her head. Her body felt heavy, as if it was collapsing, spreading puddle-like across the pavement. She thrashed, kicked out, but struck nothing, her heel scraping weakly across cobblestones.

A loud whistle – three blasts – cut through the miasma. A cry: 'Stop, police!'

No, she thought, I'm the police. She lashed out, caught material in her hand, a trouser leg perhaps. She clawed at it, pulling herself up and trying to wrestle her attacker to the ground at the same time.

Her vision cleared, and she saw the pistol slicing towards her head again. This time the pain filled her entire being.

Blinding.

Deafening.

Deadening.

CHAPTER 40

They heard the whistles as they left the Steps Bar. Three blasts cutting through the still night from the direction of the Dry-gate or Duke Street. Another three blasts sounded in response from the Trongate.

The Acme Thunderer whistle was the lifeline of police on the streets – the frequency of blasts a Morse code of sorts, audible up to a mile away. Despite being in plainclothes, Dreghorn and McDaid both still carried one, in case of emergencies. More whistles answered the call, some far off, others surprisingly close. Other officers might be telephoning in the alert from the police boxes on Buchanan Street or Wilson Street, painted pillar-box red rather than the police blue of other cities, because they were maintained by the Post Office.

The detectives glanced at each other and ran to the Alvis, turning on the bell as they drove off.

Dreghorn had quickly said good night to Rachel McAdam and they had driven to the Steps, where McDaid knew the Murder Squad were. Most of the detectives were still there, the worse for wear, but with enough stamina and bravado to go on for another few hours. Orr seemed the drunkest, which enhanced his natural charm no end. Dreghorn asked where Strachan was.

'Doing the business,' Orr slurred. 'And wouldn't you like to know who with.'

Dreghorn grabbed his tie, pulled him off-balance, repeated the question.

DS Tolliver, hat on his head, had been about to leave as Dreghorn and McDaid entered. He intervened with blessed-are-the-peacemakers tolerance and said, 'Inspector Strachan elected to walk WPC Duncan home.'

Dreghorn had shoved Orr away and headed for the door. Glasses had shattered as Orr staggered against the bar, yelling threats, but making no effort to follow them up.

With McDaid driving, they raced up the High Street, turned right onto Duke Street and screeched to a halt outside Coia's Cafe, two constables already on the scene.

Dreghorn usually scanned a crime scene with stark profes-sionalism, but now the victim was someone he cared about. The images struck him like hammer blows, tinged by a jagged, clawing rage: Ellen, lying on her side, one cheek torn open, spi-dery rivulets of blood rolling across her forehead and closed eyelids from some other hidden wound; another form, lying with his back to them outside the cafe, two pools of blood ooz-ing out from underneath him – one from his legs, the other from his upper back – and about to meet in the middle; a con-stable crouched over him, looking up in shock, saying that it was Strachan; the cafe window, splintered cracks running its length and breadth, a bullet hole at their centre.

He crouched beside Ellen, said her name. No response. He looked at the constable who was already beside her, a big man, not much older than Ellen herself.

'I heard gunshots and came running, sir,' the constable said. 'PC Murray's already gone to telephone for an ambulance. Should be on its way soon.'

'I'll radio as well, just in case,' McDaid said and rushed back to the Alvis.

Dreghorn said, 'Has she been hit?'

'Don't think so. I'm sure there were only four shots. Two hit Inspector Strachan, one went through the window and I think the other struck the pavement.' The constable nodded at a big divot that had been taken out of the concrete near Ellen's feet. 'Though there's no telling where the ricochet might have gone.'

Scared to disturb her too much, Dreghorn took Ellen's hand, said her name again. Did her eyelids flicker? Hard to say, with all the blood. He felt a rush of guilt, of remorse. If he hadn't encouraged her policing, would she be lying before him, cold and pale and bloody?

'When I got within sight,' the constable carried on, 'Inspector Strachan was already on the ground, and the young lady here was struggling with the gunman. Putting up a good fight too, by the look of things, but he struck her about the head with something – the gun, I presume.'

Pistol-whipped. Dreghorn gritted his teeth, accidentally biting his cheek. He tasted blood.

'I was too far away to help, sir. When I blew my whistle, the gunman jumped on his bike and got off his mark.'

'A motorbike?' Dreghorn asked.

'No, just an ordinary bicycle, but he was going like the clappers. I threw my truncheon at him, but missed.'

McDaid walked past, his eyes on Ellen. 'Ambulance is on its way,' he said. 'I'll check on Strachan.'

Dreghorn nodded, turned back to the constable, asked for his name.

'Kennedy, sir.'

'You did well. If you hadn't come along, they might both be deid.'

He heard McDaid's sing-song cursing and glanced over. The big man was rising to his feet after examining Strachan. The second constable, too young to have served in the war, had little familiarity with bullet wounds and looked on helplessly. McDaid unbuckled his belt and whipped it off.

'Femoral artery, I'd say. Bleeding like a pig.'

He crouched again, slipped his belt around Strachan's thigh, the blood oozing thickly, and pulled it taut into a tourniquet. There were no holes to feed the buckle into, that far down, so he maintained the pressure with his hand. He and Dreghorn shared a grim look.

An ambulance bell sounded, followed by a second one, increasing in volume as they drew closer. On arrival, one crew rushed to Strachan, McDaid handing over control of his make-shift tourniquet, while the other took charge of Ellen. The detectives gave the ambulance men a brief rundown of what had happened, the injuries they believed their colleagues had sustained and the amount of time that had elapsed since the attack.

Ellen regained a semblance of consciousness as the ambulance crew transferred her gently onto a stretcher and lifted her off the ground. She looked around with startled, fearful eyes, reached a hand weakly towards Dreghorn. He took it, explained that she was going to hospital, told her that she was going to be all right. Her lips moved and he leaned forward to hear what she was trying to say. Her breath was weak, almost a sigh. Her hand slipped free from his as her eyes closed again.

As he straightened and stepped back to allow them to carry her into the ambulance, McDaid asked, 'What did she say?'

'Didn't catch it,' Dreghorn said. 'Too weak.' He swallowed, tasted blood from his cheek again.

McDaid hoicked up his trousers with both hands as he watched the doors of the first ambulance close, his belt still tied around Boyd Strachan's thigh. Stepping into the second ambulance, Dreghorn said to McDaid, 'Take the Alvis, fetch Ellen's parents and bring them to the Royal. I'll stay with her.'

McDaid nodded gravely.

'And watch your troosers don't fall doon on their doorstep,' Dreghorn finished. 'Their night's going to be bad enough as it is.'

Dreghorn climbed inside, the ambulance man pulling the door shut behind him, and sat across from Ellen. Her body rocked gently as the engine started and the vehicle moved off.

He stared at the patterns of blood across her face, thought of the lie he had told McDaid and heard again the words she had whispered to him: 'Kitty Fraser . . . Strachan knows . . .'

CHAPTER 41

Thursday, 6 April 1933

McDaid could have sworn he only closed his eyes a couple of minutes ago. That's what it felt like, but sure enough, daylight was soaking through the curtains and he could hear the usual commotion from the kitchen as Mairi readied the weans for school.

Maybe if he lay there for another ten or fifteen minutes he could miss them, wander into the kitchen with an air of innocent disappointment. Better still, time things so that he emerged from the bedroom just as they were stepping out of the door. A quick wave cheerio and a clear conscience.

The covers beside him suddenly exploded into life as his youngest, Kenneth, jumped out from under them, yelling, 'Boo!' He giggled delightedly as McDaid started, and then flopped down onto Mairi's pillows. 'Got you!'

'So you did,' McDaid growled in the affirmative. 'When do you start school?'

'After summer,' said Kenneth. 'Ages away.'

It was actually only a couple of months until he'd be trooping out of the house with his brothers and new sister: a blink of an eye to the big man, a lifetime for the wee yin.

'I could go now, though,' the boy continued enthusiastically. 'I can read and count and everything.'

'Aye, well, mind you don't let on. Nobody likes a show-off.'

McDaid wasn't entirely sure he approved of Mairi having

taught Kenneth the rudiments of reading, writing and arithmetic, but she argued that he was keen to learn and had a genuine interest, from listening to his brothers' school stories. Also, it kept her teaching skills from getting rusty, in case she wanted to return to her old profession once Kenneth too was out of the house. Another scenario that McDaid wasn't sure he approved of, but was wise enough to hold his wheesht about for the moment.

Kenneth kicked out his feet, pressing them against McDaid's stomach. 'You've got a big tummy,' he said.

McDaid farted, easing some overnight pressure. 'No' as big now.'

'Yeugh!' Kenneth covered his nose and mouth, rolled out of bed and scampered off to clype on his father's uncouthness to the rest of the clan.

After a moment, the big man heard a chorus of children's laughter and an admonishing 'Archie!' from his wife. He pulled on his breeks and a simit and wandered through to join them, relishing the space afforded by their new home. It wasn't a country mansion like Kelpie House on the banks of the Clyde, but compared to their previous two-room tenement house, or the earthen-floored blackhouse that he'd grown up in on the Isle of Skye, it was the next best thing to a palace.

It still didn't guarantee him a place at his own table, though. Wee Archie, Bruce, Morag and Kenneth were all seated around it, tucking into bowls of porridge that shared space with a toppled trainset locomotive, a toy soldier that was being gored by a plastic tiger, a sleek racing car, homework jotters to be checked and signed, and a copy of the *Boy's Own Paper*, open at some tale of derring-do. McDaid lifted Kenneth, spoon in hand, sat down in the chair and plonked the laddie on his knee.

What was the word Conall Tracy had used? Rambunctious?
He obviously hadn't seen the McDaid household at breakfast
time. A relentlessly energetic game of dissent, dispute and one-
upmanship between the three boys, rising in volume until they
had to be shushed.

He winked at Morag, who sat quietly, enjoying the banter,
but not fully participating, although she had proved she could
hold her own. She still addressed them with a deference that
McDaid hoped would soon become a relaxed affection, and
when she said 'Mum' or 'Dad', it sounded as though she was
testing the words gingerly, wary that they could be stolen away
at any moment.

Wee Archie, Bruce and Morag finished at the same time, the
boys leaping up and bolting for the door, Morag walking her
bowl over to Mairi and thanking her.

'Bowls in the sink,' McDaid bellowed, stopping Wee Archie
and Bruce in their tracks. They slinked back, reluctantly
complying.

Bruce, still smarting from being recently bashed in the nose
by his new wee sister, said, 'She's just being a sook, so you don't
send her back.'

'It might no' be *her* we send back,' McDaid warned, earning
himself a dunt in the shoulder from Mairi as she placed a bowl
of porridge before him. She was always pulling him up about
playing the weans off against each other, even though he was
only kidding. Family life was a minefield. Sometimes walking
the beat on a Saturday night in Sauchiehall Street, with its
punch-ups, bottlings and stabbings, was less stressful. At least
then you could throw the miscreants behind bars or send them
on their way with a punitive slap in the kisser.

'No, it'll be you,' she said, 'polluting the whole house out.'

The children laughed, and Kenneth rocked back and forth in delight at the uproar that his informing on his father's flatulence had caused.

Once the eldest three had left for school and Kenneth had gone to explore whatever his imagination was turning the back garden into that morning, Mairi and McDaid ate breakfast together. It seemed like ages since they'd spent time with each other, but McDaid felt himself retreating, reliving the previous night's experiences.

The alarm on Ellen's parents' faces as they answered the door. The anguish as he said that she'd been injured only a stone's throw from where they lived. The silent journey to the hospital to meet the barely tethered Dreghorn, with Strachan in surgery and Ellen undergoing observation, having so far failed to regain consciousness. The agonizing wait, the uncertainty, Ellen's stoic father eventually telling them to go home and make sure they were well rested so that they could catch his daughter's attacker.

'She'll be all right, Archie.' Mairi had yet to meet Ellen Duncan, but knew her husband was fond of the young policewoman.

'I just keep thinking if we'd been ten minutes earlier, if I hadn't wasted time going to get Jimmy . . .'

'Then you might be the one with a bullet in you.' The things they talked about sometimes.

'Take more than a bullet to stop me, hen.'

'Archie, I know you're thick-skinned, but that's just thick.' Mairi sometimes worried about her husband's cavalier attitude to his own safety, whether his size made him overconfident or he was just too big-hearted for his own good. She loved him for it, but it also terrified her. '*McDeid* is the last thing the weans and me want you to be.'

He sighed and laughed in gentle acknowledgement.

'How was Jimmy?'

The big man's smile vanished. Dreghorn had insisted on driving him home after they left the hospital, but they hardly spoke on the journey. McDaid had invited him in for a drink, or even to spend the night, but Dreghorn had shaken his head, muttered darkly, 'You're all right, big man' and driven off into the night. The pubs were closed by that time, but there were plenty of shebeens and illegal drinking dens around, none of which would refuse entry to an angry detective who could make their lives hell, if he took the notion.

'He's kind of taken Ellen under his wing. Nothing untoward or anything like that, but he's fond of her, you know, so . . .' McDaid paused, uncomfortable with the memory. 'When he dropped me off last night, there was murder in his eyes.'

Mairi, quiet for a moment, said, 'He's a good man, but he has his demons. You need to try and keep him on the side of the angels.'

'Aye, right.' McDaid stood up, heading for the bathroom. 'Any other tall orders?'

She coughed exaggeratedly to get his attention. 'Bowl in the sink, please.'

His mouth tasted as though something had died in it. His entire body felt as leaden and lifeless as a corpse's. He might even have thought these were his dying moments, if it hadn't been for his head, which pulsed with thumps and throbs as if McDaid was clashing cymbals on his temples.

Brightness seared his vision as he peeled his eyelids open,

quickly screwed them shut again. Too blinding to work out his location. He tried again, this time raising his head from the enveloping grip of the pillows. At least there were pillows.

The curtains were wide open, probably hadn't been closed. White lilies on the bedside cabinet, an ornate Georgian-style wardrobe, a dressing table and mirror, taunting him with a brutal reflection. He hadn't been in the room before, but knew somehow that he was in Kitty Fraser's Bearsden villa. The house was unnervingly silent, and he wondered if he'd been abandoned, dead to the world.

Dreghorn swung a leg over the edge of the mattress, tapped with his toe to make sure the floor was there, and not a dizzying drop to his death. He sat up too quickly, his stomach storm-tossed, and took a breath to steady himself.

His clothes were strewn haphazardly over an ottoman in one corner of the room. He steeled himself to make the precarious crossing. He veered over to the window en route – deliberately, he told himself – and looked out. Roman Road, sure enough. And the Alvis was parked outside with as much care and discretion as his discarded clothing.

He had no memory of driving here from the city, pretty much no memory of anything after leaving McDaid. How much had he had to drink? And where? The knuckles of his right hand were grazed, but his reflection as he pulled on his trousers displayed no other injuries, so hopefully it was accidental.

He left the room and started down the stairs, shirt hanging loose, half buttoned. The maid, whose name he couldn't remember, appeared in the hallway below.

'Sir,' she said, no trace of judgement in her expression.

His mind flitted through a flurry of responses, before deciding on a feeble, 'Aye.'

As they passed on the stairs, she gestured at the coat-stand
by the front door and whispered, 'I would've picked them up,
but the mistress told me no' to bother.'

His coat and suit jacket were puddled on the floor around
the stand. Negotiating the hooks had obviously been beyond
his drunken dexterity. He smiled weakly, half shrugged, considered picking them up, but couldn't face bending over. A
wireless was playing in one of the rooms, growing clearer as he
approached, a Received Pronunciation voice reporting that, as
part of the ongoing Trade War with Britain, Free State prime
minister Éamon de Valera was threatening to abolish the constitutional Oath of Allegiance to the British Crown.

He knocked on the door gently and entered, squinting again
at the unforgiving brightness.

Kitty Fraser sat at the head of a long dining table, framed by
large windows that looked out onto the garden – another room
Dreghorn had never been invited into. She was eating breakfast, with two boiled eggs, a rack of toast and a pot of coffee
before her. She reached out, turned the radio off.

'Inspector Drunkard,' she said. 'I mean, Dreghorn.'

Normally he'd have expected amusement in her eyes, but
there was none. No malice or anger, either, just quiet confirmation of a long-held suspicion.

He acknowledged her greeting with a sheepish nod. 'Charm
personified, eh?'

She gestured for him to sit, help himself to toast or coffee.
'You battered the door about three o'clock in the morning,
woke the house. Staggered in, tried to kiss me, which I wasn't
having, then started talking about the explosion in town the

other day. The people who were injured, someone who lost an eye. It was jumbled. I think there were bits of the war in there too.' A pause. 'You mentioned my brother.'

'Billy?'

'Rab.'

'Sorry.' Sheepishness turned to shame. 'I was with him when he was, you know ... Sometimes I have dreams. It's never really left me.'

'It won't be leaving me any time soon now, either.'

He apologized again.

'You're not the first person to drown himself in alcohol rather than talk about something.'

'You keep things fairly well hidden yourself,' he said and immediately regretted it. He sipped his coffee. Burnt and bitter in his mouth.

'Quite a night you had yourself then,' Kitty eventually said. 'And it looked like it was starting so well. Who was the woman you were with in the Station Hotel?'

'A friend.' The awkward conversations just kept on coming. 'Maybe not even that.'

'She looked nice.'

'She is.'

'Respectable.' A slight edge.

'That too.' Dreghorn helped himself to more coffee. 'There was nothing in it.'

'Did I say there was?'

'She's married.'

'Yes, you seem like a man who puts a lot of faith in the institution of marriage.'

'Hot buttered sarcasm for breakfast?' He raised his cup in a toast.

That won a small smile, but Kitty quickly became serious again, business-like. 'You also said someone shot Boyd Strachan. And assaulted one of your WPCs. The one I've met?'

Dreghorn nodded, angered by his drunken disclosures. Too many blurred lines crossed. For both of them.

'I liked her; I hope she's all right.' There was less concern when she asked, 'How badly was Strachan injured, do you know?'

'Bad enough that you won't have to pay him off for a wee while. Maybe never again, depending on how things go.'

'I don't have anything to do with Boyd Strachan these days.'

'Is that Kitty Fraser talking or Sarah Hunter? Who are you today – Kitty, Sarah, Fraser, Hunter? Not sure I know.'

A long silence.

She smiled sadly, no anger, no resentment. 'Who are we trying to fool here, Jimmy?'

CHAPTER 42

Dreghorn was lighting a second cigarette outside the Royal Infirmary entrance when he saw McDaid marching towards him, having taken the train to High Street Station and walked the rest of the way.

Kitty Fraser had suggested that it would be better for both of them if this was Dreghorn's final visit to Roman Road and, despite initial immature thoughts of 'You can't sack me, I resign', he couldn't argue with her reasoning. She had hugged him without resentment as he left, and all the feelings that had pushed them together came back. Dreghorn smoked away the lump in his throat, nodded to McDaid.

'The picture of health,' the big man noted sarcastically. 'Been waiting long?'

'Length of that fag.' Dreghorn flicked the dout away and pushed open the door as wide as he could for McDaid.

'Heard anything?'

Dreghorn shook his head. 'Meant to telephone the station, but didn't get a chance.'

They had arranged to meet at the hospital to check on Ellen and Strachan before heading to Turnbull Street. The patients were being treated in private rooms under police guard, in case their attacker was determined enough to try and finish the job. Arriving at the ward, the matron informed them that Ellen's parents had been with her all night and then went to fetch the doctor.

Strachan had been operated on overnight, the doctor told them. The first shot had shattered his wrist, the impact altering the trajectory of the bullet and causing it to penetrate his shoulder rather than his torso, where it could have damaged vital organs. The second bullet, as McDaid had surmised, had nicked Strachan's femoral artery; the doctor complimented the big man's quick actions with the tourniquet. Strachan was still unconscious, but was stable and out of immediate danger, prompting an unsympathetic tut from McDaid.

Ellen had suffered a depressed fracture to her skull, as well as minor injuries, and had undergone surgery to return the broken bone fragments to their correct position. There appeared to be no bleeding or swelling in her brain, but she too remained unconscious and was being kept under observation. 'Head injuries can be tricky,' the doctor finished with solemn understatement.

Dreghorn thanked the man, asked him and the matron to telephone Turnbull Street the moment either patient woke up.

'Typical,' noted McDaid as the medics returned to their duties. 'Strachan gets shot twice and is fine and dandy, Ellen gets a bang on the head and is at death's doorstep.'

'That's not what they said.'

'Hardly jumping for joy, though, were they? Poor lassie.' The big man tutted again, nodded over Dreghorn's shoulder. 'Here we go.'

Orr was shambling furtively along the corridor, as if trying to avoid swarms of marauding germs. He nodded as he reached them, his eyes bloodshot, thinning hair lank.

'Any news on the boss?'

They ignored the appellation and quickly related what the doctor had told them. Orr fidgeted as they talked, as if the floor kept shifting under him, then glared at Dreghorn.

'Why didn't you say anything last night, if you knew he was in danger?'

'We didn't. And you were steamboats anyway – too busy trying to pick a fight.'

Orr shook his head in disagreement, but in truth probably couldn't remember clearly.

'Why didn't your boss say anything about serving with Smith and Beattie?' Dreghorn continued. 'What's he got to hide?'

'You're talking shite, Dreghorn.'

'Didn't he tell you he was in the Tans? That sounds like withholding evidence. Or trying to influence the course of an investigation. Serious stuff.'

Orr stepped around them with a dismissive wave of his hands. 'I've no' got time for this. I'm here to offer my support to Boyd's family. Speak to me at the station.'

He knocked gently on the door to Strachan's private room and entered with a venomous glance back at them. Strachan's wife and teenage daughters were inside, keeping a bedside vigil.

'Think he knows anything?' said McDaid.

'I'm always surprised he can walk and talk at the same time.' Dreghorn shrugged. 'Come on.'

Dreghorn hadn't seen Ellen since the ambulance journey the previous night. He stared at the bandages around her head, the drip feeding into her arm, the dressing on her cheek, a spot of blood seeping through, the ghostly paleness of her skin.

'She'll be all right,' he said to Ellen's parents, but the words seemed drowned by the silence of the room. She was being cared for in another private room, a few doors along from Strachan's. McDaid had elected to stay in the corridor, nodding respectfully at the Duncans.

'Do you know who did it?' Sandy Duncan asked, his words hoarse and breathing laboured. He had emphysema, Dreghorn knew, his lungs rotted by fumes in the depths of a submarine engine room, the weight of the ocean above.

'No, but we'll find him.' The words stronger now.

'See that you do.' It was almost a gasp for air.

Marjorie Duncan had risen from her seat as he entered. She touched his arm, asked, 'How's Inspector Strachan?'

'He'll live.'

'But it was him they were after, surely? Nobody would want to hurt Ellen.'

'We think so, aye. Ellen was just in the wrong place at the wrong time.'

'Strachan – he's the one that Ellen doesn't like, isn't he? Why would she be walking home with him on her own?'

Dreghorn shook his head, no answer to give. He placed a hand on Marjorie's arm. 'You're both shattered. I could send for a car to take you home, get some rest and freshen up, come back in a wee bit.'

'I'm no' going anywhere till my wee lassie wakes up, son.'

'What about you, Mr Duncan?'

Sandy Duncan's breathing seemed to fill the room. One notch lower and it would be a death-rattle. He gave a bitter smile. 'The state of my lungs, son, I'm safer here.'

Marjorie Duncan squeezed Dreghorn's hand, offering strength, tacit approval. 'You go. Do whatever you have to do.'

McDaid was leaning disconsolately, hands in pockets,

frowning deeply, when Dreghorn emerged. He pushed himself off the wall with a shrug of his shoulders.

'Jimmy, I've been thinking . . .' Normally a cue for a sarcastic comment, but not today. 'Your man from the pub, Anderson. When we asked if he knew anyone else who'd served in the Tans, he said no. He's not in the same photograph as Strachan, but he *is* in the other one, which was obviously taken at the same place and time, so they must've known each other. I reckon he needs a talking-to.'

Dreghorn put on his hat, gestured along the corridor. 'Lead on, McDaid.'

The door to the King's Arms was open, a wee cleaning woman in a headscarf and pinny bent over the edge of the pavement, emptying water from a bucket down the drain. The water was of a pinkish hue that didn't come from everyday pub grime.

'All right there, missus?' McDaid asked.

She glanced up suspiciously, continued pouring. 'Polis?'

'Aye, no flies on you. Here to speak to Ronnie – Mr Anderson. Is he inside?'

'He's gone, son. Deid. Your lot were round yesterday. Did they no' tell you?'

'We only spoke to him a couple of days ago.' McDaid removed his hat, glanced uneasily at Dreghorn. 'What happened?'

'Fell down the cellar stairs, night before last. Must've taken a tumble after he locked up. Stocious, I reckon. Hell mend him! Always knocking back fly drams when he was working. Perks of the job, he called it. Sometimes there were lock-ins and he'd get drunk and sleep over at the pub. I'd have to wake him up when I got in, and he'd try to get me to make him some breakfast. Away, I'd say, you don't pay me that much. It was me that found him.' Almost a touch of pride. 'What a sight – blood everywhere.'

Dreghorn entered the pub, stepped behind the bar to the open cellar hatch and looked down. A memory tugged at his subconscious like a strand of barbed wire, but he couldn't quite free it. Something Anderson had said when they'd interviewed him, maybe? Outside, he could hear the woman explaining that the brewery was sending round a replacement manager that morning, and she was to have everything spick-and-span before he arrived, so she couldn't stand around gossiping.

The cellar stairs were steep, no doubt difficult to navigate if you were soused. A mop stood upright at the base of the stairs. Bloody smears covered the wooden floor and had spattered nearby beer kegs. He complimented the woman on her thoroughness as she came back in.

'I've had to clean up worse,' she said matter-of-factly.

He didn't ask.

'So, did he fall or was he pushed?' McDaid mused when Dreghorn re-joined him. 'That's the question.'

'Considering two of his mates got shot in the head, what do you think?'

Back at Turnbull Street – 'in and out like a peep of gas,' McDaid observed – Dreghorn telephoned the mortuary and asked to speak to Willie Kivlichan. Urgently. Professor Glaister of Glasgow University was the Chief Police Surgeon, but Dreghorn assumed that other police doctors would have been called in to help deal with the aftermath of the explosion.

He imagined the doctor scooping organs out of a corpse, swearing angrily as he was informed of the telephone call, wiping the blood from his hands and forearms before snatching the receiver.

'It's all hands on deck here just now, Jimmy.' Harried, no niceties.

'Sorry, Willie, I need you to take a look at a corpse for me.'

'I'm up to my eyeballs in one of your corpses already.'

'Anderson, Ronald. Brought in yesterday morning. Accidental death. Fell down the cellar stairs of his pub. They probably reckoned he was drunk. Can you check his injuries, see if they're consistent with that or if there's anything that doesn't seem right?'

'Why?'

'Might be a deliberate accident, if you know what I mean.'

Kivlichan sighed. Dreghorn heard the pages of a logbook being consulted. 'Hold on,' the doctor said.

Dreghorn leaned back in his chair, stuck a Capstan in his mouth and searched his pockets for his lighter. He rolled his eyes as his hand closed around Midge McConnell's knuckleduster by mistake. DCI Monroe appeared in the doorway and told him that Sillitoe wanted to see them in his office. Pronto.

Dreghorn nodded, exhaling smoke, Kivlichan's voice in his other ear. 'Anderson, Ronald. Head injuries consistent with taking a header down a flight of stairs and colliding with a beer barrel.' The doctor paused. 'Apart from the bullet hole in the back of his skull. You're right. He was shot, prior to the fall. Similar modus operandi to Smith and Beattie, I'd hazard a guess.' He paused again. 'Something else, Jimmy. The body at the Vulcan Street explosion . . .'

'Gabriel Demspey.'

'Lucky there's anything left of him, he was so close to the blast, but there were as-yet unidentified fibres embedded in the flesh of both wrists. We've sent them for analysis and I haven't discussed it in detail with Professor Glaister, but . . .'

'What's your thinking, Willie?'

'That he might've been tied up.'

To his credit, Chief Constable Sillitoe didn't pretend the investigation into the murders of Reginald Smith and Harold Beattie was in anything other than a state of chaos. One of his lead detectives had been shot, a uniformed officer badly injured, and Dreghorn had just identified another murder victim in the form of Ronald Anderson.

Monroe shook his head when Dreghorn finished recounting Kivlichan's preliminary findings, then beamed sarcastically at Sillitoe.

'Welcome to Glasgow, sir, where you can get shot in the head and nobody'll notice.'

The chief constable stood behind his desk, Dreghorn and Monroe on the opposite side. 'To give them the benefit of the doubt,' Sillitoe noted, 'it probably wasn't an ordinary day at the office.'

Dreghorn agreed. 'Dr Kivlichan did say it would've been easy to miss, without a thorough examination. The body lay undiscovered and bleeding out for almost twelve hours. The officers on the scene naturally assumed it was an accident. Normally the wound would have been discovered on arrival at the morgue, but they were busy with the Vulcan Street blast. Identifying Gabriel Dempsey's corpse took precedence, and Anderson was put on ice until Archie and me learned of his death.'

Sillitoe leaned his knuckles on the desk. 'Any news on Strachan?'

'Still unconscious,' answered Monroe.

'And WPC Duncan?'

'The same. The hospital will contact us if there's any change to either of them.'

Sillitoe glanced at the photograph of his wife and daughter, positioned to face only him, not on open display to visitors. 'Do we think Strachan was deliberately attempting to mislead the investigation by concealing his past association with the victims?'

'We won't know until we can question him properly, sir. It's possible that he may not have immediately made the connection with the first victim, but he must surely have realized with the second. Obviously he'll have no idea about Anderson . . .'

Dreghorn said, 'When we interviewed Anderson, we asked him for the names of anyone else in Glasgow who served with him in the Black and Tans. He said there wasn't anyone, kept Strachan out of it, although we now have photographs that prove they were there together.'

'Maybe they were protecting each other.' Monroe sounded unconvinced.

'Or maybe Anderson was scared of what Strachan might do, if he did tell us.'

'Another thing,' Monroe said. 'Ballistics identified the bullet that went through the cafe window last night as .38 calibre, not .45 as in Smith and Beattie's murders. Whether that points to a different assailant or just a different weapon is anyone's guess at the moment.'

Sillitoe straightened up. 'I was in Africa during the Irish business – the Rising, the Partition – so my knowledge is limited. Atrocities on both sides, weren't there?' He gestured at the murder files on his desk. 'Could these be revenge killings, retribution for some action or event, military or otherwise, that they participated in during the conflict?'

'It might help if we could speak to Conall Tracy, sir,' said Dreghorn. 'There has to be a link.'

'The official line, Dreghorn, according to Special Branch, is that the two cases are unrelated.'

'Aye, well, maybe we need to shoogle that tightrope and shake them off it.'

'Shoogle,' Sillitoe repeated with a small smile. He enjoyed applying linguistic deduction to the abounding Scots vernacular and seemed to revel in the rough-hewn exoticness of the words. The smile faded. 'I've had the Secretary of State for Scotland on the telephone, reminding me of my duty and stressing how important it is that we extend all possible hospitality and cooperation to Superintendent Haldane and his men. Tracy is being interrogated morning, noon and night, but has so far admitted to nothing.' And to Dreghorn, 'He's employed George Garrison for the defence.'

'Surprise, surprise,' said Dreghorn.

'It may be to no avail. He's being held under the Defence of the Realm Act and I suspect they plan to have him transported to Westminster for further questioning.'

'Sir, you can't allow that,' Monroe protested.

Sillitoe responded as if quoting, ' "A cache of stolen explosives, capable of being planted anywhere in the United Kingdom, is a greater threat to national security than Glasgow's gangland squabbles." Or words to that effect.'

'Squabbles round here don't usually end in gun-play,' Dreghorn pointed out, 'and there's no evidence that the victims had anything to do with the gangs. The contrary, if anything.'

'In light of the threat to national security – impressed upon me by the highest authority – I've ordered that Conall Tracy be transported to Duke Street Gaol and held there in isolation rather than in the cells below. I've scheduled a police van to take him there at midday.'

Dreghorn glanced at his watch: twenty minutes to twelve.

'Again, in light of the threat to national security, I think it only advisable for a senior detective to accompany the suspect on the journey.' Sillitoe's expression was unreadable. 'What do you say, gentlemen?'

Dreghorn snapped to attention, resisted the temptation to wink. 'Be criminal if there wasn't, sir.'

'What, Scottish justice no' good enough for them?' McDaid exclaimed when Dreghorn recounted Sillitoe's theory that Special Branch intended to ship Tracy to London. He shook his head. 'I'm telling you, never mind Ireland – we should go it alone up here.'

Dreghorn was only half listening, gathering his hat and coat. 'Fetch the Alvis and get ready to follow me,' he ordered.

The big man frowned. 'Why, where are you going?'

'Gaol.'

'Always said it was only a matter of time.'

CHAPTER 43

'Fuckin' Fenian bastard!'

The constable drew back his fist, glanced at the torn skin across his knuckles. He gave Dreghorn a wolfish grin. 'Plenty of time to soften him up before we get there, sir.'

Dreghorn looked at Conall Tracy, whose head was still turned from the blow. He nodded at the constable, said with a bittersweet smile, 'Glasgow's finest.'

Tracy looked at Dreghorn. For a man supposedly driven by a cause, his dark eyes seemed dead. He probed the trickle of blood at the corner of his mouth with his tongue; not his first taste. He cocked his head disdainfully at the constable.

'I've been worked over in the knocking shop at Dublin Castle, lad,' he said. 'You've got a right like a wet fart, compared to those boys.'

The constable went to throw another punch, but Dreghorn stopped him, said, 'Where're the others holed up, Conall, and where's the rest of the explosives?'

He had asked the question already. Tracy's response – 'Seeing as you sneaked in here behind their backs, I reckon even Special Branch would advise me to say: go and fuck yourself, inspector' – had prompted the young constable to hit him.

'I don't know who you mean.' Tracy now shrugged helplessly. 'And I don't know anything about any explosives, either.'

'Nora and Patrick Egan, Frank Cleary, Gerry Byrne.'

Tracy shook his head as if he'd never heard of them, even though Dreghorn had seen him in the Egans' company.

'Not Gabriel Dempsey, though,' Dreghorn said. 'We know where he is. In the morgue. Blown to bits. I picked up his glass eye, rolling around the rubble like a wean's marble.'

'Eye, aye,' said the constable, to no one's amusement but his own.

'What about Reginald Smith?' Dreghorn continued. 'Do you know him? Or Harold Beattie, Ronnie Anderson?'

Tracy shook his head, face impassive.

'Smith skippered a narrowboat on the Forth and Clyde Canal. It was used to transport stolen gelignite – same stuff that blew up your pal Dempsey. We found traces on the boat. And we found Smith with a bullet in the back of his head. Beattie and Anderson, too.'

'Dangerous town, this dear green place of yours,' Tracy noted.

'It is when you're around. Smith, Beattie and Anderson were all in the Black and Tans, sent over to your neck of the woods to do their damnedest during the rebellion.'

'They did that all right, the Tans.'

'Smith and the other two in particular? Something personal there, Conall? I think you saw the opportunity to steal the gelignite for some future campaign, and to take revenge on Smith and the others, for whatever they did over there. Bang-bang-bang, back of the head, just like the old days.'

'That's a fertile imagination you have there, Jimmy.' Tracy laughed in appreciation. 'We sure are fine storytellers, us Celts.'

Quiet for a moment, then Dreghorn asked, 'What about the woman you were with in the St Enoch? Don't deny it, I was watching from the kitchens.'

'Sly bastard that you are.' Tracy frowned, probably wondering if Dreghorn was unaware of the woman's identity, or not revealing Martha Hepburn's name to avoid incriminating her in front of the constable. 'She's an old friend, that's all. Nothing more.'

'How far back do you go? Does she share the same . . . opinions as you?'

'She's the voice of reason, inspector. If we were to speak of certain affairs, she'd try to talk me out of anything unreasonable.' Tracy seemed sincere. 'She's nothing to do with any of this.'

Dreghorn took that in. 'It's only a matter of time before it all comes down around you, Conall,' he said. 'It'd be better if it was me and the big man that found Nora and the rest of them. If it's down to Special Branch – Haldane and Quinlisk especially – they might all be killed while trying to escape.' He paused. 'Last chance: where's the rest of your gang?'

'Gang?' Tracy straightened up on the bench, pressed his back against the metal wall. 'You're confusing me with your own rabble.'

The Black Maria drew to a halt with a reluctant grinding of gears. The constable flinched and snorted, as if offended by the prisoner's heavy brogue. Somewhere outside, ahead of them, the bell of a tramcar sounded; behind them, a horse whinnied. Dreghorn glanced through the barred window in the rear door and saw a horse and cart stopping, the coalman pulling on the reins. It wasn't a long trip from Central Police Headquarters to Duke Street Gaol; Dreghorn reckoned the police van was about halfway there now, stopped at the junction of Ingram Street and High Street. Not much time left.

'Squad, column, cell, army – whatever you want to call

yourselves,' said Dreghorn. 'Doesn't change the fact that we're shovelling up bodies because of you. Innocent people. There's something to be proud of, elevates you in the criminal fraternity.'

'We're not criminals.'

Dreghorn saw bodies on cobblestones, broken and bleeding from fallen masonry, tasted the dust in the air, choking and cloying.

'Murder's murder,' he said. 'Dress it up however you want, to ease your conscience. If you've got one. Do you really want more people to die, some of your own maybe?'

'Casualties of war,' Tracy stated, as if swearing on the Bible.

'War? The people in Vulcan Street weren't soldiers. They weren't anything: women chatting on the pavement, kids skip-ping, playing football, all minding their own business – until your business blew their world apart.'

'I could show you plenty like that, lying in unmarked graves, whole streets burned to the ground, the people in the North still being beaten down, oppressed.' Tracy strained against the handcuffs that locked his wrists together. He looked at the con-stable, then back at Dreghorn. 'Because of your kind, the government whose dirty work you do.'

The Black Maria moved off, rocking the passengers slightly.

'You don't know my kind.' Dreghorn leaned closer to Tracy, a quiet, deadly promise in his voice. 'You want a war? If you don't tell me where the rest of them are, I'll give you one.'

There was a screech of brakes, a cry of alarm from the driver, who was blocked off in the cabin in front of them. The side of the van buckled inwards behind Dreghorn, a giant fist that pummelled his spine, hurling him from the bench. The vehicle, he realized, was careering sideways, into the other lane, and then he struck the opposite wall, head hitting the bars, and his thoughts became jagged and chaotic, like the shattered glass hailing through the cabin.

Another impact, if anything larger than the first, a deafening crash and everything seemed to become weightless, as if the world didn't know which way to turn. Metal jarred his body to an unforgiving halt – wall, floor, whatever – and he fought to stay conscious.

Screams, more screeching brakes, shouts of anger, horses neighing in panic, short, sharp explosions that took him back in time, but had no place in the city streets. Gunshots.

Beneath the tumult, choked gasps. Dreghorn raised his head, tried to focus his vision. The van was on its side, the police constable laid out before him, kicking and struggling, his face purpling. Tracy was crouched behind the officer, his hands around the man's neck, working the manacles like a garrotte.

The constable made a hacking sound and then twitched into stillness. Tracy slipped the chain free and advanced on Dreghorn. His eyes were alive now, burning with hatred.

Dreghorn pushed himself up weakly, reaching for the detective's baton in his inside pocket, but Tracy was faster, clubbing him down again. Dreghorn felt the prisoner's knee press into his back, trapping him against the cold metal. The manacles scraped his face as Tracy slipped them over his head.

The chain bit into his neck . . .

CHAPTER 44

Flyman, McDaid had thought as he watched Dreghorn leap nimbly into the Black Maria after the handcuffed Conall Tracy.

Two Special Branch officers had brought Tracy up from the cells and handed him over to the police escort for the short trip to Duke Street. Dreghorn had concealed himself on the blind-side of the van, then darted out as the Special Branchers turned away, flashing his warrant card at the polisman in the back with the Irishman.

McDaid had followed the Maria out of the motor yard and onto the Saltmarket, but had been halted by the white-coated polis directing traffic at the junction of Trongate and Gallow-gate. He considered flashing his warrant card, muscling ahead of the vehicles turning onto High Street, but decided that would be alarmist and would only draw attention to himself and the police van.

As the officer waved the cars on and he drove past the Tol-booth Steeple, he stared ahead, watching the police van ascend the incline of High Street. There were three other vehicles and a coal wagon between him and the Maria, the coalman and his horse ambling out directly behind the police van, after making deliveries to the adjacent tenements. A couple of car horns beeped impatiently at the imposition. The coalman ushered them past with a blackened hand and the air of King George waving from the royal carriage. Horses and carts had ruled the streets long before upstart cars, so a wee bit of respect, please.

The Maria drew to a halt by the fire station as the policeman at the next junction stopped the traffic. McDaid imagined the battle of wits unfolding within the confines of the van. Dreghorn was a seasoned and incisive interrogator, able to switch from warmth and sympathy to razor-sharp ruthlessness within the space of a breath. Conall Tracy was no fool, however, a veteran of guerrilla warfare and subterfuge and a former politician to boot, adept at saying one thing while meaning something else.

Tracy had been dishevelled and unshaven when they led him out, dressed in the same clothes in which he was arrested, but he had been alert, taking in everything, examining his surroundings, counting the guards, searching for weaknesses. He had stared through the windscreen at McDaid, as if reading the big man's intentions, and had given a small, implacable nod. McDaid hadn't responded.

He instinctively scanned the pavements and shop fronts on either side – no criminals or gang members that he recognized, just citizens going about their business or window-shopping at Bow's Emporium, tempted by the neon-sign exhortation to 'Furnish at Bow's'. It was dry, but the sky overhead churned darkly, a deluge not far off. As usual.

The traffic policeman gave the go-ahead and the Maria moved off, the coalman geeing up his nag and following slowly. More car horns sounded, out of sight around the corner in Ingram Street, the commotion making McDaid uneasy. He glanced at the rear-view mirror in case he had to pull out and overtake, reached for the bell.

The screech of shearing metal cut through the horns, and a

speeding brewery delivery truck, piled high with steel kegs, ran the lights at Ingram Street. The coal horse reared in panic, kicking the air with its hooves. The traffic policeman blew his whistle, raised his hand in an insanely optimistic Stop signal and then threw himself out of the way.

The truck rammed the side of the Maria, shedding its load explosively, the impact driving the police van into the opposite lane. Kegs cascaded onto the road, bouncing and rolling like an alcoholic variation of the Dodgems, frothing beer jetting from them. Directly in their path, the horse disappeared from McDaid's sight, its legs scythed away from under it.

An oncoming car swerved violently, mounting the pavement to avoid the careering police van. The tram behind the car didn't have that option, locked into its rails, the sound of the brakes a terrifying scream. It struck the cabin of the Maria at an angle, a burst of shattered glass blossoming into the air above.

The Maria twisted and turned, the driver's cabin spinning around to face down High Street in the direction it had just come from, and then overturned, toppling onto its side. McDaid could only imagine the figures inside, hurled around with bone-crunching force.

He was jolted suddenly, his head whipped back and forth, chest battered against the steering wheel, the car behind failing to brake in time. McDaid swore, slammed on the bell and reversed, to no avail, hemmed in by the vehicles before and behind the Alvis. He glared out the back window, gave the driver behind a look of sheer bloody murder.

Three figures leapt from the truck, hats on their heads, lower faces hidden under paisley-patterned neckerchiefs, all armed with semi-automatic pistols. Two fired two warning shots into the air and then stood at the head of the traffic, sweeping their gun over the cars, threatening any driver who dared to emerge. The last gunman headed for the Maria, disappearing out of sight.

McDaid slammed on the bell, hoping to cause a distraction. He reversed again, smashing into the car behind, forcing it back until he had enough space, and then pulled out into the opposite lane and accelerated, knuckles white on the wheel.

Everything was noise and chaos. The police bell. Screams. The agonized neighing of the horse. Crashes as beer kegs struck cars, whooshes as they exploded. And McDaid's own voice, bellowing curses in Gaelic.

A gunshot, the neighing of the horse cut off.

A quick glance and McDaid saw the first gunman now standing over the horse, pistol smoking, the distraught coalman on his knees beside the animal.

'Blaigeard!' McDaid pressed the accelerator so hard he thought his foot might go through the floor. The Alvis rocked as it clipped a rolling beer keg, the steering suddenly harder to control, something damaged.

The second gunman took aim, the world around him blurring as the Alvis picked up speed. Between the brim of the man's hat and the top of his mask, there was death in his eyes. He fired, cold and calm.

McDaid threw himself to the side, his head and shoulders on the passenger seat. He held the wheel steady with one hand, kept his foot pressed to the floor.

The windscreen shattered, shards spattering him, the gunshots so close they were almost deafening. He heard the rip, felt the thump as bullets struck the chair where he'd sat upright. Something tugged at the shoulder of his coat.

There was a small initial impact, then a larger second one. He was flung off the seat, his foot finally leaving the accelerator. As he hit the floor, the front of the Alvis seemed to collapse, metal crushing and compacting to embrace him like a makeshift coffin. For a moment that seemed like a lifetime, everything went black, an irresistible darkness closing in.

McDaid snapped awake with a gasp as his lungs filled with air. The acrid odour of petrol seared his nostrils like smelling salts, bringing everything back.

'Move, yah big eejit,' he told himself. The last thing he needed was to be stuck in a car that was about to burst into flames.

For a panicked, claustrophobic moment, stuck was exactly what he thought he might be. He grunted and gasped, contorting like an oversized Harry Houdini, and gradually managed to manoeuvre himself into the driver's seat. He started grimly, suddenly face-to-face with the second gunman.

The man's eyes no longer carried death in them, they were simply dead. He was sprawled across the bonnet, arms spread, head lolling, his lower body crushed between the front of the Alvis and the roof of the overturned Maria. His hat had fallen from his head, the neckerchief torn away to reveal his bloody features. McDaid recognized him from the Sarry Heid and the mugshots handed out in the Lodge: Patrick Egan.

McDaid heard Egan's name being called, the words muffled. The name was repeated, louder now, with an air of desperation, and the first gunman came slowly into view. He stared in horror at his compatriot, then saw McDaid and raised his pistol.

The big man was already moving, slamming his bulk against

the door. He spilled out onto the cobbles in time with the gun-shot, saw a flower of burst leather appear on the seat. He scrambled to his feet, but fell again almost immediately, slip-ping on the cobblestones, slick from leaked beer. The gunman appeared, looming over him at the rear of the Alvis, swearing incoherently, taking aim, not that anyone could miss at that range.

McDaid recalled his reckless bravado to Mairi – *'Take more than a bullet to stop me, hen'* – saw Kenneth laughing in the bed beside him, the other two boys bickering good-naturedly, Mor-ag's timid, hopeful smile.

The gun fired and he flinched, but the bullet struck a keg a couple of feet away, releasing a jet of beer. Better than blood.

There was a second blur of movement behind the gunman, a sickening wet crunch, the man's head now cocked awkwardly to one side. He collapsed and a dark shape went down with him, swinging repeatedly with a working man's heavy strength.

McDaid caught the coalman's wrist on the third swing, the lump of coal in his fist glistening with blood. He pulled the man gently but firmly to his feet, turned him away from the body on the ground, the corpse laid across the bonnet and spoke softly, said that everything was all right.

The coalman's legs almost gave way, struck by the sudden horror of what had happened, what he'd done. He gasped for air, tried to find the words. 'He shot my horse.' Tears cut streaks through the coal dust that blackened his features. 'He shot my horse.'

Dreghorn hacked and choked, felt his windpipe begin to give. Panic gave him strength. He bucked and kicked against the metal, but Tracy didn't move, maintained the relentless pressure. In his head, Dreghorn heard Sandy Duncan's death-rattle breathing, felt the same sound rise in his own throat.

A huge crash filled his ears and another impact shook the Maria, sliding the detective across the metal like a curling stone shot from a cannon. The chain was torn away from his neck and he was freed from Tracy's crushing weight. He saw the Irishman flung through the air, strike the upright edge of the bench, and heard him let out a gratifying grunt of pain.

He pushed himself onto his knees, gasping for air, something heavy swinging in his jacket pocket. He reached for it, felt metal slide around his fingers, clenched his fist. Tracy was already on his feet, lunging again.

Dreghorn raised his left hand to block the chain of the hand-cuffs, swung with his right, smashing the knuckleduster that he'd confiscated from Midge McConnell into the side of Tracy's knee, buckling the leg and bringing him down to Dreg-horn's level. Dreghorn swung again, a right-cross so wild that Dougie McGinn, his old boxing trainer, would have tutted. It landed well enough, though, the knuckleduster tearing into Tracy's jaw and sending him sprawling across the interior of the van.

Unbalanced, disoriented, Dreghorn fell forward onto his hands, the knuckleduster clanging, metal against metal. The side of the van was now the floor, their world literally turned over, the rear doors horizontal instead of upright, the uni-formed officer lying between him and Tracy. He fought for breath, his neck and throat pulsating with pain.

Three urgent bangs on the door outside, a voice yelling, 'Conn, get away from the door! You hear me? Get away from the door!'

Tracy rolled away from the door, curled into a ball.

A loud bang. The doors shuddered, the bottom one falling open onto the cobbles outside, light flooding in. The top door swung up and was held in place by a man whose identity was concealed by a hat and neckerchief, a pistol in his hand. He scanned the Maria, spotted Tracy and bellowed for him to hurry, warning that they didn't have much time. Dreghorn realized he could hear police bells, had no idea how much time had elapsed.

Tracy scrabbled towards the exit, the other man training his gun on Dreghorn, cursing as he saw Conall's bloody face. Tracy lurched to his feet, struggled with his rescuer, grabbing the man's gun. He turned and fired.

Dreghorn, already moving, heard the shots fill the confines of the Maria, felt the impact of the bullets as they tore into flesh and bone.

McDaid snatched up the fallen gunman's weapon as he heard the shots, blood leaking into the cobbled grid beneath the body. He ran for the rear of the Maria, passing the upturned undercarriage. An engine roared into urgent life. He stopped behind the van to see the delivery truck start to drive up High Street, with Conall Tracy in the passenger seat.

He took a few steps, yelled for them to stop, then fired. The side window of the truck shattered, but he knew he wouldn't have hit anyone from that angle. He fired again – an empty click – then hurled the pistol after them in frustration.

He swore and turned to the van, lifted the top door. It reminded him of a coffin lid. He peered inside, yelled Dreghorn's name.

The interior was frighteningly still, the walls and ceiling crushed inwards at points from the collision, one bench almost completely torn from the bolts and hanging like a fallen rafter. And two bodies in the rear corner, one half on top of the other.

'Jimmy! Jimmy!'

The bodies twitched, and the top one – a uniformed officer – rolled off the other. Dreghorn rose into a slow, painful crouch and staggered towards McDaid, the big man reaching out to help.

'Jesus, Jimmy, we need to get you to hospital.'

Dreghorn shook his head. 'It's all right.' His voice was a croaky, lacerated whisper.

'You're covered in blood, man.'

'It's no' mine.' Dreghorn looked back at the policeman whose body he'd used as a shield. 'For once.'

CHAPTER 45

The next few hours were a blur to Dreghorn, as if he'd been stopped in time, but events were circling around him. Shock, probably. He understood that, although the knowledge didn't allow him to get a grip of himself.

The return to Turnbull Street. A quick examination by the duty physician for the day. Countless retellings to countless other officers, all of whom he knew, but the faces didn't stick, trying to piece together the exact events of the attack on the police van. Dreghorn sat and spoke quietly, every word draining more energy from him. McDaid was the opposite, pacing furiously around the squad room.

The one thing that played over and over in Dreghorn's mind was the one thing he couldn't bring himself to talk about, to admit. Throwing himself across the Black Maria as Conall Tracy raised the gun. Shielding himself behind the dead constable – *Please, God, let him have been dead* – and praying that the bullets wouldn't tear straight through the man's body and into him.

The doctor detected no major injuries, but recommended a hospital visit, to be on the safe side. Both detectives refused, insisting they were fine, but DCI Monroe ordered them to return home, get some rest and, if they felt up to it, re-join the investigation tomorrow.

*

It was 7.30 p.m. when Dreghorn arrived back at Hamilton Park Avenue, driven by Sammy Stirling, who stayed quiet for most of the journey.

He heard chit-chat and the tinkle of glasses in the reception room as he entered and sighed. Mrs Pettigrew mainly rented rooms to professionals or academics from Glasgow University, a short walk from her townhouse. Breakfast and an evening meal were included in the rent, though Dreghorn, especially in recent months, rarely took his seat.

After dinner most evenings Mrs Pettigrew enjoyed having her 'guests' gather for a drink or two to discuss politics, the arts, world events. When Dreghorn had first started lodging there – a welcome respite from the police barracks he'd initially stayed in, on his return from Shanghai in '29 – he had quite enjoyed the wee soirées, pricking pomposity, puncturing intellectual philosophizing with his pragmatic understanding of human nature and generally playing devil's advocate. One winter evening, when the other lodgers had retired, Dreghorn and Mrs Pettigrew had ended up lying on the sheepskin rug in front of the fire, kissing.

His affair with the 'Merry Widow', as McDaid delightedly described it in theatrical tones, had continued for the better part of a year – more, Dreghorn suspected, on her terms than his. There was never any discount on the rent, which delighted the big man even more.

Gradually, though, Dreghorn had felt his contributions to those evenings becoming tinged with cynicism and anger, so he had withdrawn. His relationship, if it could be called that, had petered out around the same time. Tellingly, neither of them seemed too upset, almost acting, with typical Scottish reserve, as if it had never happened.

He closed the front door as quietly as possible now, wondered if he could make it up the stairs without being seen. Mrs Pettigrew called out 'inspector' as he tried to sneak past and asked him to join them. He knew how dishevelled he looked, could smell his own sweat, the residue of fear and the coppery tang of bloodstains on his suit, which he hoped they couldn't discern in the gaslight. He suddenly felt like a pariah, intruding into the safety and comfort of their cosy drawing-room world, where disagreements were generally served with port, and not a glass to the face.

He politely declined her invitation, explaining that it had been an arduous day. She asked if he'd eaten; there were plenty of leftovers in the kitchen. He thanked her, said, 'Maybe later' and headed for the stairs. It was all he could do to stop himself climbing them on all fours.

Typically, he'd forgotten that he'd finished the whisky in his room. He held the bottle upside down to catch the final measly drops on his tongue, told himself that he could last the night without going out for another one and sat by the window, smoking. Running low on cigarettes too. Another test of willpower.

A considerate knock at the door and Mrs Pettigrew entered with a tray, as if offering Silver Service to an esteemed guest. She smiled warmly, but Dreghorn noticed that she left the door ajar. In times past she'd have closed it discreetly. Propriety over privacy now.

'I thought you looked as though you needed something to eat, inspector?' She set the tray down on the small table before him, then stepped back. 'Stovies, nothing fancy.'

'Just the ticket.' Dreghorn peeked under the plate she'd placed over the bowl to keep it warm, releasing a burst of steam, the smell making him suddenly hungry. 'Thank you, Mrs Pettigrew.'

They always referred to each other formally, an amusing affectation during intimacy, which nevertheless maintained a certain distance.

'Professor Buchan brought home an *Evening Times*. He showed me the story about the gaol break on the High Street. Were you involved at all?'

Dreghorn stubbed out his cigarette, shrugged his eyebrows self-deprecatingly. 'I have a God-given talent for being in the wrong place at the wrong time.'

'It said there were two men killed, one a police officer. Did you know him?'

Dreghorn felt the hammer blows of the bullets striking the young officer's body as he cowered behind it. 'Someone at the station,' he said, 'but no, not really.'

'Those poor men, their families. To think they'd have left for work this morning, said goodbye as normal, never knowing what was going to happen. It must take a terrible toll, your job.'

Dreghorn shrugged. 'Some days it's the best job in the world. Some days it's the worst. None of us knows what's around the corner.'

'I don't know how you . . .' She didn't finish, her eyes falling on the overflowing ashtray, the empty bottle of Teacher's.

Dreghorn's professional life had only intersected with Mrs Pettigrew's world once, a few months earlier when four men had tried to administer a professional beating to him on behalf of one of Glasgow's most powerful gangsters. It had been a rude awakening to the underside of her city, the shadows best avoided.

She folded her arms and smiled awkwardly. 'There's

something I've been wanting to speak to you about, inspector.' She glanced back at the open door, making sure no one could overhear.

'You and Professor Buchan are courting.'

Mrs Pettigrew seemed taken aback, but recovered well. 'I'm not quite sure that's what you'd call it at our age, but yes. How did you know?'

'I am a detective, remember? It was either that or you were going to kick me out. You're happy with him?'

'Early days, but he seems like a good man.'

'That helps.'

'It's a little awkward to bring up, and I'm not trying to pretend it didn't happen, but you won't say anything about . . .' She connected them with a wave of her hand.

Dreghorn almost made her spell it out, but then shook his head. 'Don't worry, your sordid little secret is safe with me.'

She glanced at the door again, whispered huskily, 'You are the sordid little secret.'

He laughed, felt a momentary lightness. 'I won't say anything. You have my word. And I wish you all the best.'

'Thank you, inspector.' She smoothed down her dress.

'I think you can call me Jimmy now, don't you?'

'Jimmy . . . How about James? A touch more class. And you can call me Mrs Pettigrew.' A cheeky flash of humour. 'I'm still the boss here. Standards, you know.'

Dreghorn saluted. 'Mrs Pettigrew.'

She paused at the door. 'You're a good man too,' she said, 'James.'

Once she had gone, Dreghorn wolfed down the stovies, unable to remember when he had last eaten. He pushed the plate away, lit his last cigarette and leaned back in the chair.

His brief contentment faded with each draw. He put Louis Armstrong's 'West End Blues' on the gramophone, the title suiting his mood and location. The music soon faded from his ears as the confrontation with Conall Tracy replayed in his mind. A violent, claustrophobic, chaotic newsreel.

He stood up and pulled the embroidered blanket off the heavy trunk that sat at the foot of his bed, disguised by Mrs Pettigrew as an innocent piece of furniture. He looked at the yellowing shipping documentation stuck to the sides and lid, listing far-off lands that seemed exotic, until you learned that human nature is the same wherever you are. Thirty-five years on the planet and, barring a few suits and hats, the trunk was about all he had to show for it.

He unlocked it, opened the lid and began to peel away the layers, the memories. Passport and travel papers to and from Shanghai, the return journey arranged at breakneck speed. Battered leather boxing gloves and a robe with the words '"Gentleman" Jimmy Dreghorn' on the back; he hadn't read the irony in the quotation marks at the time. Two Shanghai Municipal Police uniforms, dark blue serge for winter, khaki drill for summer, the cap lost at some point in his final days there. His old army uniform and an ushanka hat, supposedly made of sable fur. A present or an attempted bribe? He couldn't remember. Two books by W. E. Fairbairn – *Defendu* and *Scientific Self-Defence* – the first signed with a dedication by the author: *Keep your guard up, young Dreghorn*. An envelope containing photographs that he didn't have the heart to look at. A qipao dress of Chinese silk, perhaps still carrying some faint scent of the woman who'd worn it. He didn't have the heart to check that, either.

Finally, at the bottom, a black lacquered box with a

red-and-white dragon emblazoned upon the lid. He removed the box, the weight familiar, placed it on the table and closed the trunk, the door to his past, locked away again.

The night was drawing in outside. He switched on the small table lamp and opened the box. He unwrapped the protective cloth around the contents: a Webley Mark VI revolver, the lamplight glinting off the barrels, a whiff of gun-oil, even though it hadn't been touched for some time.

He removed the gun, cocked the hammer and pressed the trigger, listened to it click on an empty chamber, the action smooth and clean. He checked the box of .455 cartridges that was packed alongside the gun. Almost full.

A good man. Said not with an air of compliment, but as reassurance, as if there was some doubt.

Did good men spend their evenings cleaning their guns with murder in mind?

CHAPTER 46

Friday, 7 April 1933

No lying in or skiving off in an attempt to miss the weans this morning. McDaid was up as soon as he heard other movement in the household, eager to have the trauma of the previous day washed away by the warmth and love of his family.

Not that they seemed to treat him as anything other than a mountainous obstruction between them and their porridge. Mairi was the first to kick off the disrespect. And here was he, thinking they were supposed to be a united front.

'Is the bed on fire or something?' she asked.

'No, I just wanted to—'

'Out the way, Da', I need to get a spoon.' Kenneth dunted the big man aside to get at the cutlery drawer.

'Aoww!' Bruce jerked his toe out from under McDaid's heel, hopped exaggeratedly on one foot. 'Mum! Da' stood on my toe and we've got football today. Oww, I think it's broken.'

Mairi said, 'Ask if you can go in goals, then you won't have to run about so much.'

'In goals?' Outraged. 'I'm the striker!'

'Striker, my arse,' scoffed Wee Archie, then ducked as McDaid raised a hand to give him a half-hearted skelp around the ear. The oldest child, Archie was engaged in a competition to see if he could grow taller than his father. It was a long-term plan.

'Language!' Mairi's old schoolteacher voice.

Kenneth, seated at the table, said, 'Da, that's my bowl!'

'Aye, I know,' McDaid tutted. 'I'm just passing it to you.'

'Yuck! You put your fingers in it!'

'Only my thumb. Wheesht your girning – the germs'll make it tastier.'

'Archie, don't.' Mairi turned the schoolmarm glare on her husband. 'You know how fussy he is.'

McDaid threw up his arms in exasperation. 'I give up. Top of the morning to you lot, too. Shall I just go and stand in the corner and shut up?'

Morag, who had been observing quietly, piped up, 'The dunce's corner.'

Walking a gauntlet of laughter, McDaid cocked his head at the wee lassie. 'Och, you're going to fit in nicely, aren't you?'

She nodded, grinning infectiously.

And so it continued, domestic chaos, and the big man loved every minute of it.

'It's most likely that Conall Tracy and his associates will be aiming to get back to the Irish Free State, or possibly to America, where they also have supporters who would shelter them. We have officers stationed at every port, railway station and airport to apprehend him. Roadblocks and checkpoints were set up on every possible route out of Glasgow within an hour of his escape, with orders to check every vehicle leaving the city. We're certain that Tracy and his squad are currently in hiding. One of our own is lying in the morgue, another four in hospital, so mark my words: I want Conall Tracy found and brought to justice, even if you have to turn the city upside down.'

The briefing had already started when McDaid sidled in and

stood at the back, his journey delayed by a broken-down tram, earning a small nod from Sillitoe as he spoke. The chief constable had taken personal charge of the manhunt, and his cold, controlled fury at the murder of one officer and the hospitalization of two others was palpable in his clipped tones and stark gaze. Dreghorn now had a name for the officer killed inside the Black Maria: David Jardine. The driver of the police van and the traffic policeman, who was struck by a flying beer keg, had joined Ellen Duncan and Boyd Strachan in the Royal Infirmary, both of them in a critical condition.

'Gaolbreaks have long been a feature of IRA strategy,' Sillitoe continued, 'but in this case, they would have had precious little time to plan the operation; the decision to move Tracy was taken only a few hours before the escape. We cannot discount the possibility that individuals within this station passed on inside information that resulted in PC Jardine's death—'

'Weed out all the Tims,' Orr interrupted Sillitoe, then glanced back at the detectives gathered in the Lodge. 'I've said it before. If there's Fenian sympathizers, we all know where they are.'

A muttered chorus of agreement snaked through the room, louder than should have been apparent in a police force that was – officially, on paper – free of any sectarian or political bias. McDaid followed the comments, committing the speakers to memory, though there were few surprises. There were two advocacies of prejudice in the force: those who were vocal to the point of outspokenness, like Orr, and those whose silence marked a tacit, perhaps more insidious approval. Each fuelled the other, in McDaid's eyes.

The big man had been raised Free Church on the Isle of Skye, but even before the war, he had swapped those strict religious dictates for his own code of right and wrong. People should be judged as people, not as vessels of centuries-old opposing doctrines that often only had a hair's breadth between them anyway. No matter what they preached, McDaid reckoned that zealots of whatever side usually had more in common than they'd care to admit – inflexible, intolerant dunderheids, the lot of them.

Also, if McDaid subscribed to the sectarianism that coloured large swathes of the city, it would severely curtail the number and variety of social functions he could play at. The world would be a better place if everyone stopped singing hymns at each other and listened to him blasting out on the bagpipes instead.

Spurred on, Orr pointed at Dreghorn, leaning against a desk near the front. 'There was even one in the Maria with him. What was that all about, eh?'

Dreghorn breathed smoke out of the corner of his mouth. 'We were saying a few "Hail Marys" together, until he tried to put a bullet in me.'

'Missed, though, didn't he? Funny how his aim went skew-whiff for another left-footer.'

Dreghorn crushed his cigarette into an ashtray, took a step towards Orr.

'Sergeant Orr!' Sillitoe gestured curtly for Dreghorn to back down, stepped towards Orr himself. 'If it wasn't for Inspector Dreghorn and Sergeant McDaid, yesterday's loss of life would have been far greater. If I was to show the same disrespect and ungraciousness, I might well question where you were during the assault on Inspector Strachan and Constable Duncan.'

Orr started to talk back. Sillitoe raised an eyebrow in warning. Orr lost his nerve, looked away, swallowed the ball of rage.

'Sir,' he said.

Sillitoe carried on as if there had been no drama. 'Tracy came over from Ireland with a number of associates, whose names and descriptions you've already been given. Two of those associates are now deceased: Gabriel Dempsey, caught in the Vulcan Street blast, and Patrick Egan, killed during the breakout yesterday.'

Heads turned in McDaid's direction and many of the same voices that had supported Orr's comments now offered congratulations – 'Gaun yerself, big man.'

McDaid acknowledged them with a glower. Taking a life was nothing to be proud of, even if it was kill or be killed.

'Another man, Paul Kane, a member of the San Toy street gang and, we suspect, an accomplice in the Garngad heist, is also in hospital with serious head injuries,' said Sillitoe. 'Doctors are not optimistic about his chances of recovery.'

McDaid remembered the distraught coalman, clubbing Kane unconscious. What would have happened if the man hadn't intervened didn't bear thinking about. He caught Dreghorn's eye, shook his head in exasperation: Maitland Street had neglected to inform the detectives that Kane had been released after questioning, due to a lack of evidence. They certainly had enough proof now.

'That,' said Sillitoe, 'leaves Tracy and three others – Nora Egan, Frank Cleary and Gerard Byrne – on the run, whereabouts unknown, though we're certain they're still in the city. They're to be considered armed and dangerous and, in addition to the breakout and gelignite heist, are our prime suspects in the murders of Reginald Smith, Harold Beattie and Ronald Anderson, as well as the attack on Boyd Strachan and Ellen Duncan.'

The delivery truck, stolen from outside the Oriental Bar in

Finnieston Street an hour before the attack, had been found abandoned behind the St Rollux Chemical Works. Witnesses described the truck screeching to a halt, half up on the pavement. Two men – one matching Conall Tracy's description – had leapt from the cab and run to another car, which was sitting waiting, engine running. This car headed west, keeping within the speed limit so as not to draw attention to itself. Despite the suspiciousness of the event, witnesses were either too far away or didn't have the gumption to take note of the number plates.

Patrick Egan's corpse was lying in the morgue, his clothing taken as evidence and passed on to Bertie Hammond for analysis to check for possible clues – fibres, dirt stains – to whatever location they were using as a hideout. A long shot, but worth a try.

'We do, however, know that Tracy has had dealings with several of the Roman Catholic gangs in the city. In light of the political and religious climate, he can no doubt count on support from some of their number.' Sillitoe nodded at Dreghorn. 'Inspector.'

Dreghorn faced the room. 'Tracy's involved in the organization of the Irish Sweep, which, as you'll know, is illegal in this country.' He paused, knowing full well how many of the detectives liked a bet and no doubt had Sweepstake tickets nestled in their wallets. Then he remembered the one in his own wallet, a gift from his mother. 'The tickets need to be smuggled in and sold under the counter, and the stubs and profits smuggled out. We believe that Tracy is working with the Catholic gangs to sell and distribute tickets throughout the city, maybe further afield. The world's gone Sweepstake-crazy. They're even making films about it in Hollywood.

'We've established that Tracy was originally using the bookie

Les Campbell as the distributor, but then accused Les of taking a bigger cut than was agreed, which he half denies. It looks like they've gone from Campbell to using the gangs as ticket touts.' For the moment he kept quiet about Bosseye's potential involvement.

Sillitoe nodded at Dreghorn's summation. 'Start pulling in gangsters for questioning. It's likely that one or more of them aided in the gaolbreak and know where Tracy and the others are hiding out. Apply pressure to your informants to assess what rumours they might have heard. And to contacts you have in the Protestant gangs, who might be happy to drop their enemies in hot water.

'The capture and arrest of Conall Tracy is now the number-one priority of each division in the city. All departments will work towards this aim, with detectives reporting to DCI Monroe and uniforms to Deputy Chief Constable McVicar, both of whom will report directly to me.' He gestured at Haldane, Quinlisk and the other Special Branch men, who somehow managed to stand apart, even in the crowded squad room. 'Superintendent Haldane and his men from Special Branch are our acknowledged experts on Tracy and the IRA and are here to offer their full cooperation in this matter, aren't you, Superintendent?'

'Sir.' Haldane, standing to attention, was as stiff as a ventriloquist's dummy, acquiescence being forced out of him.

'And we will offer the same courtesy in return.'

Downstairs, McDaid had learned from a gossipy Shug Nugent that Haldane had attempted to assume operational command of the hunt for Conall Tracy, placing it under Special Branch jurisdiction. Sillitoe had overruled the order, humiliating the superintendent and threatening to have him and his men dispatched back to Westminster if they refused to follow the chief constable's command. A Glasgow police officer had been murdered and the Glasgow Police would bring in his killers. No one else.

Sillitoe scanned the ranks of his detectives sternly. 'Ladies and gentlemen, see it through.'

McDaid made his way towards Dreghorn as the meeting broke up.

'Nice to see you made an effort for me,' he said.

Dreghorn frowned up at him. McDaid gestured at the inspector's loosened shirt collar and slack tie-knot.

'A little slovenly for a superior officer. What sort of example does that set?'

Dreghorn said, 'Aye, well, being throttled half to death kind of gives you an aversion to tight collars.'

Sillitoe was walking towards them, fixing his cap onto his head. McDaid caught a glimpse of the scar tissue on the back of the chief constable's right hand – a souvenir from Little Willie, the semi-tamed leopard that Sillitoe had shared his quarters with while serving as a police captain and district political officer in Northern Rhodesia during the war.

'Dreghorn, McDaid,' he said. 'Your devotion to duty does you credit, but after yesterday's incident, no one will think less of you if you require a day or two's rest and recuperation.'

McDaid drew himself to his full height, affronted. 'Don't worry, sir, we'll see things through all right.'

'To the bitter end,' promised Dreghorn.

Returning to the squad room, Dreghorn telephoned the Royal to check on Ellen and Strachan. Neither had regained consciousness, though the nurse he spoke to reiterated that Strachan was stable and no longer in danger.

'Hallelujah.' Dreghorn hung up, thinking of Ellen, pale and still in her hospital bed, and of her parents' lonely vigil.

'Bad news?' asked McDaid.

'Strachan's doing well.'

'That's bad enough in my book.'

'Ellen: no change. Still under observation.'

'She'll be all right, Jimmy. She's a strong lass.'

Dreghorn didn't answer. He stood up, rolled one shoulder awkwardly, prompting McDaid to ask, 'Are you all right?'

'Just stiff from getting thrown about yesterday.' He didn't say anything about the shoulder-holster under his jacket. Hardly regulation uniform, though he could argue they were plain-clothes. 'Check in with Shug Nugent about who was in and out of the station in the hours leading up to Tracy's transfer yester-day. Check the day before as well, just in case.'

'Where are you going?'

'To test the spirit of cooperation.'

He took the stairs, forcing himself to run despite the aches and pains, felt the weight of the holstered revolver against his chest. He rolled his shoulders again as he approached the Spe-cial Branch offices, opened the door without knocking. The rapid-fire conversation he could hear from the corridor ceased immediately. The occupants froze and stared at him on a scale that started at wariness, rose through various levels of hostility and stopped at sheer bloody murder. It was like walking into the Hollywood idea of a Wild West bar, with mugs of tea instead of firewater whisky, Alexander Haldane as the owner, Eugene Quinlisk as the local gunfighter and Graham Orr as the sal-oon gal from hell.

Haldane said, 'Can we help you, inspector?'

'I thought we were all helping each other now,' answered Dreghorn.

'To be sure, we are.' Quinlisk smiled graciously. 'And a grand feeling it is, too.'

'Appreciate your offer, Dreghorn, but as you can see' – Haldane gestured somewhat dismissively at Orr – 'Sergeant Orr is already giving us the benefit of his local knowledge.'

Orr sneered. 'Boyd and me know the city better than anyone.'

'True,' Dreghorn agreed, 'if you want to know the quickest way to the cheapest pubs, Graham's your man, but if you're interested in proper police work . . .'

The gears of Orr's brain ground slowly to formulate a suitable response, but Haldane raised a finger to silence him. 'Be brief, Dreghorn.'

'So do you still think that Conall Tracy has nothing to do with the Black and Tan murders?'

'Our investigation has moved on. I now acknowledge that might be a possibility, but far from a certainty.'

'After we first spoke in Sillitoe's office, I saw you in the Lodge, smiling and shaking hands with Boyd Strachan – thick as thieves, by the looks of it.'

'The inspector and I are acquainted.'

'From where? Police work or from when you both served in Ireland?'

'I've had the good fortune to work with him in both capacities – an exemplary soldier and a sterling detective.' The latter said as if it wasn't true of present company.

Dreghorn ignored the jibe. 'Would I be right in thinking that you and Strachan were involved in operations that would've resulted in deaths or casualties on the other side?'

Haldane's face hardened further, as if iced water had been injected into his veins.

'The sort of thing,' Dreghorn continued, 'that might result in someone seeking revenge a few years later . . .'

'From your military record, Dreghorn, I'd have thought you well acquainted with deaths and casualties in warfare. And the toll they inflict on all sides.'

'You've looked at my records?'

'Know your enemies, I believe it says somewhere.'

'We're on the same side, superintendent.'

'Then I'd advise you to start behaving like it, inspector.'

They stared at each other. The silence was broken by a striking match. Puffs of sweet-smelling tobacco swirled in the air between them.

'That's better, nothing like a pipe to relax you,' said Quinlisk, taking another puff. 'All these questions about each other, when we've got more important matters at hand. I'd have thought you knew everything about us you needed to by now, Jimmy. A little bird told me that someone else has been asking after us for you, going behind our backs. A lot of people see us' – he gestured with the pipe, a trail of smoke between himself and Haldane – 'as spies more than policemen, and maybe there's a bit of truth in that, because we have to be sly. We're dealing with criminals who'd put a bullet in your head or a bomb up your arse.'

'Who wish to destroy the very society around us,' Haldane added.

'But the thing about spies is that they don't like being spied upon. If you wanted to know something, you should've just asked.'

Dreghorn said, 'You wouldn't have answered.'

'Maybe, maybe not.' Quinlisk pointed his pipe at Dreghorn. 'But that might be more down to your manners than anything else. No offence.'

'I took it as a compliment.'

Quinlisk laughed. 'Incorrigible, that's what I'd call you, Jimmy. And it's not often you can say that about someone you've only known for the blink of an eye.'

Haldane snorted imperiously, already turning away as he said, 'Good day, Dreghorn. We'll be sure to pass on any relevant information.'

As he left, Orr gurning gloatingly after him, Dreghorn made a mental note to check on Denny Knox. The journalist's enquiries into the Special Branch officers might not have been as discreet as he thought.

CHAPTER 47

McDaid caught Dreghorn as he was returning from his expedition to Special Branch, glumness and grimness fighting it out in his expression. He became more purposeful when the big man relayed what he'd learned from Shug Nugent, though to be fair, the information wasn't exactly a surprise.

'And another thing,' McDaid said, 'Mrs Hepburn's wumman, Rachel What's-her-name? She's downstairs, asking to see you.'

Dreghorn ignored the big man's provocatively raised eyebrow as they started down the stairs, said, 'Fetch the Alvis.'

They nodded to Shug Nugent, and Dreghorn approached Rachel, seated opposite the reception desk near another woman, who held a handkerchief to her face.

Rachel stood up and McDaid heard Dreghorn say, 'Miss McAdam.' A stoatir of an opening line, wee man. Step aside, Noël Coward.

Rachel said, 'Jimmy, this is Helen Jardine.' She turned to the other woman, who looked up with teary, anguished eyes. 'She's a clerk at the courts, but her husband was the officer' – she lowered her voice respectfully – 'killed in yesterday's . . .' She tailed off.

Jardine. The constable inside the van with Dreghorn. McDaid immediately regretted his flippancy.

'She came into work this morning. Nobody expected her,

but she said she couldn't stay at home. All she could think about was what had happened . . . We saw in the paper that you were on the scene. Mrs Hepburn suggested that I bring Helen here to see if there was anything you could say that might be of comfort.' Rachel shook her head, suddenly angry at herself. 'I mean, of course there isn't. I shouldn't have . . . I should've telephoned first.'

Dreghorn looked like he wanted the earth to swallow him up. He touched Rachel's arm, told her it was all right, stepped over to Helen Jardine and offered her his hand.

'Mrs Jardine? I'm Inspector Dreghorn. I was with your husband.'

He gestured for her to walk with him to somewhere more private, but she was breaking down even as she was standing up, fresh tears welling in her eyes, sobs heaving through her body. Dreghorn reached out to steady her.

McDaid looked away at the same time as Rachel, neither of them wishing to intrude. He caught her eye and nodded help-lessly, then looked back.

Dreghorn was holding Helen Jardine as she wept, the sobs racking both their bodies, anger and guilt in his eyes, fading to a slow, strange desolation.

Once the tears had subsided enough, Dreghorn led Helen Jar-dine to the nicest interview room he could find, which wasn't saying much. Rachel accompanied them, taking the comfort-ing role that would normally have been played by Ellen Duncan. As punishment for his earlier sarcasm, Dreghorn ordered McDaid to make them some tea. A double-edged sword: the big man's brews were legendarily bad.

They let Helen Jardine talk, about how she and her husband

moved from Ardrossan after Jardine had been assigned to the Glasgow Police, inspired by what he'd heard of Chief Constable Sillitoe; about how, doing prisoner transports from the courts, he had alerted her to the job she had now, where she'd met Rachel and Mrs Hepburn; how they'd recently received word that they were to be given a police house and had talked of having children. Every word drove the loss deeper.

She said she couldn't believe David was gone, but at the same time couldn't stop thinking of him being shot, the agony he must have been in. She didn't know what she was going to do without him.

In their brief moments together, Dreghorn hadn't taken to Jardine, the flashes of bigotry and violence, but people were complex. The biggest bastard in one room could be the sweetest person in a different environment.

'It's no consolation at all, Mrs Jardine,' he said, 'but I was there. It all happened so fast that it would've been instant. David wouldn't have suffered.' He knew she would have been spared the finer details of the violence that had occurred, when officers informed her of her husband's death.

This time, when she stopped crying, Helen Jardine stood up and thanked them for seeing her. They walked her outside and Rachel offered to see her home, but she said she would be fine and even managed a grateful smile.

'Thanks, Jimmy,' Rachel said as they watched the small figure walk away. 'For what you said in there. No offence, but compassion's not usually what you associate with the Glasgow Police.'

'Aye, no bother.' He tried to keep the weariness from his voice as he reached for his cigarettes. 'I'm no' a bad liar when it's in a good cause.'

'What do you mean?'

'What happened . . . it wouldn't have been as painless as I made out. But she's the last person who needs to know that.' He spoke over her. 'And you don't want to know the nitty-gritty, either, believe me.'

She nodded. 'Sorry you had to go through it all again.'

'I'm part of the investigation.' He lit a Capstan, breathed out smoke. 'There's not much else on my mind.'

'Not the sort of thing it's easy to walk away from at the end of the day, I suppose. Sorry, again. I should've telephoned, but seeing your name in the paper, I was worried, wanted to make sure you were all right.'

'Worried about me?' Surprised, touched.

'Aye, don't say it like that. It was nice having a blether the other night, remembering the old days.' She laughed. 'Listen to me, I sound about a hundred.'

'You don't look it. Not one bit.'

The comment came out without thinking. He worried that he'd crossed the line, but Rachel smiled self-deprecatingly.

'Aye, right.' She glanced at St Andrew's-in-the-Square, almost directly opposite Central Police Headquarters. A thought came to her. 'Is St Alphonsus's still open? It's the anniversary of my ma's death. I like to try and light a candle if I can. And it sort of seems right after . . .' She nodded in Helen Jardine's direction.

St Alphonsus, known as the Church in the Barras, thanks to its proximity to Maggie McIver's market, was the third-oldest Catholic parish church in Glasgow, although the current building dated only from 1905. Its rich history and the fact that it was just around the corner from Turnbull Street had completely failed to lure Dreghorn inside during his time stationed there, which probably spoke volumes. He could have told Rachel that he had to go, the investigation pressing, but instead found himself strolling along London Road at her side, the church ahead of them.

'So you're still . . .' How to phrase it: practising, a believer?

'A good Catholic girl?' She shrugged. 'I don't know about that, but it's all still in there. Are you . . . ?'

'A good Catholic girl? Not the last time I looked.'

'You know what I mean. Do you still go to Mass?'

'Not for a wee while. In fact . . .' He stopped as he opened the door and stepped over the threshold, cringed as if expecting the worst. He relaxed after a moment, breathed a sigh of relief. 'No lightning bolts from above.'

'There must still be hope for you.' Rachel dipped her fingers in the stoup beside the door, crossed herself with holy water and started up the aisle towards the altar.

Dreghorn did the same – old habits die hard – and followed. He felt the same chill he always experienced on entering a church, of whatever denomination, the weight of a moral expectation that was designed to be unattainable. To keep believers eternally striving, even though he had encountered more than one priest who liked a bet and a bevvy or had been caught shagging a parishioner. Or worse.

He looked around, at the wealth on display, and couldn't help but see it as an edifice of exploitation. Honest beliefs and a desire for goodness moulded and manipulated for power, prestige and politics. He told himself to stop it; cynicism was corrosive.

Despite all that, he still genuflected at the end of the aisle before approaching the high altar, the always-shining gold of the tabernacle and the tortured effigy of Christ on the cross above it. Just the sort of image to fill the minds of impression-able young children with . . . what: Catholic guilt? Catholic bloody terror, more like. And don't mention the Inquisition.

To the side of the altar, Rachel stood by a simple rack of votive candles, a few flames flickering weakly. She dropped a coin in the donation box, selected a fresh candle and looked for something to light it with. Dreghorn offered her his Ronson Princess. She placed the candle gently on the rack, lit it and bowed her head silently. She smiled, handed back his lighter.

'Three years ago, but feels like yesterday,' she said. 'Cancer.'

Dreghorn nodded respectfully at the altar. 'God bless you, Mrs McAdam.'

'I thought you didn't believe.'

Dreghorn shrugged. 'Hedging my bets.'

He looked at the statue above the altar, the painted blood on Christ's head, the spear wound on his side, and saw again the bullet wounds in PC Jardine's corpse, the spatters of blood over his own suit. It welled up in him, demanded a release. The candles for the dead flickered as he told Rachel about Conall Tracy strangling Jardine and then coming for him. About the impact that separated them, and Tracy opening fire with the pistol.

'I hid behind Jardine as he fired,' he said, 'held him in front of me.'

'You were trying to stay alive.' Rachel touched his arms, looked into his eyes. 'If you hadn't, you might not be here, either. From what you've said, it was already too late for PC Jardine.'

'I can't know that for sure. It could be me that killed him. That poor lassie back there . . .'

Rachel embraced him, spoke softly. 'It wasn't you who pulled the trigger, Jimmy. It's not your fault. You did what you could, you did what you had to do. All right?'

He nodded slowly, felt a sigh leave his body, couldn't remember putting his arms around her. They held each other for a moment too long. The years fell away again. More innocent times. The possibility of different futures.

His cheek brushed hers as he turned towards her. She pulled away with an awkward half-smile, wiped away the tears he hadn't even been aware were on his face. He reached up to take her hand.

Whatever she saw in his eyes made her say, 'I'm married, Jimmy.'

'I know.'

She pulled her hand slowly free from his.

'To George Garrison.'

Dreghorn said nothing.

'I use my maiden name for work, the courts, in case people think there's a conflict of interest. He . . . wasn't always the way he is now.'

She sighed when he still didn't speak, then turned and walked away, fading into the shadows, footsteps echoing emptily on the tiled floor. No backwards glance.

The real world seeped back in. Dreghorn swore quietly, congratulated himself on being the biggest eejit on the planet. He turned back to the only other witness, Christ staring down impassively from the cross, having died for our sins, so they said. Probably didn't intend for humanity to view that as wiping the slate clean so they could start all over again.

He was about to say as much out loud when he detected movement behind him. He turned to see an elderly, kindly-faced priest approaching from the direction of the sacristy.

'Are you all right there, son?'

Dreghorn thanked the priest for his concern, said he was fine. The man's warmth made him regret his earlier cynicism. The dangers of confusing the institution with the individual.

'Would you like to talk,' the priest said, then gestured at the candles, 'or are there any lost souls you'd like to light a candle for?'

'There's no' enough candles, Father.'

CHAPTER 48

'He was deid before any shots were fired, Jimmy. End of story. You've seen enough corpses to know.'

'And if he wasn't, Archie? I didn't exactly have time to check his pulse.'

'Aye, well, we'll forget about that the now.'

Dreghorn stared straight ahead. 'I won't.'

The birdcage lift shunted to a halt. Dreghorn hauled open the concertina doors with a discordant screech and strode into a wood-panelled corridor, the plushness of which would impress clients, until they realized it was their money that paid for it.

George Garrison's top-floor offices occupied the corner of Queen Street and Royal Exchange Square, overlooking the Royal Exchange, where commodities and services from coal, iron and sugar to shipping and insurance had been traded ferociously in the days before the Depression, and the horse-back statue of the Duke of Wellington, gazing imperiously down Ingram Street as if still on the lookout for would-be Gallic conquerors. It was the heart of the financial district – a 'knicker-elastic snap', as Garrison liked to describe it, from the great and good of Glasgow. Garrison liked the great and the good; they had further to fall, and he was waiting to catch them.

The detectives marched towards the door to Garrison and Associates – no other names on the sign, no chance of equal billing alongside George Garrison. The lawyer, Shug Nugent had informed McDaid, was Conall Tracy's last visitor before the breakout. Too big a coincidence, in Dreghorn's book. He chapped loudly, entered before receiving a response.

Miss Hughes, Garrison's secretary, who was employed, Dreghorn suspected, more for her looks than for her competence, was rising to her feet. Her polite expression of greeting soured as she recognized them.

'We just need a wee word with George, hen,' McDaid explained, flashing his warrant card and manoeuvring his bulk to prevent her from squeezing past and alerting her employer.

'Mr Garrison is in a meeting.'

'With the blinds down?' Dreghorn asked.

All the offices within Garrison and Associates had interior windows that allowed the lawyers to observe each other, and their boss to spy on them, simultaneously promoting both a keen sense of rivalry and a climate of professional foreboding, if not fear. Garrison's own office, at the corner of the building, was the only one furnished with interior blinds, mysteriously lowered at the moment. This time Dreghorn didn't bother knocking.

The leather admiral's chair behind Garrison's grand desk was empty, but a blur of alarmed movement at the other end of the room alerted Dreghorn to the lawyer's whereabouts, leaping to his feet from a velvet chaise longue. Not that he'd been catnapping, at least not alone.

An attractive woman in her thirties was also sitting up hurriedly, buttoning her blouse in between flustered glances at the detectives.

'Sorry, Mr Garrison,' Dreghorn said, deadpan. 'We didn't know you were entertaining guests.'

'You're mistaken, inspector,' Garrison corrected him coldly. 'Mrs Dunbar is a client. A prospective client.'

'Really? Since when did the legal profession employ the services of a casting couch?'

'Perhaps he's taken up psychiatry,' McDaid suggested. 'Although I don't think they're meant to lie down with their patients.'

Miss Hughes bustled in behind McDaid, apologizing profusely. 'I'm sorry, Mr Garrison, they just barged past me.'

Garrison gestured to silence her, then stepped protectively close to the Dunbar woman, every inch the gentleman. 'I resent your sordid implication, gentlemen. Mrs Dunbar is under a lot of pressure. Her husband has been accused of irregularities within his business, putting their family finances under great strain in this Depression. She started to feel faint while we were discussing the situation. I was trying to make her comfortable and loosened her top buttons to give her air.'

'George Garrison for the defence . . .' Dreghorn said, then looked at Mrs Dunbar with sympathy. 'Are you all right, ma'am? We're police officers, you're perfectly safe. If anything untoward happened . . .'

Mrs Dunbar stood up, smoothing down her clothing with dignity. 'It's as Mr Garrison said, officer. I felt unwell – the pressure, you know.'

'Allow me to introduce Inspector Dreghorn and Sergeant McDaid.' Garrison straightened his tie. 'Two of Chief Constable Sillitoe's Tartan Untouchables, whose dedication to law and order keeps me gainfully employed.'

'There's a stake through the heart of our job satisfaction,' McDaid muttered.

'And celebrated wits to match – not always de rigueur in the

Glasgow Police.' Garrison's voice dripped sarcasm. 'I presume there's some legal matter you wish to consult me upon. Miss Hughes, if you could escort Mrs Dunbar' – an empathetic smile – 'to reception, we'll resume business shortly. And Miss Hughes? Come straight back. It's advisable to have witnesses present in some scenarios.'

As the women left, Garrison returned to his desk, but remained standing. The office was plush and tasteful, bookshelves of legal volumes, a large globe of the world that no doubt opened to reveal an extensive drinks cabinet, and a carpet so luxurious it almost invited you to lie down and sample the pile.

Dreghorn said, 'What do you think your wife would say about the way you do business?'

'I keep my professional and personal lives separate. You meet a lot of undesirable people in the course of this job.' Garrison fixed his gaze on Dreghorn. 'It's best not to take that home with you.'

'You didn't seem to be finding Mrs Dunbar very undesirable.'

Garrison didn't answer.

'Maybe we should tell Mrs Garrison – see how good you are at defending yourself outside court. I bet she deserves a lot fuckin' better than you.'

'I would describe that as police harassment. Infidelity isn't a crime, inspector. Doesn't come under your remit. Not that that's what you saw. As we've established.'

Miss Hughes had returned, and Garrison nodded for her to close the door.

McDaid, drawing his eyes uneasily off Dreghorn, asked,

'Who did you talk to, after you visited Conall Tracy on Thursday morning, George?'

Garrison started to speak, but Dreghorn talked over him. 'Just before Tracy was the subject of a gaolbreak that resulted in two deaths, one of them a police officer, and several casualties, some serious.'

The lawyer, who was almost the same height as McDaid, looked down on Dreghorn disparagingly. 'If you're implying that I had something to do with those events, inspector, then I'd advise you to tread carefully.'

'Shug Nugent confirmed that you were the last person to speak to Tracy before he was scheduled to be transported to Duke Street Gaol,' said McDaid. 'The decision to move him was only taken that morning. How could he possibly have got word to his accomplices outside, except through a go-between?'

'I was the last person to converse with Mr Tracy? In a station full of police officers? I rather doubt it, sergeant.'

'The last civilian,' said Dreghorn.

'I note that you're conveniently exonerating your fellow officers there. As if the Glasgow Police have an impeccable, blemish-free record when it comes to bias, bribery and corruption. I think you need to cast your net wider, inspector, and not let your feelings towards me cloud your judgement.'

'I have no feelings towards you, Mr Garrison.'

'Only the joy of past experience,' McDaid announced, stepping forward to loom over the lawyer. 'Doesn't defending clients that you know are guilty keep you up at night?'

'Innocent or guilty, every citizen in this country has the right to a vigorous and rigorous defence.' Garrison gave a thin smile.

'No matter how keen the police might be to lock some people up without a trial.'

Dreghorn said, 'So you're claiming that Tracy didn't tell you he was being moved that afternoon, and that you didn't then pass that information on to associates of his who subsequently carried out the attack?'

'I'm not saying anything, inspector. As you well know, to do so would violate the confidentiality that is guaranteed by law between a lawyer and his client.'

'Have you heard from your client recently?'

'The man's on the run. Not a course of action I would have recommended.'

'But you're still acting as if you're representing him. I presume that he absconded without paying what he owes. Wouldn't that make whatever contract is between you null and void, leaving you free to help the police with their inquiries?'

'Any financial transactions between Mr Tracy and me are also private and confidential, unless you plan to produce a court order? Also, the relationship between client and lawyer is based on mutual trust. It's almost a matter of honour. If I were to renege on that trust, it would destroy my reputation, which I'm sure is what you're hoping for.'

'Honour?' Dreghorn shook his head. 'I'm giving you the opportunity to help catch the men responsible for an explosion that devastated a city street, and caused the deaths of five people.'

'I appreciate your consideration, but even if I could, I'd be unable to help you.' Garrison's shrug was almost regretful. Almost. 'We're but two cogs in the great wheel of justice.'

'The spanner in the works more like, for you,' McDaid said.

Garrison ignored the big man. 'You have your job, I have

mine, and we're both bound by the rules of those jobs. You might be willing to bend the law to suit your own aims, but I most certainly am not.' The lawyer returned to his seat, pulling the chair close to the desk, and adopted the air of a judge about to pass sentence. 'Now, unless you have any other queries or wish me to accompany you to the station . . .' He nodded at Miss Hughes, who opened the office door.

'That'll do for now,' Dreghorn said. 'At least we know where we all stand. Give Mrs Garrison our regards.'

Miss Hughes walked them to the main door, wished them a cold, curt goodbye. They tipped their hats to Mrs Dunbar as they left. Heading for the lift, McDaid asked what Dreghorn made of Garrison's performance.

'Guilty as charged,' Dreghorn said, 'and laying it on so thick that I'd say he definitely passed on the information, even if he didn't know how far things would go. But we're unlikely to get the truth, the whole truth and nothing but the truth out of him – it's a matter of honour.'

'Honour among bloody thieves.'

'Aye, nothing to do with him being scared of getting a bullet in the head if he speaks out against his client.'

McDaid hauled the cage door of the lift shut, glanced at Dreghorn as he stabbed the button for the ground floor.

'What was all that about his wife? We can hardly arrest him for shagging around, much as we might like to.'

Dreghorn stared through the bars as the lift descended. 'Rachel McAdam – her married name's Garrison. She told me earlier.'

The big man flopped against the bars, jaw dropping as he struggled for something to say.

'You really know how to pick them, don't you, Jimmy?'

CHAPTER 49

Saturday, 8 April 1933

In Glasgow, within the chasm that exists between police and gangsters, law and lawlessness, there are a fair number of compromises made. Blind eyes are turned, certain indiscretions and misdemeanours are dismissed, often in return for information related to crimes of greater import. A nod, a wink, a wee scratch of the back and everyone's happy.

Not now. Not with one policeman dead, four in hospital and the men responsible at large. Now all blind eyes were wide open and scanning the streets with predatory precision. Now it was a slap, a punch and your face mashed into a gable end at high speed if you didn't cooperate.

A grinning Chopper McKenzie of the Cheeky Forty reached for his winnings at the pitch-and-toss school he ran at Spiers Wharf on the Forth and Clyde Canal, only for a size-fifteen oxford brogue to descend, trapping his hand and the coins underneath it.

There's only one man in this city with feet that big, thought Chopper, and smiled gingerly up at Bonnie Archie McDaid.

Entering Glasser's Barber Shop to collect the fee they charged for keeping the premises safe, Bert Rowan of the Calton Entry was plonked unceremoniously in the barber's chair and tried not to tremble as Jimmy Dreghorn cancelled that weeks protection payment and shaved off his eyebrows with a cut-throat razor.

Peter MacLean and Andrew Caldwell gritted their teeth and watched in trepidation as Archie McDaid juggled precariously with the bottles of booze they were restocking the Billy Boys' London Road shebeen with. The smashing of bottles in rapid succession threatened to drown out Jimmy Dreghorn as he informed them that the gangs' illegal drinking dens were out of business until they said otherwise, or the Billy Boys started cooperating.

Vinnie Wylie of the Cheeky Forty was plucked from between his fancy woman's thighs and dangled naked – apart from his socks – out of her second-floor window by Archie McDaid. An unexpected climax to the tryst, made even more alarming by the fact that Vinnie's own hoose was directly across the road on the same floor, and that his wife's favourite pastime was leaning out the window to collect gossip on their neighbours.

And it wasn't just Dreghorn and McDaid rampaging through the underworld, it was also Sammy Stirling, Big Fartie and the rest of the Tartan Untouchables, the Murder Squad and every other squad in every division. Today the Glasgow Police comprised the biggest gang in the city, and there was only one question they demanded an answer to.

'Where the fuck is Conall Tracy?'

'Whoa!'

Dreghorn raised a hand as McDaid started to turn onto Norman Street. Further along, another police car was drawing to a halt outside Bull Bowman's tenement. The big man reversed, keeping the Alvis partially out of sight of the other vehicle, but giving himself and Dreghorn a clear view.

They watched as Eugene Quinlisk, Graham Orr and three Special Branch officers emerged from the car. Quinlisk and his men scanned the street for suspicious activity, while Orr walked straight towards Bowman's close with the confidence of the completely ignorant. He cocked his head impatiently for the others to follow.

'Beat us to it,' McDaid said. 'What do you want to do?'

'Give them a couple of minutes to get settled, then we'll join the party.'

McDaid rolled the Alvis slowly up behind the Wolseley, keeping the engine running low. Getting out of the car, Dreghorn noted movements in the windows on either side of the road. Norman Street was a primarily Catholic neighbourhood, many of its inhabitants first- or second-generation Irish immigrants, some more recent. Here the mainly Protestant police force was held in as high esteem as the Billy Boys or the Orange Order. In the current knife-edge climate, the slightest misstep could spark a riot.

Two young boys came tearing out of Bowman's close, gabbing in their best men-of-the-world voices about the 'fuckin' polis'. They stumbled to a halt, tried to slink away inconspicuously on seeing the detectives.

'All right, lads?' McDaid asked.

'Aye, till we saw you, big man,' one of them blurted out and they ran off.

'If the drums hadn't already signalled our arrival, those two smouts certainly will,' McDaid said as they entered the tenement close, dank and dark, the tiled walls cold to touch. 'Won't be long before the Conks gather, I reckon.'

Dreghorn nodded agreement, led the way up the stone stair-way, winding around towards the first-floor landing. A woman's cry, angry shouts and the sounds of a struggle sounded on the floor above: Bowman's hoose.

They bounded up the steps. The woman was swearing now, but there was an edge of fear in her voice. The struggle con-tinued, chairs overturned, feet scuffing a linoleum floor. Bowman's house was at the opposite end of the landing. Dreg-horn covered the distance at a sprint, shouldered open the door.

He almost collided with one of the Special Branchers, pushed the man back to give himself room and looked around. The officer held a shorter man by the scruff of the neck: Bosseye, eyes wide with fear, now seeing things he didn't want to see.

Bull's wife Hannah was on the floor, skirt rucked up around her thighs as she kicked and struggled, the second Special Branch officer dragging her across the room by her hair. Orr stood to one side, lowering a hand from his face, scratches down one cheek and eyelid, where she had raked his face with her fingernails. He seemed shocked, out of his depth, glancing from Dreghorn to Eugene Quinlisk.

The Irishman, in the centre of the room, gave Dreghorn a sanguine smile. He held a Smith & Wesson revolver in his hand, aimed at no one in particular, which seemed to make its presence all the more threatening. He stood over Bull Bow-man, who was forcibly seated on a wooden chair, held there by the last Special Brancher. He raised his eyes to Dreghorn, face bloodied, pistol-whipped.

With the first Special Brancher knocked off-balance, Bosseye slipped free of his grip and started for the door, chancing a weak smile and a cheerful wave.

'I just stopped in for a blether, but if you folks have got business together, it's probably best if I go . . .'

'Nowhere – that's where you're going.' McDaid entered the room, closing the door with the finality of a coffin lid, forcing Bosseye to waddle backwards like a panicked penguin.

The big man pushed past Dreghorn, took in everything. Something primal and volcanic bubbled in him. He nodded at the second Special Branch man.

'If you don't take your hand off that lassie, I'll take your bloody arm off. And you' – a hard stare at Quinlisk – 'better be ready to use that gun.'

In amongst adrenaline and cold rage, Dreghorn felt a rush of affection for the big man. He wondered how quickly he could draw his own revolver, weighed up who to go for first if things went that way.

Quinlisk shifted the gun to aim at Bowman's head, kept his eyes on McDaid.

'Oh, but I am, big fellow,' he said, cocking the hammer. 'For the right cause, in the name of the law.'

Hannah Bowman called out her husband's name. The Special Branch man jerked her hair, told her to shut up.

'Put the gun away,' Dreghorn said. 'We'll do the questioning.'

'That's all we were doing, isn't it, Sergeant Orr, asking a few questions?' Quinlisk touched the barrel to Bowman's forehead, forced him to sit up straight. 'Mr Bowman here's the one who resisted arrest. Him and his wife. Brought all this trouble on themselves.'

'Bull's got a temper on him, Jimmy, youse two know that

better than anybody,' Orr argued with a surprising lack of conviction. He touched the bloody scratch marks on his face, and the old Orr quickly came back. 'Fuckin' so does she – just as bad, if not worse.'

Hannah Bowman struggled to her feet, forcing the Special Brancher to shift his grip from her hair to her arm, ready to twist it up her back. She glared at Dreghorn, gestured at her husband's battered features. 'Look at him, look what they did to him!'

Dreghorn said, 'If you want to press charges, Bull . . .'

'Aye, right,' Bowman scoffed, 'good one.' A reaction like that would make him a target for further police intimidation and lose him respect amongst the rank and file of the Conks. You can't go running to your mammy when you're the leader of the gang. Survival of the fittest. Law of the jungle.

McDaid looked around in disgust. 'Five of you, and you can't subdue one man without drawing a gun? Call yourselves policemen?' This last question directed at Quinlisk.

'I'm whatever the situation calls for, big fellow.' A quiet chill in Quinlisk's voice. 'I'm whatever needs to be done. Understand?'

Dreghorn said, 'Putting that gun away is what needs to be done. We'll take it from there.'

'Mr Bowman here is an accomplice of Conall Tracy's. You've seen them palling about together. He needs to tell us where Tracy is. And he needs to do it *now*.'

'I already told you,' Bowman said, 'I don't know. We've only met a few times; I hardly know the man. We're in the middle of a Depression – the only struggle I care about is putting food on the table. I might break a few laws and have the odd square go in the street, but stealing gelignite and blowing people up?' He shook his head in disgust, nodded at his wife. 'Hannah's got family in Vulcan Street, for fuck's sake! Her nephew was one of the lads playing football outside when the explosion went off.'

Quinlisk smiled apologetically; a dirty job, but someone's got to do it. 'I'm not sure I believe that. See, I'm told you're a big man about town, Mr Bowman. I think you know fine well where Tracy is. And I think you're going to tell me. The alternative won't very pretty. In front of your wife, too. Break her heart, so it will.'

'Dagger Kane introduced us,' Bowman eventually said, the words dragged out of him.

'Convenient, seeing as he's lying in hospital with his brains bashed out. Not much chance of him arguing the toss with you.'

'Doesn't change the fact that it's true.'

'Dagger used to work at the Garngad Explosives Magazine,' Dreghorn said. 'We reckon he was the one who helped get them inside for the robbery, maybe even told Tracy about it in the first place.'

Quinlisk nudged Bowman with the gun barrel.

'Dagger knows Tracy from way back,' Bowman said. 'He was in Dublin for that Easter palaver and they stayed in touch. A few bevvies and a free Ireland is all Dagger bangs on about. Liked to call himself the IRA's man in Scotland, though it was mostly all talk. Tracy wanted to speak to me about the Sweep when he learned that Les Campbell was ripping him off. Dagger set up a meeting to see if there was some way of cutting Les out without affecting the profits.'

Bowman glanced at Bosseye, who maintained an air of almost beatific innocence. Dreghorn tossed the book of Sweepstake tickets onto the table, nodded at the bookie. 'Yours, I believe.' Bosseye started to calculate the odds of getting away with a denial, but Dreghorn saved him the bother. 'We got them off Midge McConnell, out selling them in the street plain as day, so the game's a bogie.'

'You can rely on Midge – drops you in it every time.'

'To be fair, it was either that or come up smelling of shite,' said McDaid, stepping closer. 'Literally.'

Bosseye raised his hands. 'I don't know where Conall Tracy is, inspector, or anything about explosives or gaolbreaks or anything like, if that's what you're getting at. I've never even met him, cross my heart.'

'But the tickets come from him, directly or not, so who are you dealing with?'

Bosseye squirmed as though his proximity to McDaid was bringing him out in a rash.

'Me and Archie were in Vulcan Street when the bomb went off, Hamish,' Dreghorn said, using the bookie's real name. 'It could just as easily be one of us lying dead in the street. All bets are off.'

'With a vengeance,' McDaid promised.

Bosseye weighed the odds again, sighed. 'Dagger Kane and two other Irish fellows – Gerry and Frank, that's what they called themselves.'

Frank Cleary and Gerry Byrne, who had been keeping Dagger company in Betty's Bar and were now fugitives alongside Conall Tracy. Dreghorn and Quinlisk shared a grim look, though the Irishman's gun-hand didn't waver.

'They never gave their full names,' Bosseye continued. 'Dagger acted like he was in charge, but I think they were just humouring him, pulling his strings.'

'What happened with Les?' McDaid asked. 'Did they suss

out he was skimming off the top by themselves, or did someone who "sees things that no one else sees" point it out to them?'

Bosseye looked hurt. 'You always think the worst of people, sergeant.'

'Aye, and maybe one of these days I'll be proved wrong. But no' the day.'

Quinlisk stared down the barrel at Bowman. 'So all the guilty parties are dead, in hospital or on the run? All this begs the question: between this Kane fellow and the lazy-eyed leprechaun over there, what did Tracy need you for?'

Bowman straightened in his chair, menacing despite the gun at his head. 'Said it yourself – big man about town. Dagger talked a good game, but without my say-so—'

There was a shout from outside, a man's voice calling Bowman's name. It was joined by others, a crescendo of angry cries, demanding to know what was going on, if Bowman was all right, if he needed help.

Orr stepped to the window, peeked out. 'It's the Conks,' he said. 'The Norman Conquerors, Bull's gang, a whole crowd of them. Looking for trouble as usual.'

Dreghorn brushed Orr aside, looked for himself. He'd have described it as a mob, hostile and bloodthirsty, men gathering from every direction, streaming out of the closes. In the days before streetlights, they'd have been carrying pitchforks and burning torches. Now Dreghorn noted a few pick-shafts and hammers, other weapons no doubt concealed. Someone spotted him and pointed accusingly. He heard his name called out, then drowned in a torrent of curses.

'Bandit country out there,' he warned Quinlisk. 'Better watch your step.'

'The Norman Conquerors?' Quinlisk laughed, as if at the

deluded grandiosity of the title. 'You don't look like you could conquer much right now, Mr Bowman. Just the opposite. Last chance. Where's Conall Tracy?'

The shouting outside grew louder, fiercer. There was the sound of shattering glass – car windows being broken or empty bottles being transformed into makeshift blades.

'What're you going to do, make your wife a widow out of sheer bloody-mindedness?'

Bowman spat blood onto the floor, enough to splash Quinlisk's shoes.

Quinlisk shook his head. 'Nobody's bloodier-minded than me.' He squeezed the trigger.

Hannah Bowman screamed. Bull Bowman jerked backwards, gasping.

The hammer clicked on an empty chamber.

Quinlisk turned the revolver on Dreghorn and McDaid, stopping them as they started forward. Dreghorn's hand was inside his jacket, closing around his own gun. Quinlisk held his aim for a moment, then slowly lifted the barrel to the ceiling and pulled the trigger on the remaining chambers, all empty.

'The looks on your faces . . .' He shook his head, smiled. 'Come on, lads, don't tell me you haven't pulled a few dirty tricks in your day.'

He returned the Smith & Wesson to the shoulder-holster under his jacket, glanced over his shoulder and, with excruciating politeness, thanked Bowman for his help. The gang leader swore back.

'The very same to you, Mr Bowman.' Quinlisk nodded for the Special Branch man to release Hannah Bowman. 'And to your lovely wife.'

'Bastard,' she said as she rushed past Quinlisk to embrace her husband.

'A not unreasonable assessment, ma'am.'

Quinlisk waved Orr and his men out before him, then stopped in the doorway. He patted the firearm under his jacket.

'The next time it'll be loaded, whoever's in my way.'

McDaid glared after the Irishman. 'I didn't think it was possible for me to dislike that wee man any more. He gives Strachan a run for his money.'

Hannah was crouched in front of her husband, hugging him, crying. Dreghorn looked away respectfully as Bowman whispered softly that he was all right, kissed her forehead and wiped her tears away.

She turned to glare at Dreghorn. 'I went to see my sister after the explosion. She said there'd been a lot of new faces hanging around Vulcan Street. No' just whoever was using the Semple lad's hoose, but others too. In suits, she said, but they looked like polismen, just like them –' she nodded after Quinlisk '– except they didn't seem interested in arresting anybody, just watching all the comings and goings.'

Bull placed a calming hand on her shoulder then leaned back in the chair and shook his head in disbelief at the detectives.

'Christ, what's the world coming to when you're glad to see Jimmy Dreghorn and Archie McDaid stepping through your door?'

CHAPTER 50

The Royal Infirmary loomed over Townhead district like a warning to the citizens of Glasgow not to get sick, its walls, golden sandstone when originally constructed, filmed with the same grime and pollution that tarred the rest of the city and seeped into the skin and hair and lungs of its residents.

The Scots baronial facade, Gothic and imposing, made Dreghorn think of the surgeons of an earlier era, advancing medical science and burnishing their God-complexes by dissecting fresh corpses supplied by unscrupulous resurrectionists, some of whom skipped the rigmarole of digging up graves by going straight to the source and murdering victims on the streets. He admonished himself for such ungracious thoughts; the Royal's doctors and nurses had more than likely saved his life six months earlier, after a madman had tried to end it with an onslaught of blade and bullets.

Injured in the same hellish night, McDaid also paused as they got out of the Alvis. He nodded at the building. 'Gies me the heebie-jeebies as well.'

Ellen Duncan's parents were still with her, Sandy asleep in a chair, worn down and weak, Marjorie by the bedside, holding her daughter's hand. Dreghorn could almost hear her bones creak as she rose to greet them, wondered how long it had been since she last moved.

Keeping his voice low, he asked if there had been any change.

'They say she's not any worse, but she still hasn't woken up,' Marjorie replied. 'I've been sitting with her, talking nonsense mainly, just so she knows she's not alone. Sometimes I think I see her eyelids flutter and I get all excited, but . . .' She couldn't continue, looked at her husband, his deathly pallor almost matching Ellen's.

McDaid placed a hand on her arm, willing some of his own strength into her. 'Well, if you ever need a break, just say. Me and Jimmy can talk nonsense for Scotland.'

They stayed for as long as they could bear, McDaid growing restless and claustrophobic as the walls closed in, rage running through Dreghorn, stretched taut, ready to snap.

The doctor they'd first spoken to when Ellen was admitted spotted them as they stepped back into the corridor. Inspector Strachan, he informed them, had recovered consciousness. The hospital had instructions to telephone a Sergeant Orr at Turnbull Street, but seeing as they were already here, could he rely on them to pass on the good news? Of course, Dreghorn assured him, nodded at the door to Strachan's room and asked, 'Are his family still with him?'

'Earlier, but they've not long gone home to get some rest and freshen up. They'll be back later.'

'Can we speak to him, doc? It's important.'

A reluctant nod. 'Not for long, though. He's still weak, I don't want you tiring him out.'

'Don't worry, we'll be gentle.'

'Fuck, it's the ugly sisters of the nursing profession.'

In contrast to Ellen, Boyd Strachan seemed in rude health. He was seated, propped up against a pile of pillows, clad in a hospital goonie, one arm in a sling. The bedclothes were pushed back off his wounded leg, his stocky thigh swathed in bandages, which had obviously been making him hot and bothered. His moustache, normally trimmed like prizewinning country-house topiary, was unkempt. Ginger-and-white stubble tinged his jawline.

'Looking well, Boyd,' Dreghorn said. 'How are you feeling?'

'Fine till I saw youse.' Strachan looked at McDaid. 'The doc said you fixed a tourniquet around my leg with your belt to slow the bleeding. Might've saved my life.' His moustache twitched; a pained grimace. 'Cheers, big man.'

'Don't remind me,' McDaid growled.

Dreghorn strolled around the bed, examining Strachan's leg like a surgeon with a propensity for amputation.

'Just passing. Thought we'd pop in and help you out with your statement.'

'I'll save it for Sergeant Orr. Or DCI Monroe. Anybody other than you, Jimmy.'

'There's gratitude for you, Archie,' Dreghorn said to McDaid.

Strachan snorted. 'It wasn't you that helped me. I know fine well how it'd have turned out if you'd been there all on your ownio.'

'No, I was too busy trying to help Ellen. If anybody saved your life, it was her. And look where it got her, lying on the ground with her head caved in, blood everywhere.'

Strachan's expression darkened.

'She's just along the corridor, did they tell you that?' Dreghorn continued. 'Still unconscious. And here you are, large as fuckin' life.'

'It wasn't me who attacked her.' Strachan's voice was level, controlled. No remorse. No regret. No weakness.

'No, but it was *you* he was after. You, Rex Smith, Harold

Beattie and Ronnie Anderson, the old pals' brigade. Ellen was just caught in the middle, wrong place, wrong time.'

'Anderson?'

'Killed the day before you were shot,' McDaid said. 'Found at the bottom of the cellar stairs in the King's Arms, head stoved in against a beer barrel, so they reckoned he'd taken a tumble when he was stocious. Didn't find the bullet till after you were here.'

Strachan didn't respond, looked straight ahead, feeling Dreghorn and McDaid's presence on either side. He seemed paler now, his skin clammy. Pain and discomfort from his wounds or something deeper?

Dreghorn said, 'If you'd come clean about your past association with the murder victims, you'd have been off the case and none of this' – he gestured at Strachan, nodded in Ellen's direction – 'would've happened.'

'Conall Tracy was under arrest. It was over. Case closed.'

'You seem pretty sure it's him behind it all.'

'Who else could it be? It all makes sense.'

'Don't know, but Tracy didn't break out of the cells, shoot you and break back in again.'

'No, it took you to let him out.' Strachan nodded at a newspaper on the bedside cabinet, its gaolbreak headlines emblazoned across the front page.

'Why did you hide the fact that you knew Smith and Beattie from the Black and Tans?' McDaid said, shooting Dreghorn a look: *caw canny.*

Strachan laughed. 'I didn't hide anything, big man. It was one possible avenue of investigation and it was being followed, like all the others.'

'By you on your own, all hush-hush, like a wee, sleekit, cowering, timorous beastie?'

'Not at all. Speak to Sergeant Orr. You'll find he was party to everything we were looking into.'

'Really?' Dreghorn said. 'He seemed fairly unsure when we mentioned it the other day.'

'Ask him again.'

'After you've had a chance to jog his memory . . .'

'Superintendent Haldane as well. I kept him abreast of our inquiries. Purely in the spirit of cooperation, you understand.'

'Over and above colleagues in your own police station?'

'We're hardly best pals, Jimmy. Your professional jealousy sees to that. That's why you only came visiting with sour grapes.' Strachan smiled, chuffed with his own wit.

Dreghorn asked, 'What happened at Tralee, Boyd?'

The moustache straightened; the smile vanished.

Dreghorn seemed to have moved closer, his voice quiet and reasonable. 'Tralee, November 1920. Black and Tans and Auxiliaries ran riot over seven days and nights, terrorized the population, burned half the town to the ground. Afterwards Smith, Beattie and Anderson were sent back to Scotland, dishonourable discharge. We know Churchill never intended the Tans to be Boy Scouts, so whatever they did, it must have been bad. Bad enough to make someone come after you, all these years later?'

'Like I said, I'll give my statement to Sergeant Orr or DCI Monroe.' Strachan stared straight ahead again.

Dreghorn smiled at McDaid as if that seemed reasonable enough, said, 'Hear that, Archie? All settled, he'll give his statement to Orr or Monroe.'

The big man unfolded his arms, suddenly wary.

Calmly, still smiling, Dreghorn clamped his hand onto Strachan's bandaged thigh, directly over the bullet wound, and squeezed, fingers clawing.

CHAPTER 51

Strachan cried out, his body bucking in agony. He swung at Dreghorn with his free hand, but the detective grabbed the wrist, pinioned it.

'Jesus, Jimmy!' McDaid started towards Dreghorn, appalled.

'Stay by the door, big man,' Dreghorn warned. 'Or step back out into the corridor and look in on Ellen. Remind yourself of the state she's in, while laughing boy here refuses to speak to us.'

McDaid held himself back, glared at Dreghorn, shaking his head.

Strachan was writhing furiously, grunting and breathing hard, but trying not to cry out again, to show more weakness. Dreghorn released him and he slumped forward, gasped for air.

'Tralee, Boyd,' Dreghorn said. 'What happened?'

'Fuck off, Dreghorn!'

Dreghorn grabbed Strachan's wrist again, held it fast against the iron frame of the bed. His other hand hovered over Strachan's thigh. A small, faint bloodstain was beginning to seep through the bandages. Dreghorn raised his eyebrow, part question, part threat.

'Did you no' hear me?' Strachan muttered through gritted teeth. 'I said—'

Dreghorn grabbed his thigh, squeezed, thumb pressing into the bloodstain. It grew bigger, the colour deepening. Strachan writhed and swore in explosive gasps of pain. McDaid turned his back, torn, unable to watch, his entire body tensed. Dreghorn curled his thumb for added pressure. Strachan looked up at him, brow furrowed.

'Stop!' he whimpered.

Dreghorn released his grip.

'Bastard!'

McDaid turned back, eyes on Dreghorn. His expression echoed Strachan's comment.

'Last time: what happened in Tralee?' Dreghorn's voice was still calm. No remorse. No regret. No sign of backing down.

Strachan glared up at him defiantly. Dreghorn reached for the wound once more, but Strachan raised a hand, the fight gone out of him.

'All right, all right,' he said. 'Give me a minute . . .'

Dreghorn heard McDaid's slow sigh of relief. He produced his cigarettes, offered Strachan one, then lit them both. The tension in Strachan's body eased as he exhaled. He stared into the smoke as it misted the air before him.

'Wasn't quite what I thought I was signing up for, but there wasn't much work around after the war, and my daughters were both wee, so I didn't have much choice. The money was some of the best going for our sort – ex-soldiers, men who'd seen action.

'We were barracked at Listowel, stuck with shitey ragtag uniforms and equipment. Under siege, it felt like. We ventured out under threat of violence, and we were the threat of violence. That's what Churchill and General Tudor wanted. Fight fire with fire. "We have murder by the throat," Lloyd George boasted. Daft bastard. Sheer bloody murder all round, that's what it was. I saw that as soon as I arrived.

'You know what mast my colours are pinned to – no Pope of Rome in my book, but over there it was different, deeper, carved into them, going back so far it's in their blood. British, Irish, Unionist, Republican, Protestant, Catholic . . . how's anybody meant to keep the peace amongst all that?'

Strachan was smoking furiously as he talked. Dreghorn passed him an ashtray from the bedside cabinet. Strachan almost didn't seem to notice, carried on talking.

'Not that that's what we were there for, no' really, no matter what the official line was. Our purpose was to intimidate and menace, but it wasn't like in the war, with the enemy over there' – Strachan nodded across an imaginary no-man's-land – 'in a different uniform. It was ordinary people, Paddys and Micks in civilian clothes, shooting at you from bushes at the side of a country lane, or from alleys and bedroom windows in streets that all looked the same. We didn't know who the fuck the enemy was, so everybody became the enemy.'

Strachan crushed out his cigarette. Dreghorn was already moving to offer him another. He accepted with a look of bitterness and resentment that seemed to encompass himself as well as Dreghorn.

'Us or them. Tit-for-tat. They kill one of us, we kill more of them. We arrest and interrogate; they kidnap and torture.' The sarcasm in his voice noted the fine line between the distinction: one person's freedom-fighter is another's terrorist.

Strachan drew on the cigarette as if it was the elixir of life. 'Except that they always knew where we were: our barracks, the roads we used, the routes we took. We were always flailing around, lashing out because we didn't know who the bastards were, where they were, who was a sympathizer, who wasn't.' He looked at McDaid as if expecting the big man to understand, empathize. 'Guerrilla warfare, big man. It's no' the same as the Somme or Ypres. You're always on edge, wondering are they friend or foe? And thinking best no' take any chances.'

McDaid gave nothing away. His war had been in Mesopotamia and Palestine, street to ruined street, hand-to-hand, under the merciless Middle Eastern sun or the icy cold of the desert night.

'Eventually,' Strachan said, 'whenever we suffered losses in an attack, we were told to target the civilian population in reprisal. Never saw written orders to that effect, of course, but that was the policy. The thinking was that if you targeted civilians – burned homes, killed livestock, destroyed crops – then they would put pressure on the IRA, force them to stop their campaign and drive their leaders to the negotiating table.'

'How did that work out?' McDaid bristled with cynicism. His own ancestors had suffered in Scotland's Clearances, homes and livelihoods destroyed when landlords put profitability over people and sent in the troops. They were forced to the towns and cities, into the iron embrace of industrial labour. Some went overseas, to America and Canada, never to be seen again. Clearances – an anodyne description for such inhumanity, as if they were an embarrassing, ill-bred mess to be brushed away and forgotten about.

Strachan's laugh became a cough, smoke catching in his throat. 'It didn't. Just made everybody hate everybody else all the more.' He glanced at Dreghorn on the word 'hate'.

'We seem to be going all around the houses here, Boyd,' Dreghorn noted.

Strachan fell silent. 'Fag,' he said.

Dreghorn fished out his Capstans. Only one left. He tossed it onto the bed, crushed the pack.

Strachan waited until the cigarette was lit before speaking again. 'You need to understand the situation.'

'Not guilty, Your Honour,' Dreghorn said. 'It wasn't me; it was the situation.'

'I'm no' making excuses. Done some shameful things. I'm sure we all have, in war and out of it.' Draw. Exhale. 'I was a sergeant, supposed to impose discipline, but it was hopeless. Smith, Beattie, Anderson, decent enough soldiers when we served in France, but over there, fired up with booze and big-otry, seeing enemies everywhere, real or imagined, they were little better than thugs. And nothing to make them think that the powers-that-be wanted them to be anything other than that.'

'But not you?'

Strachan straightened as if to attention. 'I had a bit of self-respect. I was mentioned in dispatches at Ypres and had a wife and weans I wanted to look in the eye when I got back.'

'Tralee,' Dreghorn repeated.

Strachan nodded resignedly. 'It was after the execution of Kevin Barry, the first Republican to be hanged since the Rising. Things were escalating on both sides. Two Black and Tans were kidnapped by the IRA. We put a notice up in Tralee, the largest town, warning that reprisals of a nature unheard of in Ireland would take place if they weren't returned by the next morning. Tell the truth, everybody knew they were already dead. We laid siege to the town to stop people coming or going, set a curfew and raided it night and day.

'It was the usual story on the raids. Bottles being passed around, everyone raging, so-called officers barely in control or as drunk as their men. Third day of the siege, before we set off again, a truck full of Auxiliaries and a big black Wolseley

pulled up. We weren't keen on the Auxies – a lot of the stuff
they carried out was blamed on Tans. They were just as bad as
us – worse, but they were officer class, know what I mean? A
law unto themselves. The others were Military Intelligence,
operating out of Dublin Castle.

'Haldane was in charge, a captain back then. Quinlisk was
with him, though he wasn't in uniform, puffing away on his
pipe and smiling like it was all one big joke. They'd driven
down from Dublin when they heard about the attack. I was
told that my squad would be under Captain Haldane's command for the operation. Quinlisk slipped an arm around my
shoulders like we were old pals and briefed me.

'They were after a woman – "Aren't we always?" he joked –
who was hiding out in a property in Cork. Bernadette . . .
something-or-other, I can't remember. The sister of Conall
Tracy, an IRA commander who worked hand-in-hand with
Michael Collins. She was an active force in her own right, one
of the first women into the Post Office during the Easter Rising,
Quinlisk said – a Browning semi-automatic in one hand and a
typewriter under her other arm. Really, though, they wanted
her to use as leverage against her brother, force him to surrender or become a double-agent. Conall Tracy was near the top of
the "Hue and Cry", the list of wanted men.

'She had her son with her, too young to be involved, ten or
eleven. We were told to make sure he wasn't harmed, in case
that pushed Tracy over the edge. Quinlisk showed us a photo
of him and his mother, so we'd know them on sight. She was
staying in a house in Tralee, helping to organize campaigns
for some women's movement that was allied with the
Republicans.'

'Cumann na mBan,' Dreghorn said.

'Aye, you would know, wouldn't you? Anyway, looking back, they probably wanted me and my men to pick her up to divert attention from the fact that it was Military Intelligence who were after her. And to cover their arses if something went wrong.'

'And did it?'

'By the time we got there, the main force was already on the randan – houses burning, folk getting beaten up in the streets, women and weans running about screaming, cars on fire, shops and pubs looted. Normally we'd have been in the middle of it, but seeing it at a distance . . .' Strachan took a final, bitter draw of his cigarette, stubbed it out. 'I remember Quinlisk looking at me and saying how "thorough you boys are at the old wanton destruction", like it was all a laugh. And hearing Beattie and Anderson yelling encouragement: "Go on, get into them!" '

Dreghorn and McDaid glanced at each other, wondering how reliable a narrator Strachan was, how much the story was being twisted to allow the murder detective to shine a more favourable light on himself.

'We arrived at the house where Bernadette was staying. There were a couple of weans outside. The oldest was the son, trying to keep us back from the front door with a shovel he could hardly lift, let alone swing. Quinlisk snatched it off him and we stuck a bucket over his head, told him to stay where he was or else . . .'

'You put a bucket on his head?' said McDaid.

'It was just something we did; don't ask me how it started. We kept buckets in the trucks to put over children's heads during raids, if there were any around. To spare them the sights, you know.'

To make sure there weren't any witnesses, thought Dreghorn. Or to spare the Tans the looks of accusation and corrupted innocence in the young eyes.

'We stormed the house. Big place. I went up the stairs, Smith, Beattie and Anderson searched the downstairs. Quinlisk stayed outside, smoking his pipe, letting us do all the work. In one of the bedrooms it looked like someone had been packing and was interrupted, clothes all higgledy-piggledy. There was a loaded pistol lying on top of the pile. I nabbed it, stuck it in my belt, said, "No' the day, hen." Famous last words.

'Heading back down the stairs, I heard a woman's cries from further in the house. We had orders not to hurt anyone unless we had to, especially Tracy's sister, but I wouldn't have put anything past Rex Smith . . .

'I went down the corridor, kicked open the door into the kitchen. Sure enough, fuckin' Smith and his cronies were in there. Smith was struggling with Tracy's sister, holding her over a table. Looked like he was trying to . . .' Strachan left the rest unsaid. 'And laughing away in that horrible, raspy voice of his – you know he was shot in the throat during the war?'

McDaid nodded, gestured for Strachan to continue, sickened by the way the story was unfolding.

'Anderson and Beattie were there too, holding a young fellow captive, laughing and jeering for all they were worth. He was trying to fight them off, but I didn't get a good look at him – more pressing matters, you know? I pulled Smith off Bernadette and went to hit the bastard, but before I could, she grabbed the gun from upstairs from my belt – might have been hers in the first place. Don't know if she meant to fire or if it went off accidentally, but . . .'

He paused pulled up his gown on the opposite side to his

wounded leg. Amongst the thick ginger hair that crawled across his belly was a round pucker of scar tissue.

'I grabbed Bernadette as I fell and brought her down with me. I remember us staring at each other as we hit the floor. And then a rifle butt came down on her head. Once, twice, I don't know how many times. I think it was Smith – he was the closest – but I can't be sure.

'I was in and out of consciousness after that. I came to on a stretcher outside, saw Smith crouched down, talking to Bernadette's lad. Then he whipped the bucket off the boy's head, shoved him away with a warning, by the looks of it.' Strachan shook his head. 'Everything was red and orange, fires burning everywhere. The colours of hell, I remember thinking at the time. Fuckin' hell . . .'

His voice had lowered to a dry whisper. Dreghorn poured water from a jug on the bedside cabinet, pressed the glass into Strachan's hand. He sipped tentatively.

'They shipped Smith, Beattie and Anderson back home, booted them out of the Tans. I've had no contact with them since, other than as deid bodies. I was told Tracy's sister didn't recover from her injuries. Died soon afterwards. When I healed up, I was given an honourable discharge and sent home. Joined the polis no' long afterwards. I don't know what happened to her son or the other fellow there. Never found out who he was, either. You don't ask questions in the army, you know that.'

'But being a detective is all about asking questions,' Dreghorn said. 'It didn't cross your mind that Smith and the other murders might be related to your time in Ireland? That somebody over there might have harboured a grudge, wanted revenge?'

'Aye – Conall Tracy.'

'When he broke out of the cells, shot you and broke back in again?'

'Or his accomplices. You're going round in circles, Jimmy.'

Dreghorn paced the bedside. 'You expect us to believe you defended some woman's honour out there, after the way you've treated Ellen?'

'I treat Constable Duncan with the respect due to a close and valued colleague.' Smug, now. 'As I'm sure she'd tell you. Otherwise, why would she have asked me to walk her home?'

'Asked you, my arse. She'd have run a mile. You're the last person she'd want to be alone with.'

'Sounds like you're the one who's got his eye on her. Right enough – more respectable than your current fancy woman.'

Dreghorn felt a creeping emptiness in his stomach.

Strachan looked at McDaid. 'Know where he's been spending his nights, big man? Kitty Fraser's. Her old man was the "Who's Who of Hoors". What do you think that makes her?'

McDaid said nothing, but Dreghorn could read his expression: *ya bloody eejit.*

'You're the one who's in her pocket, Boyd,' Dreghorn said. 'Hers and Teddy Levin's. We've seen the bribes, remember? The backhanders in brown envelopes.'

During a prior investigation Dreghorn had witnessed Kitty Fraser handing over a payment to Strachan and Orr. The money was from Teddy Levin, who, in addition to gaining protection from the two police officers, also occasionally acted as an informant, setting up rival criminals for arrest and prosecution and ensuring that his own power never waned.

Dreghorn had given Strachan an ultimatum: stay away from Ellen Duncan or he would reveal the murder detective's corruption to Sillitoe. It had seemed to work, but lately Strachan had become bolder, and now Dreghorn knew why. He silently cursed himself as he recalled the feeling of being spied upon that sometimes troubled him when he visited Kitty. He had been.

Strachan stroked his moustache, failing to wipe away his smile. 'That was only ever your word against ours, Jimmy. Don't think Percy would take much notice of your word now. You're in a lot deeper than her pockets . . .'

Dreghorn grabbed Strachan's thigh again, with more force than before. Strachan howled in pain, lashed out with his good hand, but Dreghorn raised his forearm to block the blows. Squeezed harder, the bandages damp with blood under his hand. Strachan was talking, pleading, but Dreghorn couldn't hear the words, focused only on his grip, on the pain he was inflicting. Felt nothing. No regret. No remorse. No—

A big hand closed around his wrist, squeezed with a strength and pressure he could never match. An arm encircled his neck from behind, not enough to hurt, but to give fair warning.

'Enough, Jimmy.' McDaid spoke quietly.

Dreghorn pulled against the big man, continued to dig his fingers into Strachan's wound. McDaid lifted him almost onto his toes, applied enough pressure on his neck to make his head swim.

'Enough.'

Dreghorn released Strachan, pulled free of McDaid's grip and stepped away. He glared at the big man, took a breath, then raised his hands, acknowledging that he was in control again.

Strachan was hunched forward, gasping, perhaps sobbing. McDaid told him that they'd send for a nurse. Strachan looked up as they headed for the door, tears of pain in his eyes, snot dribbling down his moustache. He wiped it away with the back of his hand.

'I'll fuckin' kill you, Dreghorn,' he said. 'You're a dead man, you hear me?'

Dreghorn stopped in the doorway, fixed on his hat. 'Language, Boyd. Matron'll wash your mouth out with carbolic.'

Strachan gave him a cruel smile. 'In fact I'll do worse than that. You'll wish you were dead.'

McDaid nursed his wrath until they were outside and about to get into the Alvis. He slammed his hand down on the roof, somehow didn't leave a dent.

'George Garrison's missus? Kitty Fraser – Billy Hunter's sister? The—' He bit off the rest of the sentence, unable to finish it, then threw his arms into the air. 'Who're you going to go canoodling with next: Fay Wray? Have King Kong stoating down Sauchiehall Street after you?'

'It's one of those things, it just happened. I should've told you.'

'Those things don't just happen, Jimmy. At some point it's an aye-or-no decision. And you jumped the wrong way.' McDaid's voice softened. 'Look, I know what she's been through, I know what she's lost, and you, but . . . Two wrongs and all that.'

Suddenly weary, Dreghorn leaned his elbows on the car roof, bowed his head, wondered about his life.

'If Sillitoe finds out . . .' Again McDaid left the rest unsaid, nodded back at the Royal. 'Did you believe him – Strachan?'

'Reckon he probably massaged the truth to make his own part in the affair more noble, but do I think he tried to help Tracy's sister? Much as it pains me to say it . . .'

'Pained him more.'

'Aye, I think I do. I guess sometimes bad people can do good things.'

McDaid grunted, drew his eyes off Dreghorn. 'Good people doing bad things, that's what worries me.'

CHAPTER 52

'Lucky I'm ambidextrous, eh?' Denny Knox said, stabbing at the typewriter keys with the fingers of his left hand like some native fisherman trying to impale a particularly evasive aquatic target with a spear.

He concentrated for a few letters more, then hit the carriage return and looked up at Dreghorn and McDaid in time to the resulting *ping*. A couple of other *pings* answered Knox's call, but otherwise the music of the *Scottish Daily Express* newsroom – the staccato thump of typewriter keys and the ringing of carriage returns – was muted. Most of the reporters had finished for the day, heading home or being waylaid by the magnetic pull of the Press Bar downstairs. Normally Knox would have been with them, but today he was on a go-slow, not through choice.

'Whoa, what happened there?' McDaid asked when he saw the plaster cast that encased the reporter's right hand.

'Caught it in a door,' Knox answered. 'An accident – cue inverted commas. Did your pal no' tell you?'

'What pal?'

Knox sighed, sat still for a moment, then awkwardly opened a drawer on his right-hand side and lifted out a half bottle of Bell's. He swallowed the dregs of whatever was in the chipped mug beside his typewriter and attempted to unscrew the lid of the bottle with his left hand. Dreghorn took the bottle, opened it and poured.

Knox nodded for a larger measure, said, 'Bottoms up' and took a sip. 'He didn't actually give a name – obviously didn't feel the need – but I sussed out who he and his boys were right away. Never noticed at the time, but they were waiting for me in a big black car, a Wolseley maybe, when I left the Press Bar the other night. Held off till there was nobody around, then drew up alongside and bundled me in. Two big fellows up front, a shorter one in the back, puffing away on his pipe. "Sure, and it's a grand night out you've been having, by the looks of you, Mr Knox," he said, "but you better watch out, easy to hurt yourself on the way home, pie-eyed like that."'

'Quinlisk,' McDaid said.

Knox carried on between swigs of whisky, conjuring up the quiet menace he'd felt in the car. 'All very polite on the surface, smiles, winks, compliments about my writing, a friendly pat on the knee, but underneath . . . He said he'd heard that I was asking around after him and his colleagues, but that he wouldn't dream of asking on whose behalf or demand that I give up my sources – he already knew it was you two.'

The detectives shared a reproachful look.

'He implied that he could be a good friend, able to give me far more important stories than a couple of deadbeat street-polis. As long as I remembered my place and maybe did the odd favour in return. I thanked him, said I'd think about it, and he nodded for the driver to stop. The other man got out and opened the door for me. As I was getting out, Quinlisk shook my hand, told me it was an honour to meet an honest-to-God crusading journalist, then said, "Close the door after him." Except he was still gripping my hand. I pulled free, but the door was already slamming . . .'

'Bastard!' McDaid turned away in anger, looked around as if

the Irishman might have been spying on them from the shadows of the newsroom.

'Sorry, Denny.' Dreghorn poured Knox another dram. 'We shouldn't have involved you. It's no' the same as a bunch of neds on the street.'

McDaid pointed at the reporter. 'You can have him charged. We'll back you up.'

'That'll be right. Make myself a marked man for Special Branch, Military Intelligence and any other disgruntled polisman who thinks he's been hard done by the Fourth Estate?' Knox's mild paranoia and deep mistrust of the institutions of power was part of what made him an effective investigative reporter. 'Besides, it was all very polite, veiled threats, no witnesses, and they made sure this' – he waved with his cast – 'could be construed as an accident. My own fault even. A wee bit too much to drink and I didn't quite move fast enough when one of them was politely closing the door after me.

'They even took me to the Victoria Infirmary afterwards to get it set. Most apologetic. "You should watch yourself, Mr Knox," he said. "The long arm of the law has a heavy hand. And hanging around police officers can be bad for your health." '

'Be bad for somebody's health,' McDaid promised quietly. 'I'll make sure of it.'

Dreghorn flashed him a look: *Get it together, big man.*

Knox tapped his typewriter with his cast. 'Don't worry, I'll get him back with this.' He looked at Dreghorn, determined. 'Conall Tracy's still in the wind? I want the full story when you find him: exclusive. You owe me that at least.'

'That's why we're here,' Dreghorn said. 'You mentioned Tracy had a relative that he visited in Glasgow: a nephew, his sister's son, studying over here or something. Have you got a name?'

'Somewhere around.' Knox screwed the lid back on the whisky, dropped the bottle back in the drawer and, even one-handed, flicked through the papers strewn around him with the deftness of a card sharp. Denny Knox's desk was his castle. His eyes darted across typed and handwritten notes with lightning speed.

Dreghorn had told the sulking McDaid to drop him off at the *Express* offices and then go home to his family, but the big man had insisted on accompanying him. It was long past time for knocking off, but Strachan's mention of Tracy's sister, her young son and the unidentified man who was with them during the siege of Tralee had troubled Dreghorn, a newsreel of shadowy images playing in his mind. The chances of any of that having some greater significance were painfully slim.

Weren't they?

Denny Knox whipped a sheet of paper out from one pile like a magician removing a tablecloth without disturbing the crockery.

'Here we go. Sorry, my mistake; he wasn't studying at the university, but at St Peter's Seminary, Bearsden. Owen Gerrity, son of Bernadette Gerrity, deceased. Not long ordained, so now he's Father Gerrity, of the Church of the Immaculate Conception, Maryhill.'

CHAPTER 53

McDaid nodded through the windscreen at the Church of the Immaculate Conception, its outline etched into the night.

'Think Tracy's in there?'

'Don't know,' Dreghorn admitted. 'They used to call it "sanctuary" in the old days.'

'Wherever they are, he and his cronies are bound to be armed. Might even have a few spare sticks of dynamite left.'

'Always walk the sunny side of the street, don't you, Archie?'

They had parked at a discreet enough distance to observe – with the aid of Mrs Pettigrew's opera glasses – but not to be observed. The Immaculate Conception was a stone's throw from the Forth and Clyde Canal, not far from where Reginald Smith's corpse had been discovered, another possible connection.

Collar up, hat brim pulled low, Dreghorn had already reconnoitred the location, checking all the doorways and potential entry points or escape routes. On the surface, it looked as though everything was business as usual. When they had arrived, to the accompaniment of 'Soul of My Saviour', evening Mass was drawing to a close.

Father Gerrity wished each of the worshippers a goodnight as they left, exuding a warmth that Dreghorn didn't always associate with the clergy. A decent crowd too for a weekday service; it was Lent, some of the congregation no doubt trying to squeeze an entire year's worth of devotion into forty days and nights to make up for their laxness the rest of the year. A few parishioners chatted outside, but the drizzle soon dispersed them.

Afterwards an elderly couple and three other individuals – two women, one man – entered the church by the main entrance, but all seemed innocuous enough. The couple departed after fifteen minutes, arm-in-arm as they supported each other down the steps.

Dreghorn threw his hat into the back seat, shrugged out of his coat, making sure to take his detective's baton, and opened the car door. He told McDaid he was going in to speak to Gerrity. The big man went to join him, but Dreghorn shook his head.

'If I'm not out in half an hour, call the Heavy Mob and come in after me.'

He dismissed McDaid's protests and headed for the steps. That church chill, present in the height of summer or the dead of winter, settled on him as he slipped inside, closing the heavy wooden door as quietly as possible. The church was built in a cruciform, with the confessional booths in the right-hand transept, statues of saints on pedestals on the left, towering in morally superior judgement over the congregation.

A noticeboard stated that Father Gerrity was hearing confession from 7.30 to 9.30 p.m. Two of the people they'd seen entering were seated a respectful distance from each other in separate pews near the confessionals, the third obviously unburdening herself within.

From the central aisle, Dreghorn made his way along a pew towards the penitents. He flashed his warrant card as they turned to look at him, whispered, 'Your indiscretions are forgiven, courtesy of the Glasgow Police' and jerked his thumb at the door.

The severity of his expression must have been convincing because they left without argument, genuflecting and crossing themselves with wary, sidelong glances at him.

He stood to attention outside the confessional until the door opened and a young woman stepped out. The sight of Dreghorn was penance enough and she hurried off after the others.

He waited until he was sure they were alone, then stepped inside, closed the door and knelt down.

There's nothing quite like the silence of the confessional as you prepare to reveal your darkest sins to the figure in the adjacent booth, silhouetted by a hazy screen, so that it might well be God Himself. Herself, if you had suffragette tendencies, though with the Church's sterling opinion of womanhood, that would probably have been another sin to add to the list.

'Bless me, Father, for I have sinned. It's been a lifetime since my last confession.'

Dreghorn couldn't remember the last time he'd been in a confessional – more than twenty years at least, when he was still at school, before the shipyards, the war, Shanghai. The quiet stillness, the claustrophobic oppressiveness, brought it all flooding back.

'That's all right, my son,' Father Owen Gerrity said, head bowed in patient profile. 'You're here now, that's what matters. Take your time. Whenever you feel comfortable.'

'It's funny, Father, when I was a wee boy and the school would take us to confession, I'd kneel in the pew waiting my turn and rack my brains to come up with sins I'd committed. I was more afraid of coming in without any, so I'd make some up. Swearing, fighting, breaking windows, talking back to my ma and my teachers, telling lies. Well, the last one was true, because I was lying about all these imaginary sins. Now I'm older and have done things I'm not proud of, I'd rather keep them to myself. Live with them. They make you what you are, for better or worse. Saying a thousand "Hail Marys" and "Our Fathers" isn't going to change anything.'

'It sounds as though you may have lost your way and are in need of spiritual guidance?'

'Maybe,' Dreghorn said. 'But not in the way you mean.'

'Perhaps it would be best if we spoke elsewhere, inspector?'

'No, I think it's the perfect place, it's just that the roles are reversed,' said Dreghorn. 'There is one thing I have to confess, though. I liked you, Father.'

'That's not a sin.'

'Really? I'm no' so sure.' A long pause, the silence growing taut. 'Have you ever been to Tralee, Father?'

'I travelled to many places in Ireland with my mother, but I was young. I can't always remember the names.'

'We're in confession, Father. You have to tell the truth.'

'I'm sorry, inspector, I don't understand. If something's troubling you, or there's something you think I've done, then I'd like to help. I understand you may not be much of a believer, but it's what I'm here for.'

'Oh, I'm troubled all right, Father. Let's start with things you haven't done. Sins of omission. You never said Conall Tracy was your uncle. Or that your mother was Bernadette Gerrity.'

'Is that a crime? I wasn't aware I had to lay out my family history before having a conversation.'

'Right now, your uncle's the most wanted man in Scotland, linked to nine deaths, two attempted murders and an explosion that caused dozens of casualties. Some just young lads – the very people you and Mrs Hepburn recruited me to try and help. You didn't think it might be relevant to bring that up?'

'Sometimes it seems like another life, another me. I was a child then. I'm a man of God now. My goal is to draw people away from the path of violence.'

'Aye, because that's what religion always does.'

'There are some who use it to incite division, fan the flames of hatred, there always are. But if you tar everyone with the same brush, where's the hope for a better world? You're the one who meets violence with violence. Perhaps you don't hear the rage and bitterness in your own voice. Remember how reluctant you were to try another approach?'

'What about your mother: what did she believe?'

'I like to think she'd have come to think the same way over the years, but the truth is I don't know. We view those who are gone through a veil of memories, and we're more than capable of fooling ourselves, seeing only what we want to. She died in 1921, killed by so-called peacekeeping forces.'

'I'm sorry. I know what happened – one side of it anyway. And I know you were there. In Tralee.'

Through the screen, Dreghorn saw Gerrity raise his eyes heavenwards, as if searching for strength, guidance.

'I tried to stop them, but they just laughed, brushed me aside. They stuck a milk bucket on my head, told me to stay still.' Shame in the young priest's voice. 'And I did, I stood like a statue and listened . . . to the screams, the gunfire, the beatings, the laughter of the soldiers, the smell of burning all around. It was like hell itself was calling me.'

Dreghorn felt the dark walls of the confessional close in, saw

Gerrity as a trapped, helpless, terrified child. He cursed himself for immersing the priest in the memories, making him relive the horror.

'I don't know how long I was there, frozen. It felt like for ever. Eventually one of the soldiers returned, put his hands on the bucket. When he spoke, his voice was a whisper, a rasp, as if his throat was lined with razor blades and they cut up his words on the way out. He told me I saw nothing, asked if I understood. He made me repeat it, shout it out – "I saw nothing!" – and then tore the bucket off my head.' Gerrity's voice cracked. 'I saw everything. Every cracked skull, every leaking wound, every twisted body in every muddy, bloody puddle. Every broken man and woman. Every burning house in a street of fire. Everything.'

The silence of the confessional. Sins almost too great to contemplate. The anguish that accompanied them.

Dreghorn forced himself to speak. 'The man who said that was Reginald Smith. He was found dead on his narrowboat on the canal. But you know that, don't you?'

'I know some poor man was killed, but no more than that.'

'The other victims – Harold Beattie and Ronald Anderson – were with Smith when your mother was assaulted. Bullets to the head, all of them, the way your uncle's hit squads used to do it, when ammunition was in short supply and they had to get up close to make sure. Boyd Strachan, the detective who was shot the other night and is in hospital now, he was their sergeant.

'Tell the truth, I won't lose much sleep over them, but their families will. They all had families, you know, apart from Smith. Weans who'll grow up without a father, the way you did, the way you lost your mother. They won't understand why, but they'll grow up with hate in them. That's the way it works.'

Gerrity half shook his head, as if struggling to deny the detective's reasoning. For a moment Dreghorn thought he heard something outside the confessional, but decided it was the priest, fidgeting uneasily.

'And Ellen Duncan,' he continued, 'the policewoman who was with Strachan, she's nothing to do with any of this. Innocent – in the wrong place at the wrong time.'

'I'm sorry she was hurt, but I don't see what it has to do with me . . .'

'Everyone's sorry. Doesn't change anything.' Dreghorn ignored him. 'Where's your uncle, Father? Is he here, are you giving him sanctuary?'

Gerrity started to speak, stopped himself.

'Did you find Smith and the others and then tell your uncle, for him and his gunmen to do the rest? Keep your hands clean, but not your conscience. Or did you take part? Are you a wee bit more Old Testament than I thought? An eye for an eye, and all that?'

'Please, inspector, you need to leave.'

'No, you need to tell me the truth, Father. You need to confess. Where is he?'

'Please, Jimmy—'

Dreghorn slammed his fist against the partition, rocking the entire confessional. 'Where's Conall Tracy?'

The door opened, almost torn from its hinges. Dreghorn turned, froze. It wasn't some petty sinner keen for absolution.

'Speak of the devil, eh?' Conall Tracy raised an eyebrow in gentle admonishment, a Colt M1917 revolver gripped in his right hand.

Dreghorn started to move, but Tracy shook his head.

'Uh-uh. You were lucky last time. It'd take a miracle for me to miss from here. And I don't think either of us believe in them, these days.'

CHAPTER 54

'Penance has got a wee bit more extreme since I was last here.' Dreghorn nodded at Tracy's gun as he raised his hands and stepped slowly out of the confessional. 'Used to be a couple of "Hail Marys" – and Bob's your uncle.'

'It's your sins that have got worse.' Tracy kept his distance, an old hand at holding enemies at gunpoint.

'Coming from you, that's almost a compliment, 'cos you're top of the league.'

Tracy shook his head. 'I'm a soldier in a war. What did you think when you were shooting the Huns over in France, or wherever you were? Right or wrong?'

'It didn't exactly make me feel the bee's knees.' Dreghorn kept his hands at shoulder level. He could feel the tension of the holster straps around his torso, the weight of the Webley against his ribs. There was no way he could draw before Tracy fired, not even when he was back at his Shanghai shooting peak.

'Uncle Conn . . .' Gerrity stood outside the confessional now. With his world disintegrating around him, he clung to one constant. 'This is a house of God.'

'What happens next is up to the inspector, Owen. I won't harm him if he behaves himself.'

That didn't seem to reassure the priest greatly, but before he could answer, another voice cried out, 'For fuck's sake! What's he doing here?'

Frank Cleary was leading Nora Egan and Gerry Byrne out of a door to the right of the altar. Cleary had a Colt semi-automatic in his hand, but Dreghorn figured the others would also be armed. He noted that Tracy didn't allow himself to be distracted by their arrival.

'Came for confession,' he said. 'Good Catholic boy, back in the day.'

Nora Egan shoved Byrne aside, stormed towards the detective, drawing her own weapon, a Browning .38.

'I'll do it,' she said sharply. 'No one'll hear, down in the basement.'

Gerrity stepped between her and Dreghorn. 'No one will hear because no one will be harmed in my church,' he said with surprising authority.

She glanced at Tracy, who cocked his head at his nephew. 'You heard what the man said, Nora. The peeler stays alive and well.' His eyes locked on Dreghorn, adding: *For now.*

He told Egan to search the detective for weapons, stepping aside to keep his aim clear. She slipped her gun back into her pocket, slid her hands under Dreghorn's jacket and started patting him down. She smiled almost immediately, carefully removed his revolver.

'Take his jacket,' Tracy ordered. 'He had a set of brass knuckles on him in the van.'

'Charmer, just like back home.' She stepped behind Dreghorn, grabbed his collar. He allowed her to slip the jacket from his shoulders, raised his hands again at a gesture from Tracy's gun.

Egan found the knuckleduster first, pocketed it. Egan shook

the detective's baton out of the inside pocket as she moved in front of Dreghorn again.

'Been on the wrong side of one of these a few times,' she said and drove the rounded end of the baton into his stomach, just below the sternum.

Dreghorn doubled over, gagging and coughing, but managed to stay on his feet. She drew back the baton to strike again, but Gerrity interceded, pushing her away. She raised the baton to the priest, but Tracy called her name in warning. She snorted in disgust, tossed the baton through the open door of the confessional. The impact echoed through the church.

Dreghorn straightened up, lifted his hands. Tracy seemed calm enough, but the other members of his squad were on edge, in hiding for two days now, the hours becoming increasingly desperate, the tensions between them rising.

Tracy said, 'Where's the big man?'

'Outside. With half the Glasgow Police. All armed to the teeth, waiting to blow you lot away.'

'He's lying,' Tracy told his nephew. 'If they knew we were here for sure, they'd have come in mob-handed, all guns blazing.' He spoke out of the corner of his mouth to Byrne. 'Gerry, sneak out the back and check what's going on. If you come across his big chum, invite him to the party – and don't be shy about it. Knock three times, so we know it's you.'

Byrne nodded grimly, drew a revolver from his waistband and headed back the way he had come. Dreghorn showed no concern, but silently willed McDaid to stay alert.

Tracy cocked his head at the others. 'Spread out. Watch the doors.'

Dreghorn noted the positions they took, Egan to the pews on the left side of the altar, Cleary to the right. He waited until the echo of their footsteps had faded, then said, 'This isn't going to end well, Conall.'

'If there's one thing I've learned,' Tracy said, 'it's that some things never really end. They might be dampened down with false promises and compromises, but they don't end. Just fester away, until sooner or later it all blows up again. Might be tomorrow, might be next year, might be thirty years from now. Don't pretend you don't know what I mean. You fought in the "war to end all wars". Do you still believe that today? Does anybody?'

'Not sure I ever did.' Dreghorn sighed cynically. 'Where are the rest of the explosives? If everything you stole went off in Vulcan Street, it'd have brought the whole block down.'

'Gone. Thin air.' Tracy gestured expansively with his free hand to indicate that they could be anywhere. 'They'll turn up when the time's right.'

'So you transported them to Bowling or the Firth of Clyde on Smith's boat and then what: transferred them to another boat to Ireland? Although you offloaded the explosives stored at Danny Semple's, because they were to be distributed to safe houses over here and down in England. Until the time's right.' Dreghorn glanced at Gerrity. 'And then you murdered Smith, probably more in revenge for what happened in Tralee than to stop him talking. And forced him to give you the names of the others.'

Tracy said nothing, but Dreghorn could sense his inner unease at the anguish and disappointment in his nephew's gaze.

'Uncle Conn . . . ?' Gerrity said.

'They caved in your mother's skull with a rifle butt.' Tracy's finger tightened on the trigger, his voice taut. 'They left you standing out in the road with a fucking bucket on your head, shooting and screaming all around you. Turn the other cheek, Owen? I don't think so. Kill them ten times over and it wouldn't be enough.' He focused on Dreghorn. 'The funny thing is, Smith worked out what we were up to pretty quickly. He claimed he had no love for the British government. They sent him to war, then dumped him on the slagheap, kicked him out of the Tans when things got too dirty for public opinion back home. He said we could blow up the "Houses of fucking Parliament", for all he cared.' Grim. 'He cared at the end, though, when I told him who I was. Who my sister was.'

Dreghorn was silent for a moment. 'Who was the other man in the house with your mother?' he asked Gerrity.

'There was no other man,' said Gerrity. Sharply. 'Only us.'

Neither of them spoke, but the look that passed between Tracy and Gerrity spoke of betrayals, disillusionment, guilt.

Tracy cocked his head, changed the subject. 'I don't hear any shooting out there, not even cap guns. So much for your army of police.'

'They'll be coming. Sooner or later. There's no way you can get away.'

'That's what I was thinking' – Tracy smiled – 'until you turned up. A flash of your warrant card'll get us through the roadblocks.'

'No chance. We'd be dead in a hail of bullets before we reached Paisley.'

'That'll be down to how good a talker you are, and the story you come up with; otherwise Archie – that's his name, isn't it? – will be joining your man Smith in the bullet-in-the-head club. Because once Gerry brings him in, he'll be staying here on pain of death until you get us out. If you don't . . .'

'That means you need to leave someone behind. Unless you expect Father Gerrity to take up murder as a sacrament.'

Gerrity recoiled, whether from Dreghorn's comment or the three heavy thuds that sounded at the side door, it was hard to say. Everyone jumped, even Tracy. There was silence afterwards, Egan and Cleary looking to Tracy for instructions.

The door opened and Byrne entered, a trickle of blood rolling down his forehead from where it had been cracked against the outside of the door in rapid succession.

McDaid was behind Byrne, guiding him by the scruff of the neck. The big man gripped the IRA man's revolver in his free hand, aiming it at Byrne's head. 'Shouldn't play with guns.' He gave the firearm a wee shoogle. 'They can be dangerous if they fall into the right hands.' To Dreghorn: 'The Heavy Mob are on their way.'

'You could've waited outside for them.' Dreghorn's rush of affection for the big man was tempered by exasperation that he'd just sauntered into the lion's den.

'It was getting chilly.'

Tracy manoeuvred himself so that he could see both detectives. 'You can't shoot all of us, big fella.'

'No, but I can get him. And maybe you.'

Dreghorn had seen McDaid at the police shooting range; he doubted the big man could hit any of them.

Egan and Cleary were both aiming their firearms at McDaid, the woman edging closer, Cleary sidling towards the altar for a clearer shot.

Tracy said, 'Haven't you got a family?' McDaid's silence was answer enough. 'Think of them; they'll miss you. Put down the gun and you can live happily ever after with them.'

'Is that what you told all those poor souls in Vulcan Street?'

Tracy's glare swung from McDaid to Dreghorn. 'I think you need to ask your pals in Special Branch about that.'

'What?' said Dreghorn. 'They sneaked in and blew up your man in the middle of a city?'

'Haldane and Quinlisk are the original dirty-tricks brigade. They were seen there beforehand – them or their men – sniffing around like undertakers in their black suits. Gabe Dempsey was an artist with explosives; he'd been around them all his life. He'd have made sure they weren't a danger.'

'The very fact that they were in a hoose in a busy street's dangerous in my book.' McDaid's voice grew louder. 'That's close enough, hen.'

Egan was staring fiercely at him, gun extended, in her own world of rage. 'You were the one driving the car,' she said. 'You're the one who killed my Pat.'

'I'm sorry, hen. It was him or me. He came off worse on the day.'

Her face soured, as if McDaid's regret caused bile to rise in her throat.

'Nora,' Byrne said in alarm, McDaid pulling him closer.

'I'm sorry, Gerry,' she said. 'I love you like a brother, but Pat, I loved him to death.'

She lowered her aim and fired. Byrne screamed as the bullet tore into his foot, the shot echoing through the church. McDaid bellowed a curse – another echo – swung the revolver at Egan, but couldn't bring himself to shoot. He shoved Byrne at her with all his strength, sending them both sprawling to the floor; another chorus of howls from Byrne.

McDaid glimpsed a blur of movement near the altar: Cleary changing position to get a clean shot. They opened fire at the same time, the shots deafening, gun smoke in the air. McDaid backed off as he fired, heading for the cover of the pillars on the left aisle. Cleary dropped into a crouch behind the corner pew of the right aisle.

Tracy couldn't help himself, turning instinctively to shoot at McDaid. Dreghorn lunged, his face twisting savagely, grabbing Tracy's gun-hand, forcing the shot astray, the bullet ricocheting off stone somewhere out of sight.

McDaid threw himself behind the nearest pillar, pressed his back against it, hoped his shoulders didn't stick out on either side. A small explosion of stony shrapnel as a bullet struck the pillar on his left. The same to his right, fragments stinging his face. Under fire from both sides. He tried to fix in his head the location of the firearms, risked a glance to gauge the danger.

Across the regimented pews, Gerrity stood, yelling for them all to stop, while Dreghorn struggled with Tracy, both hands on the IRA man's gun, trying to disarm him. With his free hand, Tracy drove punches into Dreghorn's kidneys. McDaid swore; he couldn't fire, for fear of hitting his partner. The wee man was on his own for the moment.

Darting a glance to his right, he saw Cleary looking towards Dreghorn and Tracy, Egan rising to her feet, taking aim.

He jerked back behind the pillar, felt the impact of her first shot even through the thick stone. The second caromed off the curve of the column, buried itself neatly in the plasterwork of the wall directly opposite him. A tad slower and it would have said just as polite a hello to the centre of his forehead. The goodbye would have been messier.

He heard footsteps, Cleary yelling, 'Hold on, Conn! I'm coming!' He fired off a shot in Egan's direction, hardly even looking, let alone aiming, then ran out from the other side of the pillar, keeping pace with Cleary, on the opposite side of the hall.

McDaid fired on the hoof, two shots, but Cleary sensed it somehow and threw himself flat. Wood splintered from the back of one pew as a bullet tore through it, the second pinging off stonework in the shadows beyond.

He slammed against another column, scrabbling to take cover as Egan fired again. Another impact against stone; a stained-glass window shattered by the ricochet. He had contacted Turnbull Street before encountering Byrne, and the gunfire must have been attracting attention, but there was no sound of police alarm bells yet. He tried to count Egan's shots; a Browning .38, he was sure, so seven bullets. More important, how many shots had he himself fired? He checked the chambers to see how many rounds he had left.

None.

Nice one, big man, he said to himself.

He glanced left, saw Cleary about to return fire, and slid around the pillar out of range. Egan, stepping into the aisle, reacted with surprise that he'd just galumphed into her sights. McDaid hurled the empty revolver at her and sprinted for the alcove ahead, the statues within the shadows gazing down solemnly. He heard Egan's shots as he ran, his body screaming at him, nerves jangling, expecting bullets to punch into him, tearing flesh, shattering bones.

Off-balance, Dreghorn struggled against Tracy's greater weight, his feet sliding and scuffing upon the marble floor. Tracy drove his shoulder against the detective, smashing him against the confessional. The wooden door cracked and buckled inwards to form an alcove, which at least prevented him from falling on his arse and losing his grip of the gun. There would have been no coming back from that.

Desperately he thrust his head forward to sink his teeth into

Tracy's gun-hand, but the IRA man twisted and jerked, smashing Dreghorn's knuckles into his own mouth. He tasted blood, blinked against watering eyes as he reared back.

He saw a smile on Tracy's face, met it with a short, sharp head-butt. It jarred him, giving Dreghorn space to kick back against the confessional and push Tracy across the aisle towards the pews.

They fell into separate rows, Tracy landing on the front bench, Dreghorn on the one behind. The detective still had a grip of Tracy's wrist, his arm stretched out, the point of the elbow upon the back of the bench. Dreghorn tightened his grip, slid off the bench, the full weight of his body now upon Tracy's forearm.

There was a crack as the arm broke, a roar of pain from Tracy. His revolver clattered onto the bench somewhere above Dreghorn's head.

Tracy fell onto the floor parallel to Dreghorn, the kneeler separating them, his injured arm flopping uselessly. Dreghorn heard Gerrity call out his uncle's name. It was echoed by another voice: Cleary's.

Dreghorn lifted his head. Through the gaps between the pews, he saw Cleary running towards him. He rolled onto his front, felt urgently for Tracy's gun. A bullet tore into the bench, narrowly missing his hand, sending the revolver skittering further away. He scrambled along the floor to get closer, Cleary's footsteps growing louder. Another shot, part of the bench in front disintegrating, the sting of splinters in his cheek.

Reach, reach. Find the gun.

His fingers brushed the butt of the Colt, footsteps so close now they were almost on top of him, his heart hammering just as loudly. One more desperate stretch and his hand curled around it. The footsteps stopped.

Dreghorn rolled onto his back, trapped in the pew as if laid out in his coffin. He raised the gun double-handed and fired.

Cleary was at the end of the row, standing over him, finger squeezing the trigger. Dreghorn's first shot hit him in the sternum, rocking his body. The second entered just under his chin, an arc of lumpy dark matter exploding into the candlelight from the back of his head.

Cleary's shot, fired with a dead hand, grazed the kneeler at the side of Dreghorn's head, exploded the marble beneath it, deafening the detective. He gasped for air, staggered to his feet, searching for McDaid. He had heard shot after shot as he'd fought Tracy, but had no idea who, if anyone, had been wounded, who was dead or alive.

The lights of the transept on the other side of the hall had been shattered by a ricochet, the shapes within silhouetted and shadowed. Dreghorn saw the outline of McDaid's hat atop one of the shapes. It looked as though his hands were raised in surrender. Nora Egan stepped into view, fired repeatedly at the big man.

Dreghorn shouted, fired Tracy's revolver as he ran, threading through the pew. Egan threw herself to the floor. He crossed the central aisle, still firing, powered into another pew. Halfway along, the hammer fell on empty chambers, small forlorn clicks as dangerous as gunshots in their own way.

Egan rose to her feet, tossing away her empty weapon, taking Dreghorn's Webley from her pocket.

'Nice of you to bring me a spare,' she said. A razor-slash of a smile, the barrel pointed at him, no chance of missing at that range.

There was a loud scraping sound, like an ancient vault being opened, a roar of effort. Egan looked back, saw a great shape toppling towards her, a form no bullet could stop.

The statue crushed her to the floor, breaking apart into large chunks, the gun leaving her hand, sliding across the cold marble.

McDaid stepped out from the plinth that the statue had stood upon. He nodded at Dreghorn, neither of them quite ready to speak yet, then retrieved his homburg from the head of the other statue, placed there as a decoy.

Dreghorn flopped down on the bench with a sigh, limbs suddenly heavy. Facing the altar, he wondered if it would be hypocritical, after everything he'd said over the years, to slide onto his knees and say a silent prayer of thanks.

McDaid stepped over Egan, who was unconscious, half buried under the rubble of the statue, the decapitated head rocking to a standstill. He bowed his head sheepishly as the statue's identity became apparent. The Virgin Mary's expression was still beatific, despite the decapitation.

'Sorry, ma'am.'

CHAPTER 55

The police bells came into earshot, growing louder as the echo of the gunshots faded. The detectives looked at each other, rolled their eyes: perfect timing.

Father Gerrity had helped Conall Tracy onto a bench and sat with an arm round his uncle. He looked around as though he no longer recognized his church, the world it existed in. Gerry Byrne was sprawled across the altar steps, wounded leg extended, moaning, semi-conscious.

Dreghorn pushed himself off the pew and crouched over Egan, felt her neck for a pulse. He told McDaid that she'd live and retrieved his Webley from where it had fallen from her hand. He slid it back into his holster as he stood up.

McDaid stared cynically at the gun. 'Just came in to talk, did you?'

Dreghorn didn't answer. An army of police was arriving outside, by the sound of things, bellowing warnings via a loud-hailer for any armed men inside to give themselves up.

McDaid ambled over, opened the doors and beckoned them inside, saying, 'Excuse me, could you keep the noise down, please? All this gunfire's given me a headache.'

Dreghorn walked wearily through the pews to Gerrity and Tracy, lifted his jacket from the floor and slipped it back on, concealing the Webley once more.

Gerrity stared towards the altar, desolate, the lifeless Christ staring back.

Tracy looked up at Dreghorn. 'It was me,' he said. 'Owen had nothing to do with any of it. We forced him to let us hide here.' Gerrity shook his head, started to speak, but Tracy silenced him with a cutting look. 'It was me,' he said again. 'Smith, Beattie, Anderson. It was me. No one else.'

Dreghorn said, 'You were in custody when Anderson was killed. And when Strachan was attacked.'

Tracy didn't miss a beat. 'One of the lads, must have been, finishing the job for me. Frank, probably. Loyal to a fault.'

'Shame he can't corroborate what you're saying.'

'And whose fault's that, inspector?'

Dreghorn's mind threw up a sudden image of Frank Cleary, framed by stained-glass, bullets tearing into him. Too tired to talk any more, he stepped back as a couple of constables approached, then nodded permission for them to take Tracy and Gerrity away.

The church was now host to a milling congregation of mainly Protestant police officers, glancing around the Catholic confines as if they'd just entered enemy territory, only to find it virtually identical to their home turf. Dreghorn nodded to Sammy Stirling and Big Fartie as he spoke to DCI Monroe, giving him a halting outline of the night's events.

Monroe warned, 'We'll need a few more details in the official report.'

'It's been a long night, sir.'

Monroe was unsympathetic. 'It's going to get longer. Sillitoe's on his way in from Kilmacolm. He'll want to see you in Central as soon as the doctors have checked you and Archie over.'

'We're fine, we don't need—'

Haldane, Quinlisk and the Special Branch squad entered, the superintendent staring coldly at Conall Tracy as the IRA man was led past.

'It's our arrest, sir,' Dreghorn said. 'When Special Branch interviews the suspects, I want to be in there with them.'

'Worry about that later, Jimmy. Get yourself checked out first.' Monroe started to walk away, paused. 'By the way, the Royal telephoned the station earlier tonight – Ellen Duncan's regained consciousness.'

McDaid stood with the ambulance crew tending to Nora Egan. Dreghorn started towards the big man to tell him about Ellen, but was intercepted by Quinlisk.

'Grand job you and the big fella did here, Jimmy,' he said with what seemed like a genuine congratulatory smile. 'Not as thorough as we might've done, but . . .'

'You mean there's still people left alive?'

Quinlisk made sure there was no one within earshot. 'Trials are a terrible expense for the taxpayer, so they are. Especially when there's no doubt about the verdict.'

'Really? What do you think happened at Vulcan Street?'

'A tragic accident for all those poor people caught in the blast. Poetic justice for Gabriel Dempsey. Play with explosives and sooner or later they blow up in your face.'

'You didn't give them a wee helping hand then? Just to make sure there was no doubt about that verdict.'

'A question from the moral high ground' – Quinlisk's eyes flicked to Dreghorn's chest – 'coming from a man with a recently fired gun hidden under his jacket.' He tipped his hat as he moved off. 'A grand job. Let's leave it at that.'

Lighting a cigarette in church was probably disrespectful, but Dreghorn had already shot a man outside the confessional, so in the grand scheme of things, smoking was a sin he could live with. He'd have to live with the shooting as well, another reel to the nightmare film that sometimes played in his sleep.

He paused to let a pair of ambulance men stretcher Gerry Byrne past, then made his way back to McDaid. He was telling the big man that Ellen was awake when the shots rang out. Three of them, followed by an oppressive silence, as if the world had been plunged into shock.

Inevitability brought them to a halt almost before they saw the body. They had known what they would find as they ran along the church aisle and through the door into the night, the cold misting their sighs.

Vehicles were parked haphazardly in the road outside: two ambulances, two police cars and three Black Marias, all with their engines still running, headlights beaming. There was no sign of Owen Gerrity, but they could hear his voice, yelling his uncle's name in alarm, one of the vans rocking as he battered the walls from inside. Silhouetted figures were grouped in silence amidst the vehicles. Dreghorn and McDaid pushed through.

Eugene Quinlisk stepped aside for them, a gun in his hand, smoke drifting from the barrel.

'We warned him,' he said. 'More than once. Didn't we, sergeant?'

Graham Orr nodded faintly, shell-shocked, unable to meet the detectives' eyes.

Conall Tracy lay on the cobbles, the headlights criss-crossing over him, harsh and pitiless.

Haldane stood over the body; his gun trained upon Tracy's head as if about to make sure. Dreghorn shoved the superintendent away, almost knocking him off his feet, cursing him ferociously. Haldane instinctively aimed the gun at Dreghorn, but the detective ignored the gesture, shook his head in disgust.

'Don't fuckin' try me. Sir.'

Dreghorn spat out the final word as if it was formed of bile. He crouched beside Tracy, felt McDaid's presence, standing guard behind him. Gerrity continued to batter the walls of the van, yelling for his uncle with increasing desperation.

Tracy's eyes were open, blood glistening on his lips as they moved silently. Dreghorn leaned over him, said his name, but there was no reaction. Whatever he was looking at, whoever he was talking to was not of this world. Eventually, life faded and Tracy's lips stilled, his expression becoming strangely sanguine, as if this was what he had expected all along.

Shot while trying to escape.

CHAPTER 56

'Inspector Strachan?'

Ellen Duncan's voice was weak. Each time she blinked, the movement was so slow that Dreghorn's heart was in his mouth in case her eyes didn't open again.

'Shot twice,' Dreghorn said. 'But he's fine, thanks to you. In rude health.'

'No other kind, with his sort,' growled McDaid.

'You were brought in together. He's a couple of doors down.'

Ellen managed a wan smile. 'I'll no' be visiting.'

She closed her eyes. Dreghorn and McDaid glanced at each other. They had left the crime scene under Monroe's supervision and driven straight to the Royal Infirmary. Nora Egan and Gerry Byrne were being loaded into ambulances and would soon follow. Father Owen Gerrity would be in a Turnbull Street cell by now, a different kind of confessional. Conall Tracy and Frank Cleary would be laid upon mortuary slabs.

On arrival, they had gone straight to Ellen's room and, after speaking to the cautiously optimistic matron, had knocked quietly on the door. Sandy and Marjorie Duncan, elated that their daughter was finally conscious, elected to step outside as the detectives approached her bedside.

'It's all right, hen,' McDaid said. 'Jimmy's already passed on your best wishes.'

Dreghorn ignored the sarcastic edge to his partner's voice. 'Strachan said he was walking you home.'

'Not at my invitation.' Ellen opened her eyes, focused on Dreghorn, seated beside her, with McDaid standing by his shoulder. 'Told him not to, but . . .' Words and thoughts seemed elusive; her eyes swam as if trying to catch them. 'Strachan said you were involved with Kitty Fraser.'

Dreghorn flinched as McDaid nudged him in the back with his knee.

'He threatened to tell Sillitoe,' Ellen continued, 'said you'd be out of a job if I didn't . . . you know . . .'

'Nothing like a bit of blackmail to win a lassie's heart,' Dreghorn said.

McDaid leaned over the bed. 'Jimmy's big enough and ugly enough to look after himself, hen. And if he can't, I'm bigger and uglier than everyone.'

'Archie's right, Ellen, you don't have to worry about me.'

'Too bloody right I don't.' She gave a small smile. 'I told Strachan to beat it. After that, though, it's hard to remember. I think he tried to kiss me . . . and I might've stamped on his ankle, like you showed me, sir, but . . . it's all confused in my head. There was a cyclist. And then—' She started, suddenly frightened. A painful rush of memories.

Dreghorn took her hand, squeezed gently, tried to calm her, but McDaid spoke over him.

'It's all right, hen. The man who attacked you – we got him. He'll no' hurt anyone ever again.'

Ellen shook her head, confused, looked from McDaid to Dreghorn.

'*Her*,' she said. 'When we fought . . . it was a woman, sir. A woman.'

CHAPTER 57

Sunday, 9 April 1933

After the night's events, the chimes of the doorbell sounded almost surreally cheerful to Dreghorn's ear. Shots were fired, lives lost, but the rest of the world remained largely innocent. Or ignorant. He wasn't sure which.

The townhouse was in Partickhill, the streetlights still burning, illuminating the tree-lined road, emphasizing the peace and quiet, unlike in the slum districts, plunged into darkness after 11 p.m. to save the Corporation money and conceal the deprivation they were so keen to condemn.

Martha Hepburn had come a long way since the wartime Rent Strikes and the march of Mary Barbour's Army. On the surface, she had always followed her conscience and never abandoned her sense of social justice. Dreghorn wondered about justice, the complexities of the law that was supposed to mete it out, and the starker nature of right and wrong. The voice of reason, Conall Tracy had called her, whatever that meant. Dreghorn knew only too well that what seemed reasonable to one person could be sheer bloody madness to someone else.

He hoped he was wrong in his suspicions, wished he was anywhere other than standing on her doorstep in the early hours of the morning, a time when good news rarely came calling. At least he wasn't battering the door and bellowing, 'Police! Open up!' – the Untouchables' usual approach.

The gentle chimes of the doorbell had an insistence of their own, however, and he soon heard movement, footsteps on stairs, then crossing the hallway within. He suddenly considered what sort of sight he presented, battered and dishevelled after his fight with Conall Tracy.

He'd expected a maid, but the door was opened by Martha Hepburn herself, blinking away the remnants of sleep and pulling the neck of her dressing gown closed against the cold. She examined Dreghorn as if he was in the dock.

'It's been a long time since I entertained gentlemen callers, inspector. Especially at this hour.'

'I think you're promoting me above my station, ma'am.'

'Wasn't that your stage name – "Gentleman" Jimmy Dreghorn?'

'Ring name. Not my idea.'

'I assume this is a serious matter?'

Dreghorn's face said it all. She sighed, opened the door wider and motioned him inside. He removed his hat as he entered, stood in the hallway, awaiting directions. A bicycle rested against one wall. His thoughts and stomach tightened.

'Yours?' As if making innocent conversation.

'It was my husband's,' Martha answered. 'Held on to it for sentimental reasons more than anything, I suppose. Now and again, if the weather's fine, I take it out for a ride in the park. If I'm being honest, I like ruffling the feathers of those who think it's unladylike.'

'It looks as though there's a few scratches . . .'

'Oh, I've had a few prangs over the years.' She gestured towards a door on her right. 'We'll use the dining room.'

Dreghorn cast a cold detective's eye over the room as she switched on the electric light overhead. A mahogany dining

table, a long matching sideboard and a well-stocked drinks cabinet along one wall, large sash windows at the far end of the
room.

'I know,' Martha said sheepishly. 'This one room alone is
almost as big as what my entire family grew up in. Do I feel
guilty? Yes. Would I change it? No. And I'm not comfortable
about that, either.'

The curtains hadn't been drawn and Dreghorn walked to
the windows, looked out. All he could see was darkness and
Martha Hepburn's reflection in the glass, watching him intently
as she crossed the room to the drinks cabinet.

'Conall Tracy was arrested earlier tonight,' he said.

'By you?'

'At first.' Dreghorn turned to face her, but she was already
turning away. 'He was killed by Special Branch officers afterwards. Shot while trying to escape.'

There was almost no reaction, only a slight stiffening of her
back, as she fumbled in the top drawer of the cabinet.

'Or so they claim,' he finished.

'You have reason to believe otherwise?' Her voice seemed to
come from far away.

'Not sure I know what to believe any more. Whenever I'm
beginning to regain a little faith in human nature, something . . . someone always shoots it down.'

Martha opened the cabinet with a small key. 'I was going to
offer you tea, but you look like you'd appreciate something
stronger.'

He didn't argue, watched as she poured a Johnnie Walker
Black Label from a virtually untouched bottle and slid the glass
across the table to him. He knocked it back in a oner. Uncouth,
but at least he hadn't bypassed the glass completely and just

snatched the bottle from her. She took the empty glass, poured him another.

Dreghorn smelled the liquid, resisted the allure, said, 'Father Gerrity's in the cells at Turnbull Street. Tracy was his uncle. He was sheltering him in the church.'

Martha Hepburn said nothing.

'Tracy confessed to the Black and Tan murders,' Dreghorn continued. 'All three of them. And the attacks on Boyd Strachan and Ellen Duncan, except that he was in prison by then. He claimed another IRA man went after Strachan, a Frank Cleary. Also shot dead earlier tonight, so he's not saying one way or another.'

She took out another glass, not meeting his eyes. 'You don't believe that?'

Dreghorn shook his head. 'I think there's more to it. I think he was protecting someone. Trying to.'

'It sounds as though you've already made your mind up who, inspector.'

'The gun*man* who attacked Strachan and Ellen Duncan was on a bike. Ellen thought he was coming to help her. Then she realized that he wasn't.' Dreghorn reached casually for his inside pocket. 'And that it wasn't a man at all.'

Martha had been standing at an angle, her right hand concealed behind her hip, near the open drawer. She brought it up in a movement of ruthless economy to aim a pistol at Dreghorn, a Browning .38 like Nora Egan's, the same one she had bludgeoned Ellen with.

'Going for my cigarettes,' Dreghorn said. 'Being shot at always leaves me gasping.'

With his left hand he slowly opened his jacket to reveal the shape of the Capstan pack in the inside pocket, and his empty shoulder-holster.

'Where's the gun?'

'There's been enough shooting for one night. May I?'

Dreghorn fished out the Capstans when she nodded, lit one, exhaled with a weary sigh and smiled wanly.

'She really thought you were coming to help her.'

'Bikes were how we got around during the Rising, carrying messages,' Martha said. 'I meant the girl no harm.'

'Funny way of showing it.'

'Things got out of hand. There was another policeman coming, she wouldn't let go of me and . . . I panicked.' Her expression became a mix of hatred and revulsion, some aimed at herself. 'You don't know what those men did. If they were on trial, you'd happily see them hang.'

Dreghorn smoked and sipped whisky, let her talk.

'But that would never happen, because they were doing their duty, loyal instruments of the British Empire. Keeping the peace, by shooting to kill. And the rest – beatings, burnings, rapes. All covered up, swept under the carpet.'

Neither of them spoke. An impasse, the Browning not quite being aimed at him, but close enough. Martha retrieved Dreghorn's glass, poured them both drinks and gestured with the pistol, indicating that they should sit. Dreghorn glanced around for an ashtray, his cigarette burning precariously.

Etiquette at gunpoint. She laughed at the ridiculousness, said, 'Flick it on the carpet, inspector, it's hardly the time to stand on ceremony.'

He sat on the opposite side of the table from her, the whisky between them. If it came to it, he wondered if he could heft the bottle at her before she fired.

CAST A COLD EYE

'A few months ago,' he said, 'Reginald Smith went up before a magistrate for unpaid docking fees, but the case was dismissed. Didn't think too much about it until I heard what Ellen told me tonight. I went back to the station before I came here, to check the court report. You were the sitting magistrate that day . . .'

'I recognized him immediately.' Her expression tightened. 'That voice, like a razor being drawn down your spine. It all came flooding back.'

'So you were telling the truth, it was a business meeting you were having with Tracy. It's just that the business was murder.'

Martha reflected on that, seemed to come to a decision within herself. 'Scotland is my home, but Ireland is my country. I've always felt as much a part of it – and it of me – as I do Scotland, for as long as I can remember. I've known Conall Tracy since childhood. He was the first boy I ever kissed' – she smiled fondly – 'and it was me who did the kissing, not that he objected. But it was his sister who was my greatest friend: Bernadette.

'My mother came from Ballydonoghue in County Kerry, my father from Listowel. Even though they moved across the water and I was born here, they each in their own way filled me with thoughts and dreams of Ireland. My father with stories of oppression and famine, the brutal realities; my mother with myths and poems and songs, all those romantic ideals.' Wistfulness and bitterness accented her voice. 'Blood for blood, sadness and loss, generation after generation. It all seeped into me – weeped into me.

'Come holidays, when I was young, I'd be taken back to the old country to stay with family in Listowel and Tralee. One year Ma would take me, the next Da'. We could never afford to all go together. The Tracy family were landlords of a pub in Tralee, old friends of my parents, so naturally I was sent off to play with their children, Conall and Bernadette. I thought Conall was the bonniest lad I'd ever seen, but you know what it's like at that age, we pretended to ignore each other whenever someone was watching.

'Bernie was my age – gallus and cunning and quick-witted. "That one's been here before," my mother used to say. She was the most daring person I'd ever met, and she dared me to be the same. I felt she knew me better than I knew myself, and I think she felt the same. Maybe it was the headiness of youth, before the complexity of life bares its teeth, but I used to count the days to the holidays, when I could see her and Conall again.

'I'd help her with her chores around the pub, and then we'd go off on adventures, exploring the countryside, staring out over the Atlantic from Tralee Bay, talking about nameless ancestors who'd left for America, making up romantic stories about what they did and who they became . . .'

There was a glow to Martha's face now, a glimpse of the innocent girl she'd once been, but Dreghorn knew it wouldn't last.

'Years later,' she said, 'we hid there and waited for a German ship that was bringing arms for the Rising. It never arrived, seized by the navy and scuttled. Sorry, I'm getting ahead of myself.' She sipped her whisky, made a face and continued. 'As we got older, we saw less of each other – life takes hold, as I said – but we did write regularly, confiding in each other about what was happening in our lives, talking about the state of the world.

'I became a schoolteacher and was active in the suffragettes, while Bernie had moved to Dublin to study medicine and had joined Cumann na mBan. She never finished her degree because she got married and had Owen. I only met her man, Michael Gerrity, a few times but never really thought he was a match for her. He was broadly supportive of Home Rule in principle, but in practice his family were well off and it suited them not to rock the boat too much, whereas Bernie – and Conall especially – had joined the campaign to break free completely of British rule and declare Ireland a republic. She wrote to me about it, and I shared her passion, her beliefs, offered to help in any way I could. Then the war came along and threw everything into chaos.'

'Has a habit of doing that.' Dreghorn forced himself to drink slowly, keep a clear head.

'I was wed by then myself and had had to give up my job, of course. Stuart was a junior engineer at Lockhart's Shipyard. A good man, but . . .' A disconsolate shrug. 'He thought he was doing the right thing by joining up, going to the Front, even though I was pregnant. "It's for the wee yin that I'm doing it," he said. "To keep the world safe for him or her. And you." God save us from blind courage! He died in 1915. Gassed at Ypres. The bairn was born a few weeks after he was killed. I called him after Stuart. Did you know I had a son?'

'Rachel said, aye.'

'Lost him to the Spanish flu, July 1919. Four years old.'

'I'm sorry.'

Martha couldn't meet Dreghorn's eyes, glanced at the window. The darkness outside answered with a reflection of herself in the glass.

'I'd lost my job, lost my husband and then was in danger of losing my home when the landlords started profiteering, raising the rents to crippling levels. I threw myself into the Rent

Strikes, alongside Mary Barbour and your mother, organizing resistance, marches, banding together to chase off the collection agents. And we won, forced the government to freeze rents at pre-war levels. After that, I think I was looking for another cause, another fight. Bernie invited me to stay with her, told me to bring young Stuart.

'She and Conn were involved with the preparations for the Rising and I joined in. I told you the Gerrity family were monied, so she had a nanny, which left us free to carry out missions, spying, surveillance, transporting weapons, sometimes disguising ourselves as young men or boys to avoid identification. It was thrilling, dangerous, but when I was with Bernie, I always thought there was nothing we couldn't do. Looking back, maybe I was just as naive as my Stuart, marching blithely off to war.

'Bernie and I were never supposed to take part in the occupation of the Post Office, but felt we had to do our bit, especially after the seizure of Casement's arms shipment. We were there for the duration, the full six days, though Conn tried to convince us to leave when the troops arrived to lay siege to the building, bombarding it with their guns. You've been to war, inspector; I don't need to tell you what it was like. I mainly tended the wounded, but sometimes anger got the better of me and I joined the defence, firing rifles, handguns. In all the chaos, I'm not sure I ever hit anyone. On the fifth day a shell burst brought the ceiling down on me.'

'I came to in St Vincent's Hospital with a broken arm and mild concussion, and learned from some sympathetic nurses that we had surrendered the day after I was injured.' She rubbed one temple, the memories paining her. 'The same nurses helped me to dress and slip out of the hospital when the police came to question me. I'd had no identification on me when I was admitted to hospital, so they had no idea who I was. No arrest record followed me home. No one back in Scotland ever even knew that I'd been involved.'

'I returned to Bernie's house. The nanny was distraught. Bernie and Conall had been arrested, and Michael had been found near the GPO, shot dead. They reckoned he'd gone there to try and talk Bernie into surrendering, but had then been caught in the crossfire, but no one knows for sure.

'I took Stuart and got the boat back home, returning to Glasgow to the news that the British government had ordered the executions of Pearse, Connolly and the other leaders of the Rising. I thought that was it, that their dream would die with them.

'Bernie wrote to me when she was released from prison a few months later. The mood of the country had changed. Outside the six counties of Ulster, support for independence in the form of a republic was growing. The ruthlessness of the executions had turned a largely indifferent population against British rule. A month after the Armistice in 1918, Sinn Fein won a landslide victory in the elections, leading to the War of Independence.'

'Did you take part in that too?' Dreghorn asked.

'Not really,' Martha answered. 'Bernie wrote to me about what was happening, but could only be vague in case her letters were intercepted by Military Intelligence in Dublin Castle. I'd lost Stuart to the Spanish flu around the same time, nearly died myself. At the time I wished I had. Everything I'd believed in seemed hopeless or no longer worth fighting for. And I had no fight left in me anyway. I was lost, inspector.'

She sounded weary to her soul, the ghosts hovering. Would

she even notice if he reached over, gently removed the gun from her hand?

She seemed to read Dreghorn's thoughts, grew more alert. 'In the October of 1920 Conall sent me a letter. He wished to engage my services to tutor young Owen. All very formal and business-like. If the authorities intercepted the message, then it would appear innocent and legitimate, a doting uncle looking after his nephew's welfare.

'I met him in Dublin before taking up the post. Officially I was to be Owen's tutor, helping him to brush up on his weaker subjects. Unofficially I was to watch over him and Bernadette. She was having doubts about her role in the war, maybe even about the war itself. A bombing had recently gone badly, almost killing the wife and daughter of the intelligence officer who was the intended target. There were always innocent deaths and casualties on both sides, but the daughter was the same age as Owen, and it had shaken Bernie.'

The irony that this might have been Haldane's family was not lost on Dreghorn. Ripples of hatred and revenge, travelling over the years.

'Conn was happy for her to step away; the last thing he wanted was for her or Owen to be hurt. But he'd received word from a spy that Dublin Castle was planning to target Bernadette to get at him, so he wanted to protect her. She refused to go into hiding with a squad of armed men for company, but Conn felt that she'd be happy to have me with her. He had convinced Bernie to leave Dublin and stay in the old family home in Tralee. I travelled down to join her.' She sipped her whisky carefully, eyes never leaving Dreghorn. 'She was pleased to see me, but I could sense the change in her.

'She was tired, disillusioned. I'd never seen her like that

before. The country was immersed in violence and she could only see it getting worse. She feared that, whatever the outcome, the land and the people would be so scarred, so riven with division and hatred, that they would never recover, that it would all have been for nothing. I disagreed, but didn't argue too forcefully in case Bernie pushed me away. She made me promise not to indoctrinate Owen behind her back, to make sure he didn't fall prey to the vengeance and violence she could see in her brother. And I did.'

'A woman of your word.' Dreghorn's voice dripped with cynicism. 'He sends his regards from the cells.'

The comment stung, but Martha pressed on. 'The weeks we spent together were happy. Bernie wrote, I tutored Owen, got closer to him than I'd had a chance to previously. We had walks in the countryside, visited Tralee Bay again. The fighting seemed very far away, and I began to understand her longing for peace, and to feel the same way. And then the Tans came . . .' The wistfulness in her voice died.

'A local IRA brigade had killed two Black and Tan soldiers, and the Tans launched a series of reprisals on Tralee. They started their assault on the other side of town, which gave us time to get away. Or so we thought. I went to get my gun, but Bernadette asked me to fetch Owen first; he was outside with some of the local children.

'The front door was smashed in as I was going to him. They overpowered me, dragged me to the kitchen where Bernadette was. It was obvious they'd come for her, under cover of the main attack. Two of them held me, while the other – the one with the voice like sandpaper on leather—'

'Smith,' Dreghorn said. 'A throat wound in the war.'

'Smith,' Martha repeated. 'He slapped Bernadette into

silence, pushed her onto the kitchen table, started tearing at her skirts. I tried to fight, called him every name under the sun, but he just laughed; all of them laughed, stinking of sweat and booze.' She pushed her glass away with the pistol barrel, the odour suddenly offensive. 'Another soldier came in, a sergeant, I think . . .'

'Strachan.'

'He pulled Smith away, yelling that Bernadette wasn't to be harmed. Nothing chivalrous on his part. She was to go to the G-Men – the Government Men – in Dublin Castle and they wouldn't be happy if a "wee shitebag like him had his way with her first". He nodded at me, though, said, "Do what you want with the other yin." '

Dreghorn felt sick to his stomach, could only imagine Martha's own revulsion. Bastard! As he suspected, Strachan hadn't told him and McDaid the full truth, attempting to paint himself in a more sympathetic light.

'Bernadette recovered consciousness as they argued,' Martha continued, her voice level, but tears in her eyes. 'She wouldn't have known who'd been attacking her, they all looked the same in those ragtag uniforms. Strachan was just the closest. She grabbed the pistol from his belt and—'

'Shot him, I know.'

'Do you? Do you know what they did next? Smith knocked her to the floor, stamped on her wrist to trap the bayonet, then raised the butt of his rifle as high as he could and . . .' She hammered the Browning repeatedly into the table, making Dreghorn jump. Eventually she stopped, blinking away the tears. 'I saw it all,' she said. 'Every blow. I was as close to Bernie as I am to you. And I've seen it every night since. Over and over and over again.'

They sat in silence until Dreghorn said softly, 'I'm sorry, again – however inadequate that sounds.'

Martha smiled through silent tears, but it quickly faded. 'Eventually they seemed to realize the gravity of what they'd done and cleared out in panic, dragging Strachan with them. I suppose they didn't see me as much of a threat, lying there sobbing.'

Dreghorn recalled Strachan's version of events. 'Were you wearing men's clothing?'

She nodded. 'We thought it might be safer to look like a family on the move, rather than two women on their own. Up close, it didn't fool them. While Smith was struggling with Bernadette, one of the others tore open my waistcoat and shirt, yelled liked he'd struck gold and . . .' She flinched as invisible hands coursed over her body.

Dreghorn lowered his eyes in shame and helplessness.

'Eventually,' she continued, 'I staggered to my feet, shouting for help. Owen was outside, screaming and yelling himself hoarse, half the houses in the street on fire. I hugged him and told him everything would be all right. Which, of course, it wouldn't be. Ever again.' A sigh almost turned her inside out. 'We got Bernie to hospital. Conn travelled down from Dublin, but couldn't get in to see her. There were G-Men posted all through the building, lying in wait for him. Couldn't see his own sister . . .

'The doctors said she would never recover, the damage to her brain was too severe. She might live for months or years, they couldn't be sure, but she would never respond to a word or a touch. My beautiful, brilliant friend. She would never give speeches or inspire and light up the world with her passion and her smile. Every day she'd have to be cleaned and washed and fed and . . . it was a living death. For someone like Bernie, that would be worse than the real thing.

'We took her back to Dublin and cared for her for – I don't know for how long. The weeks blurred together, rigmarole and numbing emptiness. One night, sitting with her, listening to Owen praying desperately in the room next door and staring into her eyes for some semblance of the woman we all loved . . . I couldn't stand it any more and put a pillow over her face.'

Dreghorn made no comment, gave no sign of emotion, but knew that Martha could sense his inner recoiling.

'After the funeral, Conn asked me to take Owen back to Scotland, to keep him away from the fight, as Bernie had wished. The lad agreed. I planned to return to teaching, but Mary Barbour got in touch and offered me the opportunity to work with her, which led to me becoming magistrate when she retired.

'When he was old enough, Owen announced that he wished to enter the priesthood. I wasn't entirely sure that it was the right path . . .' She shrugged. 'Bernadette was a believer, but I've often wondered if what happened to her pushed him too far in that direction. He's made me proud, though, and I think she would have been too. I was delighted when he was ordained and took up his post at the Immaculate Conception. He embraced the congregation and threw himself into the challenges with a vigour that reminded me of her.'

Dreghorn broke the reverie. 'And then Smith turned up, bold as brass?'

A bitter laugh. 'On another day, he might have gone before another magistrate and I'd have been none the wiser. I knew him immediately. Not so much his face, but that voice. I showed sympathy and understanding, brokered an arrangement for him to pay off his debts and made sure he walked free.'

'Did you tell Owen?'

'One day, after he'd conducted a funeral, we had a conversation about death and the nature of loss. I asked how he'd feel if he ever encountered one of the soldiers who had hurt his mother. He said he hoped he'd have the strength to forgive, which is what the Lord would want. So, no.'

'But you told Conall Tracy.'

'Everything. I had continued to support Conn over the years – small favours, nothing more – and he'd made a point of visiting Owen regularly. He said he needed to hire a boat to transport something from the east coast to the west. I suggested Smith's . . .'

Dreghorn said, 'Knowing full well what he'd do.'

'I promised Bernadette I'd shield Owen from vengeance and violence: his own or that of others. I made no such promise for myself. Conn said afterwards that Smith begged at first, in that skin-crawling voice, but not for long. He knew it'd do no good. As Conn made him kneel down, he spotted a photo of Smith and his old Black and Tan cronies, posing proudly with their weapons. He made Smith give up the names and addresses of the ones who were in Tralee that day.' She raised an eyebrow at Dreghorn. 'I daresay you know the rest.'

'Up until Strachan.'

' "Do what you want with the other yin." That's what he said, remember? After you'd arrested Conall, I couldn't bear the thought of him still going strong. A policeman, after what he'd done. I unpacked my old Browning – always kept in good working order – dressed in some of Stuart's old clothing and cycled down to Turnbull Street. I knew they'd celebrate Conall's arrest, so I waited and followed them to the Steps Bar.'

Martha took a sip of whisky, grimaced as if it was poison.

'It's funny, we met at a hanging,' she said. 'I hope you'll come to mine, raise a glass.'

He shook his head, unable to bear the thought. 'It might not come to that,' he said. 'What Smith and the others did, what you witnessed . . . you've carried it with you all these years, you're scarred inside, like a soldier with shell-shock. Maybe you weren't in your right mind, you—'

'Oh, but I was,' Martha interrupted. 'I am. We both know that. The only thing I regret is young Ellen; it was never my intention to hurt her.'

Dreghorn said, 'A couple more blows and you'd have done to her what the Tans did to Bernadette Gerrity. All too easy to become what you hate sometimes.'

The gun suddenly seemed heavy in Martha's hand. She lowered her arm, resting it on the table, though maintaining her aim at Dreghorn.

'Have you never known someone that you'd die for?' she asked, a tremulous pain in her voice. 'Or kill for?'

Dreghorn didn't answer. He thought of McDaid, blithely putting his own life at risk by walking into the Immaculate Conception earlier that night. And of Isla Lockhart, who'd died for him, even though he'd begged her not to.

'So what do we do now, Gentleman Jimmy Dreghorn?'

'Not up to me, ma'am. I'm the polis, I just catch the bad yins. Maybe sometimes I don't want to, but . . .' He pushed his chair slowly back from the table, started to rise to his feet. 'You're the one who decides whether they're guilty or not.'

'Please don't, inspector.'

Dreghorn opened his arms in an apologetic shrug, as if he had no choice. The gun was on him now, following his every step.

'You think I won't?'

'Shoot me?' He kept his arms open all the way around the table, no resistance, no threat, a clear target if she wanted it. 'Go outside and shoot Archie? He's waiting in the car. Go up to the hospital and shoot Ellen? Or maybe you'd rather put a pillow over her face?'

She stiffened as if he'd twisted a knife.

'That's the problem. Once you start, where does it stop? And it has to stop, we both know that.'

He was standing over Martha now. The pistol pointed straight at his chest. Her cold eyes were on his. A shot to the belly, to the chest, at this range, he'd never survive. A moment that lasted for ever.

She blinked as tears came again. A meagre amount, but enough.

She placed the gun on the table, slid it towards him with a sigh that shuddered her body. He picked it up, cracked open the barrel, emptied the shells into his palm, then pocketed them. As he did so, she refilled his glass and passed it to him.

'There's only one thing left to say then, isn't there?' She gave him the bitterest of smiles. 'Get me Garrison.'

CHAPTER 58

Monday, 10 April 1933

McDaid thought of Skye. Over twenty years since he'd left and he still viewed the island as home. The beauty of the landscape was never far from him – the summer blue of the sea, gently lapping onto the shore, its invincible rage in times of storm.

The seasons, their colours and smells, were distinct, each one clean and fresh. Now, outside of home and family, his world blurred together in shades of grey, starting as dark as sin, but never quite stretching the full spectrum to virgin white. Buildings, streets, smoke-choked skies; laws, lies, motivations, empty promises. All shades of grey that you had to scrape away patiently or angrily to see the truth beneath, the reality.

He stopped at the junction of Gordon Street and Mitchell Street, took a deep breath. It caught in his throat, the taste of the city. Ashes, dampened by spilled beer, or maybe blood.

He glanced at his pocket-watch – his father's, the only thing he had of the old man's – as he waited for the road to clear, and then continued on his way to the Central Hotel. Almost check-out time.

Sillitoe had called a meeting first thing that morning. In addition to McDaid and Dreghorn, Deputy Chief Constable McVicar, DCI Monroe and Superintendent Haldane were in attendance. There were no secretaries present to take 'minutes'; it wasn't that kind of meeting.

'Where's Quinlisk?' Dreghorn had asked before anyone else spoke. 'He should be here.'

Haldane addressed himself to Sillitoe, as if Dreghorn wasn't there. 'His Majesty's Government requires Mr Quinlisk's expertise elsewhere, gentlemen. He'll be leaving your city shortly. I've already debriefed him.'

Sillitoe raised an eyebrow. 'You can't debrief someone when you don't know the outcome of the meeting, superintendent.' He reached for his telephone. 'I'll send officers to fetch him. Central Hotel, isn't it?'

Haldane lifted a hand as if admitting his arrogance. 'Chief constable, please, I assure you there's no need. Eugene Quinlisk is an instrument of the British government and will abide by our decisions. You have my word.' He glanced in quiet warning at Dreghorn and McDaid. 'His loyalty and discretion are unquestionable.'

'You'd better hope so,' Dreghorn said. 'He knows where all your bodies are buried.'

'And I, his, inspector.' To Sillitoe, 'Shall we proceed, sir?'

McDaid sighed and shook his head bitterly, the seat under him creaking in protest as he shifted his weight. Not for the first time, he pictured Dreghorn leading a broken Martha Hepburn from her townhouse in the early hours of Sunday morning: the doubt on his partner's face, the lack of conviction, the lines between right and wrong and the letter of the law never so blurred. Usually Dreghorn was the loose cannon, but today cautious glances were also being cast in the big man's direction.

Sillitoe straightened in his chair and looked them over as if, for once, reluctant or unwilling to see things through. He cleared his throat. 'The chain of events as I see it, gentlemen:

Conall Tracy came to Scotland ostensibly on legitimate business. In reality, he was setting up an undercover distribution network for the Irish Free State Hospitals' Sweepstake – legal there, but outlawed here and in America. That meant recruiting local agents, primarily the bookmaker Leslie Campbell. Special Branch' – Sillitoe gestured at Haldane – 'maintain an interest in Tracy because of his Republican ideals and the part he played in the Easter Rising and the Anglo-Irish War.'

'We suspected Tracy was siphoning funds from the Sweepstake profits,' Haldane said, 'to buy weapons and explosives for what our informers termed an S-Plan, a campaign of sabotage to be carried out in Northern Ireland and here in Britain. The Republican movement has a lot of support in the west of Scotland. Glasgow, with its high numbers of Irish immigrants and their descendants, is the perfect base of operations. When we learned that Gabriel Dempsey, Nora Egan and other associates of Tracy's were also present in the city, we moved at pace to set up a surveillance operation to monitor their movements.'

'Not quite quickly enough, superintendent,' Sillitoe stated, unimpressed. 'Tracy and his accomplices staged a robbery at the Garngad Explosives Magazine with the aid of Paul Kane. They transported the stolen explosives along the Forth and Clyde Canal via narrowboat. The boat was skippered by Reginald Smith, an ex-Black and Tan who, amongst others, was responsible for the death, or mortal injury, of Conall Tracy's sister while serving in Ireland in 1920.' He looked to Dreghorn for confirmation.

'Bernadette Gerrity.' Dreghorn glanced at Haldane. 'But you already know this, sir. Smith and the others, including Boyd Strachan, were under your command at the time. They were following your orders when they tried to arrest her.'

'Participating in the same operation, Dreghorn. Not neces-sarily under my command.' Haldane addressed Sillitoe and McVicar. 'The woman was also a key figure of the IRA, but I accept that what happened was a tragedy. A casualty of war, I'm afraid.'

'Conall Tracy said almost exactly the same thing to justify his actions,' Dreghorn noted.

'You're comparing me to that murdering scum?'

'It's a fine line, from where I'm sitting.'

'I serve King and Country, damn you!'

'Sergeant McDaid,' Sillitoe spoke louder than required to derail the argument, 'this was when you and Inspector Dreg-horn became involved.'

'Aye, sir,' McDaid said. 'We discovered Smith's body a few days after the robbery, although we didn't connect them imme-diately. We also encountered Tracy through another case, one we didn't know was related at the time – an assault on Les Campbell.'

'A punishment beating because Les was siphoning off more than his agreed share,' Dreghorn explained, 'which Tracy couldn't afford, because he was already diverting funds to his own activities. Too much money unaccounted for would have raised suspicions in Dublin.'

Sillitoe tapped a finger on the open file in front of him, all the information collated so far on the case. 'So Tracy murdered Smith on his boat at some point during or after the transpor-tation of the explosives. Before killing him, he forced Smith to surrender the names and addresses of the other ex-Black and Tan Glaswegians who were present when Bernadette Gerrity was injured – Harold Beattie, Ronald Anderson and Inspector

Strachan. Tracy then targeted them for execution, one after the other. Revenge for his sister's death, correct?'

Haldane bristled. 'In principle. But Conall Tracy was in your custody when Anderson was murdered. And when the attack on Strachan took place.'

Sillitoe said, 'That would have been one of his accomplices, acting on his orders.' Dismissive, but with an edge.

'One of the dead ones?'

'Highly likely, I'd say.'

'Tracy fingered Frank Cleary for Anderson's killing.' Dreghorn said. 'No reason to doubt him.'

'Really,' said Haldane. He and Sillitoe stared at each other, neither backing down. McDaid noticed McVicar looking from one to the other, gauging which was the most politically astute to support.

'What about the explosion in Vulcan Street?' the deputy chief constable asked.

'Some of the stolen explosives were stored there,' Monroe said. 'We're assuming the detonation wasn't deliberate.' He too fixed his gaze on Haldane.

'Then the resident of the house . . .' The Vicar glanced at his own file, open on his crossed knee. 'This man Semple – he's another accomplice.'

Dreghorn shook his head. 'He had no idea what they were up to. Only agreed to let them use the place in return for them paying his defence costs. He's up for attempted murder.'

'And for trying to stick a knife in my belly,' McDaid piped up, in annoyance. Nobody seemed particularly bothered by that bit.

'I believe we're all familiar with the chain of events after that,' Sillitoe continued. He gave a summary: Tracy's arrest and subsequent escape; Dreghorn and McDaid's discovery that Father Owen Gerrity was Bernadette's son, and Tracy's nephew; the shoot-out with the fugitives in the Church of the Immaculate Conception; and Conall Tracy's final moments, bleeding to death in the street outside.

'Shot while trying to escape,' Sillitoe finished, voice clipped.

Dreghorn shot a cynical look at Haldane. 'A man with a broken arm tried to steal your gun and run off?'

'Desperate men are capable of desperate actions, inspector,' Haldane responded coldly. 'Perhaps he hoped to die that way instead of facing the rope. The Irish love a martyr.'

'Or maybe you wanted him dead before he could face a trial,' Dreghorn snapped.

McDaid didn't believe a word of Haldane's story about Tracy's shooting and doubted anyone else did, but for the moment that truth was unspoken. In his experience, that was often the outcome when politics and the law clashed.

Sillitoe cast a cold eye over the group. 'Does everyone agree with my summation?'

'It has all the elements of a penny dreadful, chief inspector,' Haldane scoffed. 'Or what do they call them these days . . . a pulp thriller?'

'Which parts do you find unpalatable, superintendent?'

'The priest, for one.' A sharp look at Dreghorn. 'He's an accomplice and a sympathizer.'

'He'll be charged with aiding and abetting a fugitive, but his involvement ends there. A hapless victim, if anything, taken advantage of by Tracy, and torn by conflicting loyalties to his uncle and the memory of his mother,' Sillitoe stated. 'Certainly no killer.'

'The Hepburn woman is, though. Or could have been. Why

isn't she a suspect in Anderson's death, chief constable? She's a far more likely candidate than Cleary, if you ask me. She started the whole bloody affair by furnishing Tracy with the victims' identities, and her attack on Inspector Strachan proves she's capable of pulling the trigger herself.'

'Until recently Mrs Hepburn has been a fine, upstanding member of our society, who it seems has been compromised by a past relationship with Conall Tracy and his sister, and by acts of violence that you and Eugene Quinlisk were party to. The extent of her complicity is still under investigation. A prison sentence is unavoidable, but the charges she'll face will be determined when that investigation is completed. By the Glasgow Police. No one else.'

'A scandalous affair, and I can appreciate that you and your superiors might wish to play down the significance, but it has ramifications beyond the so-called second city of the Empire. A matter of national security. If her involvement with Conall Tracy is as deep as it appears, then she deserves to face the death penalty.' Haldane stood, brushed down his suit. 'I intend to see that she does.'

Sillitoe spread his hands magnanimously. 'Continue inquiries as you see fit, Haldane. Of course we would then be forced to pursue further investigations of our own.'

Haldane was quiet for a moment. 'Such as?'

'Complaints of excessive brutality on the part of your officers. The unofficial sanction of a shoot-to-kill policy.'

'Really? I've already given my statement on the circumstances surrounding Tracy's death. I stand by my actions.' Haldane cocked his head at Dreghorn and McDaid. 'As for brutality, I have it on good authority that your own men are prone to heavy-handedness on occasion.'

'The difference being that they're *my* men.' A dangerous pause. 'When I stated earlier that the detonation of explosives in Vulcan Street wasn't deliberate, I meant on the part of the suspect. Gabriel Dempsey's corpse was ravaged by the blast, but the doctors who examined it nevertheless found strands of hemp embedded in the wrists, leading to suspicions that he had been bound by ropes prior to the explosion.

'If Dempsey was tied up, then it would have been impossible for him to set off any explosion, deliberately or otherwise. Several witnesses also claim to have seen well-dressed individuals in dark suits, not unlike those favoured by your men, in the area in the days before the explosion, spying on the comings and goings in the street.'

'You're accusing us of detonating an explosion in a British city?'

'It certainly begs the question: if you knew where the suspect was hiding, why didn't you arrest him sooner? I'd like to believe that the security forces are incapable of such brutality and deceit, that they would never condone the sacrifice of innocent lives for political gain or to turn public opinion against enemies of state. I would dearly like to believe that. And I can only imagine how damaging it would be, were someone to prove otherwise.'

Dreghorn said, 'Or maybe it was just one way to make sure Tracy didn't escape the noose again. Good old-fashioned revenge for the bomb that injured your wife and daughter.'

Haldane remained silent. McDaid looked around, but no one would meet his gaze. Eventually Sillitoe said, 'Do you agree with my summation, superintendent?'

Haldane smiled humourlessly, stepped forward and extended his hand.

'It's been enlightening to work with you, chief constable,' he said. 'I won't forget it.'

Sillitoe rose slowly and shook hands with Haldane. McVicar and Monroe did likewise. Haldane turned to the detectives, offered them his hand. Dreghorn refused, but McDaid accepted.

And squeezed.

At first Haldane did well not to show the pain, but eventually he flinched, tried in vain to pull away. Sillitoe took his time in saying, 'Sergeant.'

McDaid released Haldane with a nod and a smile.

'Sorry, sir,' he said. 'The firmer the handshake, the greater the respect.'

McDaid moved from Gordon Street into the hustle and bustle of the station. He glanced at the glass roof for a hint of brightness, but saw only more shades of grey, dark clouds scudding across the sky, threatening rain. An everyday threat in Glasgow.

He held open the hotel door for a haughty woman in a fox-fur stole, the hapless creature's head still attached, and an equally hapless porter, struggling under the weight of her luggage. At reception he was informed that the parties he was enquiring about had already checked out, but were in the bar on the first floor, having a drink together prior to catching their train. The receptionist remarked that they seemed to be in a celebratory mood.

McDaid tipped his hat to her as he backed away. 'Well, think how chuffed they'll be to see me.'

He took the stairs, which were wide and grand, designed to offer a stunning view of the enormous crystal chandelier that hung overhead, if that was your sort of thing. McDaid promised himself that he would bring Mairi here soon – if he wasn't barred after today. Could a police officer be barred? Wouldn't a flash of a warrant card shatter any such restriction? He'd have to ask Jimmy. If anyone had encountered a scenario like that before, it would be Dreghorn.

The hotel was quiet, no unruly sounds sneaking in from the arrivals and departures on the concourse beyond. The battlement-strength walls, luxurious furnishings and thick carpets cocooned guests from the harsh realities of the world outside. The only noise consisted of the voices and laughter from the bar, tinged, to McDaid's ear, with an undercurrent of cruelty.

Eugene Quinlisk was clinking glasses with the three dark-suited Special Branchers. For the entire duration of their stay, the other officers had never identified themselves, on purpose no doubt.

'Slainte!' Quinlisk toasted, and they knocked back their whiskies in unison. It wasn't their first; empty glasses lined the bar, being cleared away by an attentive young barman.

McDaid stood in the doorway like a roadblock, said nothing.

One of the Special Branchers nudged Quinlisk. McDaid recognized him as the man who'd held Hannah Bowman captive, dragging her along the floor by her hair. Quinlisk stepped away from the others, placed his glass on the bar.

'Come to make sure we get off safely, sergeant? Very considerate of you.'

'Didn't want you to leave without a proper Glasgow goodbye.'

'I didn't think you were from here.'

'The place rubs off on you.'

Quinlisk glanced at his colleagues, who spread apart slowly. 'You'll take a drink?' he asked innocently.

'I'll get my own.' McDaid slammed coins onto the bar. 'Large whisky, please.'

Quinlisk ordered the same again for his group. When the barman had finished serving, McDaid told him to go and check the barrels. The lad said he'd done it earlier, but McDaid flashed his warrant card and repeated, 'Go and check the barrels, son.'

He then knocked back his whisky in a oner as the barman left. Quinlisk left his drink untouched.

'Sore about that wee ferrety fella, Knox?'

McDaid said, 'That'll do for starters.'

'Fair enough, I suppose. He didn't seem a bad sort, but in our game you can't take chances. We had to have a wee word. You brought him into it. If you wanted to know more about us, you only had to ask nicely.'

'As nicely as you asked Bull Bowman and his wife?'

Quinlisk sighed sadly. 'You're sure you want to do this, big fella? There's four of us.'

McDaid made a show of counting to confirm their numbers.

'Aye,' he said. 'Normally I'd wait until you went and got some more men, but I'm in a wee bit of a rush.'

CHAPTER 59

'I'm sorry, sir, I know you liked her.'

'You've got nothing to be sorry about, Ellen.' Dreghorn managed a gentle smile.

'Doesn't really make me feel any better, sir.'

Ellen Duncan was sitting up in bed, her eyes bright and alert, though there was a touch of doubt, of sadness. There was minimal bandaging around her head now, the bruising and abrasions on her face healing well. The doctors had warned that she might have some minor scarring on one cheek, but otherwise she was expected to make a full recovery. Another day or so in hospital and she would be allowed home.

Sandy and Marjorie Duncan had returned to Dennistoun for a change of clothes, confident now that they could leave her side, albeit briefly. It was the first chance Dreghorn had had to visit, being mired in bureaucracy and compromises, shame and doubt and guilt over his own actions. He had told Ellen everything, and yearned for a cigarette, but figured it would be a poor show to light up and pollute a private hospital room.

'It was what I said that led you to Mrs Hepburn, though, wasn't it?' Ellen continued.

'I think I already suspected. You just flicked the light switch on.'

'Even with what she's done' – Ellen gestured at her injuries – 'I still can't help but think of her as a good woman, especially after what happened to her and her friend in Ireland. Who knows what you'd do in the same position? Glasgow needs people like her.'

'Needs the likes of you more, Ellen.' Dreghorn shrugged. 'Sometimes good people do bad things, simple as that.' He realized McDaid had applied the same observation to him.

Ellen sighed. 'I'm beginning to wonder if it's ever simple, sir.'

He tried to think of something reassuring to say; she was too young to be growing jaded and cynical. All he came up with was an even more uncomfortable question.

'Ellen, the night of the attack, you said Strachan tried to kiss you. How hard did he try?'

'I'm not sure, sir. After leaving the pub, my memories are all . . . fragmented. I don't know now that I could even say for sure it actually happened.'

Dreghorn was good at spotting lies – he'd seen and heard enough – but she stared him straight in the face, showed no signs of it, of anything. Afraid? Suffering from genuine confusion or loss of memory? Planning a quiet revenge? He couldn't tell.

'Don't be feart of him, Ellen.'

'Oh, I'm not, sir.' Grit in her voice. 'Don't worry about that.'

Before he could respond, there was a knock at the door and Marjorie and Sandy Duncan entered, both beaming.

'Sorry, inspector.' Marjorie nodded at her daughter. 'What do you think: picture of health, isn't she?'

'You all are.' Dreghorn offered her his chair. 'Looking better than me, though that wouldn't be hard. And I think you can start calling me Jimmy now.'

It was true, Ellen's recovery had worked wonders on the Duncans. Marjorie plonked herself down on Dreghorn's chair, chatting ten to the dozen and emptying pokes of Ellen's favourite sweeties from her bag onto the bed. Even Sandy's breathing seemed less laboured as he patted Dreghorn's back avuncularly.

'There's a woman out in the corridor asking for you,' he said, raising an eyebrow, man-to-man, in appreciation of her attractiveness. 'Said she didn't want to interrupt when you were with Ellen, but seeing as we were coming in . . .'

Dreghorn thanked him and headed for the door, paused before opening it. 'We'll see you back in Turnbull Street in a few weeks then, sergeant.'

Ellen, sooking a soor ploom, looked at him curiously.

'Didn't I say?' Dreghorn said. 'Due to your courage in the line of duty, Chief Constable Sillitoe is promoting you to the rank of sergeant with immediate effect. Up to you, but I suggested you might like to be attached to the Special Crime Squad with me and Archie.'

'P-plainclothes?' she stammered.

'That is what detectives wear, sergeant.'

The warmth he felt from Ellen's exhilarated smile evaporated as he stepped into the corridor and Rachel McAdam rose from her chair to face him.

'Jimmy,' she said. 'I telephoned the station, but they said you were unavailable.'

He had refused the calls. Not because he didn't want to talk to her; he didn't know what to say.

'Then I went in, and the sergeant at the desk said you were up here, visiting.' She nodded at the door to Ellen's room. 'I saw inside, when one of the nurses opened the door to check. She looks as though she's on the mend. Ellen, isn't it? She's a bonnie lassie.'

'I suppose.' He found he'd never really taken notice. 'Under all the cuts and bruises.'

Rachel suddenly looked as though she was about to snap at him, accusation burning, but bit back as a pair of nurses finishing their shift came down the corridor, gossiping excitedly. By the time they passed, the anger had flooded out of her.

'It's true then?' she asked, bereft. 'Martha was Conall Tracy's accomplice – she was the one who attacked Strachan and Ellen?'

'She never intended to hurt Ellen, but that's the thing with violence. Once you let it go, it's hard to control. It spreads and infects, hurts people you never wanted to hurt . . .'

'I thought I knew her.'

'You did. You do. She's still the same person. I know that's hard to take in, but she's still your friend, Rachel. What she's done doesn't change that. And she probably needs friends now more than ever.'

She paced up and down the corridor as if trying to escape her thoughts. Dreghorn reached for his cigarettes and lighter.

Rachel said, 'They've asked me to take over as acting magistrate. For now, at least.'

'Good.'

'I can't do that. It'd be like betraying Martha. Abandoning her.'

'You don't have a choice.' Dreghorn removed the cigarette from his mouth without lighting it. 'It's what Martha would want. Not doing it – that would be betraying her.'

She stepped in front of him, close, accusing again. 'She could hang, you know.' As if it was his fault.

'Maybe not,' he said. The old anger flared suddenly. 'Your man might get her off. Garrison can sell sand to the Arabs. You must know all about that by now.'

She slapped him, and then kissed him just as hard. She stepped back and they stared at each other until it became uncomfortable. If she wanted him to say something, he didn't know what it was. Or maybe it was the other way round.

Dreghorn didn't watch her walk away, and she didn't look back. He slumped against one wall, the unlit Capstan in his mouth, drawing suspicious looks from passing nurses, as if he was the Reaper himself, waiting for his next victim to expire.

When he was certain he'd given her enough time to leave the building, Dreghorn took the stairs and wearily made his way down to the foyer. Outside, he tilted his hat back on his head and lit the cigarette, bitter smoke scouring away the sweetness of her kiss.

As he exhaled with a deep sigh, the smoke misted his view of McDaid, coming towards him with all the grace of a lead-booted deep-sea diver on the ocean bed.

When they'd left Sillitoe's office, McDaid had stated curtly that there was something he had to do and that he'd meet Dreghorn later at the Royal. From his grazed knuckles, black eye, split lip, torn shirt collar and dented homburg, Dreghorn realized what that something was. He felt a rush of affection for the big man, but said nothing, just smoked.

'What're you smiling about?' McDaid said.

'If I didn't laugh, I'd cry.'

Author's Note

In 1921, a police van en route to Glasgow's Duke Street Prison was attacked by armed men attempting to free a senior member of the Irish Republican Army's County Sligo Brigade, arrested while on the run in Scotland. The breakout was unsuccessful, and the ensuing gun-fight saw one policeman wounded and another killed. Recounted in newspapers of the day, it also features in the excellent Glasgow Police Museum (http://www.policemuseum.org.uk) – well worth a visit.

This, and later incidents involving the theft of explosives from Scottish collieries, as documented in Chief Constable Percy Sillitoe's memoir *Cloak Without Dagger*, acted as the springboard for *Cast a Cold Eye*.

The history of Ireland is deeply complex and highly emotive, and the particular period referenced – the War of Independence, the Partition of Ireland, the Irish Civil War – continues to have ramifications today. I hope that I've done the subject justice, and that those moments of artistic licence that fiction necessitates are not too jarring.

The writing of this book involved a great deal of research, including from my other half, Deborah Tate. Already having a personal interest through family stories and her Scots-born mother's Irish heritage, she immersed herself in the wider history, and amassed enough material for a book of her own.

Other sources: the BBC documentary series *The Road to*

Partition; Charles Townshend's *The Republic*, Diarmaid Ferriter's *A Nation and Not a Rabble*, and his 2020 *Irish Times* article about the Black and Tans; and the works of Tim Pat Coogan, especially *The Twelve Apostles*, as recommended by our dearly missed brother-in-law, Belfast boy Hugo Fagan.

Especially insightful was journalist and war correspondent Fergal Keane's *Wounds*, spotted by Deb on display in a Shropshire National Trust second-hand bookshop. Powerful, poignant, fair-minded and compassionate, Keane's prize-winning 2017 'memoir of war and love' personalizes the conflict through the story of his grandmother and her involvement in those tumultuous events.

The Irish Hospitals' Sweepstakes was a phenomenon, referenced in countless books and the subject of Hollywood films. Tickets sales were indeed illegal in the UK and the US during the period of the novel. It generated vast sums of money and, while funds did certainly go to the good causes it was set up to aid, it also made some people very, very rich – a fact that caused no little controversy. The siphoning-off of funds to contribute to sabotage campaigns is a plotline of my own invention.

As with *Edge of the Grave* – the first book in the Inspector Jimmy Dreghorn series – I've taken certain liberties for dramatic effect in the portrayal of the Glasgow Police and the criminal underworld, such as introducing radio-cars to the streets pre-1936, when they first appeared.

Sadly, a great deal of Glasgow as it appears in the novel has vanished, enough to bring Elizabeth/Betty to tears when she was given a tour of her old haunts by her nephew Raymond in the 1980s. The glorious structure that was the St Enoch Hotel and Duke Street Gaol have long since been razed to the ground, and no doubt some imaginative flourishes on my part have gone into recreating them. I have also, at times, played with distances, layouts and locations to make the story flow more smoothly. The Church of the Immaculate Conception, for instance, is not intended to be its real-life namesake, built at a later date.

A part of Scottish life is the Scots–Italian community, so apologies for shooting out the windows of Glasgow institution Coia's Cafe in Dennistoun (https://coiascafe.co.uk/coias) – another establishment that's well worth seeking out.

Sticklers amongst you will notice that the *Inverness Courier*'s famous Loch Ness Monster story appears some weeks earlier in the book than in reality, but it was impossible to resist Dreghorn's sardonic dig at McDaid.

As for the book's title, I confess I'm no expert on the works of William Butler Yeats, and owe thanks to the actor Adrian Dunbar for his inadvertent suggestion. During an episode of *Coastal Ireland*, he visited Yeats' grave at Drumcliffe in County Sligo and read out the poet's epitaph, taken from 'Under Ben Bulben'. Deborah and I looked at each other and piped up, 'Now that's a good title!'

GRATITUDE AND ACKNOWLEDGEMENTS

A big tip of the hat from Jimmy, 'Bonnie' Archie and me to:

Editor Alex Saunders, Philippa McEwan, Charlotte Tennant, Hemesh Alles, James Annal, Lucy Hale, Gillian Mackay, Jon Mitchell and everyone else involved at Pan Macmillan. My agent Jane Gregory, and the team at DHA, including Camille Burns, Stephanie Glencross, Mary Jones and Penelope Killick. Those authors who welcomed me into the crime fiction world with kind words for *Edge of the Grave* (*EOTG*), including Mark Billingham, David Bishop, John Harvey, Peter James, Adrian McKinty, Liam McIlvanney, Abir Mukherjee, James Oswald, Mary Paulson-Ellis and Craig Russell. Cheers also to Janice Forsyth, Teddy Jamieson, Rob Kraitt, Bob McDevitt, Stephen McGinty and Breege Smyth.

As mentioned in *EOTG*, I earned a living for over two decades as a comic-book writer before trying my hand as a novelist, and I'm mighty grateful to those readers who follow my work, then and now. I may not have reached that point without initial guidance from comics legend Alan Grant, who passed away in 2022. Writer of iconic characters such as Batman, Judge Dredd and Strontium Dog (often in collaboration with the equally legendary John Wagner), Alan was an early mentor to me and countless other budding writers and comics artists. Few of us get anywhere without mentors who discern, encourage and develop potential, and the world of writing, storytelling in general, shines less brightly without him. He once told me that he began his working day by writing a letter of complaint – highlighting injustice and hypocrisy – as it fired him up and got the creative juices flowing. Great advice, though where would you start these days?

On a personal note, thanks to Hibs devotee the late Raymond McMaster; my Aunt Evelyn and singer/songwriter Uncle John (www.johnmorrison.org.uk) – who like Jimmy Dreghorn began his career in the shipyards; artist extraordinaire Cam Kennedy and his wife Isobel for whipping up interest on the Orkney Islands; and Elizabeth and Robert Sutherland – former head of Marvel Comics UK, founder of Redan Publishing – Deb's own much-missed mentor and our dear friend.

Discover Robbie Morrison's first dark historical crime novel featuring Inspector Jimmy Dreghorn...

WINNER OF THE BLOODY SCOTLAND CRIME DEBUT OF THE YEAR

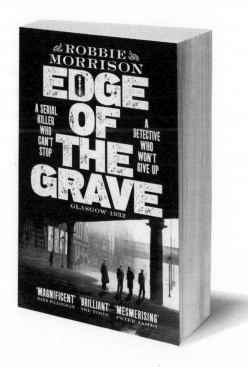

'Tense, absorbing and dripping with gallus Glasgow humour, this book is absolutely wonderful'
Abir Mukherjee, bestselling author of the Wyndham & Banerjee series

'A magnificent and enthralling portrait of a dark and dangerous city and the men and women who live and die in it. I can't wait to spend some more time with Jimmy Dreghorn and Archie McDaid. Robbie Morrison has produced an astounding debut'
Mark Billingham

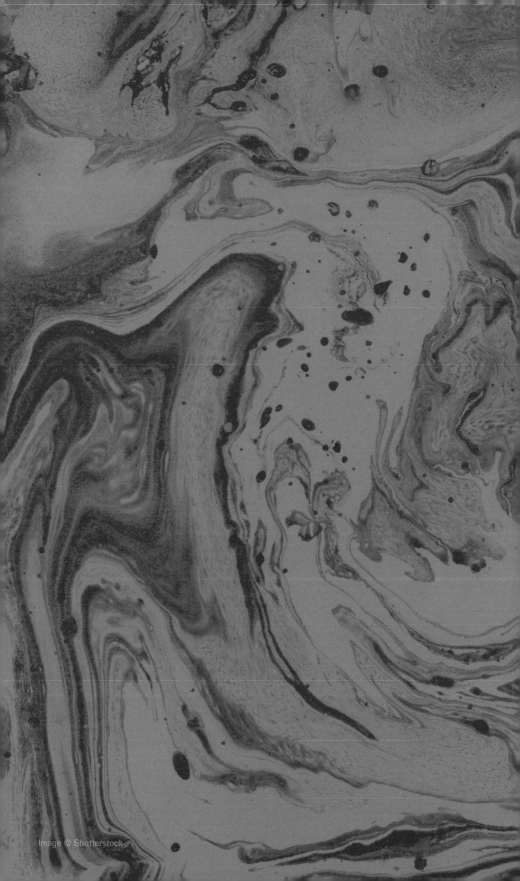